The Girl with the Faraway Eyes

Ric Wasley

Dedicated To

My publisher, Elizabeth,
My cover artist, Taria,
And as always, my special editor and partner, Barbara.

Author's Note

This is the story of a woman who some claim is a myth, someone who never existed at all. A character made up from a composite of representative metaphysical personalities prevalent in occult groups at the turn of the last century.

And yet... there are others, many others, perhaps millions who have seen her face on hundreds of UFO and paranormal web sites and TV shows. They have gazed at images of the enigmatic woman called Maria and are convinced she is real and her story is real too.

Real or myth, her story is compelling and as strange and incredible as the times in which she is purported to have lived. A time when events, inconceivable and unbelievable in their own rights, happened while deluded, self-proclaimed messiahs and dictators plunged the world into a conflagration of war that could have ultimately destroyed all life on this planet.

Perhaps that's why we have always felt, in our desire for answers, compelled to explore the edges of the impossible, and in doing so blur and redefine the eternally wavering line between myth and reality. For the purpose of this fascinating story, that's exactly what I have done.

Foreword

The following is based on a story about a woman who lived in Germany during the tumultuous years of the first half of the twentieth century.

Her name was Maria Orsic, sometimes spelled Oršić, Ortisch, or Orschitsch and, according to many sources, she was a famous medium in Germany before and during the Second World War. Born in Zagreb in 1895 to a Croatian father and Viennese mother, by the time Maria had reached her teens, she was acknowledged by all who saw her to be an incredible beauty of grace and charm.

In 1919 it is thought Maria moved to Munich, Germany to be with her fiancé. It was there when she became part of an occult group called the Thule Gesellschaft, which was involved with the occult crazes of the day. These included psychic mysticism, ancient wisdom, and the long awaited "New World Order" first postulated by Edward Bulwer-Lytton in his 1871 novel, *The Coming Race.*

One of the key pursuits of the Thule Gesellschaft at the end of Germany's humiliating defeat in the First World War was the belief among seers that an untapped source of unlimited power from the cosmos existed. It is interesting to note that the popular *Star Wars* movies called this same sort of theoretical power source "The Force."

In the years directly following the war, chaos reigned in Germany with constant street battles among Communists, Socialists, and Fascists. The currency fluctuated wildly, and to the average German, it seemed as though all institutions and social order had broken down. Thus, when groups of scientists, spiritualists, and intellectuals began saying the glorious, new "Age of Aquarius," offering peace and prosperity to all, was right around the corner if the power of the universe could be harnessed, it was naturally appealing.

They called this free, benign, and unlimited power Vril.

Maria became so fascinated with this possibility that shortly after arriving in Munich, she and several of her spiritualist friends, Traute and Sigrun, formed a new group, which they called *Alldeutsche Gesellschaft für Metaphysik*, The All-German Society for Metaphysics, or the *Vril Gesellschaft*.

From 1919 through the early twenties, the information coming from these groups hinted they were in psychic contact with otherworldly entities who were supplying them with information presented in ancient Sumerian. These out-of-body visions supposedly gave detailed instructions on the construction of devices that would enable the dawning of the new day and usher the transcendence of man to a higher state of being.

This was a hopeful and comforting message for people who believed their own world was falling apart. These occult societies began to attract a lot of attention, especially from a group that was failing in their own efforts to appeal to the average German. It was not hard to understand why. The group in question was formed around a core of frustrated workers, angry Socialists, and bitter soldiers. The name of the group was the *Nationalsozialistische Deutsche Arbeiterpartei*, more commonly known as the Nazi Party.

Soon, many of the names that would emerge into infamy began to take an interest in the *Vril Gesellschaft*. They started to warp the *Vrilerinnen's* (the Ladies of the Vril) optimism of the elevation of mankind into their own central tenant that the superman, *der Übermensch*, was indeed coming—and he was German—The Aryan.

Men such as Hess, Göring, Himmler, and even Adolph Hitler began to monitor the *Vril Gesellschaft* meetings, and it wasn't long until they found another use for the *Vrilerinnen*—the technical knowledge they were receiving, which purported to unlock the secrets of manipulating time, space, energy, and matter itself.

Thus, by 1942, the *Vril Gesellschaft* had gone from being a loosely affiliated collection of spiritualists, psychics, and mystics to a pseudo-scientific appendage of the state under the control of SS Reichsführer Heinrich Himmler's far-flung empire of both brilliant and crackpot projects he used to assure Hitler would win the war for Germany. This brings us to the final act of the *Vrilerinnen* and the start of the legend of Maria Orsic.

For several years, she had been associated with various projects centered around the famous physicist Dr. Schumann's attempts to develop a working prototype of a flying machine, the *Haunebu*, or disc device, based on his antigravity technology.

An offshoot of one of these experiments was something called "*Die Glocke*" or "The Bell" because of its curious, bell-like shape. To this day, no one really knows for sure what the purpose of this object was or the technology behind it. All we do know is that the Nazi government and the SS considered it important enough to grant it almost unlimited manpower and funding as part of a weapons project administered by the SS Armaments office, or *Forschungen Entwicklungen*. The later stages of the project took place in lower Silesia within the old

Wenceslaus mine complex. The tests of the Bell itself were performed within a large, open-air structure of reinforced concrete, and many who saw it said reminded them of Stonehenge.

The SS also made liberal use of slave labor from the nearby Grosse Rosen concentration camp. Many of these inmates were worked literally to death in the construction of the facilities. Also, reports began leaking out that, even after construction was completed, an alarming number of workers and scientists began to die from the effects of working on the Bell. Why? What caused it, and what was the purpose of the object? There had to be people in the government, scientists, and technicians directly involved with the project who must have known. And what about Maria and her *Vrilerinnen*? After all, they were reportedly supplying the information behind the technology. Surely they must have known the true purpose of the Bell. During the last 70 years someone must have talked.

But no one ever did.

Because in early spring of 1945, just ahead of the advancing Red Army, the site was abandoned overnight. All the Russians found when they got there were abandoned equipment, a dynamited mine, and more than sixty white-coated technicians, all apparently executed by the SS to prevent their capture and to ensure the secret of the Bell.

Even stranger was the absence of the high-ranking SS generals and Maria Orsic herself. They, and the Bell apparatus, had vanished, never to be seen again.

Except for two odd things:

One: the Bell is reported to have reappeared in a heavily wooded area of Kecksburg, Pennsylvania on December 9, 1965.

Two: according to eyewitnesses, Maria herself was seen and photographed in Germany almost seventy years after disappearing, and she hadn't aged a day!

This photo is on a number of websites. There is even a YouTube video utilizing modern face-recognition technology to make the case that an attractive young woman is the same one who vanished in 1945 who, if alive now, would have to be more than 120 years old!

Those are the main facts agreed upon by the majority of the sources I reviewed when writing this book.

However, it should be noted: there are hundreds more who assert even more fantastic claims involving ancient aliens, UFOs, time travel, interstellar travel, secret bases at the South and North Poles, and, of course, massive world government cover-ups and conspiracies. Whether any of these claims are true or not, I leave up to the reader to make their own judgment.

This book suggests merely one possibility out of the (literally) thousands postulated as to what the Bell was and what happened to the beautiful and enigmatic Maria Orsic when she vanished in 1945.

Even though many of the facts can and have been verified, it is a strange and incredible story—more bizarre than any story of the most fantastic tale science fiction could create. Nonetheless, from all of the available information I came across in thousands of pages over hundreds of sources while researching this book, the link between the occult and advanced Nazi technology appears to be more or less true.

Like all unexplained mysteries, the unusual nature of this tale lends itself to speculation. I have done so. The majority of the facts, up until the abrupt disappearance of the woman purported to be Maria Orsic, are true. Whether my speculation on the conclusion of these facts are correct is something readers will have to decide for themselves.

Prologue

Lower Silesia, Greater Germany - March 1945

Tank Commander Comrade Sergei Popov craned his neck to see over the 85mm barrel of his T-34 median tank, trying to take in the entire sight stretching out before him.

Though the ground was, for the most part, still frozen, the muddy surface was dotted with slushy puddles amid the small hummocks of dirty, soot-covered snow, and irregular white lumps dotting the approach to the large cement structure where the tank headed.

As they narrowed the distance, Sergei realized the white color of the lumps were different than the rest of the melting snow; they were speckled with blotches of red—a red he and his men had become all too used to over the past five years.

Blood.

About fifty meters from the strange structure, Sergei held up his hand and the squadron came to a clanking halt.

The clusters of uneven shapes were thicker now, and he could make out individual outlines lying scattered in front of the looming structure and reminding him of a picture he had once seen in State School Number 43 as a boy in Kiev. The photo had been of England's Stonehenge, the ancient circle of connected, upright stones. But this strange circle was located near an abandoned Polish mine, probably just another in the growing list of work camps and death camps abandoned by the fleeing Germans.

The photo of his childhood had shown an edifice constructed of prehistoric, lichen-covered irregular stones surrounded by a pristine, grassy plain. This structure was obviously brand new—poured concrete strengthened by steel rebar and marked by the familiar symbol of an eagle clutching a swastika, and underneath, the stark runes of twin lightning bolts—the emblem of the dreaded SS. It was equally obvious that, whatever it was, it had been built to withstand tremendous forces both inside and out. And there was one more difference. The wind-swept plain in the photo of the English stone circle had been untouched, serene—peaceful. The scene before Sergei was anything but. Oh, it was quiet all right, perhaps even peaceful. But it was the peace of the grave and the silence of the dead.

He halted his tank to within fifty meters of the circular structure. Clearly, what he thought were lumps of dirty snow were bodies, and despite the silence of the deserted site, the lumps that had been men hadn't died peacefully. Their bodies were contorted in agony and terror and riddled with powder-burned bullet holes framed by splotches of dried black blood.

He climbed down from the tank's turret and turned one of the bodies over with the toe of his boot. It was a man of perhaps fifty with steel-rimmed spectacles twisted over the bridge of his nose. He was dressed like most of the others in a white lab coat with an identity badge clipped to the pocket. It read: *Engineer Doctor Hermann Hoffmann—Scientist—VRIL Project.*

Sergei checked a few more bodies. They were a few malnourished slave labor prisoners dressed in the usual tattered blue-striped pajamas, but mostly scientists and engineers in white lab coats and nametags designating them as members of a project with the enigmatic name of "VRIL."

Sergei shook his head. On the Red Army's victorious drive through the Caucuses, Ukraine, and Poland, he'd enough examples of the Nazi's cruelty in the burned villages and death camps to provide him with nightmares for the rest of his life. But among the piles of half burned or buried corpses, he'd never come across any that looked like they were German. And not just German—high status Germans—with lab coats and identity badges.

He shook his head and climbed back into the tank. Why would the SS murder their own people? It didn't make sense.

Sergei waved his hand in a circle to indicate to the rest of the squadron that they should turn around and rejoin the main force bearing down on the heart of the Third Reich.

He gave one last glance at the field of corpses. He didn't know who they were or what they were killed for, but one way or another, they would have the satisfaction of knowing that those who sent them to their death would be joining them in Hell soon. Very soon.

* * * *

Boston, Massachusetts—Present Day

Everybody has dreams; some are realistic, most are not. And some dreams are so fantastic that you have to remind yourself they are only dreams. But it doesn't stop them from being true.

There are those who tell me I should not be writing this. I should be smart and let big, old, shaggy, smelly "sleeping dogs lie" because some secrets need to stay secret. So, if I know what's good for me, I should keep my mouth shut and use my computer to play video games, shop the Internet, or meander around Facebook. And they're probably right. Unfortunately, I've never been able to do what's good for me, as many of the "sleeping dogs" I've tripped over could tell you.

Having grown up as the only child of a divorced mother who could never quite decide between being a Hippie flower child or a '70s disco queen, I've always felt most comfortable with all things retro; from the music, TV and especially film. Mom also felt that prescribed bedtimes were stifling to creativity. That, coupled with the fact that she was gone most nights to clubs, classes, and New Age groups meant the I grew up watching a lot of old movies and TV shows. Ever see the old movie with Jimmy Stewart called *Mr. Hobbs Takes a Vacation*? In it Jimmy plays a guy who, every year, with the best of intentions, takes his family on a vacation. And every year, despite these best of intentions, it turns out to be a disaster. And the only thing he can do to "get it off his chest," as it were, is to write about it. After which, by the way, he promptly tears it up. But it's OK because he got his catharsis and it makes him feel better.

Well, that's sort of where I am—in the market for a nice, cleansing catharsis.

And then, there's the other thing...

Like a vast New World Order, multi-national corporation, secret society, Illuminati, Rosicrucian, Free Mason, Bilderberg, Opus Dei, and various government-world-conspiracies—just to name a few.

And what, do you ask, could all of those groups that seem to exist only to make us paranoid have in common?

Just one thing: they all want me silenced or dead. Probably both.

That's the other reason I'm writing about the events of the past several months. Because if they do decide to shut me up for good, they're going to find a nasty surprise because I'll go viral with this, and in a few minutes, every detail of what they've planned and plotted and killed to protect will be sizzling through the Internet for billions of people to read.

Unfortunately, I will probably not be one of them.

Or perhaps, just perhaps, they will decide that the story I have to tell is too fantastic for anyone to believe and I'll be left alone to go my merry way along with millions of others who are also dismissed as "kooks." In which case, this manuscript will stay on my hard drive, and no one will ever know about how history has been changed and mankind has been—

But I'm getting ahead of myself.

Best to let you decide for yourself.

Chapter One

My name is Chris—Chris Brennan, not that it's particularly important in the scheme of things. Neither was my life—at least not until the cold, rain-wet night when I met a young German grad-student named Dieter and the woman he introduced to me as Ria in a smoky Munich beer cellar.

I had come to Germany to do post-grad study in computer science and had been promised a job by Deutsch Technische Daten Wissenschaft Gesellschaft when, or at the rate I was progressing, I should say "if," I completed the required program they had set up for their prospective software engineers.

I had originally started out in college to be a writer, but halfway through my English degree, I realized that outside of doing a long stint as an overworked and underpaid assistant professor or high school teacher to a bunch of bored, smart-ass kids, there wasn't a whole hell of a lot I could do with a degree in English. Thus, I switched my major to computer science, but I guess the urge to write was still there because I spent more time as a freelance stringer for *Weekend Trekker Magazine* and a bunch of blogs than buckling down to the finer points of software programming. That's why, when I looked around and saw the big 3-0 staring me in the face, I decided I need to grow up—or at least try and buckle down to find a regular job with regular pay. But the writing bug lingered below the surface of my good intentions.

Perhaps it's why my writer's antenna started twitching two minutes after my new friend Dieter introduced me to his date, Ria.

It was a raw, damp night in late November when the tourist-influenced face of jolly Bavarian *Gehemshelicht* had long since worn off, and the beer halls had gone back to being what they had always been—a place for cheap, filling sausage and beer. Lots and lots of beer.

At least it was why I was there.

I had entered down a half a flight of slick stone stairs, propelled through the door by blasts of a sudden, wet wind at my back. The place smelled of beer, sauerkraut, and damp wool, but I didn't care. I was cold, wet, and hungry, and headed straight for the long bar against the back wall. I wedged myself between two thick-bodied workmen, and though they both gave me dark looks, through a lot of frantic hand waving and a continually muttered string of, "*bitte*" and "*danke,*" I finally managed to catch the attention of the beleaguered barmaid. She took my order for bratwurst and hot German potato salad, and when she came back several minutes later with my food, I also ordered a stein of their house dark beer, which I greedily drained half of before I even glanced at the food.

The pair of laborers whom I had inserted myself between gave me a hard look that said, "If you think you're gonna stand here and eat, you got another think coming, *Schatzi.*"

I mumbled another insincere apology, took my plate and beer, and went to find an empty table. There wasn't one.

Not only was every table filled, but all of the chairs and benches were too.

There I stood; a half-filled stein in one hand and a plate dripping knockwurst juice in the other. I must have looked pathetic, but in the typically German way of not giving a crap about the plight of their fellow men, no one called out or offered to make room for a pitiful sausage-holding waif at their table.

I was beginning to give serious thought to trying to see if my standing in the middle of the room and sticking my nose into my plate like a dog might nudge someone's conscience in the right direction when fate, always on the lookout for a good laugh at the expense of one of us poor mortals, intervened.

At a small table built for three against the wall, a short, rotund man pushed back his chair and got up. A businessman in a trench coat spotted the movement at the same moment I did and made a beeline for the now-empty chair. But I had the advantage of youth and a good pair of Nikes. Before he made it halfway across the room, I slid into the hard wooden chair and began introducing myself. In Germany, unlike the States, it's perfectly acceptable for people to sit at a stranger's table if there are no other seats available. Even better, the guy and girl at the table were about my own age, meaning I wasn't going to have to feed my face amid the elbows and sputtering shouts of a table filled with fat Munich burghers.

While the guy introduced himself as Dieter and his stunning girlfriend as Ria, I shed my soaked fleece jacket, gulped down the remainder of the beer, and in a generous gesture I really couldn't afford, signaled the waitress and ordered a round for the table.

"Thanks." Dieter smiled. His girlfriend didn't say anything but she smiled too. It was enough.

"I'm Chris, by the way." I leaned over the table and extended my hand. Dieter shook it and Ria wrapped the tips of her fingers around mine. Her skin was soft, warm, and dry, and a tiny tingle like a mild shock of static electricity surged through me. But the air inside the crowded, smoky beer cellar was damp and dank—hardly a breeding ground for static electricity. I mentally shrugged. Maybe I was falling in love. That wouldn't be too unusual since, having grown up being told that, "all you need is love," I lived up to Mom's teaching by careening in and out of relationships with alarming speed.

The drinks came—a refill for me, a pale lager for Dieter, and a glass of Liebfraumilch for Ria. I raised my fresh stein at my new friends, and over the rim of the mug watched Ria's eyes. She noticed and raised one eyebrow with an amused smile. I started to wink but Dieter looked up with a puzzled frown, and I quickly buried my pass attempt in the foam of the dark lager.

To draw attention away from my aborted flirt, I asked Dieter, "Are you guys students?"

He nodded. "*Ja*, I am in my last year at the university and sadly must leave this pleasant life to go work in *mein Vater's* factory selling—of all things—plumbing fixtures!"

The girl Ria patted his hand and made a sympathetic face. "Poor Dieter." She glanced at me then turned back to him. "If only you could make your father understand that you have a brilliant future right here in Munich."

He took a sip of his beer and nodded morosely. "*Ja*, Ria, if you could save me from a life of selling faucets and brass-plated shower handles, I would be in your debt forever."

She put the tip of her forefinger to his lips and smiled. "Be careful what you wish for, *Schatzi*. Forever can be a very long time."

There was something in the way she said it. The tone was light and her smile was winsome—almost sultry. But something else fluttered behind those bright blue eyes. Like the answer to questions most people didn't want to ask. Now I was curious.

Between mouthfuls of bratwurst and sauerkraut I asked. "How 'bout you, Ria? Do you go to the University?"

She took a sip of her Liebfraumilch and smiled. "Not for quite a while I'm afraid."

I paused in mid-chew. "Well, if you don't mind my saying, it couldn't have been too long ago."

She blew me a kiss. "That's sweet, *Liebling*. I'll bet you have all the local *Fräuleins* swooning at your feet."

"Only those who don't know me well."

She laughed and raised her wine glass in a salute. "And witty too."

I raised mine back while Dieter stared at both of us as if there was a joke of which he might be the punch line.

Ria saw him and gave him a quick peck on the cheek. He beamed and held up three fingers for the waitress to bring us another round. While he fumbled for his wallet, Ria watched me with amusement as if daring me to find out exactly what was going on. I wasn't sure, but I must admit, I was intrigued.

For one thing, she was probably the closest thing to the definition of "classic beauty" I'd ever met in the flesh. Maybe it was her high cheekbones and heart-shaped face, or long graceful neck, or flashing cobalt blue eyes, or the soft shimmer of pale gold hair with amber highlights that curled around her shoulders. It was all that and more. And then there was her accent: a soft, German lilt not uncommon in Bavaria, or even Austria, but with a hint of Eastern European behind it. And then there was the way she spoke. She obviously had great command of the English language, but some of the words and phrasing she used sounded a bit...old fashioned. Something from a generation or two ago. There was certainly none of the "awesome, dude" slang my American friends and most of my German ones peppered every sentence with. Let's face it, she was beautiful and intriguing and I was hooked.

She looked over the rim of her glass again. "Have I perhaps suddenly grown a third eye in the middle of my forehead, Herr Chris?"

"No, sorry. I guess I was staring—bad habit of mine. Must be the frustrated journalist in me."

Now her eyebrows really did rise in speculation. "You are a reporter? You write for the newspapers—the media then?"

"No—not unless you consider newsletters, Internet media, and blogs, reporting."

I couldn't tell if she was disappointed or relieved.

"Well," Dieter piped up, "if you want something truly interesting, you should write a piece about our Ria." He put his arm around her.

But she shrugged it off and said, almost a bit too brightly, "Oh, stop it, Dieter. Our little group is not newsworthy. It is just an amusing way to pass the time."

"Really? Tell me about it. I'm always on the lookout for creative ways to fritter away more of my life. What sort of a group is it?"

I was sure Ria was about to change the subject, but Dieter jumped right in.

"A group for studying the mysteries of the universe, past lives of the spirit—the occult." He turned to Ria, a mixture of adoration and infatuation playing across his face. "And she is the most talented medium our group has ever seen."

"Medium, huh? As in old gypsies with séance tables and crystal balls?"

"Gypsies?" Her eyes flashed with contempt for a moment and then it was gone. "Hardly. No, nothing that melodramatic. We are merely a group of like-minded pursuers of ancient truths and cosmic wisdom."

"*Ja*, but I still say I have never seen anyone who could know the most deeply personal detail about a perfect stranger merely by touching his hand."

Ria shrugged and almost succeeded in keeping her expression mildly amused.

But, much to her increasing annoyance, Dieter continued. "You really must come to one of our meetings and see our Ria in action. She can not only tell you things about yourself, but things about people long dead, and most amazingly, things about life far beyond our comprehension."

I was about ready to start making the *Twilight Zone* sound, but figured Germans might not have spent many hours watching old American TV re-runs while growing up. Regardless, I was hooked. Pretty woman, séances, sci-fi, and genuine German wack-doddles? Sign me up!

Chapter Two

The rest of the evening passed in a pleasant haze of conversation, speculation, semi-serious banter punctuated by laughter, and many more steins of lager. At least, at first.

Dieter was convivial, earnest, and endlessly curious. And though slightly on the pedantic side when the conversation touched on something he knew about, he looked at the world through rose-colored glasses of wonder for the things he longed for but knew deep down he could never have—which, after an hour of conversation, I realized was Ria.

It was painfully obvious that he adored her, and if it wasn't true love, it was certainly something beyond infatuation. It almost made me reconsider making a play for her myself.

Almost.

They say all's fair in love and war, and while what was going on at the table was certainly not war, it hadn't really turned down the winding back street towards love either.

Dieter's expressions of devotion reminded me of a faithful St. Bernard. If he wasn't seated at the table, he would have wagged his tail every time Ria smiled at him.

She smiled at me too, but while her lips turned up in the classic gesture, her eyes were guarded and seemed elsewhere; somewhere far away—far, far away.

By the time the bulk of patrons had trundled off to their warm beds with visions of sausages, sugarplums, and schnapps, the conversation had passed from polite to speculative to intense.

In other words, it had turned to the metaphysics—where science and faith stomped on each other's toes.

It began innocently enough when I mentioned a freelance assignment had been suggested to me by the owner of a popular, worldwide eNewsletter. The website and blog attracted a lot of sci-fi and UFO aficionados, and the online entrepreneur who owned it was a former classmate back when I still thought I could write for a living. He wanted someone to do an open-minded, unbiased piece on Erich von Däniken, the famous UFO hunter who wrote the popular *Chariots of the Gods* books.

To this day, I can't say for certain what my motivation was for throwing this topic into the conversational stew pot. Perhaps an overabundance of beer mixed with whimsy, but I suspect the real reason was that I wanted to see what kind of a reaction I could get from Ria. After an evening of conversation, I was beginning to pick up what my poker-playing friends refer to as "tells"—those little, involuntary signals we all give off when something takes us by surprise.

Oh, she was good. I could tell she had perfected being able to hide her reactions behind a carefully constructed mask. If I wasn't watching for it, I would have missed it completely.

But I had set up the question to see if it would produce a reaction, and for a split second, it did.

I threw it out casually enough—right after Dieter had been waxing poetic about their "New Age-Spiritual" group's attempts to channel the essence of famous Greek philosophers such as Socrates, Aristotle and Plato.

"Well," I said leaning back in my chair, "why stop there? I mean if you're doing Plato, why don't you go all the way back and see if you can raise some high priest or exotic princess from his most famous work?"

"Atlantis," Dieter breathed with a beatific expression. "Yes, Ria." He turned to her. "We really must try again."

"Again?" I was looking at Dieter but my antenna was tuned in to Ria. Her mask was still in place.

"Yes," Dieter continued. "Several months ago we almost succeeded in making contact with the spirit of one of the members of the High Council of Elders."

"You don't say? Sounds fascinating. Did you happen to ask him whatever happened to the island? Did it really sink into the Atlantic, or did they simply get tired being the only advanced civilization on a planet filled with cavemen and go off to teach the Egyptians how to pile up stones in a triangle until they formed a pyramid?"

Dieter slapped his palm down on the beer-wet table with a soggy splat. "You must not poke fun at such things, Chris. There are many who have gone before us, and it is our duty to reach out in every way possible in a never-ending quest to bring to light once more their lost knowledge. I do not possess the skill, but within our group there are some who have been working for years to penetrate the veil of ages and bring such knowledge forth for the betterment of all mankind."

Dieter fell squarely into that eternally hopeful and inevitably disappointed collection of utopian dreamers. He was so intense, I kinda hated to burst his bubble. But on the other hand, he gave me a perfect opening—and I took it.

"Supposing that's true? Where would the ancients have picked up all that cool knowledge? Certainly not from some guy smacking cave bears over the head with a club."

"No, no—of course not." He stared at me solemnly. "Surely you must know that in the wide universe there must be many more advanced beings then us."

"Oh, I get it. You're talking about the stuff von Däniken writes about in his *Chariots of the Gods* books. Since we're here in Germany, maybe the next one should be called *Volkswagens of the Gods*. What d'ya think, Dieter? Would that one catch on?"

Dieter didn't answer. He shook his head and muttered in German about "smart-ass Americans who never take anything seriously." I glanced over at Ria and asked casually, "How 'bout you, Ria? Do you think the pyramids, Stonehenge, and all those cities in the Mexican jungles were built by little green men from outer space who visited here thousands of years ago?"

She shrugged. I threw a little more gas on the fire.

"Some people think they're still here."

For a fraction of a second, her mask slipped, and her eyes bored into mine like a laser that could slice open my head and take a peek to see if there was anything more than random, beer-fueled conversation in there.

I was momentarily taken aback by the intensity of her stare, and then it was gone as suddenly as it had come.

But I had my answer. There was something else going on behind those faraway eyes, and I was going to find out what.

* * * *

Just before they threw us out, Ria kissed Dieter on his cheek and gently moved his head onto the sleeve of his jacket and out of the wet puddle of beer on the table where it had fallen.

She glanced over at me and smiled. "I think it's his bedtime. How about you, Christopher? Are you ready for dreamland or are you still curious?"

I leaned back in my chair and gave her what I hoped was a devil-may-care wink. "Put me down as curious...eternally."

"Hmmm...you recall, of course, what curiosity got the cat."

"Of course. But then again, no one has ever accused me of being a pussy."

She laughed—whew. I had learned to my chagrin that American idioms didn't always go over well in Europe. But Ria seemed amused—and something else. The something else was what interested me.

The barmaid was clearing away the empty glasses and shooting us dirty looks as if to say, "It's late and I'm tired and you'd better get the hell out of here before you get a wet dishrag slapped up alongside your head."

Ria stood up and gestured to me. "Come. Help me get Dieter home and then..." She shrugged and gave me a sideways glance as if daring me to discover what else might lurk behind those enigmatic eyes.

I came around the other side of the table and got under Dieter's right arm while Ria took his left.

We half-walked and half-dragged the mumbling, stumbling Dieter out the door, up the stairs, and down three long blocks to a grey stone building of a dozen small flats. I helped Ria manhandle him into the tiny elevator and finally into his place where we dumped him on the couch. Ria propped a pillow under his head and kissed him on the cheek.

"Sweet dreams, my plumbing fixture prince."

We exited, and as she closed the door with a click, she glanced over her shoulder.

"So, *Liebling*, are you ready for bed or perhaps some adventures?"

"Is that an 'either, or?' Funny, I always considered them one in the same."

She half closed her eyes and looked at me briefly before answering. "Yes, I'm sure you do. But my question is, do those who share your adventures consider them worth the journey?"

"Well, my first response would normally be, 'You'll have to ask them,' but somehow, I think I'd better bow out of this verbal joust before I come up *hors de combat*, and no, I'm not going to touch that double entendre with a ten foot Thesaurus."

This time she really laughed. "You can make a woman laugh. That's a very special talent, Christopher."

"I've got others, if you'd like to see a few samples."

"Who knows? Perhaps. But for the time being, walk with me."

We left the building and walked through the small park on the other side of the street. She took my arm and leaned her head close to mine. "Back in the beer cellar, you made a joke about the little green men from another planet coming to earth. But you also said you were doing an article on Herr von Däniken. Do you think he is a fool or perhaps a charlatan?"

"If I only wrote about non-fools, my list of potential subjects would be rather short, and as for a charlatan—I always try to reserve judgment."

She nodded. "Yes. Very wise. One man's charlatan is another's prophet."

"Are you speaking from experience?"

"Is not experience the best teacher?"

"Probably—but by the time you've got enough of it, you're too old care."

She looked up at me with an odd expression. "Not always. Things are seldom as simple as they appear at first glance."

"Ah, so speaks the voice of experience. But if you don't mind my saying, from what I can see from my humble viewpoint, as intelligent and clever as you are, you don't appear like the years of wisdom have hung very heavily on your delicate shoulders."

"As I said, things are rarely as they appear at first glance."

She stopped and looked up at the sky. The rain had finally stopped and the clouds had parted. She took my hand and guided it up to a dim cluster of stars in the northern sky.

"When men first looked up in the sky, they thought the stars were points of light just beyond their grasp. So they climbed mountains to get closer and shot arrows at the moon in hopes of bringing it down." She drew my face closer to hers and whispered. "But then they came to realize that they might be the home to other things—fantastic things, wonderful things—gods."

"Hey, you didn't tell me you were Erich von Däniken's sister."

But she didn't react. She kept staring up into the night sky. "You say you are a journalist, a writer—but how open is your writer's mind I wonder?"

"You're the psychic, Madam Ria. Why don't you tell me?"

"Is that what you want, Christopher?"

"Among other things."

"Ah, then perhaps we should talk. Do you like coffee, Herr Christopher?"

"It dependents on who makes it and where it's served."

She took my hand again. "Then let us see if we can find a place where the coffee and conversation are both stimulating."

"And what place would that be at 4 a.m.?"

She started walking and called back over her shoulder. "My place."

* * * *

But I never got that coffee, and we didn't really talk, either. We made love.

I must have dozed afterwards because when I opened my eyes again, the mid-day sun was streaming through the curtains and she was gone.

Chapter Three

When I got home, I sat at my kitchen table until the late afternoon shadows made the note I'd found on my pillow when I awoke too hard to read. It didn't matter. I had memorized it hours ago.

You are very sweet boy, Christopher, and I think you should follow your dream to be a writer, but if you want to be something more than merely another journalist, meet me at the beer cellar tonight at 9…
Ria

I was there at eight thirty, and nine o'clock came, but she didn't. She didn't come at nine-thirty or ten, either. I waited until closing, but she never showed. By then, I would have even settled for Dieter, but he was likewise a no-show. I asked the barmaid if she'd seen them when she came over and handed me the check for my two beers and a sandwich. But all I got was a shrug before she hurried off to shoo the remainder of the lingering customers out the door. Without looking at the bill, I stuffed it into the back pocket of my jeans, threw ten Euros on the bar, and left.

The next morning I retraced our footsteps from the park, down eleven blocks to what I was sure was her building. But when I reached the third floor and knocked on what I was also certain was her door, it swung open.

I walked inside and looked around. It was empty. Clothes, furniture—even the pictures on the wall—were gone.

I went down to the first floor and knocked on the landlady's door. She spoke a little English, and although my German was better than passable, she apparently needed to practice her limited English skills on an obvious American. Between us, we made a broken conversation that would have embarrassed Tarzan and Jane.

"*Entschuldigen Sie, Frau*, but I am looking for the woman who lives in the flat on the third floor—front unit facing the street. Do you know where she has gone?"

She looked at me funny and started to close the door.

"Wait! *Bitte*—please, it's very important that I find her."

She shook her head. "You have made mistake, *mein Herr*. No *fräulein* on third floor. Flat in front empty for last two months. You want rent—*ja*?"

I shook my head, bewildered. "That can't be. I was with her in there only one night ago."

"*Nein*, you mistake make. Flat vacant. You want rent, you come back—I make you good rent. Until then, *mein Herr*, *auf Wiedersehen*."

She closed the door.

* * * *

The rest of the day and most of the night were spent replaying the time we were together and trying to figure out what went wrong. That got me nowhere. Then I tried not to think about it. I did my best not to think about anything.

I made an attempt at being philosophical. Maybe this was the grand, cosmic scheme's way of sending me a wake-up call to stop messing around with things unlikely to put a dime in my pocket and get my ass back to studying and passing the computer courses of my future employer.

For the next two days I lost myself in a frenetic round of studying, seeing long-neglected friends, and an orgy of cleaning, organizing, and tidying up. I washed dishes and had the cruel thrill of condemning millions of moldy microorganisms to a hideous death at the hands of the German equivalents of Lysol and Clorox. I chased without mercy entire colonies of dust-bunnies from their hither-to-undisturbed sanctuaries under my bed, couches, and tables, and it was this manic round of compulsive tiding up all the frayed edges of my life that ultimately did me in.

Towards the end of the second day, somewhere between organizing my sock drawer and sorting through which clothes would finally get washed, I found the note.

I had filled my laundry bag with a miscellaneous collection of stray socks, underwear, and T-shirts and was stuffing one last pair of jeans in when I felt something crinkle in the back pocket. Thinking it might be a stray Euro that I could certainly use, I pulled it out and was disappointed when it was only a folded piece of paper.

I assumed it was one of the hundreds of notes I constantly wrote to myself. Instead, when I pulled it out, I realized it was the bar bill from my last night in the beer cellar. I started to crumple it when I noticed there were actually two pieces of paper. Tucked inside of the flimsy check was a heavy, cream-colored paper of the type normally used for writing formal notes back when people still did that sort of thing.

I unfolded it and it was indeed a note, written in a beautiful, feminine hand. But what really set my pulse racing was the signature—"Ria."

Dearest Christopher,

I am so sorry I couldn't say goodbye in person. Something has come up and I must leave, but perhaps we will meet again someday.

Until then...thank you for a lovely evening and keep watching the stars.

Auf Wiedersehen, Liebling

Ria

PS... If you are serious about pursuing a writing career and would like some new perspectives on your von Däniken article, you might wish to visit an old friend of mine. His name is Max Becker and last I heard he was residing at Neuturmstrasse 211. Ask him if he still dreams of Aldebaran.

I reread the note three times, hoping for a clue as to where she went, and as I was about to refold it, I found one.

Embossed into the paper at the top of the page were two raised, intertwined letters—an "M" and an "O."

An "M" and an "O"—but no "R" for Ria. Either she had borrowed a sheet of monogrammed writing paper from someone, or the woman I knew only as Ria had a different name.

* * * *

For the next week I haunted the beer cellar hoping Ria would complete whatever "came up" and return to share some more schnapps and smoldering glances with me, but for six nights, she didn't show.

However, on the seventh night, Dieter did.

He looked terrible—worse than I felt.

His eyes were bloodshot, face unshaven, and his formerly crisp clothing looked like he'd been sleeping in them for the past week. After I bought him a cognac for his shakes, he confirmed that he had.

"Ria, huh?"

He nodded. "I knew she was not in love with me, but I thought I would at least have time to try to change her mind." He looked up at me. I was disappointed, but he was really hurting. "I never thought she would leave without a word."

"Nothing? No phone call—note?"

"Now that you mention it, yes, there was a note."

I stiffened and tried to ask casually, "What did it say?"

He shrugged. "Nothing really. Just that she had to go away and she wished me well."

I took a deep breath. "Did she say you might meet again?"

He shook his head. "No, why?"

"No reason." But somehow I was glad. Maybe our one night had meant something after all.

Dieter rubbed the stubble on his chin.

"Here, let me buy you another." I steered him to a small table and signaled the waitress. "Tell me a little more about this occult group you and Ria belonged to."

He continued to stare at the tabletop until the drink came and then swallowed it down in one gulp. He gave a shudder, but a bit of color had returned to his face. He held up the glass. "Another, *bitte*?"

"*Natürlich, mein Freund,* but how about a little trade. Another cognac for a little information?"

He shrugged. "Why not? Ria didn't like us talking about the group to non-members, but now she is gone..."

His face devolved into the look of a basset hound discovering the cat had eaten his schnitzel.

I held up two fingers to the waitress, and she handed me two more glasses as she passed by our table.

Dieter reached for one, but I set both glasses down and folded my hands. "You were going to tell me about the group?"

He glanced around and then sighed and nodded. "You have heard of the Thule Gesellschaft?"

I pushed one of the glasses across the table to him and took a sip from the other.

"Wasn't it one of those crackpot groups that flourished before the First World War and believed some master race had come from the Arctic and the Earth is hollow?"

He pushed his chair back and took on the faintly pedantic air he'd had the first night I met him.

"The original Thulists believed the ancestors of the Nordic races had come from a land the Greeks called Thule, or Θούλη in Greek. The Romans referred to it as Ultima Thule, the most distant northern land, or edge, of the known world, though some have claimed it was Iceland. In the late nineteenth and early twentieth centuries, various groups of Germanic mystics claimed Ultima Thule was really ancient Hyperborea, the lost, ancient landmass in the extreme north, as postulated by your own United States Congressman Ignatius L. Donnelly at the turn of the twentieth century."

He paused and took a drink.

I was correct. Once Dieter got rolling on a subject, nothing short of a nuclear blast could stop him.

"It was Herr Donnelly's writing concerning the true fate of Plato's Atlantis that heavily influenced such notable occultists as James Churchward, the English explorer, and Madame

Helena Blavatsky, the famed Ukrainian mystic, during the second part of the nineteenth century.

"In the early twentieth century, another German occultist, Rudolf von Sebottendorf, saw an opportunity for the Thulists to gain some support and prestige and integrated them into another group he headed, the *Germanenorden Walvater* of the Holy Grail, who saw themselves as the descendants of the medieval Teutonic Knights, and the Thule Gesellschaft was born.

"By 1919, the Thule Gesellschaft had succeeded in attracting many new members, some of whom were very talented and very attractive, young women. Soon, they had formed another, and even more mystical, offshoot of the Thulists called the *Alldeutsche Gesellschaft für Metaphysik*."

He looked over at me. "That is the group I belong to; the Pan-German Society for Metaphysics." He smiled almost sheepishly. "As you can see, it is not so very mysterious or 'out there,' *ja*?"

"And that's the group Ria belonged to?"

"*Ja*—among others."

"Like what others?"

He frowned and bit his lower lip, whether in reluctance to say more or because he wasn't sure, I couldn't tell.

"Well...there was one she did mention—once. And then I think it was quite by accident, because when I asked her about it, she said it was a special meditation group closed to new members unless you were related to one of the initiated." He paused and rubbed his forefinger across his upper lip. "Now that I think about it, I do believe she mentioned her great-grandmother was one of the founders."

"And what polysyllabic, ponderous, German name was this group called?"

He smiled again. "Not so complicated. The Vril Gesellschaft."

"OK—I know *gesellschaft* means 'society,' but I'll be damned if I ever heard the word Vril. What's that German for?

"It's not. The word Vril is not German."

"Then what is it?"

Suddenly, he became uneasy and glanced nervously around the room. When he turned back, it was as though someone had pulled down the shade and turned off the light behind his eyes.

"I really must be going, Herr Chris. I must return to my father in Dusseldorf at the end of the week, and I have much packing to do."

"Hang on—what's the rush? Come on, have another. You must have some idea what Ria's group was about. I mean, is this Vril animal, vegetable, or mineral? Is it a place or a person—or maybe some mystic chant, or even a lost seer from Atlantis? Go on. Give it your best guess. I love a puzzle."

"Perhaps you do, but I do not. Yes, some puzzles can be entertaining..." He looked around again. "But the more I study, the more I am of the opinion that some puzzles do not wish to be solved."

I tried not to show it, but if he had hoped to cool my interest, he could have done it better by dousing himself with a bottle of schnapps and setting his hair alight.

Two couples sat down several tables away from us and began talking in low tones. One glanced over at us. All of a sudden, Dieter stood up and said, with Teutonic formality, "I thank you very much for the drinks, Herr Christopher, and now, if you will excuse me, I must be going home to bed. *Gute nacht.*"

I watched him as he headed towards the door and lost himself in the crowd.

I sat there at the table sipping my cognac and doodling on a napkin. After a few minutes, I looked down at what I had been unconsciously writing—a single word written over and over.

Vril.

Chapter Four

When I got back to my now overly pristine apartment, I tried to sleep, but my mind kept spinning off in a thousand different directions, most of which were only partially fueled by my frustrated lust for the enigmatic but totally hot Ria.

I was curious too. The more I thought about it, the more puzzled I became. At the top of the list of questions that wouldn't leave me alone was the word, "Vril."

Naturally, I Googled it and stopped first at the always interesting, if not always correct, Wikipedia. But when the page popped up on my computer screen, what I read made me embarrassed for my own gullibility in listening to the nonsense Dieter and my sweet Ria spouted during our first meeting in the beer cellar.

It read:

Vril, the Power of the Coming Race is an 1871 science fiction novel by Edward Bulwer-Lytton, originally printed as *The Coming Race*. Many early readers believed its account of a superior, subterranean master race and the energy-form called "Vril" was accurate, to the extent that some theosophists accepted the book as truth. Since 1960 there has been a conspiracy theory about a secret Vril Society. *The Coming Race* was originally published anonymously in late 1871, but Bulwer-Lytton was known to be the author. Samuel Butler's *Erewhon* was also published anonymously, in March 1872, and Butler suspected its initial success was due to it being taken by many as a sequel by Bulwer-Lytton to *The Coming Race*. When it was revealed in the 25 May 1872 edition of the *Athenaeum* that Butler was the author, sales dropped by 90 percent because he was unknown at the time.

I slowly closed the lid of my laptop. OK...who's the asshole now? Taking this shit seriously just because the girl spouting it had a nice butt. Idiot!

And yet... Yeah, I'd always been a devoted fan of the Syfy Channel and cut my teeth on the old masters like Edgar Rice Boroughs, H. Ryder Haggard, Sir Arthur Conan Doyle, H.G. Wells, and Jules Vern. So, was it very strange when a pair of whack-a-dos teased me into a paranormal mystery, I was gonna bite—hook, line, and sinker?

My finger hovered over the touch pad mouse then stopped. Did I really want to meander down this path to zoned-out, stoned-up weirdness? And more importantly, could I really afford this sort of intellectual masturbation right now?

No. Not unless I could get Ria to join me.

But she was gone, and for the time being, I had to put aside the mystery, and all of the other jagged, little pieces of the puzzle that wouldn't fit, and get back to what I was supposed to be doing in Germany—learning the friggin' finer points of software programming. The first of the course exams was coming up, and if I didn't pass, I might find myself without a meal ticket. For the next two days, I reprised the old college cramming routine, and when the big day came, I aced the test with flying colors.

Believe me?

Yeah, right.

Oh, I did pass—but just barely. And my less-than-stellar performance earned me a session with the HR Director of my potential, but becoming-less-likely, employer.

"*Guten morgen*, Herr Brennan."

I was greeted by a typical, expensively dressed, and perfectly coiffed executive—the quintessential *Deutsch Verantwortliche Mann*; the company man. He began in well-modulated and almost completely unaccented English. "And how are you enjoying Germany so far?"

"Couldn't be better. Nice scenery, good food, and great beer."

He managed a faint smile that said, "OK, *Kinder,* you get one smart ass remark and you've used up yours."

His smile faded quickly and so did mine. This was "Uh-oh" time.

He held up a sheaf of papers, glanced at them and then at me. "I have here the results of the exam you took." He sighed and shook his head.

See what I mean? Definitely, "Uh- oh."

I tried to keep the panic out of my voice. "Umm, yes, so I see. I haven't had the chance to look at them yet. I was told I passed."

He shrugged. "Passed? Yes. But just barely, and to be quite candid, Herr Brennan, we are not actively seeking new software engineers who passed 'just barely.' Which is why we are puzzled by these results. When we first accepted you into our program, we did so because both your college grade point average and test scores were of superior quality." He put down the papers and gave me his best HR "concerned" look.

"Are you happy, Herr Brennan? Has something happened to distract you from your work? Perhaps a death in the family or..." He winked—which was a bad idea because he wasn't very good at it and looked like someone had poked him in the eye with a sharp object. "Or, maybe some romantic problems?"

I stifled desire to blurt out, "You got it, Fritz. I'm climbing the walls 'cause this hot chick I banged a week ago took off without so much as Bye-Bye kiss."

Instead I gave him what I hoped was my most contrite look and nodded. "Yes, you're correct. My mother has been very ill and I'm quite worried."

Now the truth is, the last time I'd heard from Mom, she was partying on the beach in Cancun with her new boyfriend Ernesto, but as far as Herr Wetzel from HR was concerned, poor old Ma was a little old lady gasping out her last breath and pining away for sonny-boy across the sea.

"Ah, I suspected as much." He said with a satisfied smile. "In that case, what I propose is this: we will keep you in the program for another three months to allow you more time to study and prepare for the next round of exams." He stood up and offered me his hand. "I trust this will be satisfactory?"

I assured him it would, thanked him profusely, and left his office before he could change his mind.

But as I waited for the elevator that would take me down to the street, I kept wondering why I didn't feel more relieved.

The answer didn't hit me until I was almost to my flat, and then it struck me so hard, I stopped in the middle of the street, forcing honking drivers to swerve and pedestrians to break their stride.

I really didn't like software very much.

* * * *

When I got back to my place, I killed the next four hours and a bottle of schnapps watching re-runs of *Gilligan's Island*–in German. I was that depressed.

Along about midnight, I rolled the empty bottle under the couch, and while considering if it was worth the effort to go and hunt up another one, I closed my eyes to, no doubt, give the problem the deep contemplation it deserved, and when I opened them again, the morning sunlight was streaming into my eyes.

I stumbled over to the window. The day was disgustingly bright and cheerful. I pulled the shade, lurched back to the bed, and pulled the covers over my head.

The next time I awoke, the sun had gotten the message and had discretely slipped behind the buildings across the street, enabling me to pull the shade up and make a very late breakfast or early-bird dinner out of a half box of stale cornflakes and condensed milk—which I promptly threw up.

This was not going well at all. Either I needed to spend some quiet time doing introspective things to figure out what bothered me and get in touch with my inner nitwit, or go out to someplace where the music was so loud you couldn't hear yourself speak, let alone think.

I chose the latter.

When I woke up the next morning with a tall, buxom blond who told me her name was Gretchen and that we were in love, I realized I really did need to have a serious conversation with myself.

I bought her a nice lunch and a dozen roses and told her I'd see her back at the club where we met this evening. Fortunately for both of us, she never asked if I had the slightest idea where the club was or even its name; consequently, after wandering through unfamiliar parts of the city, I finally made it home just before sunset.

This time, I gave the schnapps a night off and got a decent, non-drunken night's sleep, and when I woke up sober and *sans* headache the next morning, I finally accepted what I had known all along. I wasn't going to be a software engineer. I was—and always had been—a writer.

* * * *

I won't pretend I wasn't tempted to take Herr HR Director's generous offer of another three month's stipend and make believe I was studying for the next round of exams, but in a rare flash of self-righteous virtue, I sent a professional and business-like email stating that, for personal reasons, I had to drop out of the program. When I pressed the "Send" button, I felt very honorable and quite the "captain of my soul," though I wondered how I'd feel when I was broke and scrounging for crusts of pumpernickel behind the beer cellar.

With the cheery specter of starvation looming on the horizon when my savings ran out in a month or two, I decided to get busy doing the piece I wanted to write and was sure I could sell to one of the sci-fi or UFO mags. The fact that my only two connections to the paranormal/mystic groups had flown the coop was only a minor inconvenience. The several hundred times I'd re-read Ria's note had convinced me that the place to start was with the only name Ria had mentioned. Max Becker.

In the end, I decided not to call first. Calling would give him a chance to say no.

When I showed up on Saturday at the small pensioner hotel where he lived, I was half expecting he'd be out in a park somewhere, throwing a Frisbee or kicking a soccer ball around with his buddies. But no, he was in, said the concierge, and even more surprising, he agreed to see me.

But he was not what I was expecting—not at all.

In the first place, he was more than twice as old as the 20-30 something I'd expected to be one of Ria's friends. I mean, she did say he was an old friend, but I never suspected that she meant it literally.

After recovering from my original shock of the old man standing in the doorway, I took the seat he pointed to and studied him as he took the chair opposite me and began filling an intricately carved Black Forest pipe from a tobacco humidor.

At first glance, all I'd been aware of was white hair spilling over a lined forehead, but when I looked a little closer, I realized that, despite the white hair and lines, the man sitting across the wooden table from me, calmly lighting on old-fashioned pipe, was in great shape for an old guy.

Though the hair was pure white, there was plenty of it, and he wore it thick and long, curling over his collar. His face was lined but without the jowls most old people had, and his nose was thin and hawk-like. Although his expression was mild enough, his eyes were piercing blue and I doubted they missed much. I quickly revised his age downward to mid to late 60s while hoping I'd look as good at his age.

I also realized that while I'd been studying him, he'd been studying me. He lit his pipe, took a long puff, and settled back in his chair.

"And so, Herr Brennan, the porter told me over the intercom you had been sent to me by a young lady of our mutual acquaintance."

When I nodded, he took another puff and smiled. "Perhaps that is why I agreed to see you. I don't get many visitors any more. Most are in nursing homes or graveyards, and very, very few are young ladies." He put the pipe down and leaned forward. "Who is this *fräulein* who is a *freund* with old Max, eh?"

I had planned out the whole Q&A before I came, complete with notes and pithy, probing questions. But that had been based on interviewing someone around my age, or maybe at the most, ten years older; thus, the whole grandpa thing kinda threw me. For lack of anything better to say, I blurted out, "Her name is Ria and I'm guessing she's your granddaughter or niece or some family friend, right?"

He regarded me curiously. "I'm afraid you may have me confused with someone else, *jungen*. I know no one by the name of Ria."

That's what his lips said, but his eyes said something different. They said there was the ghost of a memory, but he didn't want to recall it to life. His brow furrowed momentarily and then cleared as if he refused to consider a three-letter nickname might have a connection with someone from his past.

I pulled out the letter, unfolded it, and pointed to where she had written his name. "No mistake, Herr Becker. Look, it's right here in Ria's own handwriting."

He shrugged and smiled without even glancing at the letter.

Frustrated, I shot the only arrow I had left.

"She told me to ask you if you still dream of Aldebaran?"

The indulgent smile left his face. "Let me see that."

He reached out slowly, and picking up the letter, stared at it as if mesmerized by some hidden message only he could see. He read it over several times before he looked up at me, all humor gone, with his face pinched and pale. "Where did you get this letter?"

"I told you—from a girl named Ria. Pretty, about thirty...long, blondish-brown hair. In fact, make that very pretty, with a great smile."

"Yes," he whispered. "That would be her."

He sat quietly for a long time, the only movement his fingers tracing the words over the heavy, cream-colored paper.

Just when I was ready to give up on the whole interview and write him off as a strange, old guy slipping into early senility, he spoke.

"Yes. I do believe I know the woman of whom you speak."

I straightened up and got out my notebook and micro-recorder.

"But," he continued staring off into space, "her name is not Ria. Do you see the letters embossed at the top of the page?"

I looked where he was pointing and then went back to testing the sound level on the recorder. "Yeah, I did notice those. An 'O' and an 'M.' She must have borrowed someone else's stationary."

He shook his head and pointed at the letters again. "No. This is her stationary, embossed with her name. Not an 'O' and an 'M,' but an 'M' and an 'O.' Her name...I understand now— the modern nickname, Ria—short for Maria, or Marija in her father's native Croatian tongue. Her name, young man, is Marija Oršić."

I spent the next hour trying to persuade the man, who now looked to have aged twenty years since I first saw him, to tell me who the hell was Marija Oršić and what she had to do with the girl I knew only as Ria.

But all he did was shake his head and stare at the letter muttering, "All this time... after all this time."

Finally he said, "I need time to think. Come back tomorrow, young man, and we shall see."

With a weary sigh, he closed his eyes, put his head down on the table and didn't look up when I closed the door and left.

Chapter Five

When I showed up the following morning, I half expected him to be gone. That seemed to be the pattern of everyone I'd met lately. But he was there and told me to come right up.

He looked much better. His color had returned and he appeared to have regained most of his earlier vigor. But the sparkle behind the blue eyes was gone, replaced instead by a kind of fatalistic resignation.

He was, however, willing to talk—more than willing. In fact, in some odd quirk of fate, my visit yesterday had jarred loose some memory of guilt, longing, or something else, and he needed to talk about it.

We sat at the table in his small kitchen and I took out my recorder and notebook once more. I indicated the recorder and he waved his hand in dismissal. I clicked it on.

He opened an old, yellowed file folder with something written on it in faded brown ink, and then took out a photo and pushed it across the table towards me. "Is this the girl you call Ria?"

I picked up the photo. It was her and yet...

"Is it her?"

I nodded. "Yes...I think so, but she looks different."

I studied the photo. It was an old black-and-white, almost sepia, of the formal portrait type–slightly frayed around the edges. The girl in the photo was beautiful. Her hair was long and honey-blond and mostly straight with a slight wave where it was tucked behind one ear. I closed my eyes and tried to picture Ria's face. Her hair had been wavier and a little browner, though it was hard to tell the exact color in the slightly yellowed black-and-white photo in my hand. The long, graceful neck arched up from an old-fashioned lace collar. The lips were perfect and kissable and a twinge stabbed through me as I remembered our night together. But the eyes...they were compelling. And though her expression was serene and maybe a bit aloof, no man could look at those eyes and not wonder how they would look back at him.

I glanced up and saw Max watching me intently. "Is that her?"

I nodded slowly. "Yes. I think so. But like I said, she looks different. I mean, it's her, and yet it's not. The features are the same, especially the eyes. But the girl I met was dressed differently, more make-up, laughed a lot. This girl looks, I don't know...more serious than Ria."

He shrugged. "Maybe we took ourselves more seriously then. Perhaps too much so."

I stared at him. "Then you know this girl?"

He gave sharp laugh. "Know her? I was her fiancé."

I don't know how long I sat there with my mouth open, but when I finally gathered my wits I said, "In that case, this must be Ria's—what? Mother? Grandmother?"

He took the photo and leaned back in his chair. "Open your notebook, young man. Is your recording machine turned on? *Ja? Gut*, so we begin."

* * * *

"It was in Vienna towards the end of the war where I first met Maria."

I stopped with my pen poised over the page. "That was in 1945, right?"

He shook his head. "*Nein*, not that war, the one before it. The Great War."

I put down my pen. "What? That war ended in 1917, almost a hundred years ago!"

"It ended in 1918," he corrected calmly.

"But you couldn't have been around then. I mean that would make you…"

"I am older than I appear." He folded his hands and stared across the table at me. "Now do you want to hear my story or not?"

"Ah, yes—of course I do."

"*Gut*. Then do not interrupt me again. Now, where was I? *Ach, ja*—so as I said, it was in late October of 1918 when I first met Marija Oršić—Maria—and like in the fairy tales my *Mutti* had read to me as a child, I fell instantly in love with her the moment I saw her."

* * * *

Vienna, Austria, October 1919

I was then a *Leutnant*, a lieutenant, in a Hussar company that had long since been reduced to freezing in rotting trench boots and fighting for a few meters of churned-up mud on the Western Front. But because of my family connections, I had been invited to one of the last balls to be given in the disintegrating remnants of the Austro-Hungarian Empire. My father, a general, had been wounded early in the war and never recovered full use of his leg, but even though he and mother could not come to Vienna, they got me an invitation and even sent me a new uniform. I looked most dashing, I must say. But when I first beheld Maria, I was as awkward as the most ragged private and barely had the courage to approach and ask for a dance. She was dressed in a deep blue velvet dress that matched her eyes, and her long hair was piled atop her head. She was radiant.

She was talking with a middle-aged *Oberst*, a colonel. I waited until he went to fetch her some punch and quickly stepped up to her with more confidence than I possessed and introduced myself. I was so stiff and formal, I believe I clicked my heels and bowed, which made her laugh. Fortunately, I had enough wit to smile too, and I asked her to dance.

She looked at me coyly for a few moments with those mesmerizing eyes. A few moments, I must add, that to me felt longer than being under three days of enemy shelling. But finally she smiled and whispered, "Very well, Herr Leutnant, but we must be quick before *Oberst* Kessler returns and has you shot."

I fear I must have grinned like an idiot because I would have gladly faced a whole army of *obersts* and firing squads to hold her in my arms. And so we danced.

She was so beautiful and I wanted nothing more than to take her hand and leave the ballroom, leave Vienna, the war, and find some quiet, secluded place where we could be together forever.

But of course, it could not be. Her father had accompanied her. He had come from the eastern part of the Austro-Hungarian Empire and was, if anything, more traditional than the easy-going, pleasure-loving Viennese. And although not a member of the Austrian titled class, he worked for the prestigious University of Munchen, so we were firmly boxed in by protocol on all sides. I did, however, in the brief time we danced, learn her address, and by the time the *oberst* returned and stood frowning at me, I had persuaded her to meet me the next afternoon for coffee and *sacher tortes* at a small café I knew of. And the next day, when she entered the café, the sight was sweeter to me than all the cream filled pastries in Vienna.

We talked for I don't know how long, but by the time we'd finished our coffee and sugar cakes, the sun had dipped below the rooftops. I knew she would have to leave soon, but all I wanted was to continue to gaze at her and hear her voice, so I kept asking her one question after another. Such as, "What do you do to keep yourself amused, Miss Orsic?"

She laughed. "Please, Herr Leutnant, do not confuse me with one of those well-bred but boring young ladies of quality who were at the ball. We have no family estates or hunting lodge, and my father must work for a living."

I smiled back. "Well then, since you are not required to be hostess at the family *Jagdschloss,* do you have any hobbies or avocation?"

"Ever since I was a little girl, I have wanted to be a ballerina."

She ran her hands lightly down the contours of her shoulders and hips. "But now, alas, I fear I am too old."

This time I laughed out-loud with delight. "I know it is not polite to ask a lady her age, but if I may be so bold, what great, advanced span of years could you have reached to render such a lovely form too decrepit to dazzle all of Vienna with your dancing?"

She picked at the remains of her cake and then whispered in a mock conspiratorial tone. "If you must know, Leutnant, I have achieved the ripe, old age of twenty-three."

"Well, as your older and wiser friend—by a full year—my advice is to continue with your dreams."

She shook her head. "No, I must accept that path is closed. Though I do hope to teach ballet and dance. However, there is one talent I have discovered that fascinates me more each day."

"Then it must be fascinating indeed to spark the interest of one clever as you."

She raised one eyebrow. "And I must say, Herr Leutnant, I likewise suspect you have many hidden talents yourself. Perhaps one is spinning pretty words for young ladies to swoon at, *ja*?"

"If I did, I foreswear them all now as callow, schoolboy nattering. But please, tell me about this special interest."

"You must promise not laugh."

"Cross my heart."

"Very well. For some years now I have had what some would call–visions."

"What sort of visions?"

"Often, before sleep comes or when I am quiet and lost in thought, I see images of strange and ethereal places and beautiful, elegant beings."

"Perhaps you were dreaming, or maybe you were seeing visions of angels and heaven?"

She shook her head, quite serious now. "No, they are not of heaven. The heaven of the Bible does not exist."

"And how can you be certain?"

"Because they told me so."

"The people of your visions?"

"Yes."

"Then if they are not angels and do not come from the spirit world, where do you think they come from?"

"From another world–another sun–another galaxy."

* * * *

Munich – Present Day

That little tidbit almost killed the whole project for me right then and there.

I stopped my furious scribbling in my notebook and glanced up.

Max's eyes were closed and he had a slight smile on his face. I could tell he was thinking of her—the woman he called Maria—the woman he implied was the one I knew as Ria.

Perhaps he recalled a memory from a time of lavish balls and genteel cafés. A time of aristocracy dripping with titles and dashing officers festooned with gold braid; a time long gone and faded from living memory. But apparently not from the memory of Max Becker. Either he was one of the most convincing liars I'd ever run across, or I should be contacting the *Guinness Book of World Records* not only for the world's oldest man, but the best preserved. And that bothered me too.

Watching him I thought, for the hundredth time, there was no way he could be within a half century of the age he'd have to be if his story was true. And yet…there was something about him and the way he told it that convinced me if it wasn't true, he certainly believed it was.

I coughed and he opened his eyes and sighed. He noticed me staring at him and picked up his pipe. He lit it with a kitchen match and studied me through the clouds of aromatic smoke.

"*Ja*, forgive me. It has been so long, but I can still see her as I held her in my arms that night in Vienna." He smiled sadly. "Such are the dreams and fancies of young men, eh, Herr Brennan?"

I thought about it for a moment and nodded. "Yeah, and sometimes those dreams end way too quick."

"But it does not make their ending any less painful, does it?"

After a minute or two he set the pipe down in the ashtray. "You have a question, Herr Brennan?"

What I wanted to say was, "You bet. For starters, about half a century of living appears to be unaccounted for by the looks of you." But I didn't want to have that conversation yet. Not before I'd gotten the story of why the girl I'd fallen for in Munich more than a week ago was a dead ringer for the one the man across the table from me had met in Vienna almost a hundred years ago.

Instead I answered, "No, just a little writer's cramp. Tomorrow when I come, I'm gonna bring my laptop."

He looked at me strangely then finally nodded. "Yes. Tomorrow."

* * * *

As I walked home from Max's flat, I decided to give it another day or two. Maybe I wanted to find out if ol' Max was messing with my head, or was merely an old guy who spun a great story, or maybe was just plain nuts.

I also couldn't get Ria out of my mind. That part of the mystery had become personal. Deep down, a part of me wanted to see this through. My track record for finishing things I started wasn't great, and I figured that if I was going to be any kind of a journalist, I would never get anywhere if I couldn't separate the bullshit from the strange-but-true. And this certainly covered the "strange" part of the equation. I needed to find out if any of it fell into the "true" category.

I had a vague feeling that if I didn't talk to Max now, I might not get the chance later.

With all those thoughts and feelings rattling around my brain, there was one other I should have been paying attention to: the uneasy feeling that I was being followed.

Chapter Six

The next morning, I shook the last sucrose-encrusted frosted flake into my cereal bowl and came to a painful conclusion. Despite my state of near penury (see, I told you I had been an English major), it was time for me to scrape together a few of my rapidly dwindling stack of Euros and replenish my depleted larder. In other words, I went shopping.

On my way back, while wrestling with two colorful plastic bags filled with sausage, cheese, and assorted breakfast cereals, I turned a corner and bumped into Dieter.

I retrieved my fallen loaf of pumpernickel. "Hey, Dieter, man. What are you doing back in Munich? I thought by now you'd be settled in Dusseldorf supplying the world with gold-plated faucets?"

But when I looked up, he was backing away. "Hey, Dieter! What gives?"

He turned and crossed the street and ran/ fast-walked, into a small park, and despite my repeated calls, he didn't look back.

Short of running after him while carrying two bags of groceries, there was nothing I could do. I didn't know whether to be puzzled or pissed at not only being snubbed, but being treated like Typhoid Mary.

"The hell with him," I muttered, re-gripped my bags, and continued down the street. But before I turned the next corner, I noticed two men in dark suits standing on the corner at the far end of the park.

There was nothing remarkable about them, and perhaps that in itself drew my attention. They were non-descript. Maybe a little too non-descript. They were simply standing on the corner smoking. Not walking or even talking. Just smoking. One was looking across the park towards where Dieter had disappeared, and the other was looking at me. I stopped and stared back and he quickly turned away, but in that brief glance, I was sure I'd seen him somewhere before. I closed my eyes, recalling the expression on Dieter's face as he backed away from me. It was the same expression he'd had that last night at the beer cellar–panic and fear. That expression crossed his features when two couples sat down a few feet away from us. And the two non-descript men with their non-descript dates who'd sat there and glanced over at us that night were the same men standing across the street. Watching.

OK. If they wanted to watch me, I'd let 'em get a real good look. I hefted my bags and started across the street. I had to dodge a Porche and a BMW, and by the time I darted around the hood of a white-panel truck, whose angry driver cursed me out in colorful German idioms, I was in time to see the two men pile into a taxi and move off into traffic.

I stood at the curb feeling slightly foolish. Was I letting this whole mystery thing turn into a self-fulfilling prophecy?

I finally crossed back over and continued home. Several times I stopped, whirled around, and scanned the street behind me. But no one was there.

* * * *

I had started out for Max's flat the next day when my cell phone rang. He asked me to meet him at a small café instead, about two blocks from his building. He was seated at a small table in the corner when I arrived.

He looked tired and distracted, and his eyes kept darting around the café, as if he was expecting someone. Someone he wasn't anxious to see.

When I sat down and pulled my laptop out of my backpack, he put a hand on the case. "Please, Herr Brennan, you are a nice young man, and I am thinking maybe you waste your time with a wild story told by a foolish old man, *ja*?"

"Is that what it is, Max? A wild story?"

He looked like he wanted to say yes, but he shook his head. "No. Strange as the story is, the reality is stranger than the most outlandish tales of the Brothers Grimm. It is all too true. And I must warn you that like many strange tales, with knowledge come consequences." He stared at me, but when I didn't respond, he sighed. "And you still wish to continue?"

"Are you kidding? With that kind of a build-up, how could I not?"

He sighed again and shrugged resignedly. "Very well. I tried. All right then, if you are ready..."

I nodded.

Munich, January 1919

As much as I wanted to stay in Vienna, I had to return to the front. I was there in November when the German army asked for an armistice and subsequently signed the humiliating Treaty of Versailles that was to become the catalyst for descent into madness. But at the time, I cared less about defeat than getting back to Maria, who, by the time I was mustered out in January of 1919, was all I could think of.

Of course I had to see my parents. Consequently, my first stop was my family's *schloss* outside of Salzburg. I stayed there for two agonizing weeks while my father tried to persuade me to take an interest in running one of the salt mining operations that had produced much of the family income since our ancestors had acquired the rights back in the Middle Ages. But that was the last thing I wanted to do.

On a bitter, cold morning, I boarded the train for Vienna with the firm intention of asking Maria for her hand the moment I saw her. Imagine my despair when I arrived at her home only to learn that her father had secured her a position giving ballet lessons to young girls and she had joined him in Munich.

But young men are natural optimists, and my despair turned quickly to determination. That very day, I boarded the train for Munich.

My long-fantasized romantic scene of sweeping Maria off her feet and making her my wife never materialized.

Oh, I tried.

When I got to Munich, I went straight to the flat she shared with her father, and I cannot say she was not glad to see me—she was. But she was distracted, almost removed from the everyday mundane. She said she was flattered by my proposal and certainly cared for me, but she demurred from marriage at that time because she said it would not be fair to deny me the sole attention a husband deserved. When I asked why, she told me quite readily. She had formed a group with several other young ladies for the study of various psychic phenomena. A group they called the *Alldeutshe Gesellschaft fur Metaphysik.*

It all sounded quite harmless, even a trifle silly to me at the time. But as I was to find out later, I could not have been more wrong. For the first few weeks, I'd asked to accompany her and she had demurred, saying I might be disconcerted by the process.

"Maria, I love you and want to share in all things important in your life."

She finally agreed, but not before extracting a firm promise. "You must neither comment on, nor in any way intrude in the conduct of the meeting."

I laughed. "Please believe me, my dearest, after three years in the trenches, there is little that can disconcert me."

I was wrong.

The first time she finally agreed to allow me to accompany her to a meeting, it all looked innocent enough; almost charming, if not a bit melodramatic.

They met in an old three-story building leased by Maria's partner in the group, a very self-confident young woman who called herself Sigrun.

The assemblage consisted mostly of young woman, and after entering the room with Maria, I sensed they wanted to keep it that way. Maria introduced me and had me sit on a chair against the wall.

I won't say they were hostile to me, rather more like uncomfortable with the presence of one who was not only a man, but also not an initiate into the group itself. Not rude or unkind, but I had a distinct impression I was inhibiting the proceedings for them to do whatever it was they did when they met...and I soon found out what it was.

From the little Maria had told me, it sounded like they studied a psychic potpourri of spiritual medium, channeling, and Eastern Mysticism. It also appeared to me that she had been deliberately vague about the precise method they employed to achieve this communication.

The meeting began.

Each of the half dozen women stood behind one of the heavy, ornate chairs ringing the table, and in unison, loosened the combs and clips holding their hair in place.

In those days, only very young girls ever allowed themselves to be seen with their hair down. I had only seen Maria's hair done up in a neat bun or peeking out from beneath the brim of a fashionable hat. Thus I was completely unprepared for what happened next.

When Maria removed the last comb, her shining, blond hair cascaded over her shoulders and down her back until the pale gold tips brushed the floor.

I stood with my mouth open. In my entire twenty-four years I'd never seen anyone with hair that long. But in the next two minutes, I saw five more young, attractive women with hair as long or longer. Nonetheless, it was eerie to see them all with their long hair swaying free, clasp hands around the table and begin some sort of chant in a strange language I'd never heard before.

Suddenly, without warning, Maria's body began to shake. Her eyes rolled back in her head and she stared unseeing at the ceiling. I started to go to her, but an angry glance from Sigrun sent me back to my chair. Instead, the ladies gripped their hands tighter and shut their eyes as though trying to project their powers into Maria.

And then Maria began to speak. The hairs rose on the back of my neck because the voice coming from this delicate, beautiful girl was not hers. It was deep with bass and a lilting timbre as though it emanated from a deep well or dark cave. It echoed through the room, and I swear the walls rushed back and the plaster ceiling was replaced by stars and milky constellations. I felt for a moment displaced in time and space and then it passed and I was seated back in the third-floor room in Munich listening to Maria, or rather the voice coming from Maria's throat. The tone was becoming smoother, the words flowing into one another in rhythmic, melodious sentences punctuated by short, sharp consonants. The language was at once familiar and strange.

I cast my mind back to my university days when I studied ancient history and attended a lecture by the famous explorer and archeologist Dr. Hugo Lieberman about the root languages of ancient Sumer and Chaldea. While most the words issuing from Maria's mouth were not familiar to me, occasionally one or two were reminiscent of what the professor had identified as being one of the first spoken languages of the cradle of civilization in Mesopotamia. I also recalled his theory had been controversial. He claimed the eventual language that emerged from the valley between the Tigris and Euphrates, from those earliest known cities, was really the evolution of a far older language—the very first of civilized man. The language of lost Atlantis.

Many of my classmates had laughed and asked the professor mocking questions, but others had been quite enthralled by the idea of some ancient, master race of a superior civilization. It had provoked many a lively debate in the cafés and beer halls later.

Could this be what Maria's group was all about? Had all of these young women succumbed to one or more of the crackpot theories emerging from the popular press and lecture halls?

I considered intervening, but I was afraid. If I did, not only might I be asked to leave, I would risk losing the affection of the girl I loved. Thus, I remained silent and listened.

Abruptly, Maria's tone changed and she spoke in her own voice.

"Tell me, great Assurbanipal, what is this secret knowledge you wish to impart to me?"

Again the strange voice spoke, and Maria rasped to Sigrun, "Quickly, bring me paper and pencil."

She did and Maria began to write, drawing diagrams with strange symbols on sheet after sheet of paper. I was too far away to see clearly, but it appeared as though she was drawing blueprints for some fantastic machine.

The pencil moved faster and faster

"Yes, yes." She gasped. "I understand. Yes!" Suddenly, she stiffened, closed her eyes, and slumped unconscious in her chair.

I jumped up and ran over to her. Her face was deathly pale and her skin cold to the touch. I scooped her up in my arms and laid her on the couch in the adjoining room. I was rubbing her hands to restore some circulation when Sigrun came in with a small silver cup of peppermint schnapps.

"Do not be concerned," she said in a brisk, business-like way, "this often happens after a communiqué with our spirit guides."

Her off-handed manner rankled me. "All the more reason why Maria should not be subjected to this nonsense."

That was a mistake.

Sigrun stiffened and set the cup down on the table. "If that's the way you feel, then perhaps the better solution would be for you not to be present." She stalked out of the room.

Now I was certain I would never be allowed to participate in another of the group's sessions, but quite frankly, I was far more concerned about Maria's health and state of mind than any thoughts of that strange and disturbing gaggle of mystical women.

With my arm still around her shoulders and the glass of schnapps pressed to her lips, Maria soon came around, but we didn't really speak until the taxi ride back to her father's flat.

I learned that participation in the psychic group required the members never to cut their hair.

"I know it sounds fantastic," she said, "but we have determined that our hair acts as some sort of antenna for picking up psychic signals from other planes of existence."

Since I was familiar with the operation of wireless radio, I tried to convince myself that a similar principle might be extended to whatever messages might be floating out in the ether.

"Maria, I'm not sure what to make of everything I saw. In fact, I'm not really sure of what I did see. But I do know these kind of—trances, or whatever they are—can't be good for you."

I hated the way I sounded—chiding and a trifle pompous. But I was concerned.

She didn't speak but stared out the window at the slushy street for such a long time I wasn't sure she had heard me.

"Maria...?"

"Perhaps we shouldn't see each other for a while, Max."

"Maria, how can you say that? I love you. I want you to be my wife. I'm concerned for you—for your health and well being. I—"

She turned and took my hand. "And I am very fond of you too, Max. I may even love you. But you must understand, my work—the group Sigrun and I have created—is the most important thing to me right now." Her large blue eyes opened wide. "It may be the most important thing to the entire world."

"What, Maria?" I cried, totally frustrated. "What could be more important than our love? What you are doing? What is it you think is so vital that it can change the whole world?" I swallowed and asked the question bothering me the most. "That voice...when you were speaking in that strange tongue. Who was speaking and what did they say?"

Maria's face took on a beatific expression and she stared at something only she could see. "The voice was that of the Sumi. Beings of incredible compassion and wisdom whose voices speaks through me from a distant world that orbits the sun Aldebaran in a star system 68 light-years away in the constellation Taurus. The same beings who visited our earth tens of thousands of years ago and gave rise to today's modern man."

Chapter Seven

I stopped typing. The group Max had mentioned—the *Alldeutshe Gesellschaft fur Metaphysik.*

I had heard that name before—from Dieter—the last night I spoke to him. I tried to recall what he had told me about it, but Max continued speaking so I typed in the German name and drew a yellow highlight through it to mark it for further investigation once we were done. I turned my attention back to the old man sitting across the table.

To say that I had lots of questions for Max is putting it mildly. As I walked him back to his flat, I peppered him with queries, but he looked nervous and tired and responded to me with one-word answers, which finally degenerated into shrugs.

On the steps of his building I studied his face. He looked worried and his skin had a grey, pasty pallor.

"Are you OK, Max?"

"*Ja, ja.* Just tired, that is all. You know how it is with us *alten kämpfers*, old fighters. We like to talk, but the fires burn low and we need rest."

"Sure, absolutely. Get a good night's sleep and—tell you what—tomorrow morning, I'll come by with coffee and some nice pastries, say about nine?"

"*Ja, natürlich.* That would be nice."

"OK, then, I'll see you tomorrow."

He nodded, but he wasn't looking at me. He was staring off towards the horizon at something only he could see.

* * * *

That night, the dreams began.

I had spent some time organizing my notes, and then placed a call to my old English professor who had left academia to start an online sci-fi fantasy, and paranormal website, newsletter, and eBook publishing company. When I got through explaining my idea for an article and book, he was not only excited, but told me he was sure he could syndicate it internationally.

By the time I put my cell phone down, for the first time since I'd changed majors, I was finally doing what I was meant to do. I had a fascinating topic, told by an eyewitness who, if he could be believed, was a story unto himself, and even if not, it would still make a damn good yarn.

I had promised myself an early night, but was so pumped, I decided to change my mind about an invitation to a party a guy from my computer class had mentioned a few weeks ago. I'd logged the date into my iPhone calendar along with the address, and at about ten o'clock, I headed over.

A couple of brews, I told myself as I walked through the open door and nodded to my host and a few other people I knew. And that's probably the way it would have wound up except...

I was halfway through my second double Bock and thinking about leaving, when I noticed the faint scent of a peculiar perfume. A tingling surged through my body like an electrical charge and a cool hand stroked the back of my neck. I turned around.

"Ria!"

She wore a long black dress, black spiked-heel boots, and an intricately crafted silver charm tied around her neck with a black velvet ribbon. She looked fantastic.

"Where have you been? Why did you leave? What have you been doing?" It all came out in a rush until she put her fingertips to my lips.

"Shush. Don't talk. Kiss."

And we did.

Sometime later, I resumed breathing. "OK, tell me what the hell is going on?"

She laughed and kissed me again. "A bit of this, and a bit of that, but tell me. How are you getting on with Max?"

"He's either got the story of the century or he's as wacked out as I am for listening to him."

"But you believe him?"

"I'm starting to, but there's a bunch of things I can't get my head around."

"Such as?"

"Such as the picture of the girl he claims was his girlfriend in 1919—a girl who looks exactly like you."

"Ah, well, you know it is said that each of us has a doppelganger."

"Maybe, but never one who was born more than a hundred years ago."

"It is also said one should never say never."

"Are you saying it is you?"

She changed the subject.

"I must be serious for a moment. Has Max mentioned anything to you about either a *Jenseitsflugmaschine* or a *Vril Flugscheiben?*"

I struggled with the unfamiliar word and came up with a translation of something like "beyond flying machine" or a "Vril flying discs."

When I told Maria, she smiled. "Yes, that would be a literal translation, but taken inclusively, a better one would be 'Other World Flight Machine' or 'Flight Discs.'"

"Tell me you're not talking about flying saucers."

She cocked her head to one side and smiled enigmatically. "I'm not talking about anything. I'm merely asking questions."

"Which you do most of the time while providing me with damn few answers."

"But if you are to become the writer you wish to be, finding the answers to questions will become your stock and trade, *ja*?"

"I suppose. But my life would be made a whole lot easier if someone would provide me with an occasional answer, or better yet, a fact."

"*Ach,* all right, here's one." The smile disappeared from her face. "Don't delve too deeply searching for details about what Max tells you. Take it as an interesting story about a time long past."

"Why? You were the one who put me on to Max. I thought you wanted me to tell his story."

She nodded slowly. "Yes, you're right. I thought someone should pass on the great discoveries that were made in paranormal research in Germany during the first half of the twentieth century."

"And now?"

"Now...I think maybe there might be great danger involved."

"Danger? Like what? Little green men who want their flying saucers back, or UFO nut cases who want the little green men to take them for a ride?"

I expected Ria to laugh and, although she gave me a brief smile, it was obvious she was staring over my shoulder at something or someone who had walked into the room.

"Ria? You-hoo, Earth to Ria. This is your space ship calling. What gives?"

She continued to stare at whatever was behind me. I turned to look, but I saw nothing except a great crowd of milling people talking, drinking, and laughing.

I turned back to ask her what the hell was so interesting on the other side of the room, but she was gone.

* * * *

I cursed myself all the way home and swore that if she ever showed up again, I was gonna handcuff her to me.

Rather than cursing fate or feeling sorry for myself, I should have been thinking, not about the fact she disappeared without warning, but why she disappeared.

But when all you can think about is blond hair, blue eyes, and a seductive smile, you should be prepared for the unexpected. I shouldn't have been surprised by what happened next—but I was.

The next morning I was late getting to Max's building and was only one block away when I remembered I'd promised to bring coffee and pastry. I stopped in the middle of the sidewalk and yelled, *"Scheisse!"* in deference to the German-speaking population around me and cut across the street to a small bakery.

The upshot was that it was almost noon by the time I finally rang his buzzer in the building foyer. Balancing a cardboard tray with two large cups and a half dozen waxpaper-wrapped pastries and *Sahnetortes*, I was trying to remember more German curses when, after the third ring, he had still not buzzed me up.

Then, one of the *Sahnetortes* slipped off the sagging tray and landed on the spotless tile floor with a forlorn plop. The scowling face of the *Portiersfrau* appeared around the corner. Several moments later, she was back with a mop and began rubbing at the frothy mess with short strokes, punctuated with grumbled comments of "*Dummkopf*" and "*Schwachsinnige.*" Not exactly words of high praise.

It wasn't until I tried pressing the buzzer a fourth time, almost adding both coffees to the mess on the floor, when she stopped pushing the mop.

"If you are looking for Herr Becker, you waste your time," she snapped. "He is here no more. He moved out this morning—very early."

I couldn't believe it. Déjà vu all over again. This was becoming a pattern—no, make that a trend. Should I be considering changing my deodorant or toothpaste, or was I a one-man people roach bomb?

"Where did he go?"

She shrugged angrily. "I should know? Am I now being his *Mutti*? The only thing he says to me is that he goes to live with his daughter in America. Now you will move your foot, *bitte*, so I can finish."

* * * *

I left the pastries and one coffee with the *Portiersfrau,* which at least earned me a grudging, *"danke,"* and I took the other coffee and slowly sipped it as I walked back to my flat.

I tried to add up the list of people who'd bugged out on me over the past week and realized it added up to almost everyone I'd met in that time period: Dieter, Ria, and now Max. What did they all have in common? Me.

Was all this my fault? Something I did? OK, then what was I doing? Hmmm... Asking questions, probing for information about a weird but very interesting story about mediums, channeling, and UFOs. A strange story to be sure, but nothing to induce everyone involved to get away from me as though I were poison. Unless...

The whole way home I kept going over the details of what Max, Dieter, and Ria had told me, looking for a connection for something that might have repercussions for someone, somewhere.

The one thing I kept coming back to was UFOs. Other than making interesting documentaries on the History, Discovery, and Military channels, was there anything to them that could affect real people in a real way? Oh sure, there were tons of UFO clubs and societies, but most of them where for hobbyists and people convinced that the government is lying to them in a thousand ways—which, of course, it is—and keeping the little grey men under wraps in Area 51. That one I had a little more trouble with. But could that really be what this was all about? Nah, this story hadn't really gotten to any conclusions yet, and looked like it never would. Probably wouldn't have turned into anything anyway, simply the ramblings of some old man who told a good tale but had gotten his chronology scrambled. As much as I hated to admit it, maybe it was time to put the writing thing away and see if I could salvage my software career.

It was in this frame of mind that I turned the key and opened the door to my flat. All thoughts of coincidences and senile old men vanished. My flat had been ransacked.

Chapter Eight

They were gone. All my notes, the micro recorder, and my frigging laptop. Gone. All gone.

After spending an hour doing a half-assed job of straightening up the mess, I searched for anything the bastards who'd tossed my place might have missed. I was forced to conclude that, story-wise, I'd been cleaned out. Not only did the bastards steal my work, they took the goddamn tools of my trade. Or, to be more precise, what used to be the tools of my trade. I not only had no story, but nothing to write it on.

The fact that I might never have made much money on the story in no way stopped me from glumly watching my dreams of gigs on Letterman and Jimmy Kimmel evaporate like last night's spilled beer. And speaking of spilled beer, I saw no reason not to do what I did best when faced with setback and calamity. I went out to get wasted.

Six hours later, I was back at my door fumbling for the key while Gretchen, the blond, buxom, Bavarian waitress from the Rathskeller, played kissy-face with my left earlobe.

It wasn't until after much struggling to get the door open when I dimly realized what the problem was. Every time I turned the key in the hole, it locked the door, which could only mean one thing: the door was already unlocked.

Hmmm… Somehow it didn't seem terribly important then. We were inside and Gretchen was "ooh-ing" and "ah-ing" over my only mildly interesting framed samples of the capitals of Europe, back when I thought I might be harboring latent talents as a photographer. Turns out I wasn't. But either

Gretchen was under the delusion I was, or she was feeling extra frisky, 'cause after one shot of Jägermeister, we had gotten all nice and cozy on the couch when...

"Christopher, I think perhaps we should stop now for a little bit."

"Ummm? Hey, why? It was just starting to get nice, and to quote Robert Frost, we've still got 'miles to go before we sleep.'"

She shook her head and got up unsteadily. "I am thinking that maybe I had better go now."

"For God's sake, why?"

"Because," she put her hand to her mouth and swallowed hard, "I think I am going to be sick." And a moment later, she was—nosily—into a large, imitation, classical Greek vase I'd picked up last summer in Athens.

"Ah, yeah. You know, Gretch, you may be right. Want me to call you a cab?"

But she was already halfway out the door. "No, no. I just need to get some fresh air—away from here; far away from here. I don't know what it is, but there is something here, something about this place that makes me... *Ach, mein Gott!*"

She clapped both hands over her mouth and ran, staggering down the hallway.

I slowly got up, shut the door, and then opened it again. I took the imitation Greek vase and dumped it down the waste chute at the end of the hall. I closed the door, finished my shot of Jägermeister, and shuffled into the bedroom. I managed to kick off my shoes but was too tired to undress. I flopped down on the bed and rubbed my hands over my eyes. "Christ, now I've got to try to sleep when I'm horny *and* drunk. Why in the hell did she get sick so quick?"

"Because she wasn't anywhere near good enough for you," answered a voice from the other side of the bed.

"Holy shit!" I rolled off the bed and went scrabbling under the bed for the old cricket bat I'd discovered in the back of the closet when I'd moved in.

By now my eyes had adjusted to the dark, and I could see a form lying curled up on the bed, head propped up on a single pillow, and as near as I could tell, staring at me.

I hefted the broad wooden bat and said in what I hoped was my best no-nonsense voice, "OK... you've got two seconds to tell me who you are and what the hell you're doing here before I start rearranging what are probably very attractive features. Now talk."

"And here I thought you were fond of me," said a low, throaty voice.

"Ria?"

I could see now the dark form was certainly all female. She threw back the covers and whispered, "Get in."

I sat down on the edge of the bed and reached for the light switch, but her hand closed over mine. "No, don't turn on the light."

"Why not? I've seen you naked before, and I kinda like it."

"Then close your eyes and think of that while we make love."

And we did.

Later, when we should have been feeling all warm and cuddly, she was distant. Sort of quiet, almost sad.

"Was it something I said? Something I did or didn't do?"

"No, nothing like that."

"Well, I hope not. After all, I do have a reputation to maintain. You know, ninety day money back guarantee if not completely satisfied."

She chuckled. "I can assure you, were I not satisfied, you would know it long before ninety days."

"Phew, there's a load off my mind...and other key, performing portions of my anatomy."

She chuckled again and I noticed, again, how her voice sounded a bit lower and throatier than it had only a few days ago—more like Lauren Bacall than the Ria I'd met in the beer cellar that cold, rainy Tuesday evening on the night when my life became far more complicated.

I couldn't say exactly what was different, but something was. She acted more world- weary, resigned, remote. And then the moon passed from behind a cloud, washing a pale, silver light over both of us.

I felt her shrinking away from me and the moonlight as she pushed herself toward the far side of the bed. But in the split second before she did, I caught a glimpse of her face.

She looked to have aged over the several days since I'd seen her last, and not by a little, but by ten or perhaps even twenty years.

"Ria!" I gasped, unable to control my shock. "What..." I didn't know what to say. I reached out and pulled her towards me, but she shook off my arm.

"*Damnen-Scheisse*," she shouted, "I told you not to look at me."

"Hey, sorry for my inability to control the movements of the clouds and moon, but if you can put your hissy-fit on hold for a minute, I've got a question or two of my own. Beginning with: what in the hell has happened during the two days since we were last together?"

The anger flowed out of her like air from a punctured balloon.

"It hasn't been two days. It's been twenty-two years."

There was something about the way she said it that, as incredible as it sounded, made me believe her.

"But how? How can it be possible? What could have happened to age you twenty years in two days? No, wait, that's not right. You said, 'it's been twenty-two years.' But if it's true, why do I recall, quite vividly, being with you only the day before yesterday? I guess what I'm trying to ask is, which one of us is nuts?"

The ghost of a smile returned to her face. "Probably both of us."

Then she became serious again. "What do you know of another countryman of mine, Herr Albert Einstein?"

I shrugged. "The same as everyone else. Big-brain German scientist who fled to America when the Nazis came on the scene. During World War II, he and a bunch of other scientists came up with the atom bomb. After the war he went on to teach at some Ivy League school. I think it was Princeton."

She smiled. "Very good. You have summarized it quite correctly, except for two things. One, he was not German, he was Austrian, from Vienna, like me, and two—the atomic bomb was not his only project of genius."

"OK, I'll bite, what's the other one?"

"There were many, but the one scientists are still wrestling with today centers around the theories he postulated about quantum mechanics and the nature of time and space."

"You're losing me, Ria. The only thing I know about time and space is that I never have enough of it."

She smiled wistfully. "Sometimes you get more than you know what to do with." She shook her head as if to clear it. "But as the work of Einstein has shown, if one was able to manipulate the quantum template of the cosmos, it would be possible to not only change the way time flows, but the very nature of it."

"And you've been able to do it?"

She shook her head. "No, I have not, nor do I suspect anyone else born on this planet could either."

She bit her lower lip and a worried look crossed her face. Then she said, almost to herself, "Though I'm afraid there are some who are all too willing to try."

"Really? Like who?"

She stared at me, unaware she'd spoken out loud. Her brow furrowed and she took a deep breath before finally answering.

"Ruthless people, dangerous people, evil people." She took my hand and squeezed it hard. "People who have been involved with this technology for more than seventy years who now feel it should be theirs alone. Believe me when I say they will stop at nothing to gain the few remaining bits they need to implement their ultimate agenda."

"Which is?"

"A new world order under their hegemony, enforced by unimaginable power."

I laughed. Relieved to hear of something so prosaic it had become the stuff of James Bond villains. "For a minute there you had me worried, Ria, but this sounds like another nut group of comic book bad guys stalking Indiana Jones for the lost Ark, or the mad scientist with a death ray."

She sighed. "I knew I shouldn't have mentioned anything. It's just that I'm worried for you, Christopher. Now even more so, since you take as a joke something others take with deadly seriousness." She glanced up at me. "You laugh when you say 'death ray,' but have you heard of Nikola Tesla?"

"Mmmm, yeah. Wasn't he the guy who competed with Edison for the technology that would be adopted as the standard for electricity?"

"Yes. He was a brilliant mind, but what most people do not realize is that he didn't stop with developing A/C power. He created hundreds of other inventions, including one referred to by him and others who observed it as a 'death ray.'"

"OK, so what? As far as I know, no one has ever used it or anything like it."

"Just because they haven't does mean they will not."

The direction of the conversation was taking on a decidedly "kook" tone. I gently tugged on Ria's hand, trying to pull her back down to the pillows, but she pulled her hand away.

"You must try to understand. These people are more brutal and evil than anything you could imagine, as they have already proved to the despair of millions."

"Whoa, you make them sound like a combination of the Hell's Angels and Attila the Hun."

"They are far worse. When they first arose nearly one hundred years ago, they were allied with a splinter group of the Thule Gesellschaft who wanted to bring back the old Teutonic Knights of the Middle Ages. They called themselves, *Die Herren vom schwarzen Stein*, the Men of the Black Stone.

Several members of the group became the nucleolus for a new political party that took shape in 1919 called the *Nationalsozialistische Deutsche Arbeiterpartei,* or as it came to be known to the rest of the world, to its ever-lasting sorrow, the Nazi party."

* * * *

We talked for the rest of the night until the sun came up, but Ria wouldn't tell me anything more. She kept saying it was too dangerous. Instead, she spoke of a lot of what sounded suspiciously like New Age psychobabble, like the old, hippy, flower children "peace, love and harmony" crap of the sixties.

To change the subject as much as anything, I finally suggested we go out to breakfast, but she shook her head.

"No, no, I really must leave. I have already stayed too long."

"Oh no you don't, my little strudel. I'm not letting you out of my sight again because every time I do, you pull a vanishing act."

She looked down at the floor. "I know, and I'm sorry, but it can't be helped. I probably should have never returned, but as you must be realizing by now, the ones who broke into your flat are very dangerous. So yes, I am fearful for you." She touched my cheek. "And yes, I am fond of you too."

Her face softened and she looked twenty-five again. Then she squared her shoulders and the set of her jaw firmed. "But there are others who I am fond of too, and to whom I have a responsibility."

She buttoned her jacket and headed to the door while I stood, torn between pleading with her not to go and tying her to the bedpost.

She put her hand on the doorknob, but then turned back to me.

"One more thing. If we should meet again and I look younger—as when we first met—you must promise me something."

I crossed over to the doorway, pulled her close, and kissed her. "Sure. You name it."

"Do not, under any circumstances, comment as to my changed appearance or in any way refer to this meeting. Let it be as if this night had never happened."

She kissed me once, and was gone again.

* * * *

After she left, I got a bowl of my usual Frosted Flakes and spent the next hour sitting at the small Formica kitchen table, watching the soggy flakes slip, one by one, beneath the white waves of milk and come to rest like some sunken corn frigate on the bottom of the chipped china bowl.

Gradually, depression gave way to anger. I grabbed the bowl off the table and threw its contents into the sink. This was the last time I was going to let her waltz into my life and out again with yet another quivering piece of my heart and my ever-dwindling peace—no, make that "piece"—of whatever was left of my mind.

I had no reason to stay in Germany anymore. I went into the bedroom and started to pack. The only problem was that I had no idea where I was going. London, Paris, Rome? Or maybe somewhere like Budapest or Prague where my remaining supply of Euros would go further.

My cell rang, and I snatched it off the desk hoping it was Ria, cursing myself for wishing it.

But it wasn't. It was Dieter, and he didn't sound good.

"Herr Chris, you must come and meet me."

"Nice to hear from you too, Dieter, and why must I meet with you?"

"Because I know who spent the night with you."

"Hey, hang on a sec. Who I spent the night with is none of your damn business, but if it makes you feel any better, she split on me this morning. If you want to go chasing after her please, be my guest."

"No, no. You misunderstand me. It is not Ria I wish to speak with, it is you."

"Yeah, and why is that?"

"Has anyone broken into your flat?"

"How did you know?"

"Do you remember the night in the beer cellar when those people sat down close to us and I had to leave?"

"I remember your leaving, but I didn't pay much attention to those people at the next table. Why, are they important? Do they have something to do with Ria?"

As usual, he answered with yet another question.

"Have you noticed anyone following you? A man, perhaps? He looks about fifty, tall, thin, cold, *ja*? Like a snake?"

I thought for a moment. The restaurant. The men on the street.

"Maybe. Why? Who is he?"

Dieter spoke quickly as though he needed to get all the words out before he changed his mind.

"His name is Hans Kammler, and trust me when I say he is someone to be afraid of, very afraid. We must meet, Chris. Right now."

"Sorry, Deiter. I've had it with trotting off to secret locations for clandestine meetings that never turn out well."

"*Ja,* I understand, but this time I think you will want to come, because the one who has given me instructions to give to you something of great importance, is Maria herself."

Crap!

"OK, when and where?"

"One hour at the small travelers' café in the railway Bahnhof."

Chapter Nine

It took me little more than a half hour to get to the train station, but he was already seated at the far end of the counter when I entered the café.

I sat down on the stool next to him and offered my hand, but he didn't take it, and he didn't look at me, but his eyes darted from one end of the café to the other.

"Christ, Dieter, you're as jumpy as a cat. What's going on? Is it that Kammler dude you're worried about?"

"Keep your voice down," he whispered sharply. "They have people everywhere."

"Who? Who has people everywhere? Kammler?"

This time I was sorry I said it. Dieter looked as though he was going to be sick. I dropped my voice to a whisper. He was getting me spooked too. "OK, as you obviously know, I had a visitor last night, a mutual friend."

He stopped looking around the room and nodded slowly. "Ria."

"Yeah, Ria. But she looked different. No, I take that back. She looked like Ria but as though she'd aged twenty years overnight."

"Yes...I wondered if something like that might happen. It confirms what my own research has indicated." He nodded solemnly, more to himself than me. "She would never tell me, you know. Every time I asked her, she would shrug or change the subject, but I knew where she had been. I think I even know *who* she has been, and if I'm right, then I also know why she doesn't want me to know...why she doesn't want anyone to know." He rubbed the back of his hand over the stubble on his cheek. He hadn't shaved, and that wasn't like Dieter either.

I sighed. "Dieter, you're being obtuse, even for you. What the hell are you talking about? Where has Ria been to age her twenty years, and for that matter, where is she now? She took off on me again, and this time, I'm not even sure I want to find her. However, I keep getting sucked deeper and deeper into whatever you and Ria have been up to, and if there are some nasty people who might want to do nasty things to me, I deserve to know who, what, where, when and why."

The old rules of journalism didn't translate well into German. Dieter sat there looking at me, head cocked curiously to one side like the dog in the old RCA Victor ads.

"I don't think I understand you, Herr Chris, but I do know that you might be in danger. I'm afraid both of us may be."

"Over what?"

"This."

He took a small, thin key from the top pocket of his shirt and nervously slid it across the counter to me.

"It's the key to a post office box. As soon as I leave, you must go to the other exit and then proceed straight to the *Postamt*. Go to postal box 899, this key will open it, and inside you will find an envelope addressed to me. I want you to take it."

"Why? What's in the envelope?"

"My insurance policy. You see, I intend to tell them, if they ever come to get me, I will have arrangements in place to send the information they covet to the press; which is you, and if anything happens to me, it will be made public."

"OK, I'll bite. Just what is so damned important? And if it's that earth shattering, then how come it all fits into one crappy envelope? I mean, how much startling information can one little envelope hold?"

He looked at me with ghost of a smile. "About 16 gigabits of letters, diaries, photos, blueprints, and film footage of truly extraordinary achievements."

I leaned forward. This was more like it: secret files, beautiful women who came and went when the mood struck them, and shadowy, but all-too-real bad guys who wanted to get their hands on—

"A memory stick. That's what it is. A 16-gig memory stick. Am I right, Dieter?"

His eyes darted from me to the café entrance and back again before he inclined his head towards me and whispered, "Yes."

"And all this data contained on the stick; what is it? Where did you get it and why do the bad guys care so much about it?"

I glanced over at him but he wasn't looking at me. Instead, he was staring, lips slightly parted, face pale, and knuckles clenched white, at three men outside of the café's one dirty window. I could barely make out their figures through window's decades of accumulated grime, but Dieter recognized them and was terrified.

"Is that them?" I said softly out of the corner of my mouth.

He swallowed once and whispered, "Yes."

He clutched my hand. "Don't get up or look at them. Perhaps they don't know we're here. It could be a coincidence." But his panicked expression told me it was not. "We need to leave, but I don't dare turn around to see if they have gone or perhaps wait for us just outside the door."

"I might be able to help there." I looked at the large steel coffee urn on the counter to my right and I could see their reflection in the polished surface. I saw a lot of hand gesturing, and then two went off in one direction, and the tallest in another.

I waited a full minute before I turned to Dieter. "OK, they're gone."

I thought he'd be relieved, but if anything, he seemed even tenser. He closed his eyes, drew a deep breath, and let it out slowly.

"All right, I'm going to leave first in case they have anyone still watching the café. They will follow me. Give me five minutes and then go quickly to the *Postamt*. Once you have retrieved the memory stick, you must take it to this man, whom I believe you already know."

He pulled a paper napkin from the holder, scribbled a few lines on it, folded it several times, and slid it over the counter to me. He drew one more deep breath, muttered, "*auf Wiedersehen,*" and quickly walked out the café door.

I placed two euros on the counter for the coffee and unfolded the napkin note.

It read: Herr Maximillian von Buchholz, c/o Madeleine von Buchholz Kruase at 1547 Beacon Street, Apartment 2B, Boston, Massachusetts, United States.

Huh? Maximillian von Buchholz? Dieter said I already knew this character, but I didn't remember any Maximillian von... hang on a sec. Maximillian...Max. Maximillian von Buchholz was really Max Becker. And he was now living in the US in my old hometown of Boston. And that was where I was going next.

If I survived that long.

* * * *

All the way back from the post office I was nervous and jumpy as if someone was following me. And they probably were.

The plain envelope with a few grams of memory stick felt as though it weighed a hundred pounds. It wasn't until I returned to my flat and double locked the heavy wooden door that I opened the envelope and looked at the contents.

There was the ordinary-looking memory stick, which I had expected, and a note, which I had not. The note was in Dieter's handwriting and scribbled on a piece of memo pad stationary: *Hoffsteader & Söhne, Sanitärgroßhandel-und Geschäftsausstattung;* Hoffsteader & Sons, plumbing supplies and fixtures. The note said:

Take this to Maximillian von Buchholz now residing in Amerika. He will know what to do with it. Do <u>not</u>, under any circumstances, let it out of your sight.
– Dieter.

Great. I was glad Max would know what to do with it, because I sure as hell didn't. I started to put the small storage device back into the envelope, but paused. What the fuck? If I was gonna play messenger, I might as well know what I was carrying. I fired up the second-hand laptop I'd bought to replace my stolen one, and pushed the device into the USB port. When the screen came up, I clicked "open" and was rewarded with page after page of unfolding data. There were scanned-in images of old newspaper clippings, letters, mathematical formulas, and blueprints. Dozens and dozens of blueprints. Almost all of them were for different types of rockets or flying machines and something that looked like a cross between E. T.'s flying saucer and a Ferris wheel.

There was a knock at the door and I froze. The only one who could even conceivably be calling on me was Dieter—and he didn't know where I lived. This couldn't be good. I moved to the doorway, my hand hovered over the doorknob, and silently cursed my cheap landlord for not springing for a peephole in the door. I was about to call out, "Who is it?" when a cold trickle between my shoulder blades changed my mind. I didn't want whoever was outside the door to know I was on the other side. Then I heard something click in the lock and the doorknob began to turn.

Shit! I reached out to slide the chain lock into its receptacle, but stopped. If they jimmied the lock and saw the chain was in place, they would know I was here. Shit!

I backed away, looking for a place to hide. Franticly, my gaze swept the room. Where? In the closet? Under the bed? What did I think, they were ten years old and we were playing hide and seek? I heard the last tumbler on the lock click and the door started to swing open. I grabbed the laptop and my backpack and took the only escape route I could think of—out the window.

It would have been much nicer if the building had a regular fire escape instead of a rusty iron ladder, but beggars and cornered rats couldn't be choosers. As I clung to the flaking, pitted rungs, I heard them moving through the apartment and talking in low voices.

"He is not here, *Herr Obergruppenführer.*"

"Keep looking."

"*Jawohl, Herr Obergruppenführer.*"

The sound of doors opening and furniture being overturned came from inside. Then it struck me. *"Herr Obergruppenführer?"* That was an old Nazi rank from WWll. One of those weird SS ranks where everybody was called *"Führer."* I wasn't sure, but I think I'd read where that rank was pretty high up, maybe even a general. I heard a second man speak in English.

"Still nothing, Doctor Kammler."

My fingers tightened around the iron ladder. Kammler? Wasn't that the name Dieter had mentioned? Yeah, and the context was not complimentary. Something like, "he is someone to be afraid of–very afraid."

Now, I knew he was a doctor, so how much of a bad ass could he be? Then I remembered that the sadistic Nazi war criminal Joseph Mengele had been a doctor in the SS, and they had called him the "Angel of Death." Not good.

And with that cheery thought, a gravelly voice called out, "Check the fire escape."

A few moments later, a head popped out the window, looked down at the alley below and then withdrew. "There is no fire escape, Herr Doctor, only a ladder."

I let out the breath I'd been unconsciously holding and eased myself back around the drainpipe over the window where I'd been hanging out. Good thing he hadn't looked up.

I listened to them kick over a few more chairs and then heard the door slam. A few minutes later, I saw the front door to the building swing open, and I dropped back inside the apartment as three men exited and got into a black Mercedes waiting at the curb.

I took off my backpack, flipped a chair upright, and sat down, waiting for my hands to stop shaking.

Whoever had tossed my place the first time must be connected with this guy Kammler, who was apparently a doctor, and if I heard right, held the rank of *SS Obergruppenführer*. The only problem was the last time that rank had been used was 1945.

* * * *

Have you ever been dumb enough to think that things couldn't possibly get any worse? Of course they can. So I shouldn't have been surprised when Dieter didn't answer his cell. I left him a voicemail, telling him I had retrieved the envelope and memory stick and wanted to know what it was all about, and why these bad guys were trying to get their hands on it, and for all I knew, me. He didn't call back.

That night, I slept in the closet.

If they were watching my building, they wouldn't see me come back to my apartment and thus would not be likely to search it again. However, it didn't stop me from finding the longest, sharpest butcher knife in the kitchen drawer and putting it under my pillow. The closet was cramped and smelled like old shoes, but I wired the door shut with picture wire, figuring that if they tried to open it in the night, it would make enough of a racket to wake me. What I would do with a kitchen knife against three, probably armed guys, was one I was too tired to think about, but thankfully, they didn't come.

In the morning, I got on my computer and booked an evening flight to Boston. I finished the last of my stale cornflakes and turned on the TV. The announcer was halfway through the morning news and I was standing at the sink rinsing out the bowl when I heard:

"And in other news, a young man from Düsseldorf was brutally murdered last night. His body was found early this morning at the Kaiser Hotel by the maid. Police have asked that anyone who might have had contact with this man, please contact them."

A picture flashed on the screen of a photo of a young man with blond hair and a serious expression. It was Dieter.

* * * *

For a moment, I was so upset I seriously considered calling the police. But only for a moment.

It didn't take me long to figure out that the people who were after me were most likely the same ones who'd killed Dieter. They wanted the memory stick and were prepared to kill anyone to get it. That much I got; it was the "why" that puzzled me.

All I knew about them was that they were merciless, relentless, and deadly. They were either some type of neo-Nazi group, complete with all the weird titles and ranks, or else they thought they were the real thing, which made them a bunch of nut cases. Dangerous nut cases.

All right then, why didn't I go to the cops? Maybe it was because I'd always had nightmares about Arnold Schwarzenegger in *The Terminator* saying, "I'll be back," and then walking through the cop house blowing everyone to smithereens. More likely, I was just plain spooked about everything that had happened over the past week and simply wanted to get the hell out of Dodge—or in this case, the merry old land of *München.*

I had the uneasy feeling they still might be watching the building to see if I came back. If I was gonna be stuck in some third-rate spy movie, I might as well go all the way—secret meetings, cryptic messages, and disguises. I decided to try one out. Since they'd be watching for me coming into the building, they'd pay little attention to someone going out. All I needed was a reasonably effective disguise, and I had a good idea of where to get one.

The old man across the hall was very absent minded and usually forgot to lock his door. I knew, because he'd asked me to throw the latch anytime I passed by and saw it open, like now.

Yup, I peeked out into the hallway and his door was open several inches. I quickly darted across the hall and snatched an old raincoat, twenty years out of date, along with a battered tweed cap and a beat up cane. I ducked back into my apartment and threw my backpack into an old canvas shopping bag and tossed a newspaper and half-empty bottle of schnapps on top of it. I had no theatrical make-up, so I sprayed a bit of wet, white paint onto a paper towel and dabbed it on my hair. Not very professional, but then again, it only had to get me out of the building and down to the metro and to the airport.

I wanted to leave right away, but I knew I'd have a better chance at twilight, so I waited. It was the longest afternoon of my life. While I waited, I started going over the contents of the memory stick. Most of it looked like gibberish to me. As I'd glimpsed briefly the day before, there were long, complex formulas, blueprints, drawings of strange-looking machines, and page after page of peculiar writing in languages I'd never seen. Some looked like ancient cuneiform while others were in some type of bizarre text.

Frustrated, and increasingly apprehensive about getting out of the building with my skin intact, I pulled the memory stick out and shut down the laptop. I held the thin two-inch rectangle in my hand, turning it over and over. I needed a place to hide it on me, but where? I thought about the place where prisoners always hide their drugs when smuggling them into prison, but the thought of prison showers and body cavity searches made me discard it just as quickly. I ran through the limited options I had—in my backpack or on my person—and rejected each idea in turn.

Finally, in desperation, I took my black leather jacket and ran my hands over it. I could slit the lining and slip it in somewhere. Somewhere that anyone searching the coat wouldn't find or feel, but where...? Then I saw it. Maybe not perfect, but given the time and my need to get the hell out of here, it would have to do. I took a steak knife out of the kitchen drawer, quickly picked out a few stitches, and slid the stick in. I pulled on the jacket, and over it, the old raincoat and hat.

It was time to go.

Chapter Ten

I thought I was going to get away clean.

From my admittedly limited experience as an actor, including my role in the senior class play as the "dustman" in *Pygmalion*, I played the part of an old man rather well. I hunched over, clutched my shopping bag, and tottered right by the two heavies watching the building. I was about to turn the corner when one of them pushed off from the hood of the Mercedes he'd been leaning against.

"Hey... *alter Mann, was in der Tasche*?"

The bag. He wanted to see what was in the bag, and if he looked under the newspapers, he'd find my laptop. Then they'd search me and...Shit!

He crossed over to me and reached for the bag. "You just came out of the building. Did you see a guy in his twenties, brown hair, medium build, wearing a black leather jacket?"

"*Nein*," I mumbled continuing to hobble towards the corner.

"Well then, let's take a look at what you have in your bag."

He started to grab for it so I played my only card.

"*Ach, meine Lebensmittel*," I wailed and nudged a large jar of pickled pig's feet out of the grocery bag. The jar shattered on the sidewalk, drenching his shoes and cuffs in rank-smelling vinegar and dubious pork.

"*Du dumme Arschloch*," he screamed and kicked the cane out from under me.

I pretended to stagger and wailed, "*Meine gebeizt Schweine Füße!*" over the mock tragedy of my lost pickled pig's feet.

He picked up the cane, snapped it over his knee, and threw the pieces at me. "Get the hell out of here, you old *Dummkopf*, before I smash your fucking head in!"

I scooped up the bag and, still moaning about my lost jar of pig's feet, stumbled to the corner and the dark street beyond. I peeked back around the corner and saw a BMW pull up to the building and the tall, thin man get out. I saw them gesturing and pointing to my building and then to the corner I'd just turned. The tall man started towards my corner. Half a block away, a cabbie was delivering his fare. I sprinted for the cab and jumped inside.

"Drive!"

"Where?"

"Airport."

The light turned and he sped away from the curb. I turned and saw the hawk-faced man round the corner and stare at the receding cab. He stood there, hands on hips like some old WWII German general surveying a battlefield.

I continued watching him watch my cab until we turned the next corner, but I had a sinking feeling that he hadn't been fooled by the old man. Not at all.

* * * *

I got to the airport three hours before my flight and headed for the security screening line. But one look at the hundreds of people snaking back and forth between the maze of ropes convinced me to hit the men's room before I committed myself to the check-in shuffle for the next hour.

I chose a vacant stall, latched the door, and took off the raincoat and cap. I began rubbing at my white, paint-tinged hair with a paper towel and some nail polish remover that had been left in my apartment a month earlier by an enthusiastic grad student, who'd, no doubt, hoped she'd be invited back to retrieve it, along with some very skimpy black lace underwear.

Suddenly, the sound of stall doors being opened and closed, and then, "*Was machst du, Arschloch?*" followed by a soft "pop," like someone pulling a cork from a champagne bottle made me freeze. I had a sinking feeling. No one had decided to celebrate with a bottle of bubbly in a Munich Airport bathroom.

A split second later, the door to my stall in crashed inward with the sound of ripping hinges. I grabbed my backpack to make a run for it, but the grinning thug filling the space where the door had been shook his head.

"*Nein, du nicht mein kleiner Freund.*"

And "little friend" or not, the next thing I knew, he dragged me out and was tugging at my backpack.

"*Übergeben sie, Arschloch.*" He snarled at me to hand it over.

How low on the social scale must I be to be called an "asshole" by a real-life example of one?

"*Scheisse,*" I muttered, "talk about the asshole pot calling the kettle black."

He was not amused.

I drew in my arms tighter around the straps and struggled to twist out of his grasp. Then I caught sight of the second stall from mine. There was a widening red puddle seeping slowly across the tiled floor. The popping sound I'd heard had been a silenced pistol, and the poor bastard who had probably been mistaken for me was dead.

I had no illusions left that they would not hesitate to kill me to get the contents of my backpack.

He saw my look of horror and grinned. "*Ja*. That will be you in five seconds unless you hand it over. Now, *geben*!" He pulled a WWII Lugar 9mm automatic from his suit coat and pulled back the cocking mechanism.

I made a break for it. And I would have made it too except...

He lunged forward and caught the lifting handle on the backpack. There was nothing I could do. I let my shoulders slump and wiggled out of the pack. Then I banged open the men's room door and sprinted back into the terminal. I glanced back and saw him grinning at me, the middle finger on his right hand extended while his left clutched my backpack.

* * * *

There was no more pursuit. Why should there be? They had gotten what they'd been after, which was of course, not my backpack, but the computer in it. They'd already gotten my first laptop, and now assumed I'd downloaded whatever information Dieter had given me onto the used laptop. And they were right. I had.

But how long would it take them to figure out I had downloaded the contents of the flash drive onto the second laptop but kept the original source—the memory stick?

An hour later, as my flight finally took off and the jet gained attitude, I sat in the window seat with my face pressed against the Plexiglas and fingered the thick leather of my jacket's right shoulder epaulette tab. It was imperceptibly wider than the left one.

Because that's where I'd hidden the memory stick.

Chapter Eleven

Boston, Massachusetts

"Actually, this is not Boston."

The rental agent looked at me as if I'd said the apartment had roaches, which it probably did. I even toyed with the idea to switch off the lights for a few minutes to see what crawled out from beneath the stove and refrigerator, but then, what if we turned the switch back on to find a whole colony of the little critters break dancing on the counter?

It was late and I was tired. Having already viewed three other downtown apartments that probably were infested, not only by roaches but large rodents too, this was probably the best I could hope for given my budget. And the painfully thin woman with the smoker's cough was losing enthusiasm for showing me any more places I couldn't afford.

That's probably why she'd dragged me all the way out to Brighton, which most people lumped into Boston along with its more upscale neighbor, Brookline—but not me. I'd lived in Boston, and this wasn't it.

She looked annoyed, her only expression outside of boredom and impatience. "Perhaps not technically, but it is right on the Green Line and only minutes to downtown Boston."

Sure, if you got a hundred or two of those minutes to spare during peak commute hours. But I didn't say it. I was tired too, and she was right; it was all I could afford.

"And it has a nice bow window with views of Commonwealth Avenue, which runs all the way from here to the Public Gardens."

She waved her hand towards the street as if giving it permission to continue its eastward journey to heart of the city.

"Plus, there is a washer and dryer in the basement. I really don't think you're going to find a better bargain anywhere in the city for the money. Now, if you can spend a little more, I can show you—"

"I'll take it."

* * * *

It didn't take me long to move in for one simple reason: I was carrying everything I owned in my new backpack, refilled at a downtown Army Navy store across the street from the realty office. After I gave the rental agent a check, and her nicotine-stained fingers dropped the key into my hand, I was, for all intent and purposes, home.

The good news was the apartment came furnished, so I had something to sit on and something to sleep on. That was also the bad news. Think college dorm furniture but not nearly as sturdy and twice as old, and you've got a rough idea of the quality of the furnishings decorating a cramped, one-bedroom apartment in the section of Brighton mostly occupied by college students.

I quickly learned which of the sagging chairs not to sit in and that encompassed all but one. My other preemptive strike was focused on the mattress. It was not that there were stains on it, the stains looked as though someone had had some very wild nights or had been murdered on it. At first, I was concerned. It might have bedbugs. Then I decided no self-respecting bed bug would take a chance on making a home in something looking like it had been used to line a cat litter box.

The first night I threw some blankets on the bed and slept like the dead until I awoke itching. Perhaps the bed bugs were more egalitarian than I imagined. At any rate, I felt better after I moved the blankets to the floor and slept the rest of the night in what I hoped was solitude.

The next morning, after calling 1-800-Mattress, I got down to the business of tracking down Max Becker, or Maximillian von Buchholz as I now knew was his real name, though the whys and wherefores of the need for an alias eluded me. No matter. I had an address and that was the logical place to start.

The address proved to be a stately, well-kept, red brick three-story apartment building surrounded by an ornate, Victorian wrought iron fence. Three apartments fronted on Beacon Street, all with large bow windows. According to the address Dieter had given me, Max's sister's unit was number two, which should be the one with hanging plants in the window on the second floor.

I had considered calling first, but figured I'd have more luck showing up unannounced rather than giving Max Becker, who wasn't Max Becker, time to be conveniently out when I arrived.

I buzzed the door in the lobby and was surprised when a young, feminine voice came over the intercom,

"Yes?"

Fortunately, I'd come prepared and had invested in a tie and a clipboard and a somewhat official looking blue windbreaker.

"Ah, hello. I'm with the EPA and we're doing a census of heating systems to check for efficiency. It won't take long. All I need is to check your radiators and stove."

"No problem, but you gotta make it quick 'cause I'm leaving for a class in about ten minutes."

The door buzzed and I pushed it open with a click.

The girl who answered the door looked even younger than she'd sounded. About nineteen or twenty I guessed, and damned hot, in a wholesome sort of way. She was about five-four but sweetly proportioned with green-gold eyes, silky, long, honey blond hair, high cheekbones, and an infectious smile.

"C'mon in, Mr. EPA Man." She opened the door with a little mocking curtsey and waved in the general direction of what I saw was the kitchen. "You can go ahead and poke around while I finish making myself gorgeous for my creative writing class that, like I said, I gotta bolt for in about ten minutes."

I nodded and she trotted off down a long hall that probably led to the bedrooms.

"According to our records," I called after her, "this apartment is registered to one Madeleine von Buchholz Krause. That wouldn't be you, would it?"

I heard a door close, then opening again quickly. "No, that's Gram."

"Ah, OK, and you are…?"

"Katy. Katrina Krause, though I'm using Kat now 'cause it sounds much cooler in the alternative rock band I'm singing with. Kat Krause, awesome lead singer for Changing Lanes."

I caught a brief glance of her darting from the bedroom into another room across the hall, which I assumed must be the bathroom. Sure enough, I heard a toilet flush and she came out, smoothing down a red top that left her navel and gold belly button ring nicely exposed.

"Umm, yeah. Very cool."

She came bustling into the living room where I stood and looked at her watch. "Oh crap, I really gotta go. I mean like, right now. Sorry, Mr. EPA Man, but you're gonna have to come back another time 'cause I gotta run and Gram and Uncle Max are both out."

"Uncle Max? Oh, then your uncle lives with you?"

"Actually, my great-uncle, and yeah, kinda. I mean, like, he just got here a few days ago, and I don't know what he and Gram have decided. All I really know about him is that he's Gram's kid brother from Germany, but for now, yeah I guess he lives here."

She struggled into the straps of her backpack and gave me a one-eyebrow-raised smile as she watched me make some scribbled notes on my clipboard. "Wow, you EPA guys sure are snoopy."

"I'm sorry if it seems that way, but we need lots of information if we're going to be able to make a difference in global warming," I lied.

"Oh sure. Save the planet and go green. I'm vegan, you know."

"Ah, that explains the faintly green glow."

She laughed and then stuck out her tongue. "Not bad for a man from the government."

I smiled back and walked with her as she moved toward the door. "Maybe it'd be easier if I came back when your grandmother or uncle are here. They're probably home a bit more often then you, I'm guessing?"

She nodded, following me out to the hallway and turning the key in the lock.

"When do you think, for instance, your uncle will be back?"

She glanced at her watch again. "Yipe! Damn, I'm gonna be soooo late." She turned and clattered down the stairs two at a time, calling up to me, "Probably tonight. Ciao."

* * * *

I spent the rest of the day scouting out the neighborhood between my student-populated Commonwealth Avenue neighborhood and the upscale area of Brookline's Beacon Street. I found some good, reasonably priced places to eat, even though the majority of the cuisine ran towards pizza, subs, and burgers, along with an overpriced liquor store, and a CVS.

The remainder of my time I devoted to stopping to gaze in shop windows where I searched the reflection of the street behind me for any skulking figures who might be carrying concealed weapons in their pockets. I didn't see anything. But that didn't mean they weren't there.

Having gotten myself duly paranoid to the point where every guy in a raincoat with his hands in his pockets made me duck into doorways, I stopped in at a kitschy brewpub catering to college kids and young, ex-college working people who wished they were still in school.

Over a beer and some greasy nachos, I decided to operate under the assumption that the Third Reich wanna-be's were still in Munich, muscling little old ladies off the sidewalk, and I should get on to doing what I'd come back for.

A bored waitress dropped the bill on my table and I surveyed my dangerously dwindling supply of cash. I needed to find a very rich lady with loose morals and low taste in men, or find myself a job. Option B was more likely than Option A.

Fortunately, I still had a few friends in town, and one of them happened to be the editor of one of Boston's longest running "alternative" newspapers.

I finished the last of my draft beer, powered on my smart phone, and leaned towards the window for better reception. He answered on the third ring.

"Hey, Jason, it's Chris—Chris Brennan. How are you doin', man?"

After a bit more chitchat, I hit him up for a writing job, hinting that I was working on something big. At first he told me, "No way, what with all the free blogs and online news and events, we're struggling as it is."

But when I told him about how I'd switched majors to computer science, he got interested and told me I could write and submit—if I'd put in a few hours every day on their backload of computer programming. After settling on a freelance scale for whatever they took of my writing, and an hourly pay only marginally above minimum wage for the programming, he told me to come by in the morning and he'd get me started. I clicked my cell off, feeling better as the prospect of scrounging in garbage cans with the homeless receded slightly.

I left the pub and stepped out into the growing darkness. The sun had dropped below the roofline of the buildings and was setting in a sullen, ocher red against the trees of Chestnut Hill in the distance.

It was time to get a few answers.

* * * *

I stood in the small foyer of the Beacon Street apartment. Would the girl who answered the door this morning answer it again? I surprised myself hoping she would. She didn't.

"Who is it?" A low, querulous voice crackled over the small, tinny speaker.

I dusted off my story from the morning and once again I was buzzed up. But when I got to the door, the elderly voice behind the peephole demanded to see my badge. It was all I could do to keep from blurting out the old line from *The Treasure of the Sierra Madre*. "Badges? We don't got to show you no stinking badges."

I managed to restrain myself. Fortunately, I'd prepared for this question. I held up an impressively intricate laminated plastic badge, which had been issued for computer room access when I'd been interning at the German software company. It had lots of stamped markings in very small print, which I was counting on could not be read very easily, and I was right. The door opened a fraction and a rheumy blue eye looked me up and down. The clipboard, jacket, and my mostly clean cut, earnest young man appearance must have convinced her because the door shut, the chain scraped in the lock, and it swung open.

The woman at the door looked about eighty. She was thin and her skin was very pale as though she didn't spend a lot of time in the sun, which probably accounted for its relatively unwrinkled condition. For an octogenarian, she looked pretty good.

"Vell, vhat is it you vant?"

Her thick German accent told me she hadn't come to the US until she was an adult, and English was most definitely her second language. She had a low, rasping voice, which back in her prime, probably made her sound like Greta Garbo.

"Ah, I'm with the EPA and we're doing an energy audit. I was here this afternoon. Perhaps your granddaughter might have mentioned I'd be returning?" I glanced around the hallway hoping the cute girl I'd met earlier might be able to rescue me, but no such luck.

"She is not home. You know how it is with young people. They come, they go, and no one knows vhere or vhen."

She led me back to the kitchen and I noticed that, despite a slight unsteadiness in her gait, she held her back straight. I was likewise struck by the still-graceful arch of her long neck.

"You vant to check the gas stove, *ja*?"

"Absolutely."

She folded her arms and stared at me while I made a great show of scribbling furiously on my clipboard.

I moved around the kitchen, pretending to check fittings on the stove. "All right then, is it just you and your granddaughter living here?"

"Vhy do you vant to know?"

"Well, ma'am, that's one of the most important parts of the Green Initiative program. We're researching the energy consumption per consumer." I smiled. That even sounded plausible to me.

"Humph." She snorted but finally nodded. "*Ja*, it is myself and my granddaughter who live here all the time."

I flipped a couple of pages on the clipboard and frowned. "Hmm, that's odd, because when I was here this morning, your granddaughter told me her uncle lived here too."

"If you know already, zen vhy do you bother me *mit* stupid questions?" She turned and walked away. Damn!

I followed her out of the kitchen. "Then your brother is here right now?"

She opened the door. "You are all done here now."

It was not a question.

I clutched my clipboard and sighed as I walked down the stairs. Now I was going to have to go about it the hard way.

* * * *

It took me two days of watching the apartment before I was able to catch Max coming out the front door. He'd probably come and gone before, but what with working for Jason at the paper and trying to catch a few hours of sleep, there was a limit to the amount of time I could devote to watching the Beacon Street building from the cement-and-wood bench on the opposite side of the street.

I was dozing off when a taxi's horn jerked me back to alert. A man came out and started walking down the street away from me.

When I realized the figure rapidly disappearing down the block was Max, I got up and trotted off behind him.

Fortunately, I was in reasonably decent shape, thanks to lots of adrenalin fueled by running and scrambling to stay alive, but by the time I caught up with Max, I was winded. I turned the corner where Harvard intersects Beacon Street and saw him standing underneath a green-striped storefront awning, waiting for me.

"For an old guy, you move pretty damned fast." I said by way of greeting.

He smiled his little twinkle-eyed Bavarian *bürgermeister* smile as though running into me on a street corner three thousand miles from where we'd met was the most natural thing in the world. Apparently it was.

"I've been expecting you."

I drew in a deep breath. "Silly me. Just because you skipped out without a word, and I had to flee Munich with a bunch of crazy Nazis on my tail and spend the better part of another week and a lot of good storytelling and outright lying and energy in tracking you down, I kinda thought you might have been avoiding me."

He kept smiling and opened the door to the lunch counter under whose awning we'd been standing. "Nonsense, it was good for you. Teaches you how self-reliant you can be." He held up two fingers to the counter man, and he came over to our small table with two cups of watery, tan liquid that might have been coffee in another life.

"OK, Max." I took a drink of the coffee-flavored water and stared at him. "I'm all gooey and dewy-eyed with the joys of accomplishment and self-worth, but now I'd like some answers."

He made a gesture that could have been interpreted as either, "Certainly, I'm at your service," or "Fat chance, Charlie."

Regardless of what he meant, I was taking it as the former. "All right then, let's start with why you left Munich is such a hurry, though I think I know the answer."

"Yes, you do. Because from what you just said, it sounds like they came to visit you too."

"If you mean Colonel Klink and Sergeant Schultz, yeah. We had an enjoyable game of hide and seek while hanging out the window. Just who are those dorks anyway? All I know is that they have no sense of humor and are suffering under the delusion that the Third Reich has risen again and they want get in on the ground floor as Nazi Storm Troopers."

The tiny smile never left his face, but his eyes grew cold and distant as if he was watching something he hoped he'd left far behind. "They are not deluded, and they are something worse than those low-browed street thugs who made up the SA the Storm Troopers in the late twenties and early thirties." He shook his head. "No, the men who came after you were no *Sturmabteilung* Brown Shirts. Those men you saw were blood-oath members of the one of the greatest concentrations of evil to have ever walked the earth. They were *Schutzstaffel*, demons in black shirts—the troops who wore Death as their cap badge. The SS."

He was quiet and I tried to digest what he'd said. It was obvious ol' Max was having a senior moment, maybe more than one. He was a sharp old guy, but when we'd talked before, I'd noticed that his dates didn't match up with his age, and now he was obviously letting those jumbled ghosts from the past spill over into the present. I decided to try tact, or at least what passed as tact for me.

"Ah, Max? I don't want to make too big a deal out of it, but I think you might have gotten your chronology a bit muddled. Hitler's SS thugs got put out of business by the Allies in 1945, and even if these monkey brains had belonged to that lot, they'd be in their nineties by now. These boys look much too spry."

He shook his head. "No, you're wrong. They are SS, and every bit as deadly as they were seventy years ago."

I sighed. If we were going to get anywhere in the information department, I was going to have to humor him. "OK, let's say these guys are pretending—or even think they are the original SS—what's the deal? I mean, is this one of these neo-Nazi, Forth Reich conspiracy things Robert Ludlum writes about in his spy novels? Do they work for some Ernst Stavro Blofeld-type villain and have gotten me confused with James Bond? Though, I do have to admit, the resemblance is stunning."

Max didn't laugh.

"How do I make you understand?" He sighed. "I cannot fault you for your skepticism. If I had not lived it, I would not believe it either." He gazed at me intently. "Maybe what would be best is if you were to go away and lose yourself in this big, beautiful, free country and forget you ever met a strange old man named Max Becker."

"Sounds attractive, except for one small problem. I never met Max Becker. All I met was a man who used that name, a man whose real name is Maximillian von Buchholz."

He looked down at the table then back up at me with a small, sheepish grin like a kid caught lifting spare change off his old man's bureau. "*Ach*, so you know, then."

"No, not really. All I know is you're not who you say you are, and now I'm involved in it, and whether I like it or not, I'm very much afraid that these delusional Nazi doorknobs are going to be coming after me."

"No, I don't think so. Why would they care about you?"

"Because I've got this." I pulled the memory stick out of the watch pocket of my jeans.

He took it and turned it over in his fingers. "Amazing, the technology, isn't it? If this is what I think it is, then it once took an entire room of filing cabinets to hold the information contained in this tiny bit of plastic and silicone." He looked at me. "That is what is on the device, *ja*?"

"If you mean hundreds of pages of mathematical formulas, pages of blueprints, and long, incomprehensible lists of specifications in particularly dense German, then, yes."

He grabbed my hand, his eyes darting around the empty room, but we were only ones there, even the counter man had gone back to the kitchen where I could hear the sound of talk radio and vegetables being chopped.

"You must learn to be more careful, Herr Chris, because now you are correct. They will be coming for it."

"Then I think you owe it to me, Max, to tell me straight up, and no bullshit, the truth about Nazis and little green men. What the fuck is going on?"

He sighed and finally nodded. "Yes, you are right. I do owe you that, and probably more. Very well. Let me take you back to Germany in 1919."

Chapter Twelve

Southern Bavaria, December 1919

It was more than a year after the anticlimactic ending of the Great War, and Germany was still smarting under the humiliation of defeat and punitive reparations of the Versailles Treaty.

To assuage wounded national pride, many previously skeptical realists had found comfort in heroic Germanic myths of the sort Herr Richard Wagner based his fanciful operas on. And, I suppose, what was the most frightening, though I did not recognize it at the time, was that many of these men, who were pure genius in science, physics, and mathematics, had started to incorporate these myths into their formerly pristine technological disciplines. The first and foremost of these genius had joined the Thulists after the war, and by now, the political men who were struggling to unseat the Weimar Republic had started sniffing around some of our meetings.

I say "our" though, I must confess, I was more of an observer, a hanger-on, truth be told. But Maria was one of the group's leaders and I loved Maria, so...

We had outgrown the third-floor apartment parlor, but fortunately, the Thulists had now made connections with some wealthy patrons, and on this day in late December, we and the DHvSS men of the "Black Stone"—but more about them later—were meeting in a rustic Bavarian hunting *schloss* in the vicinity of Berchtesgaden.

Maria was very excited because only the week before she had awoken me in the middle of the night.

"Max, they were here," she exclaimed breathlessly, pointing to her head. "In my mind I mean, and they told me things. Wonderful things."

Now she and Sigrun had the rapt attention of everyone gathered before the huge stone fireplace in the great hall. She was explaining to them that the first message she'd received had been in a script unknown to her, but was later identified as a secret Templar code from the Middle Ages, which Sigrun, her friend from the Vril Gesellschaft, had helped to translate.

The most recent transmission she'd received, she suspected, was in some ancient language also unfamiliar to her. That was why her previously small circle had expanded to include the Panbabylonists, a group close to the Thule society and based around the study of ancient cultures. Maria and Sigrun had presented the unfamiliar writing to the Panbabylonists, which included such notables in archeology and philology such as Hugo Winckler, Peter Jensen, and Friedrich Delitzsch among others. It turned out that the apparently strange language was actually ancient Sumerian, the language of ancient Babylonia. But what had everyone in the lodge speechless with amazement was how both sets of the now-translated documents contained references—actual detailed instructions—for an unknown type of disc-shaped flying machine powered by the mysterious form of energy they called Vril.

Being madly in love with Maria, I naturally believed every word she'd related, but even had I not been enamored of her, the evidence she and Sigrun presented was so startling and detailed, no one could have made up anything so elaborate without expert working knowledge of not only arcane, extinct languages, but physics, mathematics, and aviation engineering too.

That day, the members of both groups pledged to provide the funding and technical expertise to start work on building the machine.

Both Maria and I left the meeting elated. We would soon be able to build a machine that might perhaps reach the stars. However, it took more than three years merely to gather the parts, and another two to begin the first stages of the actual construction. By that time, Rudolf von Sebottendorf, the founder of the Thule Gesellschaft, had begun to dabble in politics and had thus invited the man who was to become Hitler's Deputy Führer, Rudolf Hess, to attend a meeting. It was during the meeting in November of 1924 when Maria suddenly went into a trance. At first, I wasn't alarmed because a trance or during sleep was how she always received her messages. This time, however, quite without warning, shortly after we sat down, her eyes rolled back and she began speaking in an elderly, masculine voice. I was unfamiliar with the voice, but the effect on the circle was electric. Von Sebottendorf paled.

"She is speaking with the voice of Dietrich Eckar," he said.

I had heard Maria mention his name once or twice as part of the Thule membership but not recently, so I shrugged. "Why is that significant?"

"Because he has been dead for more than a year."

This unnerved Hess.

Suddenly, the voice of Eckart announced, "We have something of great import to tell you." Without warning, the voice changed to a soft, lilting woman's voice.

"Good evening my friends."

No one spoke, so I asked the question everyone wanted answered. "Who are you and where are you from?"

Maria replied in the same soft voice. "I am of the Sumi. A race that dwells on a distant world that orbits the star Aldebaran in the constellation of Taurus."

The woman Maria was channeling continued speaking.

"We Sumi are a humanoid race that colonized the Earth 500 million years ago on a now-submerged continent we called Atlantis. Our race guided your ancestors in building the great cities of Larsa, Shurrupak, and Nippur in Iraq, and those inhabitants, who were genetically improved by our science, were installed in those new cities. You see, we foresaw the sinking of Atlantis and subsequent great flood and thus took those steps to protect our hybrid progeny. They were the progenitors of the modern day Aryan race."

This had an immediate and profound effect on Hess, and from that day forward, he always regarded Maria with a new mixture of awe and fear. Although we didn't realize it at the time, that single reference to "Aryans" would open the door to a nightmare called the Third Reich.

* * * *

Munich, November 1923

Hess was not our first contact with the National Socialists. In November of 1923, Gudrun, one of the other Vrilerinnen, those handsome young ladies of the Vril Gesellschaft, invited us to a mass meeting.

Gudrun begged Maria, Sigrun, and me to accompany her to a political rally to hear a brilliant young speaker she had met at a lecture based on Edward Bulwer-Lytton's book, *The Coming Race*. This was the book that had first sparked the interest of German romantics at the turn of the century and had given rise to the Thulists. It also provided fuel for the increasingly strident rhetoric many of the Nationalist groups used to battle the Communists in the steadily escalating violent street clashes.

Gudrun was quite taken with their leader's oratory.

"Ach," she gushed. "You mark my words. He will become a champion who can bring the spiritual message of a new Golden Age to the masses and the importance of working together to implement the Thulist goals of achieving a more perfect and transcendent German race."

We were naive enough to believe Gudrun. At least at first.

The man was speaking that night at a working man's beer hall. We came in and took seats on a long, wooden bench in the first row. When the man stepped up to the small speakers' platform, I found him disappointing after Gudrun's build up. He was not tall or in any way striking, and seemed nervous, not looking at the crowd, eyes downcast.

I recall how he started...slowly at first. Quietly, almost hesitantly, as if unsure of himself, but as he began to speak, it was as though he drew strength from his own words and his voice rose. His blue eyes began to flash as he accused Jews and Communists of betrayal at Versailles. His face became infused with an almost-divine madness as he insisted that the greatness of the German people had been lost and how they needed to find their way back to the Nordic past, to the

Germanic roots of pre-history, to the ancient, god-like people of Thule.

"Do you see what I mean?" Gudrun turned to me breathlessly, face flushed with excitement. "He cites many of the very beliefs of our society. I am going to invite him to one of our meetings. I'm sure he could help us to broaden our membership."

I didn't answer her, but I felt uneasy. There was something about the man's manner. His eyes frightened me. Yes, he was putting forth many of the same theories espoused by our philosophers and professors, but in a strange, twisted sort of fashion only a hair's breadth from violence.

No, from the first time I saw him, the man filled me with dread. I did not care at all for Herr Adolph Hitler.

He only came to one meeting and did not come alone. He was accompanied by Dr. Krohn who was one of the founding Thulists and the man who helped to create the "blood flag" of the NSDAP, the *National Sozialistische Deutsche ArbeiterPartei;* the Nazis. Krohn took much of the design from the 1919 Thule Gesellschaft banner featuring the ancient Buddhist and Hindu symbols for good luck; the swastika.

Hitler didn't speak or stay long, and after listening to one of the on-going discussions about the possible connections of the Aldebaran and the power of the Vril to our northern peoples in the distant past, he spoke a few words to Krohn, nodded in our direction, and left. But he did not forget about us, and when he became chancellor in 1933, he gave our group the full political and financial backing of the new Third Reich.

But that was ten years in the future. For now, our challenge was finding the necessary funds to keep the

Jenseitsflugmaschine (Other World Flight Machine) and the *Vril Flugscheiben* (Flying Discs) projects going.

Herr Hitler had his problems too, and when he was arrested and sentenced to Landsburg Prison for his failed Beer Hall Putsch, I think we all breathed a sigh of relief.

Herman Hess had chosen to accompany his leader into prison and served as his secretary while Hitler dictated his rambling tirade about race and power into what became *Mein Kampf*. Hess also kept up a steady stream of correspondence with the leaders of the Thule Gesellschaft, and when Hess and Hitler were released after only nine months, more and more of the Nazi leaders were becoming interested in our work.

Over the next few years we had more and more visits from almost the entire rogue's gallery of party bosses. In addition to people like Hess and Göring, there was Nazi theorist Alfred Rosenberg, Hitler's personal physician; Dr. Theodor Morell, and of course, that odious little toad, Heinrich Himmler. All expressed interest in the mystic speculations of the Thulists, but even more in the experiments regarding Vril and especially the *Jenseitsflugmaschine*.

Fortunately, or perhaps unfortunately as it turned out, we did not concern ourselves with the Nazi machinations and power struggles over the next few years. All of our efforts were focused on translating the information coming from the Vrillian ladies and applying it to complete the *Jenseitsflugmaschine*.

Now, I will freely admit that the Thulists had many wealthy and influential supporters among the upper classes who had much to gain from a re-emergent Germany, which, of course, suited the Nazis too.

But perhaps the single most valuable asset between the Thulists and the Vril *Gesellschaft* was Maria herself. In fact, she was in such demand with channeling masses of data from Aldebaran and providing spiritual readings for some of our wealthiest patrons, I began to worry about her health.

On several occasions I chided her and told her she must cut back on her psychic activities or face exhaustion.

She would only smile and kiss me. "You must understand, my love. This is not merely a thing of interest for scholars and those of our group, but shining knowledge to bring mankind closer to the utopian society of the Sumi and other advanced beings of the Aldebaran star system." She touched my cheek. "So please, dearest Max, such an end is worth any personal cost I might have to bear."

But it wasn't to me.

I loved her and was torn between wanting to protect and provide for her, and wanting to support her in something she passionately believed. It still shames me to say that, were it not for the money we received from her wealthy patrons, we would have starved in those early days. I, myself, had a difficult time finding steady employment in the Weimar Republic, and the little I made from teaching didn't go very far. Through family connections, I managed to stay on the active rolls as a reservist in the Austrian army after the war, but it was only at half pay, and with inflation and economic uncertainty, we relied on Maria's income. That was probably what kept me from pushing my suit with her. If I pressured her to marry me, it would appear as though I merely wished to secure my meal ticket. It was perhaps as much from my feelings of guilt as well as love that I poured myself into helping her and the society with our project over the next few years.

And despite my initial skepticism, the first prototype of the *Jenseitsflugmaschine* began to take shape. The original concept, as conceived from the translated messages Maria and Sigrun had received, was not for a flying craft, but rather an inter-dimensional, channeled flight disc.

Maria believed whole heartedly in the vision of wonders she saw through the minds of those she channeled and hoped that the successful completion of the ship, or rather portal device, would allow us to journey instantly across the vast distances of interstellar space to learn the ways of the Sumi and return as their ambassadors to usher in a new and enlightened age.

She could not see that such a use was not what the political arm of the Thulists wanted. What they desired above all was power and the advanced technology of the stars harnessed to help them crush their enemies and rule the world.

Thus it came as no surprise to me when, one year later, after having shown promising, but inconclusive, results, the Inter-dimensional machine concept was scrapped in favor of the levitator unit known by then as the Schumann SM-Levitator.

Slowly at first, but with ever increasing pressure from our investors, the National Socialist Thulists began shifting the emphasis of the project towards the construction of a *raumschiff*–or some sort of spaceship capable of reaching the stars—or controlling the skies here on earth. This was what Hitler and Himmler really wanted, and over the next five years, the RFZ (*RundFlugZeug*), or "Round Aircraft" project came under the complete control of Himmler's SS technical branch, *Entwicklungsstelle* 4, known as Unit E-IV. This was the SS special projects group charged with producing a viable, working flying disc for war.

Chapter Thirteen

I couldn't help myself. I laughed. "At least that part didn't come true. I mean, can you imagine little green men wearing Nazi armbands zipping around in flying saucers?"

He didn't laugh back.

"Yes, I can. Because it almost happened and may happen yet."

"Hang on a sec. I'll admit, I've gone from being a total skeptic to accepting the fact there is something pretty strange going on, but are you telling me the Nazis actually perfected a flying saucer? If that's true, what happened to it? I mean, we took their jet planes, rockets, and most of their scientists after the war. Why not these so-called flying saucers?"

"What makes you think you did not?"

"OK, then where are they?"

"Have you ever heard of Area 51?"

I pushed my now-cold, watery coffee away and stared back at Max. He was serious, and I was convinced he was telling the truth, at least as he knew it. I was still confused by his chronology, but now I was beginning to think the confusion might be on my end rather than his.

He took out his pipe and began to fill the bowl from a worn, leather pouch until he seemed to recall where he was. He sighed and put the pipe back into his pocket.

"I sometimes forget I am here in America where there is plenty of freedom, but not for us smokers, *ja*?"

I wasn't interested in discussing the dangers of second hand smoke. "Go on, Max. You were talking about Hess and doors you and your mystics wished you hadn't opened."

His eyes glowed fiercely and his normally calm voice turned angry. "How could we? How could any sane person have imagined what would happen once we let those murderous thugs into our life?"

"But you did."

He nodded slowly. "Yes, we did." He turned and stared out the fly-specked window. "Worse still, we did not realize until later that, despite Hess's apprehension of Maria, or maybe because of it, he began to carry tales of our discoveries back to others."

"Others...what others?"

"A drug addicted former flying ace of the Great War by the name of Herman Goring; a failed chicken farmer and mystic Heinrich Himmler; and yes, an angry, disillusioned corporal...our future *führer*, Adolph Hitler."

His eyes looked out on the busy Brookline Street, but I doubted he saw it. Those eyes were focused on the past—on chaotic, angry mobs that made up German politics during the Weimar Republic—a time when common sense was locked in a death struggle with madness.

Max scanned the small lunchroom uneasily. When he glanced at me watching him with a puzzled expression, he smiled sheepishly and shrugged. "Old habits die hard, but you must remember that I spent the next twenty years speaking of Hitler's failings, only in hushed tones, and even then only to a small circle of trusted friends."

Max paused, took his unlit, empty pipe, put it in his mouth, and sucked moodily on it.

"Hey, are you guys gonna order something or what?"

We both looked up, startled at the counterman standing next to us, his food-stained apron bulging over his belly and a dirty dishrag thrown over his shoulder.

"I mean, you two have been here more than an hour and one cuppa' coffee. Christ, gimme a break."

Max glanced up at him and nodded. "*Ja*, you are quite right. Apologies for overstaying our welcome." He pushed a five-dollar bill across the table and stood up, gathering his coat and hat.

I reluctantly followed. I suspected that with the addition of another fiver, we probably could have bought the dump outright. Max was buttoning his coat when I joined him on the sidewalk.

"Walk with me," he said.

We turned right and I noticed he was heading back towards his Beacon Street apartment. I hoped he could wrap up his story in a half dozen blocks. If only.

As we waited for the crosswalk light, he resumed.

"You must understand. Maria never wished to become involved with anything that could be used for the purpose of making war. She told me violence was the furthest thing from the hopes of those who were in contact with her. She told us the technology they were sharing with us was to bring about a more peaceful and prosperous world, as they had tried to do when they first visited our planet thousands of years ago."

He pointed to a bench next to a corner bus shelter and we sat. He stared at the passing buses and Green Line trolley cars for a few minutes as if gathering his thoughts to decide what he would or would not tell me. The afternoon shadows grew longer, turning the red brick of the Federal style bow-front buildings a muted shade of burnt orange. People hurried by along Beacon Street; all anxious to get somewhere or to leave something else behind, and I wasn't sure which of those categories I would place myself in. All I knew was I'd been captured by Max's story. It was like a poison ivy itch; I knew I shouldn't scratch, but I couldn't help it.

It's amazing the way in which our minds, when confronted by the unbelievable, can quickly regain their equilibrium by retreating to the mundane.

I got up from the bench and tapped Max on the shoulder. "All this talk about saucers has made me thirsty for a really good cup of coffee."

We were only half a block away from a nice little deli I'd discovered the day before, and when we sat down at the counter, I decided to indulge one of my guilty pleasures for hot pastrami and Swiss on rye. Max ordered a Ruben, and while we waited, he continued.

Chapter Fourteen

May 1934

By 1934, after ten years of planning and work, the first prototype of the *Jenseitsflugmaschine* was ready for testing. For this, the Nazi bosses insisted that the honor of making the first flight should be given to their resident flying hero of the Great War, Hermann Göring. But at the last minute, he had second thoughts and instead "volunteered" the services of another World War I ace, Lothar Waiz.

The aircraft, christened the RFZ-1, wobbled to an altitude of 60 meters then began spinning uncontrollably and was quickly brought back down. Upon landing, the craft's spinning increased, and Waiz was barely able to scramble out before the ship ripped herself to pieces.

Surprisingly, Göring, Hess, and Himmler, who had come to observe the test flight, did not seem at all upset. Instead they insisted we try again, and to that end, work began on a second craft, the RFZ-2. This time the test was successful.

It wasn't until a week after the first test flight I finally figured out why it had failed. You see, unbeknownst to me and most of the group, Maria, aided by Thule member and scientist Dr. W.O. Schumann of the Technical University in Munich, had secretly installed the first crude components to open the inter-dimensional channels once the craft had achieved flight. She and the other Vrilerinnen were certain they could then use the ship to make direct contact with citizens of Aldebaran and thus keep the technology with the greatest potential for misuse out of the hands of the Nazis.

But the Nazis got wind of it, and as time went on, I became increasingly suspicious there was a National Socialist working for them within the circle of the Vrilerinnen themselves!

At any rate, knowledge of Maria's plans obviously reached the ears of the party bosses, and I am certain the machine was sabotaged when Himmler and Göring made their inspection tour the day before the flight.

Hitler had come to power in 1933 and the whole country had become a vast network of spies and informants. You could not laugh at a joke or listen to American Jazz without having some waiter or block warden denounce you to the Gestapo.

* * * *

Munich – June, 1935

Maria, Sigrun, Traute, and I were out at a cabaret when a group of SA Storm Troopers came in. During the two years since Hitler had inaugurated the new Thousand Year Reich, the thuggish collection of former butchers' boys and shopkeepers had gone from being a comical group of brown-shirted malcontents to a paramilitary force that not only terrorized without interference from the police, but often with their full cooperation and participation.

On this particular night, we went to see a jazz quartet performing for the last time, because under the increasingly repressive Nazi regime, all sorts of entertainment were being condemned has "degenerate" and banned. The other reason was because one of the quartet musicians was a Jew.

I knew there was going to be trouble from the moment they entered. They didn't sit down, but stood against the back wall of the club, arms folded over their chests, eyes made crimson by the cabaret's red spotlights. They reminded me of jackals sizing up their prey. We did not have long to wait.

When the quartet finished the song and was about to begin their last set, the largest of the Storm Troopers stepped forward and yelled, "Get off the stage, Jew!"

The club grew silent in an instant, and even in the red spotlight I could see the diminutive clarinet player tremble. The group's drummer stepped up to the microphone.

"How dare you come into a place where people have come to be entertained and disrupt the show? Please refrain from further disruptions or I shall have to ask the manager to tell you to leave."

The little Jew shook his head and tugged at the drummer's sleeve, but it was too late. With a feral grin, the SA leader nodded and they began moving towards the stage, knocking over chairs and shoving people out of the way as they came. Only a few men made any attempt to stop them. I was one.

As they passed our table, I stood up, but one of the SA contemptuously pushed me back down in my chair. Outraged, I jumped up and started after them, but Maria grabbed my hand.

"No, Max, please don't. Those men are vicious. They will hurt you."

I tore my hand out of her grasp. I was angry and my blood was up. "Maria, someone needs to stand up to those pigs, and my time is now."

Brave words, but there were five of them and only one of me. I must confess, I expected some of the other patrons to join me, but by 1935, most people had seen what these bullyboys could do and were too cowed to interfere. I knew it too, but at that moment, all of the frustrations of life in a totalitarian society boiled over. I was no longer thinking of the future or even the next five minutes, I just reacted.

By now, the Brown Shirt leader had reached the stage, grabbed the poor, little clarinet player by the collar, and was shaking him like a rag doll. I strode up to the leader and ripped his hand away from the little man. "Is this what National Socialism is? Beating up harmless, little musicians?"

"He is not harmless. He is a Jew."

"And I am still an officer in the Austrian Army and I order you to release him."

It was a desperate move, but it was all I had. Unfortunately, they weren't impressed. In fact, their leader's lips twisted with scorn as he sneered.

"Do you think that intimidates us? Soon, you Austrians will be taking all of your orders from us."

Unfortunately, he was right, but I wasn't thinking about future geo-politics. All I wanted to do was to get them to leave and, hopefully, without rearranging my facial features. It didn't look like either of those was going to happen.

"Karl. Otto," the leader barked.

Two of them reached out to grab me, but I whirled, punching the first one in the stomach and he fell off the stage. The second swung at me and missed and I drove him back with a blow to his jaw followed by another to his solar plexus. Then two hands grabbed each of my arms and one went around my neck. Their leader leaned close to me. I could smell the reek of garlic sausage and stale beer on this breath.

"Now let's see how little sugarplums who style themselves as Austrian officers can take a beating." He drew back his big, meaty fist.

"I think you had better release him."

Maria stalked up to the stage; long, blond hair flowing behind her like an avenging Valkyrie.

The hands didn't open, but they relaxed a little.

"Who are you? This one's doxy?"

Maria walked up and stood in front of him. "No, Herr Sturmabteilung Leader. I am the one who will report you if you do not release him and leave this club."

He laughed and sneered. "Report us? To whom? Some pathetic police official? Most of them are with us."

"No, not to the *Polizei*, someone far more important."

He laughed again. "*Ja, Schatzi*, and who could that be?"

Maria gave him an icy blue stare. "Does the name Heinrich Himmler mean anything to you?"

I heard his breath catch and felt a tremor pass through him, but he recovered quickly.

"I don't believe you. How could a little chit of a girl know the Reichsführer?"

She didn't answer but produced a folded note on heavy, cream-colored paper, and as the SA man opened it, I noticed the SS runes at the top of the page. But it was the words she read aloud from the last paragraph that made everyone on the stage fall silent in shock.

"'And therefore you are hereby ordered to give the woman, Maria Orsic, who is involved in vital research for the Reich, as well as her associates, every consideration and assistance... Signed, H. Himmler, *Reichsführer SS*.'"

Chapter Fifteen

We didn't talk much on the walk back from the deli to Max's apartment. I was still trying to picture life in Nazi Germany.

Like most people, I'd seen the movies and read the books about what a bunch of pricks they were, which was why everyone always cheered when the Allies kicked their butts. But also, like everyone else, outside of a few documentaries on the History and Military channels, it was hard to imagine what it must have been like living every moment as though someone evil was watching your every move, which, in most cases, was true.

No, as someone who'd lived through that terror, I couldn't blame ol' Max for maintaining a healthy degree of paranoia. In his case, and for that matter, mine too. It was probably justified.

He stopped on the sidewalk across the street from his apartment building, and like a careful schoolboy at the crossing light, looked both ways, scanning the length of the street before walking quickly across. He glanced over his shoulder to make sure I was following him. I was.

When we got to the front entrance, he scanned the street one last time before sliding a well-worn key into the lock of the frosted glass door. I entered behind him. He didn't wait for the hydraulic piston to slowly close the door but gave it a sharp tug and didn't release the handle until it clicked shut.

"Wow, Max, is it me or are those guys with faces like an old pickle jar following you too?"

He gave me a thin smile and punched the elevator button for a different floor than his and sent it merrily on its way...Empty.

"Ah, I get it. If the Three Stooges show up in a few minutes, they'll think you're in the elevator and search a floor where you aren't."

He nodded and held open the door to the stairs. "Correct."

We started to climb.

"It won't fool them for long of course," he called back over his shoulder, "but it might give me a few minutes' head start to lead them away from the building."

"And then what?" I asked, but he didn't answer. Before I could decide if I wanted to ask again, he pushed open the door to his floor and motioned me to hurry.

Once inside the apartment, he threw the deadbolt and turned the key in the lock.

He smiled for the first time that afternoon and motioned me towards the living room.

"Come. I think maybe we would both benefit from a nice schnapps, *ja*?"

* * * *

Max poured my schnapps and set it down on a small, walnut pedestal table next to a heavy, old-fashioned chair complete with a lace antimacassar, but he took his and walked to the big bow window facing the street. After a few minutes, I got up and joined him. Standing next to him, I finished my schnapps and was about to ask for another when I noticed he hadn't touched his. The second thing I noticed was that he looked worried.

I moved a little closer, trying to see what he was looking at so intently. I peered out at the rapidly darkening street and saw... nothing. At least, nothing that meant anything to me. But then again, I hadn't spent the better part of the twentieth century looking over my shoulder for Nazis and little green men—or maybe it was little green men who were Nazis. I was rapidly getting to the point where nothing would surprise me. But then again, I still had a lot to learn.

"Whadd'ya see, Max? Are those guys watching the building? Have you spotted them?"

"*Nein.*" He scratched his chin and gave one last glance out the window before pulling the curtains tightly closed and stepping away. "And that is what bothers me. I know they are out there, but if they are concealing themselves, it means they are satisfied they know where I am and feel they can come for me at any time."

He turned and looked at me. "It could also mean they are aware of your whereabouts too, Herr Brennan."

Marvelous. That was all I needed.

"Maybe we both need another schnapps, Max."

He looked at his still un-tasted glass and smiled. "My apologies. I am not being a good host, *ja*? Come, *mein junge Freund.* Let me refill your glass and we will talk of other things."

But we never got the chance. There was a fumbling at the front door of the apartment, and a few seconds later, it banged open and Kat came rushing in followed by the old lady. Kat bustled into the living room and started to smile when she saw Max but it abruptly froze when she spotted me.

She paused and looked at me from under pale lashes; one hand resting on a sleek, tantalizingly rounded hip—green-gold eyes sparking in the filtered, setting sun streaming through bay window, and honey blond hair with auburn highlights curling carelessly over her right shoulder. The effect on me was not atypical of any red-blooded American male; that is to say, an intense desire to cover the six feet separating us and kiss her until she, I, or both of us forgot about everything else. Almost as if she could read my panting, little mind, her brows knitted then arched to accompany an amused smile.

"Well, Mr. EPA Man, I'll give you this: you are nothing if not thorough. I mean really, twice in two days? What is it? Are Gran's cabbage and pigs knuckles causing global greenhouse gasses?"

I smiled. At least as much of a smile as is appropriate for a sweet young thing being watched by her hatchet-faced grandmother.

"Ha! Yes—I mean, no. I mean, now if you lived on farm, then we might be interested in what we in the EPA biz politely refer to as 'cow flatulence.'" I gave her what I hoped was a surreptitious wink. "Why, do you know that cow flatulence is responsible for over ten million pounds of methane each year?"

"Hmmm, no, I didn't but thanks for sharing."

The little lines around her eyes crinkled with a smile. The kind of smile you see on a girl when you're not sure if she's going to giggle or if she is politely humoring you. I hoped it was not the latter, and then wondered why.

Maybe that's why I added, "And if you're really a fan of hot air, let me buy you an overpriced Starbucks latte sometime, and I'll fill you in on what me and Al Gore intend to do about cow farts."

This time she did laugh. Right out loud. And I don't know who was more amused, me or Max.

"OK, Mr. EPA cow flatulence man," (not my most coveted title, but what the hell?) "It's a date. Coffee and bovine humor. When and where?"

I glanced at Max. He was still smiling, but he was also sending me caution signals with his eyes. Was he pissed or just being protective? Or was this another of the endless stream of mysteries and strange events going on outside the periphery of my increasingly befuddled mind? Suddenly, I didn't care. What I wanted more than anything in the world was a simple date with a pretty girl.

"Hmm, me and the cows are off until tomorrow, so how does now suit you?"

This time she giggled and arched one eyebrow. "Do you think you could give me 'til ten minutes from now?"

"Hey, we boys from the Cow Fart Brigade are nothing if not generous. Take fifteen."

She gave me a mock curtsy and headed down the hall. "Back in a flash."

I grinned back foolishly. One of my signature moves.

But when I turned back to Max, he wasn't smiling. And his expression was positively mild compared to the old lady's.

"What?" I whispered nervously.

He shook his head. "This is not a good idea."

"Which one? A Starbucks latte or a harmless little date with Kat?"

"The latte would be better alone, I think."

"Hmm....If I didn't know any better, one might almost conclude you're trying to tell me I'm not good enough to date your niece." I said, only half joking.

"*Nein*, no, mine *lieber Freund*, not at all. It's only—"

"Yes, it is!" A sharp, guttural voice snapped out from across the room. "That is exactly correct. I do not think you are good enough for her. What do you think? That we let our Katrina go traipsing off with every jumped-up functionary who comes knocking at our door?"

"Jeez... Don't hold back or anything." I mumbled. But Kat bounded into the room, pulling on her brown leather jacket.

"OK, EPA guy, you ready to roll?" Then she turned and saw all the unhappy faces. "Huh, did I miss something? What? Did the EPA uncover lead paint or roaches?"

I winked at her. "Not me, sweet thing, but I'm getting the impression that if I was carrying a roach bomb or two, they might be lobbed my way."

Kat looked puzzled, Max looked embarrassed, and the old lady looked daggers at me.

Kat's gaze darted from one face to the other but settled on her grandmother. She sighed. "Oh, Gran, have you been trying to play watchdog with my dating life again?"

The old lady's eyes looked down but then snapped back colder than before. "*Ja*, yes I am. I must. Better I should become your *kettenhounde* than shirk my responsibility for your welfare and the promises I made to your...mother."

Watchdog or not, I caught the way she paused over the word "mother," and I wasn't the only one. The old lady glared back defiantly, but Kat's eyes narrowed and she appeared about to speak when suddenly the old lady sighed and shook her head in resignation. "But I suppose you must do as you please, which is also just like your... mother."

There it was again, that hesitation.

Kat nodded, her eyes cold. "Yes, Gran. Just like my mother."

The last word was clipped and rang of determination, but there was also something else in the way she said it. Something almost wistful.

I also got the impression this debate had little to do with me. I was just the latest excuse in an ongoing battle. Since every good beat cop knows that the surest way to get yourself in trouble is to get in the middle of a domestic squabble, I decided to gracefully withdraw while I had the chance with both my skin and ego intact.

I cleared my throat. "Hey, guys, you know it's getting kind of late and I've got reports to write. I think I'll just hit the road." I turned to Kat. "Can I get a rain check?"

She nodded absently, still glaring at her grandmother.

I moved towards the door, calling back over my shoulder. "And, Max, why don't we meet tomorrow for lunch. Same place as today?"

Kat looked puzzled that I seemed to know her uncle, but the EPA dodge was wearing thin and I had planned on telling her anyway.

Max caught Kat's look too but only nodded. "*Ja.*"

I let myself out, closed the door behind me, and walked down the stairs.

Stepping out onto the building's front stoop, I scanned the street, and sure enough, across the street was a silver BMW with three people inside. The darkened windows obscured their faces, but I had little doubt they were in Coolidge Corner to sample a corned beef on rye at one of the famous local delis. My immediate suspicion was that they were looking for me. Or Max. Or both.

And it was confirmed a few moments later when a tall, grey-haired man accompanied by two stocky hard cases, got out of the car and started across Beacon Street towards me.

I started to move to the left, but as soon as I did, one of the two goons angled off to intercept me. The second one did the same on the right.

With three out of four directions blocked, the only way I could go was back. I twisted the knob to the building's outer door. Locked.

I didn't have enough time to buzz Max to let me in. They were moving in and would be on me in a moment.

Then I heard the door behind me click. Simultaneously, a hand tugged on my collar and I took a stumbling step backwards. I felt soft hair and smelled expensive shampoo as a low voice whispered in my ear.

"C'mon, there's a back door and maintenance shed that opens onto the next street where there's a cab stand."

I turned quickly. "Kat? What are you doing here? I thought you had an argument to win."

She grinned while motioning me to follow her down the stairs to the basement level. "It was gonna end in a draw anyway. It always does."

We clattered down the stairs into a musty basement and up a short flight of stone steps to emerge into an overgrown garden filled with rusting lawnmowers and chipped birdbaths. As we entered an old, single-story brick garage at the back of the property, I turned in time to see the basement door swing open and a shaved, meaty head appear. I couldn't tell if he saw us 'cause Kat pulled me into the garage.

"This way, quick!"

A minute later, we emerged onto another pleasant, tree-lined Brookline street and Kat made a beeline for the cab stand at the end of the street.

As the cab pulled away from the curb, I shot another glance back, but this time, no bullet head appeared. We were safe. For now.

Chapter Sixteen

"Where to?" Kat asked me.

"Harvard Square."

We rode in silence for a few minutes. Finally, she tilted her head and made a gesture pointing behind us. "Friends of yours or just people you owe money?"

I shrugged. "I wish I could say it was either of those, but I've got a hunch it's a little more serious than that. Fact is, I don't really understand it myself. Maybe you'd better ask Max."

"I did."

My eyebrows rose. "Really, and what did he say?"

"He told me to help you." She looked out the rear window. "And I'd say I'm off to a flying start on that front."

"You'll get no argument from me, there. Did ol' Max tell you who he thinks these guys are?"

She gave slight shrug of her shoulders suggesting he might have and it didn't matter. Or it mattered more than she wanted to admit to me or to herself.

"Oh, there's all kinds of family secrets that get mentioned over the years, and since I'm never sure how much of it is true and how much has evolved in the telling, I take them all with a grain of salt."

I shook my head. "I don't know. From what Max has told me, and from what I've witnessed, I'd be more inclined to take these guys seriously."

She shrugged again and stared out the window as we took the Harvard Bridge over the Charles River into Cambridge.

I tried again. "He must have told you all about him and the Nazis and all that occult stuff?"

She gave another noncommittal nod. "A few things, but like I said, I take it all with a grain of salt. I mean, scratch any German over the age of seventy and they'll all tell you stories about how they were lied to or how they stood up in heroic resistance to the Nazis. I've never met any who claim the Third Reich was a great idea and really deserves another shot."

"Yeah, well, if we had hung around your building a few minutes longer, I get a feeling that 'shot' you mention might have come on a lot closer terms than you'd ever want."

"Okay, there may be a few skinheads, white supremacists, and bitter old men who babble about a Fourth Reich, but they're mostly nutcases who do nothing but make noise."

"Then what about the guys after me...and for that matter, after Max too?"

"It wouldn't surprise me if he hadn't picked up a few enemies along the way, but as to why they've got it in for you too...well, you tell me."

* * * *

Over a double espresso and a chicken wrap for me, and a vegan wrap with avocado and sprouts for Kat at a funky little bistro with a window on the Square, that's exactly what I did.

By the time I finished, I was working on my third espresso and she had switched to cappuccino.

I drained the last bitter dregs from the tiny cup and placed in back in the equally tiny saucer.

"And that, Miss Kat, is about where you came in."

"Hmmm," she said, licking the thin froth of cream from her upper lip like an animus of her namesake. "Sounds like I missed all the good parts."

"If your idea of 'good parts' runs to hiding, ducking through airports, and trying not to get murdered, and if you have an adrenalin junkie's death wish, then I guess you could say so."

She made a mock sultry face and lowered her eyelids. "Danger is my passion, *Herr* Brennan."

She took a long, slow sip of her cappuccino and then burst out laughing. "I think you've been reading too many spy novels." She giggled again and winked. "C'mon dude, lighten up."

"You don't believe me." I was on the verge of being pissed at having my unwelcome adventures of the past week and a half come off as some college kid's half-assed attempt to impress a girl with a bunch of macho bullshit.

Kat caught my beginnings of a snit and sighed. "OK, Mr. 'Dude,' Ms. Smart-Ass officially apologizes."

"And, Mr. Way-too-sensitive says, you're right. I definitely need to lighten up. I guess being stalked by Nazis gets me a wee bit on the cranky side."

"No problem. I get off on teasing, as you can probably tell. But...." She flashed me a grin and a wink. "It also means I kinda like you."

"Ah, then that calls for some return teasing." I arched my eyebrows. "And for the record, do you mean 'like' as in middle school I-want-to-hold-your-hand liking, or as in all-grown-up-and-find-you-sexy-as-hell like?"

"Hmmm...well, it's been a long time since I was engaged in the former, and if you think you have a shot at sampling the later, you're gonna have to invest in more than a veggie wrap and coffee."

"Cappuccino." I corrected.

"Duly noted." She pushed her chair back. "Want to give it a shot?"

I stood up. "That's the best offer I've had all week."

* * * *

As soon as we stepped outside, I couldn't help it. Despite my promise to myself to "make love not war," once you start spending the majority of your waking hours running and hiding, it becomes a hard habit to break. I scanned the street up and down, eyeing the crowds for big, nasty looking men with no necks.

"Stop it!" Kat poked me and took my arm. "C'mon, James Bond, you're gonna buy me a drink." She dragged me past a row of locked bicycles and out into the streaming traffic rushing through the square like demented kamikazes.

Notwithstanding my firm belief that a gonzo cabbie would soon put an end to my worries about neo-Nazis and little green men, we made it to the other side and were soon strolling down tree-lined Mt. Auburn Street. Another ten minutes brought us to a funky little club called Past Tense. It was small and crowded and looked like a good place to get lost in a crowd. We went in.

Two beers and a white wine later, my life was looking brighter. I hadn't felt this romantically inclined since the last time the mysterious Ria popped in and out of my life.

Kat and I had progressed to the giggle-and-whispers stage, and my mind was starting to conjure up erotic scenes featuring a firm body and honey blond hair.

And I, quite frankly, was more than content to let our future happy trails together meander down that path for the foreseeable future, or at least to an ending of the evening between some reasonably clean sheets—but I had awakened some inner Emma Peel in Kat. Between giggles and leaning in so I could be duly tantalized by her perfume that smelled of incense and sex, she continued to bounce back and forth between sweet nothings and speculations about homicidally inclined thugs.

"Alright, Mr. Dangerous, what else do you have to offer the world and an innocent little girl from Brookline—aside from battling the forces of evil?"

I shrugged and smiled weakly. "My boyish good looks and sparkling personality?"

She leaned back in her chair and gazed at me from half-lidded, pale eyelashes. "Perhaps, or then again, it might be your *Austin Powers: Man of Mystery*-aura."

I had just enough time to get out the required anachronistic "groovy" rejoinder before she winked and whispered, "C'mon, mystery boy, let's find out what sort of secrets you have to share."

A short cab ride and a panting thirty-second tour of my apartment later, I did.

Chapter Seventeen

And thus, Kat and I fell madly in love, and in due course, were married, bought a house in a Boston suburb and had 2.3 lovely, charming children. The End...

Yeah, right.

The love thing, though, did get off to a nice start. Her delightful, firm body lived up to all of my expectations and then some. And by the time we got to round three or four and I was about to break the news to her and myself that I was no longer a teenager, she asked me if I ever studied the *Kama Sutra.* Although the closest I'd ever come was a salacious poster on a dorm room wall, I, of course, nodded knowingly—which prompted her to ask if I'd ever tried position number thirty-six.

"Hmm...that might have been the day I missed a class due to a conflict with teaching Tantric breathing techniques at the Sorbonne."

She grinned wickedly. "Well, you could probably use a refresher course." And she proceeded to lead me into a responsive review of positions thirty through forty, inclusively.

By the time Mr. Sun poked his head through the dirty, white aluminum blinds, I had developed a newfound respect for the males of old India for having survived the rigors of the considerable sexual athletics of *Kama Sutra* to be able to populate the country down to the present day.

As Kipling so aptly put it, "You're a better man than I am, Gunga Din."

Kat called a cab to take her home and kissed me good-bye while I was still trying to unglue my eyelids and determine if my rubbery legs could carry me as far as the kitchen and the coffeemaker.

"Call me." She blew a kiss as she went out the door.

I may have mumbled, "Absolutely." Or maybe not.

No matter. I was going to see her again. Unless a bunch of bullet-headed, bad tempered, modern day Teutonic Knights found me first.

After the third cup of black coffee, my brain began to fire on a few cylinders and I started cataloging what I knew about the mystery I had been dragged into, kicking and screaming...it wasn't much.

There was an old German who appeared to be an anti-Nazi, but also had a lot of inside information for one who was supposedly on the outside. And then there were the thugs; neo-Nazis, skinheads, or whatever unpleasant group they were hooked up with, who, for some equally unfathomable reason, wanted to do bodily harm to yours truly. And lastly, at the very bottom of the mystery, what I found myself staring into was...the girl who had launched me into this whole trip down Alice's rabbit hole. The enigmatic and tantalizingly inscrutable girl with the faraway eyes—Ria.

And despite the coffee, the more I thought about Ria and whatever esoteric but all-too-real madness she, Max, and I were involved in, the more my bewildered brain continued to scamper through a dizzying chain of events and conclusions leading nowhere. And despite the perpetual feeling of imminent and impending disaster, my eyelids began to droop.

I'll just close them for a minute, I told myself.

When I opened them again, the late afternoon sun shone in my face.

I yawned and stretched. Great. I had missed my meeting where I was supposed to evaluate the newspaper's servers and get started on updating the aforementioned.

Yeah, it's not like I need the money or anything. My stomach growled by way of ironic comment, prompting me toward the kitchen in the vague hope of finding a couple of Slim Jims and corn chips I might have missed during my last ravenous ransacking of the depressingly bare cupboards.

I pushed open the kitchen door and stepped into infinite vastness of the cosmos.

Literally.

One minute, I was staring down at dirty black-and-white checked linoleum, and the next...I stared into the swirling spiral of galaxies churning their way through the star-flecked void and my befuddled brain oscillated between feelings of wonder and fears of raging insanity.

Holy fuck, this is it. I've finally cracked. All those little neurons have gone into stress overload mode and are now kicking the crap out of the synapses. Who knows how long I've got before I start dribbling and babbling and running naked down Comm. Ave, flapping my arms and proclaiming myself the ghost of Timothy Leary.

Mmm hmm... Hey all you hipsters, "tune in, turn on, and drop out." Apparently I had taken a wrong turn on the road of reality and was doing exactly that.

I almost wished I'd gone over the edge. It would be preferable to the nagging little worm of panic telling me that I wasn't crazy and had stumbled, instead, into the center of the universe. Wasn't this how Buddha and prophets got started?

And look at what happened to most of them. Regular folks didn't appreciate people who tripped through infinity and came back to tell the tale. Stonings, crucifixions, and other unpleasant deaths usually followed. But how the hell do you escape from the heavens in your kitchens when you can't find the damn door?

And then, as if in answer to a prayer I hadn't figured how to form, I heard a voice. Thin, soft, and tentative; a girl's voice. Frightened and searching, just like me. Speaking in German, but with a soft, lilting accent. Bavarian...possibly Austrian.

"Hello? Who is there? Can you see me? Can you help me?"

I strained my eyes, drifting in lazy circles, knowing neither right nor left, up or down. And then, off in the distance—who knew how far? A few feet, a few miles, or light years—stood a slim figure in a long, old-fashioned summer dress. She had a long, graceful neck, and long, shimmering blond hair flowing down past her waist and streaming out from behind her. As she got closer, I could see that she was also beautiful.

She floated, or morphed, next to me and touched my hand. "Are you real or are you one of them?"

"Them?" My voice echoed off walls in another dimension.

The vision in white solemnly looked into my eyes with hers. Her eyes changed from gold to green to blue before shifting back through the spectrum, all in an instant.

"The god-like beings who are masters of the Universe, the old ones from Aldebaran, the ones who taught our ancestors writing and science and how to harness the greatest force in the cosmos. The force they call the Vril."

Vril! Either I was truly insane, or this was beginning to make sense in an incredible and unbelievable way.

I grabbed her soft hand. "Your name? What's your name?"

She swallowed and answered in the same low, soft voice. "Maria."

Maria? There was something in the way she said it, so familiar and yet different.

I stared at her, floating before my eyes. She was young, a teenager. Sixteen, seventeen? A high school girl but from a different time, perhaps the beginning of the twentieth century.

"Please, can you...will you help me?"

She spoke softly but with the intensity of someone who wanted answers—answers to important questions. Answers I didn't have.

"I'm sorry. I can't help you. Christ, I don't know where I am or who you are, or for that matter, who the fuck I am! For all I know, you could be a sexy-looking flashback to a bad acid trip. If so, will you stick around? But maybe you could tell the stars and the Milky Way to take a hike."

She squeezed my hand tighter and shook her head. "I have this feeling that somehow I know you, and I think you know me too."

She was right. I knew it the first moment she looked into my eyes and I recognized promise of the beautiful woman she'd grow into. A woman who'd shared my bed and started wheels in motion that now had me chased across two continents. A woman who almost made me not care that any moment could be my last.

Ria.

But she wasn't Ria yet. She was a pretty, sweet schoolgirl from what appeared to be perhaps the early 1900s, and right now she was as frightened and confused about being a speck of human plasma floating in an infinity of time and space as I was.

I had to do something to get us back to whatever reality we belonged to before it was too late and we went insane—which the small knot in the pit of my stomach told me wasn't far off.

I tried to concentrate on the pretty, fearful face in front of me instead of the mind wrenching disorientation of spinning galaxies and stars winking in and out of existence. It wasn't easy.

I put both arms around the young girl, whom would one day become the stunning and enigmatic Ria, and pulled her close to me. She smelled of violets and peppermints. I held her until she stopped shaking. Though a moment here—wherever, "here" actually was—could have been an instant or an aeon. That's why we had to get out.

"Do you remember exactly what you were doing just before you came to be here?" I asked.

"I was riding on the trolley, in Vienna, my home, on my way to school. We had come to my stop. I got up from my seat, went down the trolley steps, touched my foot onto the pavement, and in the next instant I was here."

"And I went through a kitchen door. No help there."

Somewhere, a billion light years away and a billion years ago, a star system exploded and showered the universe with white-gold light. I looked at my hand on her shoulder. It was becoming translucent, shimmering with a thousand tiny suns. I felt like I was drifting away—becoming unglued from space and time. I didn't know if I was dreaming, going insane, or was already there. I needed to put an end to this—and fast.

"You spoke about the 'old ones,' the 'god-like beings.' How do you know them?"

"From dreams," she whispered. "They have come to me in dreams ever since I was a child."

"Why?"

She shook her head. "All they have ever told me was that I am very important to them—for the messages they want me to deliver to all mankind."

"And what are these messages? Have you delivered them?"

She paused, then slowly shook her head again. "No. They say the time is not right yet." She looked up anxiously. "But they have told me it is coming soon."

I had more questions, but I couldn't remember what they were. My blood pounded in my ears and my heart fluttered against my ribcage making me dizzy and sick.

"Then you can't tell me anything about these beings? About their power? The Vril?" My voice sounded like it was coming from a long way off.

"They don't tell me much, but I can feel it. The power of the Vril. It is everywhere. And soon, I'm sure, they will give me information about how to access it. They have told me they will share with me the great secrets. The way to the stars and unlimited power, and I, in turn, will share it with all mankind."

Now her eyes were shining with an iridescent light sparkling with the brightness of the universe. But I was trying to remember what Max had told me about Maria and the occult, and the Thulusts and the Vril.

I had a thousand questions but I couldn't formulate the words. They kept drifting away with little parts of me, and I noticed, with an amused detachment, that she was too. We were both fading away like Alice's Cheshire Cat, becoming "star-stuff" just like Crosby, Stills and Nash sang about.

I had one last glance of Maria/Ria and then she was gone...and so was I.

* * * *

When I opened my eyes, it was dark and I had a splitting headache. A fucking dream. That's what it was. A goddamn fucking dream brought on by stress and lack of sleep. I got up from the couch and rubbed my eyes, shuffling towards the bedroom, then stopped. I put my hand up to my nose again and sniffed.

The scent of violets and peppermint.

* * * *

After a half hour of staring into the mirror to make sure I was really there, I decided to call Max and arrange a meeting. I was going to give back the flash drive with its dizzying pages of blueprint drawings, mathematical formulas, and arcane, enigmatic scraps of unknown writing. I was going to resign from the whole affair, not that I had voluntarily signed up to begin with. I mean, it was bad enough being chased halfway across the globe by fascist thugs bent on personal mayhem, but throw in a generous helping of madness and hopping in and out of the space-time continuum, and you reached the point where Mrs. Brennan's baby boy says, "Thanks very much for the ride through the looking glass, but here's my stop on the cosmic highway and I'm getting off."

I called Max and Kat answered.

"Hmmm... You just squeaked in under the deadline, but I guess a win is a win."

Totally baffled, all I could reply was, "Huh?"

"Please tell me you're calling me because you know the unwritten rules of hooking up require a guy, who isn't a total, selfish asshole, to call the girl within the first twenty-four hours."

I had a second of confused panic before the natural bullshit response most guys are born with kicked in. "Ah, yeah, absolutely."

"Ahhh ha…"

"No, seriously, I really did call to—"

"Invite me to an expensive dinner?"

I could hear the smile in her voice and see mischievous little twinkle in her eye. She had me.

"Sure… That was right at the top of my list."

"Proceeded only by a root canal?"

We both burst out laughing

"Hey, I really do want to take you out. But the five-star restaurants are probably out of the picture until I receive my inheritance from a long, lost uncle, who is so long lost he doesn't even know he's leaving his vast fortune and collection of pornographic playing cards to me."

I now had her on her way to a full-fledged giggle fit, and my chances for getting lucky again at the end of the evening were rapidly improving. So, it was with no small degree of trepidation and concern at blowing a good thing when I asked Kat, as casually as I could, if Max happened to be around.

"Please tell me that isn't the real reason you called?"

"Absolutely not," I lied. "Though you can't blame a guy for being efficient; two birds, one stone and all?"

It sounded lame to me too, and she left me sweating for almost a full minute before she sighed. "Oh, OK. I supposed we modern, liberated, *Sex and the City*-type gals have to take what we can get. And yes, he's here. And yes, I'll tell him you're coming over and want to talk, but you still owe me one damn good veggie burger."

* * * *

Slipping on my jacket, I grabbed my wallet and keys and emerged onto the front steps of the building. It was drizzling and I was trying to decide if I should treat myself to a cab or hoof it down to the T-stop on the corner when I glanced down the street—and had my mind made up for me.

There, at the edge of the misty pool of light cast by the flickering streetlamp, was someone sitting in a parked car smoking a cigarette. The black Mercedes had a window open part way, letting out a thin stream of strong-smelling tobacco smoke. I had smelled the sharp, acrid odor before when that trio of German nasties had tried to rearrange my anatomy.

They found out where I lived. Well, duh! I should have seen it coming, but that's what happens when you're too busy chasing multifarious romantic entanglements and letting, "the little head think for the big head," as my old buddy from the Italian North End had been fond of saying.

Damn! Repentance may be good for the soul, but it wouldn't do much for my body if they got their hands on me. I only had one small chance: not let them know I'd made them.

I stood on the steps adjusting my jacket and pulling up my collar as though deciding which way to go. I moved off towards Commonwealth Avenue and the T-stop. Behind me I heard the tires of the Mercedes squelching along the wet pavement about half a block behind me. I got to the corner, caught the tail end of the crosswalk light and crossed to the westbound trolley tracks. Out of the corner of my eye, I saw the Mercedes at the light, ready to come across the tracks where I stood alone at the T-stop, to hustle me into the big black car. The light turned green, and sure enough, the car started towards me. Almost without thinking, I bolted to the eastbound side of Comm. Ave. and franticly waved my hand at a cab parked across the street.

Fortunately for me, the cab was on duty, and without hesitation, cut across three lanes of eastbound traffic. I jumped in, and without even asking me where I wanted to go, the dreadlock-sporting cabbie whipped around the approaching Mercedes and turned left onto the westbound side of Comm. Ave., leaving the black car heading the wrong way towards downtown. Through the rear window I watched their taillights merge into smeared red drops in the distance and let go a long-delayed sigh of relief.

That's when I noticed I wasn't alone. There was a man sitting in the shadows on the other side of the back seat.

"Aw, shit!" was my first and most sincere reaction.

"Maybe not." The man on the other side of the seat reached over and shook my hand. "Steve Novak, colonel, USAF. We need to talk."

Advanced Research Projects Agency, were experimenting with a theory that a transmitter could warp space and time just like gravity. According to one of the scientists, Preston Nichols, they were able to find a time vortex that would tunnel them back and forth between the present day and the time of the Philadelphia Experiment in 1943. According to his calculations, this vortex, if properly expanded, had the potential to teleport objects and even humans as far as 100 light years away, to and from any time in the past or future. They experimented, but found anything beyond the year 2021 was unrecognizable and no tangible future beyond 2021. Because by having knowledge about the future, this knowledge has now altered the present. Preston also explains that if someone were teleported back into time, they would eventually meet themselves—and explode."

"Whaaaaat?" I looked hard at the colonel to see if he was bullshitting me, but either he was a world class, straight-faced liar, or he believed the bizarre crap he was spouting. Either way, I'd heard enough. No, make that more than enough. I stood up.

"Listen, guys, it's been real, but like I said, I've got places to be where hopefully no little green men, mad scientists, or crazy Nazis are gonna show up. Give my regards to Mulder, Scully, and Indiana Jones when they drop by." I walked to the door and turned the nob. It was locked. Naturally.

I turned back to the colonel, but before I could speak, he beat me to it.

"Sit down and shut up."

"OK, but someone is gonna have to tell me what the crap is going on, what the hell you're talking about, and exactly what the fuck it has to do with me."

Chapter Eighteen

And we did. Or rather I talked—in the form of a hundred non-stop questions—and he listened—without answering any of them.

When I finally ran out of steam, he took out a black box of cigarettes marked Dunhill Fine Cut, put one in his mouth, and lit it. Fortunately, having spent a considerable amount of time in Europe over the past year, I was resigned to an early death from second-hand smoke being blown in my face, usually at those charming sidewalk café tables where the chain smokers of Europa frittered away their lives, and yours, by collateral damage, in a cigarette-induced nicotine smog. So I only coughed a little, which he didn't acknowledge but did crack the window a bit.

Finally, frustrated and more than a little pissed, I pulled out a couple of bucks, tapped the cabbie on the shoulder and said, "OK, let me out at the next light."

The cabbie turned his head in the opposite direction and raised his eyes in the rearview mirror towards the reflection of my non-communicative fellow passenger

"MIT Center for Theoretical Physics, 77 Mass. Ave., Building Six," he said.

Now it was my turn to raise my eyebrows. "Other than being kidnapped by a group of mad scientists who plan to tie me to a centrifuge and use me as a human video game for a bunch of MIT geeks, why in the hell would I ever want to visit MIT, and even more important, why would they ever want me to?"

He almost smiled but covered it with a long drag on his cigarette, saying softly more to himself than me, "You don't know how close you really are."

"Huh? What's that supposed to mean? MIT wants me as a human guinea pig to test centrifuges and video games?" But he had reverted to the silent routine.

I put my hand on the door handle. "Hey, either I get some answers or take my chances rolling into traffic."

His laugh was somewhere between a grunt and a snort. "Try it."

My fingers pulled on the handle, but I heard a click. It had been remotely locked, and when I looked for the release button, I saw it had been removed altogether.

I sighed and leaned back into the seat. "OK. It looks like the Massachusetts Institute of Technology is the next stop on our happy little tour. If it wouldn't violate your secret oath to the president, scientologists, or the local Moose lodge, who the hell wants me, and what the Christ am I supposed to find there?"

"Maybe some answers."

"That would be a nice change. And precisely who at that esteemed bastion of science and technology might be equipped to give them to me?

"Dr. Jerzy Dombroski, professor of quantum physics."

At the mention of "quantum physics," little alarm bells went off in my head and I wracked my brain trying to recall the snippets of half remembered and less understood scraps of conversations with Max and Dieter.

Then it hit me.

"Holy crap! MIT, a physics professor, and an Air Force colonel...please tell me this has nothing to do with Project

Bluebook and you don't have Mulder and Scully locked in the trunk!"

Once again the "almost" smile. "The professor will answer all your questions."

"Why don't I believe you?"

He shrugged before he turned away and stared at the traffic whizzing by on the rain-wet streets. The driver hung a left and crossed over to the Cambridge side of the Charles River. I watched while the first of the imposing, in a Stalinist sort of stark grey, buildings of the MIT campus appeared on our left. The cab took another left, and I watched the Boston side of the city recede behind us.

I turned back to my silent partner. "If I've gotta see this Professor What's-his-name-ski, at least let me call my very hot and soon-to-be-pissed-off date to let her know I'll be a little late."

He didn't answer, which wasn't comforting.

"I am going to be only a 'little' late...right?"

When he continued to stare out the window, I pulled my cell out of my jacket pocket. But before I could dial, he took the phone from my hand and ran a small silver disc, about the size of a quarter, over it and handed it back, shaking his head. "Sorry. Looks like you're out of juice."

He was right. No signal, no bars, and no battery. I'd had it on charge all last night, and when I'd left the apartment, it had been at 99%. No more. I couldn't even get it to turn on.

"What the hell did you do to it?"

"Like I said, save your questions for Dr. Dombroski."

Oh boy, this was gonna be fun.

* * * *

A bored security guard at a small metal desk in the building's lobby wasn't going to let us in, but a quick flip of the colonel's ID changed his mind. He quickly scribbled out passes for us.

"Take the stairs," he said with a vague wave of his hand, indicating the stairs at the end of the corridor, "the elevators are turned off for the night."

Given our surroundings, and the cheap spy/thriller unreality of the situation, I half-expected some mad scientist who looked like a cross between Albert Einstein and Boris Karloff. But the good doctor, standing at an interactive white board when we walked in, looked perfectly ordinary: a blue oxford shirt, kakis, and brown loafers. Receding white hair, he was probably in his mid to late seventies, thin and fit looking, except for one shoulder slightly lower than the other, but all-in-all perfectly commonplace for an academic. That is, until he turned and looked at us. There was an almost imperceptible nod at the colonel, but I got the stare he must save for disagreeable strangers and unpleasant specimens under his microscope.

As a result, I didn't know whether to shake his hand or slither out under the door. He solved my dilemma by pointing to the couch on the other side of his office and with the command of "Sit."

I discretely scanned the room for signs of any large canines for which the order had been intended. Nope. No one here but us mutts, and of course, the colonel.

The professor sat down in a worn, green leather chair behind his desk and reached for a pipe from an intricately carved walnut rack with an old, cut-glass humidor in the middle. Between cold, appraising glances in my direction, he made a great show of fiddling with a long-stemmed briar pipe; scraping the bowl and then filling it with a pungent tobacco smelling of apple and pecans. As he tamped it down, he continued staring at me from under bushy salt-and-pepper eyebrows. And for all of his fiddling and tamping, when he finally finished, he returned the pipe to its rack without lighting it, which told me the entire ritual had been more about gaining time to look me over than smoking the damn thing. His next words proved me correct.

"Very well, Colonel Novak. Since you have succeeded in breaking my concentration and pulling me away from a very important piece of research that you, of all people, should be anxious for me to finish, you may tell me what was so damned urgent that you needed to bring this *głupiec* over to meet me this instant."

Call me cynical, but I had a strong hunch the term *głupiec*, was not only in some language I wasn't familiar with, but probably was not a synonym for "awesome."

The colonel confirmed it with his less-than-ringing endorsement.

"Despite his appearance, what we've vetted on him so far indicates that he's not a fool and seems to have a pretty fair talent for getting himself out some nasty scrapes."

"Thanks, Colonel...I think."

He didn't acknowledge my comment or presence but went right on talking as if I wasn't there, which, right now, sounded like a pretty good idea to me.

"It sounds like you two have got a lot of important things to discuss, now if you'll excuse me, I have a hot date that's rapidly cooling and I need to sweet-talk my way back into her good graces. *Adios* and *adieu* boys, it's been real." I stood up.

I didn't get far before I felt the colonel's hand lock around my wrist in vise-like grip.

"Sit down and shut up."

"Shit, with an invitation like that, how can I refuse?" Trying not to rub my sore wrist, I sat back down. How many more people could I run across who liked to interact with me by bruising various parts of my anatomy?

Colonel Novak went back to ignoring me in the third person.

"According to our Munich source, they believe our person of interest has passed on what may be a complete set of plans, drawings, and translations confirming the three prototypes of the *VRIL-7-GROSSRAUMSCHIFF* from *HAUNEBU I* through version III."

Dombroski grunted dismissively. "You forget, Colonel, I have read and thoroughly interviewed all of the remaining team who worked on Operation Paperclip; your government's less-than-noble program to bring top Nazi rocket scientists to America after the war, including two who worked with its supposed VRIL scientists, Dr. Viktor Schauberger and Dr. Ing Schumann."

"And that, Professor, is why you are vital to this project and why we need you to debrief this young man and discover if the documents contain any references to the Philadelphia and Phoenix experiments."

"Bah! The Philadelphia Experiment was a fool's errand when they performed it in 1943, and the passage of seventy-five years has not made it any less foolish."

The colonel remained expressionless, but I noticed how the back of his neck reddened.

"Perhaps, but according to the data we have from the Navy, the follow up to it, the Phoenix Experiment, did produce tangible results."

"Philadelphia Experiment, Phoenix Experiment?" I broke in. "My guess would be any city activity with the word 'experiment' tacked onto it probably would not be sponsored by the Chamber of Commerce. Would someone mind terribly giving me a clue as to what they were?"

The colonel sighed. "Both concerned certain aspects of temporal displacement, although initially the Philadelphia Experiment, begun during the Second World War, was working to enable our ships to evade Nazi subs using a type of an invisibility cloak."

The professor snorted with disgust. "And all your scientists succeeded in doing was scrambling the atoms of a dozen crewmen to the point that when the field finally shorted out, their bodies had been fused into the hull of the ship!"

The colonel bit down hard on his lip but said nothing.

"The Phoenix Experiment," the professor continued, "really began after the war in 1947 as a continuation of the Philadelphia Experiment...and produced the same lack of positive results."

"Now that's not fair, Professor." The colonel leaned forward. "It opened our research into many previously, only-suspected avenues of spatial and temporal research."

"Ahhhh, and if I'm not being too obtuse, what experiment, and more to the point, what does it have to do with me?"

The colonel turned to me. "From 1947 to 1987 in Montauk, out on Long Island, the boys from DARPA, the Defense

The colonel snapped. "What part of 'keep your mouth shut' didn't you understand?"

And suddenly I was mad. Really fucking pissed. I stood up and kicked back the coffee table in front of the couch. "You know what? Fuck you, Colonel. Fuck both of you, your stupid secret projects, Nazi nut-jobs, and Max Becker too. I am so outta here, and if you don't like, it you can suck my—"

The colonel started to rise, but I'll never know if he was going to shoot or arrest me because the professor grabbed his arm.

"What name did you say?" he growled at me.

The professor's slight Eastern European accent increased with the question, but I was too angry to consider why.

"Max. Max Becker," I snapped back, "the German son of a bitch who got me mixed up in this mess. Which, as of now, I am officially resigning from, and you or the crazy krauts chasing me can have that damn flash drive. I don't care which. I am fucking done!"

The professor slowly came around from behind his desk and stood in front of me. "This Max Becker. How old is he? What does he look like?"

"I dunno, late sixties, seventies. White hair, blue eyes, but in pretty good shape for an old guy. Why?"

For the first time since I'd met him, the professor looked unsure, confused.

"No, that would be too young. He would have to be in his nineties by now." He shook his head and stared out the big second floor window at the traffic lights on Mass. Ave. He remained like that for a full minute until he slowly turned back to me and stared at me. No, make that looked right *through* me.

"Unless...," he began. "Yes, unless he was using the same device as Kammler. They must all have had access to it. Only that could explain it." He turned to the colonel. "Colonel Novak, forgive me. I am starting to think you may be right. And yes, I most definitely wish to speak with your Mister...?"

For the first time, the colonel smiled. "Brennan. Christopher Brennan." And gestured to me in a way that had me wondering if he expected me to bow, tap dance, or sing "The Star Spangled Banner."

But after searching my emotions, all I could really feel was a vast, increasing, stinking swamp of confusion.

Chapter Nineteen

The next two hours spent with the colonel and Professor Dombroski flew by in a mind numbing series of stories I couldn't believe and explanations I didn't understand.

They all centered around the crazy tale I'd first heard from Max about the Thulist Occult movement after World War I and its connection to the early Nazi party. Not the least of which was the influence it had over political, cultural, and even scientific decisions, by the rouge's gallery of murderous crackpots and thugs, who would later emerge as the party "Bozen" - the fat cats - of the German National Socialist movement of the twenties and thirties.

Their names, and those of the corpses of their ten million victims, were written in blood throughout Europe and Russia by the murderous pack of misfits whom, those who knew better, should have moved heaven and earth to insure their rants were confined to rubber rooms tucked safely into the dark pines of the Black Forest.

But as history continues to show us, more often than not, it is the inmates who run the asylum. And as Max had been telling me, the illuminati and freethinkers of academia and the occult, found ready and willing empty vessels among the disillusioned and dissatisfied mass of former soldiers and workers after the humiliation and economic chaos brought about by the Treaty of Versailles. It was that disaffected mob that rallied to this group of unknown misanthropes and made sure the world would learn, to their eternal regret, their names. Names that would come to strike terror into the rest of the world: Hitler, Himmler, Hess, Göring, Gobbles,

Heydrich, Eichmann, Mengele and the other faceless bureaucrats, storm troopers, and sadists who put wholesale murder on an assembly line.

However, among this litany of madmen and butchers were two names that struck personal cords with me: Max Becker and the illusive, mysterious, and hauntingly beautiful Maria Orsic.

"She was nothing more than a charlatan and a Nazi whore." Dombrorski spat in response to my questions about Maria's part in the mystic ideals co-opted by the nascent National Socialists.

"Whoa...that's not what heard."

"Hah! From that 'friend' of yours? The SS stooge who now calls himself Max Becker?"

"Yeah, I know about the name change to Becker from von-something-or-other, but what are you talking about, 'the SS stooge?' Max was never in the SS. He told me he fought against them during the thirties."

The professor made a disgusted sound and shook his head. "Pah, Colonel, you have brought someone who is either a fool or hopelessly naive, and neither is of any use to us."

The colonel finally spoke up. "That's not fair, Jerzy. He's only met Becker in a vacuum and never heard any accounts other than his."

"Yes, but..."

I stood up and waved both hands. "Hello? Hey, I'm right here, and if you two go back to talking around me and leaving me abandoned in the third person, I'm gonna pick up what's left of my marbles and go home."

The colonel treated me to another of his wary smiles. "Point taken. Let's talk about what we need from you. We—"

I made a "T" out of my hands. "Time out, Colonel. Either you guys answer my questions or there's never gonna be any 'we' to need anything."

"What is it you want answers to?" The colonel was back to being the guarded government official.

"Since you think Max has been leading a double life, you can start by telling me who you think he really is."

The colonel raised his eyebrows and gestured to the professor. "Jerzy, why don't you tell him what you've pieced together?"

The look of disgust on the professor's face deepened into raw hatred. "The man calling himself Max Becker is a former SS Sturmbannführer by the name of Maximillian von Buchholz. He was born in Vienna and served in the First World War. After the war, he moved with his doxy, Maria Orsic—a so-called medium—to Munich where they both became Thulists and great friends of the vicious madmen who founded the Nazi party, including Adolph Hitler."

He took a deep breath and stared through the window as though he was seeing lines of goose-stepping storm troopers on the mist-wet street below. Who knows? Maybe he was. Then he snapped back and continued.

"In 1935, perhaps to escape the repercussions of an altercation at a nightclub with several SA storm troopers, he apparently called in a favor from Himmler himself and secured an officer's commission in the Ahnenerbe Section of the SS."

"Ahnenerbe? What's that?"

"It stands for Deutsches Ahnenerbe—Studiengesellschaft für Geistesurgeschichte, or, 'German Ancestral Heritage— Society for the Study of the History of Primeval Ideas.' It was a section Himmler created to establish a connection between Germans and the ancient Aryan race. They reported directly to Himmler, and he lavished funds and resources on their expeditions to everywhere from Tibet, the Near East, and all the way down to Antarctica. Only the needs of war on two fronts finally curtailed their crackpot research. But even though they could no longer pursue their myths in exotic locations, they didn't abandon them. They instead took advantage of the SS's almost-unlimited supply of slave labor and began excavations all over the Reich for so-called 'mystical artifacts,' such as the Spear of Longinus, the Ark of the Covenant, and the Holy Grail."

"Sounds like something out of an Indiana Jones movie. Are you trying to tell me all the stuff in Spielberg's movies was real?"

He shook his head and glared at me. "Those film makers didn't know the half of it. If they had, they would have hung themselves in despair before shooting a single frame."

He was breathing heavily now. Something was really starting to piss him off. I probably shouldn't have stirred the pot, but I needed answers.

"Hmm...that brings me to another question. How come you know so much about it?"

If looks could kill, his would have burned me to ashes.

"How come, Mr. Brennan? I'll show you the fuck, 'how-come!'"

He took off his jacket and savagely pulled at his shirt cuff, ripping off the button in the process. And there it was, in faded blue ink, blurred and washed out by seventy years of living, suffering, and probably wondering why he'd been spared: a string of numbers tattooed onto the underside of his left upper forearm.

"Auschwitz/Birkenau."

I wasn't quite sure of how to respond—or if he cared whether I did.

Like everyone else, I'd read the books, seen the movies, and even watched documentaries on TV, but I knew enough to know that no one who hadn't been there could truly imagine the horrors of everyday existence spent trying to survive for a few more days or even hours.

All I could say was, "Sorry."

He glanced up at me. "Perhaps you are." Then he shrugged. "No matter. Every day of my life since then has been due to the fact that my father, a former professor of physics at the Technical Institute of Munich, somehow bribed a guard to get me assigned to the Buna Werke, a labor camp located near Oswiecim, Poland."

The professor stared blankly out to the dark drizzle beyond the window before continuing. "I asked him why he could not come with me to the factory. He made up some excuse, and I learned years later that the amount he had for a bribe was only enough to secure one place. For me."

He turned away from the window and went on, his tone bitter and voice clipped. "The plant produced synthetic oil and Buna-N, or rubber, using slave labor from the Auschwitz/Birkenau_concentration camp. By the time I arrived in 1944, the Buna factory had some 80,000 slave laborers. I was a skinny, starving boy of ten, so they set me the task of crawling under the machines to glean the little scraps of rubber that fell behind them."

He looked at me with dead eyes. "Do you know I still sometimes wake with the smell of burning rubber and corpses in my nostrils?"

I cleared my throat. "I mean, like I'm sorry for what you went through and all, but what does it have to do with Max, and especially me?"

"One day, when I was carrying my basket filled with rubber scraps, I spotted a crumpled piece of wax paper on the floor underneath one of the machines. I could see through the paper it contained a small rind of cheese that one of the guards had been munching on and tossed in the pile of dirt and debris under an extruding machine. So without thinking, I bent down, slithered under the machine and grabbed the precious piece of refuse. But as I backed out, picked up my basket, and turned to stand up, I bumped into one of the Lithuanian SS guards. He smashed me across the face with a fist of iron, and followed it up with a kick to the stomach with his hobnailed boot. He raised his truncheon and would likely have beaten me to death on the spot when the director of the factory rounded a corner with a group of SS officers and eastern Gauliters. The guard immediately came to attention and was suddenly all smiles as one of the SS officers asked him a question about the extruding machine, which made him forget all about me. And as softly and quietly as I could, I scuttled away, but as I got to my feet and looked back, I saw the young, handsome SS officer who was talking to the guard. He looked like a Nordic god with his blue eyes, blonde hair, and black uniform with the silver death's head cap badge. It was only later when a friend of mine who was working in the records division for Operation Paperclip told me the name of the man." He glared at me. "It was Maximillian von Buchholz, the man you know as Max Becker."

I sighed. "Look, Professor, I know you went through some real bad shit...some unbelievably bad shit I can't ever understand or even imagine. But I wasn't there. Maybe everything you say about Max is true. Maybe he was some kind of Nazi SS monster, but I have to be honest. All I've ever seen is kind of a nice, old guy with a lot of unbelievable stories to tell. So if you guys really need me to help you, you're gonna have to fill me in on how the guy you call von Buchholz and I know as Max, gets from the SS to UFOs and little green men."

Dombrowski glared at me, and then for the first time his expression of hostility softened, and the anger drained out of him like a deflating balloon.

He sat back down behind his desk and rubbed his eyes. "Colonel, you tell him. I am suddenly feeling very tired."

Without preamble the colonel started to speak. "As previously stated, your friend Max is really a former SS officer who was deeply involved with the SS and Himmler's vain attempts to win the war by securing mystical 'weapons of power.' Not only that, but according to our information, he acted as a liaison officer among the Ahnenerbe, the Haunebu, and VRIL projects."

"And what exactly does that mean? I mean really, Colonel, what would a liaison officer between the Indiana Jones branch of the SS be liaising about with a bunch of nut jobs running around creating flying saucers in hopes they could visit little green Nazis?"

I didn't even draw a smile from the colonel. I guess the military trains you to leave your sense of humor at the recruiting office door. With barely a raise of his eye, he continued.

"Yes, part of the position seems to have been created specifically for him; however, according to our best information, he—shall we say—'grew' into the position? After 1935, there was a huge increase in SS expeditions to India and Tibet and the Middle East. Your pal Max became quite a rising star in the group sent to find and decipher the ancient Sumerian and cuneiform texts. These texts were then sent back to his girlfriend, the self-styled medium, Maria Orsic, who supposedly used them to channel technical information from some mysterious star people for the purpose of creating an interstellar flying craft that would allow them to meet these 'aliens.'" The colonel gave a small snort of skeptical disgust. "And gain access to even more technological wonders."

"So, I'm going out on a limb here, Colonel, but without belaboring the obvious, you apparently think all of this is bullshit?"

The colonel didn't say so directly, but his look said the equivalent of, "Uh, yeah, duh..?"

"With that being the case, would it be too much for you guys to finally tell me why I'm here, and what the hell you want me to do?"

They looked at one another. The professor gave a slight nod to the colonel who bent down and opened his briefcase. He took out rolls and rolls of faded, yellowed blueprints and unrolled them onto the coffee table. They were about three feet long, old, but in pretty good shape, all except for the last two. One of them had the end third ripped off, and the other that had been on the outside of all the rolls, had the entire middle badly scorched, or in some places, completely burned out. The colonel motioned me over and tapped on the two partially destroyed blueprints.

"Do these look familiar?"

I peered down at them. "Yeah. I don't know whether these are all the same ones. I only saw them for a couple of minutes, but yeah, these kinda look like what was on the flash drive Max gave me."

"And that, Mr. Brennan, is the answer to your question of what the hell you're doing here. We need to see the original, undamaged copies of those two blueprints, and as far as we know, there are only three people who have at least some of them. One was one of the top ten Nazi bigwigs and a purely evil son of a bitch, an SS general named Hans Kammler, then there's your buddy Max, who may or may not be a war criminal, and of course...you."

* * * *

Our happy little trio went on in the same vein for another hour until the colonel was mostly convinced that I didn't have the flash drive on my person—at least until he could upgrade his cursory pat down of me and my personal possessions into a full strip search with a body cavity chaser.

Before he could whistle up some big boys with clubs, side arms, and MP written on their helmets, I took a shot and asked, with as much sincerity as could muster, if I might be allowed to continue on my formerly, merry way.

"Sure," said the colonel in what I surmised was the same reasonable tone of voice he used when asking the condemned if they'd like a blindfold or a last cigarette. "As long as you are heading to wherever the flash drive is."

Shit!

I pasted on my sincerest smile and replied, "Absolutely."

I stood up and began moving to the door. I wanted to leave before he changed his mind. I mean, this was too good to be true. And of course it was.

I had expected that he would put a tail on me, but figured I had at least an even shot at shaking them off. But he wasn't about to give me the chance to try. He stood up and pushed the speed dial on his cell phone.

"Sergeant, I'll be down in a minute with the young man I accompanied here. I'd like you and Lieutenant Emerson to take him wherever he wants to go—within reason."

The colonel gave me a smile used by people who don't smile very often; in other words, somewhere between disingenuous and insincere. "In plain terms, Mr. Brennan, we don't want you wandering off or losing your way in the dark."

Seeing as how my choices were limited between taking up permanent residence in the professor's office, or being dragged off to some secret Air Force Base where they'd strap me to a table and perform a preemptive alien autopsy on me, the most attractive choice was to get a ride across town at the government's expense.

As the colonel put me into the back seat of a nondescript government car, he leaned in and said, with only the slightest trace of irony, "We'll stay in touch."

Oh, yes. Of that I was certain.

* * * *

More out of boredom than any real interest, I tried to engage the sergeant and the lieutenant in small talk, but the sergeant was too busy threading his way through the last streams of late-night Boston traffic, and the lieutenant merely answered me with taciturn grunts.

With little expectation of success, I had nothing to lose by giving my only plan a shot. We came to a stoplight.

"Bang a right on Harvard Street," I said.

"Why?" they asked—in unison.

"I've got to take a wicked piss and there's a Dunky D's two doors down on Harvard Ave. And because they sell so much damn coffee, they actually have an unlocked restroom that isn't totally disgusting."

The lieutenant looked at me as if he discovered something unpleasant on the bottom of his shoe. "What do we look like to you? A pair of fuck-ups who fell off the turnip truck?"

I was gonna say, "No, you look like a pair of fuck-ups who think saying, 'fell off the turnip truck' is cool." But since I was trying to bullshit them with my sincerity, I kept my big mouth shut. Instead, I put on my best twenty-something "Please, Mommy" whine.

"Hey, really man, I gotta go—and like right now! I mean, I'm serious man. In about two seconds, we're going to be up to our ankles in piss."

The sergeant driving looked in the rearview mirror and raised his eyebrows inquisitively. The lieutenant regarded me for a moment before nodding once. The light changed and the sergeant took a right onto Harvard and stopped in front of the Dunkin' Donuts sign. I opened the right-hand passenger door, and as I did, the lieutenant opened his and came around the back end of the car.

"I'm coming with you."

"Sure, no problem, except it's a one-holer and like, really small."

We walked to the back of the store where there were two cheap, brown, hollow doors; one with a sign marked women, and the other men. He opened the door to the men's room and stuck his head in, quickly observing that what I said about the size was true. He looked up at the window and noted it was too small for me to squeeze through.

"Okay, make it quick."

I went in, locked the door, and went to the sink. Quickly, I plucked my multi-tool out of my jacket pocket and scraped the paint out of the slots of two large screws inset into the wall of a small space next to the sink. After a few seconds, I had the screws backed out enough to be able to slip the blade of the multi-tool along the inside of the piece of quarter-inch wallboard and gently ease out the 2' x 3' section. It was barely large enough for me to squeeze through, and with one more step, I was into the back of the maintenance closet on the other side of the wall. The door was locked, but only to those trying to open it from the outside. I opened it quietly and stepped out into a short corridor lined with shelves of coffee and paper supplies. So far, so good. And I was damned glad that the last time I'd been here, I'd watched a repairman replace that section of wall a late-night patron, trying to sober up with many cups of black coffee, had kicked out in a fit of pique after being told he was not allowed to piss in the sink. I'd been waiting in line to use the men's room and had seen, the next day, the owners replace the blue-board so if this happened again, it would be easier for them to unscrew a simple one-piece panel and replace it. And, fortunately for me, for some inexplicable reason my brain likes to store random bits of information like this and is able to dredge them up at opportune times—like now.

I tried the handle of the steel fire door leading to the alley but it was locked. Damn! Just then, I heard a voice behind me.

"Hey!"

Damn....Again!

I spun around and a short, swarthy man stood there, wiping his hands on his apron. "What you doin' man?" He growled in broken English.

"Hey, sorry," I deliberately slurred my words in the same post-drinking, pre-sober stage that at least half of the patrons were in. "I was looking for the back door."

I gave him a bleary smile and rattled ineffectually on the steel door's handle. Then a voice called from the kitchen.

"Hey, Manny! Where's that fucking Columbian roast? Come on, move it dude."

He looked at me, then up to the shelf crammed with one-pound bags of coffee, and a second later inserted the key from his ring into the lock on the steel door and pushed me out into the alley.

The whole process had taken only two or three minutes, but by now I was sure the lieutenant was starting to pound on the Men's Room door. I guessed I would have no more than five minutes before they got around to figuring out that somehow I'd gotten out of there and gone into the alley. So I started off at a quick jog and at the end of the alley, climbed over an old wooden fence, made my way to a side street, and from there, back out to Comm. Ave.

My luck still held and I saw a cab dropping off a fare. As the female passenger got out and handed him a few bills, I hopped into the back.

"Beacon Street," I told him before he even had a chance to say "where to?" while glancing out the rear window and hoping none of the bobbing headlights of the cars behind us contained two really pissed off Air Force men.

Chapter Twenty

I'm not the kind of idiot who, when faced with an unpleasant set of options, figures it doesn't really matter since things couldn't possibly get any worse. No, I'm a different kind of idiot. The kind that is thoroughly convinced things not only can, but, in all probability, will get a lot worse; therefore, it really doesn't matter which set of unpleasant options you take because they'll probably all be bad.

Thus, "in sure and certain hope" that I was gonna wind up with my nuts in a vise no matter what I did, I told the cabbie to head over to Beacon Street and Kat.

What's the worst she could do? I mused. A little yelling, followed by abject apology from yours truly, followed by some great make-up sex. Hey, I could do worse. Or so I thought.

My first problem was I had to get her to see me and my cell phone was dead. Or was it? I pulled it out, and sure enough, it was back on and showed almost a full charge. Whatever the colonel had done to it must have been merely temporary, or perhaps it only killed the power within the effective range of that device he used. Maybe the government had picked up a few little pieces of alien tech while chasing after bigger prizes? At any rate, I was not about to look the proverbial gift horse in the mouth, so I called her from the cab. And she promptly hung up on me. I hit re-dial. This time, she picked up.

"You inconsiderate asshole!"

No argument there.

"Kat, please. Let me come over to explain."

"I've had it with waiting around for you. I'm going to bed. Alone!"

Then she hung up on me. Again.

Sigh...

I continued on anyway, and ten minutes later, I was standing in the Beacon Street Apartments' lobby. With the fatalist aplomb of a doomed French aristocrat stepping up to the Guillotine, I pressed the intercom buzzer, and a minute later it crackled with the query, "Chris?"

"Yup. Your wandering boy is standing in the lobby with a big 'pretty please?' on his chapped lips, waiting to beg your forgiveness."

Silence followed by an aggrieved sigh. "Oh, all right, but you better be prepared to do some serious groveling."

"I've got on my best knee-pads."

The door buzzed open.

When I stepped inside her front door, I tried to give her a big, contrite, but passionate kiss, but she shook her head and backed up a step. She wasn't about to let it go that easily.

"OK, pal, let's hear it, and it better be good."

"Ah, sure..." Hmmm, how much was I going tell her? I had thought about it on the cab ride over and still hadn't come up with a clear plan, so I did what I usually did.

Wing it.

"First of all, it wasn't my fault." Her expression told me that the last refuge of a coward wasn't going down well. "I mean, I was on my way when I sort of got kidnapped."

"Kidnapped? Oh, pul-eezeeee! You're not even trying to come with a plausible excuse. What's next? Shanghaied by pirates?"

No, I was definitely on the point of crashing and burning. No other option but to switch over to the last refuge of the truly desperate—the truth—at least part of it.

Big sigh. "OK, Kat, let me level with you."

"In addition to being a novelty, I agree that would be a good place to start."

"You remember when I told you about the stuff me and your uncle had been, ah...talking about?"

She looked me up and down. "Yeah?"

"There may be a few parts of the story I may have left out."

"Really?" The sarcasm had definitely been turned up several notches.

"Ah, yeah....You see, when I met your uncle back in Germany, before I began a life of being chased through alleys by the Katzenjammer Kids, he told me about some really weird shit. I thought he was just a nice old guy who'd been reading too much UFO stuff in the German tabloids. But then things started happening. Especially to me, but now I think about it, also to a bunch of other people I knew. And let me tell you, it was some pretty damned spooky stuff from some even spookier people. And I know this is really gonna sound 'out there,' but these guys have been chasing me all the way from Germany. I think that somehow they were in the SS!"

"The SS? Like as in the SS in all the World War II films? The bad guys in *Schindler's List*? The guys in the black uniforms and shiny boots?" She took a step back and rolled her eyes. "The guys who would now be well into their nineties?"

"Um....Yeah."

She shook her head. "You know, Chris, standing me up is bad enough, but don't make it worse by shoveling shit on top of one of the worst excuses I've ever heard."

"Kat, first of all, I didn't mean to stand you up. And secondly, you know your uncle had some pretty dark experiences in Nazi Germany."

"Sure, but nothing like the kind of BS you're talking about. Uncle Max was just another German who was also a victim of the Nazis."

I watched Kat's adorable, heart-shaped face. The color rose in her cheeks, tinting them a shade a cosmetician might have whimsically called "pretty in pink." But I knew if I kept up my current line of questions about her great-uncle, it was gonna turn to a bright, pissed-off red. So it was with great reluctance, and more than a little regret for being on the verge of blowing our entire nascent relationship, that I shook my head.

"Sorry, Kat. From what I've read and seen firsthand, no one joined a murderous outfit like the SS by mistakenly thinking it was gonna be pleasant times spent drinking beers with a bunch of guys in funny hats with skulls on 'em and beating the shit out of all and sundry on a regular basis."

If she had been a firecracker, she would have exploded. She stood in front of me, her eyes flashing and a curl of tousled, honey-colored hair hanging over one crimson cheek like an angry question mark directed at me and my unsolicited conclusions.

Damn! She was so hot!

My brain was where random and inappropriate thoughts go to die. She put both hands on her sweetly curved hips, and her chest was heaving (also sweetly).

"You think I'm gonna let you stand here and spout bullshit that my great-uncle, Gram's kid brother, was some sort of a monster? You can take a flying leap through that friggin' window!"

She pointed across the fussily decorated, if somewhat outdated, living room to the bow window and the rain damp street below. And all I could think of was her hand, shaking with righteous anger, smelled like lemon and jasmine.

"Kat..." I reached for her hand but she pulled away.

"You know what, Chris, just go. I don't think I wanna date a guy who thinks my uncle was some sort of big-shot Nazi official in an SS uniform."

She spun on her heel and yanked open the front door. "Go! And for the record, you are totally, one hundred percent wrong!"

"No, he's not."

We both turned. It was Max. He nodded.

"Everything he said is true, Kat."

His voice was deep with the rasp of regret. He shuffled over to where she stood, stunned, still holding the door open, and put his arms around her. I watched as she stared up at him, hurt and bewildered. Then she stiffened and pulled back.

"Uncle Max...what do you mean? That can't possibly be true. But if it is, how could you? And most of all...why?"

"I wish I had one good and easy answer, but like most things in life, it is very complicated and filled with compromises and all of those 'good intentions' with which the road to hell is paved. And trust me. I came to know that road well."

He motioned to the living room where the darkness and lights from the street beyond were beginning to fade with the softer gray of approaching morning.

"Sit, please. There is much to tell you." He stared at the street below, but his eyes were fixed on something far away and a lifetime ago. "And," he added softly, "there may not be much time."

* * * *

"Everything I told you about the first twenty years of my life is true. All except my name. Max Becker is a name that I, like many ex-SS men..." He gave a snort of disgust. "Suffice to say there were a lot of new names in Germany after the war." He bit the inside of his lip but then continued.

"In fact, I kept my name, proudly, right up until the time I 'joined' the SS in 1935. After that, not so proudly. But at any rate, yes, I was born Maximilian von Buchholz of old, but tired, nobility. And Austria was indeed my birth place, just as I told you, Herr Chris, and you, my kleine Prinzessin." He smiled at Kat but she was still too stunned to smile back.

His smile turned into a resigned sigh and he went on. "It was a name I bore proudly during the First World War and I—"

"Hang on a sec, Max. As long as you're in the mood to clear up mysteries about your past, I've got a big juicy one for you. If you served in World War I, how come you don't look any more than eighty? No, I'll take that back. Maybe you're taking steroids or something, but looking at you right now, you look even younger than when I first met you. Sixty-five maybe, certainly no more than seventy. Math was never my strong suit, but it doesn't take a genius to figure out that even if you lied about your age and joined up when you were fifteen or sixteen, it would still make you over one hundred and fifteen years old. I don't care how much steroid you shoot, no way are you gonna knock fifty years off your age. So what gives?"

He looked like he was going to answer and then decided against it. "Yes, that is a very valid point, Herr Chris, but let me table that for the present and merely say things are not always as they appear."

"Jeeze, thanks for the news flash," I muttered but gestured for him to go on.

"And I have told you both about my life in Munich with Maria and the Vril society while the Nazi's began their mad grab for power." He looked at Kat with sad eyes. "Though I did skip over much of that when I told you stories whenever you and your...Grossmutter came to visit me in Munich. Forgive me, Liebling, but I did not want to tarnish your young dreams with the horrors of such terrible times. You see, many of us had to do things then that would have outraged all sense of decency in a normal world."

I noticed how he stumbled over the word Grossmutter, "grandmother." The little light of puzzlement flickered at the back of my mind but was quickly extinguished. There were bigger fish to fry. Much bigger and far more worrisome.

Kat said nothing, merely watched the man she had always known as her "sweet, old Uncle Max" with eyes that were turning more wary and troubled with every word.

For the next half hour, Max summarized everything he'd already told me for Kat's benefit. When he finished, the wary look was still in her eye, but I could tell she was trying to reserve judgment until he was finished with his explanation. But before he proceeded to the second part of his story, he turned to Kat.

"Liebchen, will you be a gut Mädchen and get your old uncle Max his pipe?"

This earned him a raised eyebrow from his grandniece, but after only a few succinct comments about smoking, and especially smelly old pipes, she got up and went down the hall.

"It's in my bedroom on the night stand." he called after her, then quickly turned back to me, whispering, "There are things I can only share with you because I do not wish to put my niece in any more danger than she already is. So if you think I may be leaving out some important details, understand that I will tell you later, when we are alone."

"And exactly when might that be?" But, I was silenced by a finger he placed before his lips. Kat had returned with his pipe and a worn chamois tobacco pouch. Pretty good ears for an old guy. I jotted it down on my mental list of things concerning Max that didn't quite add up.

He made a great show of stuffing and tamping down the tobacco in his pipe and clamped it firmly between his teeth, but didn't light it.

"Where was I?" he said, scratching his full head of tousled white hair.

"The part where all was about to be made clear," I deadpanned.

"Ah, yes, of course." He tried to give us an avuncular wink but failed to quite pull it off. So with another sigh, he leaned back in the chair and continued.

"After the incident at the club with the SA Storm-troopers, word must have gotten back to the SS how I had played my trump card by using Himmler's letter. I was awakened the next morning by one of the most dreaded sounds in Nazi Germany. The knock at the door."

Chapter Twenty-One

Munich, June 1935

Bang! Bang! Bang!

The door reverberated from the sound of a jackboot or truncheon crashing against the thin oak panel.

I had been startled out of a lovely dream where I had been making love to Maria beneath the cool, green canopy of a forest willow tree. But now, I scrambled to the door, pulling on my shirt and managing to get one brace of my suspenders hooked over my right shoulder as the heel of a jackboot splintered a five-centimeter sliver out of the lower panel of the door.

"Open this damned door, or we'll kick it in!"

"Yes, yes, I am coming as fast as I can." I fumbled with the lock, but before I could pull it open, it was violently pushed out of my hand by the same jackboot which, as the door flew open, I saw was on the foot of a stocky SA officer standing, glaring at me, flanked by two serpent-eyed men in black trench coats. The sick feeling in the pit of my stomach told me they were Gestapo. They confirmed it when the two men pulled out copper identity discs with their ID numbers.

"Well?" the SA officer called over his right shoulder. "Is this the man?"

This time my stomach turned over completely because standing right behind them in the hallway was one of the troopers from last night. He clicked his heels and answered.

"*Jawohl!*"

The portly, florid-faced officer with the red swastika armband pointed at me and turned to the two Gestapo men.

"Arrest him."

The one on the left started to move, but the one on the right held up his hand.

"And one more time, Commander Vogel, exactly what is this man accused of?"

I thought the plump officer would puff up and explode, but after a few seconds he collected himself and spoke.

"This shirker, who is not even in the uniform of the Vaterland, threatened my men with a phony letter purported to be signed by Reichsführer Himmler himself!" He cleared his throat and spat on my floor. "It is probably a forgery anyway."

When the Gestapo men made no move towards me, the SA officer spun on his heel and shouted, "I demand you arrest him. We'll give him something to write about, though I doubt he will even be able to hold a pen after we finish with him at Dachau."

"Well," the one on the right spoke up again, "I should like to see the letter in question myself." He gestured to me. "You will produce the letter."

I hurried to the bedroom and could hear the SA officer sputtering about, "outrages," and "he needs to be taught a lesson." But when I arrived once more at the front door, the Gestapo man silenced the complaints with a slight raise of his right hand. The other he held open, and I put the Reichsführer's letter into it. Maria had wisely surmised that the SA might not want to give up on dragging me off to a "reeducation" camp and had finally persuaded me to take the letter, which protected her and her "colleagues" from interference. Good thing too, because had I not possessed the letter, I would have found myself hustled off on a one way trip to the Gestapo interrogation cells in the basement of Prinz-Albrecht-Straße. As it was, even with the letter, the SA official was not ready to throw in the towel. The taller of the two Gestapo men quickly skimmed it until his gaze fell on the signature and his eyebrows rose a millimeter.

"This is the Reichsführer's signature. I think you owe Herr von Buchholz an apology, Herr SA Commander."

But the pompous, fat toad was having none of it. There were innumerable power struggles going on between the SS and the SA, and the fool was determined that the SA should emerge victorious, so he piped up.

"Then we shall go see Herr Himmler himself and see what he has to say about his minions misusing his name to prevent the guardians of the Vaterland in the their sacred duty to rid Germany of Jews and the Communist filth."

And so we all went off to see Reichsführer Heinrich Himmler, the deadliest man in Germany.

At that time, Hitler spent a lot of time in his Munich headquarters, The Brown House, so naturally Himmler found a reason to be there too. And after a wait of only fifteen or twenty minutes, we were ushered in.

Himmler stood with his back towards the door, staring out the window, and it made us fidget and feel uncomfortable, until finally he turned to us with his cobra-lidded eyes and asked in a deceptively mild voice, "Yes?"

The taller of the two Gestapo men came to attention and stiffly handed my letter to Himmler. Without looking at it, Himmler adjusted his wire-rim spectacles and looked at the four of us standing in front of him. His voice stayed mild, but his implications were not. And he soon made us all understand that.

"Are any of you aware of why I am in Munich?"

No one spoke, and now he looked directly at the fat, little SA leader. "I know you of the SA labor under the delusion that all of us fellows in the Schutzstaffel merely spend our time polishing our boots and providing color at boring civil ceremonies."

I noticed sweat beginning to appear on the SA commander's upper lip.

"But let me assure you all, this is not the case." Himmler glanced at the two men of the Gestapo and raised his eyebrows before refocusing on the perspiring SA leader. "It might interest you to consider how closely the Gestapo and SS are going to become when we have completed the program so dear to the Führer's heart—unifying the SA, Gestapo, and the SS into one seamless organization dedicated to the preservation of National Socialism and our Führer."

While the SS had decisively won the conflict between the SA and SS back in 1934, the ongoing power struggle between the SS and the Gestapo, which was under the heavy heel of Herman Göring and his Prussian police force, was common knowledge at the time. Few people had any doubts that Himmler was going to emerge victorious there too. And for all of the bombastic talk concerning a "unified" front of dedicated followers of National Socialism, the three men standing next to me should have been well aware of how thin the ice upon which they trod really was. Unfortunately for the SA man, he had not done his due diligence, unlike the pair from the Gestapo. So, despite Himmler's thinly veiled threats, the officer stuck his brown boots further into the pile of scheisse he was leaving behind him.

Following the mass executions carried out in '34 as part of the June 30 "night of the long knives," the SA officer, as a loyal party member and brigade commander, believed he was safe. More the fool was he. No one in Nazi Germany was safe, least of all any officers in the SA.

A plodding little nobody by the name of Victor Lutz had been appointed leader of the SA after Hitler had ordered their charismatic leader, Ernst Rohm, to be executed, and I think Himmler was looking for a chance to put the waning power of the SA firmly in its place—under his boot heel.

So when Himmler invited the red-faced little commander to explain to him, exactly, what this was all about, the fool took the bait.

He prattled on for about five minutes, during which time Himmler remained ominously quiet. Finally, using the same deceptively mild voice, Himmler spoke.

"Let me see the letter."

He scanned it briefly then turned the letter over, walked two steps forward, and held it in his right hand until it was about an inch from the SA commanders nose.

"Perhaps you could help me, Herr Commander. As you can tell, I have weak eyes and am forced to wear spectacles, so my eyesight might not be as keen as yours."

The SA man started to smile sympathetically, but when he noticed the grim faces of the two Gestapo men, the smile waivered around the edges.

"Please, if you would be so kind," Himmler continued, "tell me whose signature is on the bottom of this letter?"

Now he was the one smiling—like the cobra about to strike.

With dawning horror of the pit into which he was stumbling, the SA man swallowed hard and said, "Why, I believe it is your signature, Herr Reichsführer."

Himmler smiled. "Then why, may I ask, do you have the unmitigated temerity to come into my office and waste my time, and the time of these men from the Gestapo, to question an order which bears my signature?" His voice rose with each syllable. He spat the last word and slammed his fist down on his desk so hard, the framed portrait signed by Adolf Hitler wobbled in its gold-and-silver frame.

By this time, the SA man finally realized what he had gotten himself into and had turned a satisfying shade of gray. Himmler walked behind his desk and straightened the desk photo.

Without looking up, Himmler motioned to the two Gestapo men.

"Perhaps a weekend in Landsberg prison, or better yet, Dachau, will give our friend here a chance to reflect on the best uses of his time and that of this office."

The officer sputtered and protested as the Gestapo clamped their hands around either arm and led him away to disappear down the corridor.

Himmler then turned to me, reverting back to the mild and slightly pedantic tone, but retaining the underlying hint of menace.

"And now, my dear von Buchholz, I think it would be a good time for us to have a little chat."

Himmler motioned me to sit. I took the chair on the other side of his desk and immediately sank down until my chin was level with the desktop. I had heard how this was a common trick of both Himmler and Hitler. Hitler used a low chair for guests while his own was raised on a slight platform hidden behind the desk, thus giving him an imposing image and putting them at a psychological disadvantage. Apparently Himmler's devotion to his boss included copying the Führer's deceptions.

"And so to business." Himmler folded his hands carefully upon the desk like a prim schoolmaster preparing to talk to a promising student about his future endeavors. "Do you recall when I gave Maria this letter?" He pushed the letter towards my side of the desk.

I shrugged, and then nodded. I actually didn't remember the date, but fortunately it was typed on the top of the letter.

"Yes, Herr Reichsführer, it was in January 1933."

Himmler leaned back in his chair and beamed. "Yes, yes the dawning of a glorious new age for Germany. And do you recall the occasion upon which I granted you and die schöne Maria the not-inconsiderable protection of this office, which I might add, you have clearly witnessed?"

This one was going to be tougher, and while I wracked my brains to recall the exact circumstances I quickly said, "Yes of course I do, and I am very grateful."

Himmler remained sitting there, hands folded waiting for me to continue. My stomach began to knot as I pictured myself winding up in Dachau along with the fat SA Commander. Then, suddenly I remembered.

"Yes, *natürlich*, Herr Reichsführer. It was on Christmas Eve of 1932."

Himmler frowned. The Nazis no longer approved of Christian holidays in their systematic program to replace the soft, and in their eyes, suspiciously Jewish-inspired religious holidays with their own hodgepodge of Viking and Germanic ones. So I quickly added, "Yes, it was only a few days after the Solstice Ceremony in Nuremberg where you had invited Maria and Gudrun to speak to a group of anthropologists about the religious connections between ancient Aryans and the Anunnaki of Sumer."

"Indeed, and you and your Vrillian folk were kind enough to reciprocate with an invitation to the delightful soiree you held on...Christmas Eve." His mouth twisted slightly when he said, "Christmas."

"And that was the night when you so graciously offered Maria and me the protection of the SS. And true to your word, your letter came two weeks later."

My flattering, oozing speech produced the desired results when the small, pinched face broke into an indulgent smile.

"Yes, yes. Keeping one's word is important. A fine Germanic trait, you know."

He cleared his throat and was all business again. "And now that you've seen the importance of our work and the necessary power we must wield to accomplish our tasks, I'm sure you will be pleased to learn I have in mind a position for you to aid us in these bold endeavors."

I didn't like the sound of this but I tried to smile.

"Sir?"

"I'm sure you are familiar with the Ahnenerbe." Himmler leaned back in his chair and laced his hands behind his head, pontificating on a subject obviously dear to his heart. "The name comes from a rather obscure German word, meaning 'something inherited from the forefathers.'"

I, as with most Germans, knew all about the incredible array of crackpot science springing up around the Nazis' muddled blend of anthropology and myth, but of course, I kept my mouth shut and he droned on.

"The official mission of the Ahnenerbe is, of course, to unearth new evidence of the accomplishments and deeds of Germanic ancestors through the use of precise scientific methods, but it goes beyond that." He looked at me meaningfully, and all I could do was nod.

He learned forward and whispered conspiratorially, "We intend to prove that the Anunnaki were the founders of the Aryan race and they are returning to Earth to give their descendants, we National Socialists, the secrets of their science and technology."

His eyes shone with the type of fervent zeal one usually sees in religious fanatics, and if it doesn't frighten you, then it should. He went on.

"As I'm sure you know, from the psychic research done by your comrades of the Vrillian, according to ancient Sumerian texts, the Anunnaki were extraterrestrials who were mistakenly thought to be angels by early men. These same texts tell us these angel-like beings, who, according to the Sumerians, 'came from the heavens,' were an extremely long-lived race, living 200,000, 300,000 perhaps even as long as 500,000 years! And even more, the texts say this god-race came to Earth several hundred thousand years ago from a distant planet called Nibiru."

Himmler's face flushed and his right hand gripped the gold pen from his desk as though he was waving a holy relic.

"And the Reich has been most fortunate to have your extraordinary young woman, Maria, as one who, with the aid of her remarkable psychic abilities, is uniquely capable of translating these writings for the Fatherland!" He slapped the desk again, this time with his open palm, and beamed triumphantly at me.

I had long suspected he was mad, just like the rest of them, but this confirmed it. Unfortunately, it was the inmates who were now running Germany, what could I do?

He told me.

"And that, my dear von Buchholz, is where you are now to have the honor of likewise serving the Fatherland."

He walked around the desk and put his hands on my shoulders.

"I am commissioning you into the Ahnenerbe and the SS with the rank of Sturmbahnführer. Your primary duty will be liaison between the Ahnenerbe in the field, and Maria and the Vrillians, whose work will lead to the wonder weapons of the Anunnaki and the ultimate domination of the world by National Socialist Germany!"

Chapter Twenty-Two

Max leaned back in his chair and closed his eyes. "And that, Lieblinge, is how I came to join the SS."

"Son of a bitch," was all I had to contribute to the moment.

Several minutes passed, and finally Kat said, "So what did you do for the next ten years?"

He sighed. "The first thing I did was go home and tell Maria I was going to refuse the commission, which of course would mean I'd probably have to leave Germany, and, of course, I would want her to come with me. But in the end, she talked me out of it by saying that if I remained in the Ahnenerbe with my SS rank, I wouldn't have to engage in any of the paramilitary activities of the SS and I would be able to protect our friends. And so I was persuaded and began my decade-long journey on the road of good intentions which leads ultimately to hell."

I whistled. Despite the current skepticism in which I held his role in the Third Reich, I had to admit that Max's brush with one of the greatest villains of the twentieth century definitely had stirred my interest.

"So the chicken farmer made you cock of the walk, Max?"

Kat cocked her head quizzically. "Chicken farmer?"

"Yup," I said. "Before he appointed himself arbiter of who was a superman and who was not, our little murderer Himmler had only exercised the power of life and death over nothing more complicated than the hens on his chicken farm."

Kat still looked puzzled, but it would take a far better pop psychologist than I to explain the giant lunatic asylum Germany had become between the two wars.

For the next hour we—well, mostly me—asked questions and Max answered them. How truthfully? I think he tried his best. How completely? I had my doubts.

He did manage to save many of their friends and smuggled more than a few Jewish families out of Germany. But as the small hours of the morning got larger, I became increasingly nervous about the current crop of neo-Nazis, not to mention the ticked off members of our own government, whom I thought would have been hammering on our door by now. Finally, I cut Max short.

"Why are the US military and other assorted clandestine agencies so interested in you? And please don't tell me it has to do with little green or even big-head gray aliens."

He actually smiled at that one.

"All right, but it does have quite a bit of bearing on their interest, which began even before the end of the war. You have heard perhaps of Operation Paperclip?"

I thought for a moment. "Umm...yeah. Something to do with grabbing all the Nazi scientists at the end of the war before Uncle Joe Stalin could get his hands on 'em. Right?"

"Yes." He nodded. "Correct."

"And from what little I know about the operation, the US was more interested in getting the science behind the V2 rocket to keep us number one in the new Cold War that was heating up. Though, I gotta tell you, I still think it kinda sucks that we had to take in a bunch of Nazi assholes to do it."

Max picked up his unlit pipe and fiddled with it in a distracted manner as if he was trying to find the right words. Finally, he put the pipe back down and looked up.

"You've got to understand that despite the brutality, barbarity, and evil of the Nazi regime, German science was miles ahead of the rest of the world. And nowhere was that lead more apparent than rocket science. I am sure in your school you must have studied the works of the famous scientist Werner von Braun, whom the Americans captured at the end of the war in 1945 and brought here to America to work on the rocket program being set up at White Sands."

"Yeah, sure, we studied Von Braun on the whole thing; Sputnik, Moon landing, etc. What's your point?"

"My point, Herr Chris, is the question the Americans should have been asking themselves when they captured the Nazi rocket scientist along with much of their equipment and research. Specifically, why were the Germans so far advanced in comparison to every other modern, technological nation?"

"Okay, I'll bite. What's the answer?"

"Instead of giving you my answer, I will repeat something von Braun told a US State Department official when asked the same question. It was reported von Braun smiled a bit, pointed his finger towards the sky, and said, 'We had help.'"

Max smiled. "Yes, I know it sounds like a joke, and no, I cannot vouch for its truth. I was not there."

"But what you're implying is that Werner von Braun, the 1960s hero of the US Space Race, and quite possibly an un-indicted war criminal who was most probably complicit in the brutal conditions and subsequent death of thousands of prisoners, said the German superiority in rocketry came from aliens?"

He shrugged. "I didn't say it, you did."

My head began to hurt. "Look, Max, I don't have the time or inclination to play word games with you. I'm still waiting for you to tell me how all this fits together into something that will explain why old Nazis, the US Air Force, and who-the-fuck-knows-who-else are all chasing after me, and for that matter, you too?”

“And while you're at it, I guess you'll have to include me as well.”

I'd forgotten about Kat. I turned to her. “Look, I'm sorry about the date and showing up five hours late, and the trouble that pinned itself to my ass is now splashing over on you. But maybe if I leave here and find myself some quiet work somewhere, as a dog walker or a street-corner mime, these guys will leave you alone.”

But before she could answer, Max shook his head. “No, sadly. Even if you had never shown up, they would have tried to use Kat to get to me.”

“Then damn it, you better tell us what the fuck we can do to stop it!” My patience was wearing thin and frustration was becoming an all too familiar companion.

Kat looked disturbed too. “Uncle Max, I know we haven't spent much time together, what with you living in Germany, but I've got to admit, not only is this all new to me, but the whole thing is getting me seriously creeped out.” Her eternally kissable lips frowned and she hugged her arms as if warding off some spectral chill.

Max nodded. “Very well, but for that we must return to Germany in the third year of what Propaganda Minister Joseph Goebbels had christened The Thousand Year Reich.”

Chapter Twenty-Three

Northwestern Germany, April 1937

With each passing day, The Vrillian Damen, Maria and Sigrund in particular, were becoming more important to the Nazis, especially the SS. And I had come to the reluctant conclusion that, had I not taken Himmler's offer, I would have definitely joined the growing list of grumblers against the state in Dachau.

Ironically, despite my distaste for all of the gaudy but sinister trappings of the apparatus of the Nazi state, I was beginning to warm to my work with the Ahnenerbe. Oh, much of it was tainted with mythological nonsense, along with the standard National Socialist trash concerning Aryan supremacy and the inevitable triumph of the Nordic Ubermann. But either out of self-interest, self-advancement, or plain, old self-preservation, many surprisingly talented and reasonably competent archeologists, linguists, and anthropologists had also found a home in the Ahnenerbe.

Of course, another big draw, in addition to protection and job security, was the almost unlimited budget for research and archeological expeditions to anywhere in the known world. All that was needed was to spin an interesting tale to Himmler, who proved to be fertile ground and surprisingly gullible to the most outrageous theories and half-baked science.

He personally organized a lengthy and monstrously expensive expedition to Tibet to prove that the people of Tibet were really survivors from Atlantis and the progenitors of the Aryan race. He was also an enthusiastic supporter of a lavishly equipped expedition to Antarctica to search for the entrance that supposedly led to the hollow earth inhabited by the "god-race" postulated in the book, *The Coming Race*, by Rosicrucian author Edward Bulwer-Lytton, which many of our few remaining philosophers believed had inspired the formation of the Thulists and ultimately, the Nazi Party.

The Nazis even set up a base on that continent at what they called New Swabia, and there were those who claimed they had actually found the entrance and evidence of an advanced civilization, though I never saw any proof.

I didn't participate in any of these expeditions other than to coordinate meetings between the scientists and leaders and the Vrillian ladies, who were much in demand to relay psychic clues or interpret findings. It was interesting, in a fanciful sort of way, and though Maria believed whole-heartedly in the reality of her visions and messages, I remained quietly skeptical until....

It was a bright, spring Tuesday in 1937 at a cozy chalet near the Oder River in northwestern Germany. Maria woke me up.

"Come on, lazy bones." She smiled. "We have an important appointment today. Reichsmarschall Göring and Deputy Führer Hess, and perhaps even Himmler, will be flying in to Hauneburg today to join us to see the test flight of the next generation of the SS E-IV."

Maria dressed quickly and looked ravishing as always. I, on the other hand, struggled with the webbing of my Sam Brown belt and spit-polished black boots. Normally I would have worn an old pair of corduroy trousers and rolled neck sweater, but with the party Bozin bigwigs arriving today, I had to make sure I was turned out in my Schutzstaffel best.

Most of us simply called the H-Gerät (Hauneburg Device), the Thule Disc Project. Hauneburg was the spot the Nazis had chosen for the secret base where we had been translating the writings and diagrams from the Vrillian ladies to build and test flying disc prototypes.

Since late 1934, the SS technical branch, Unit E-IV (Entwicklungsstelle 4), had been pushing the Vrillians to come up with a reliable "disc craft" that could be outfitted for air combat. And while some of the ladies of the Vril were enthusiastic supporters of the Nazi aims, Maria kept hoping Himmler and his crew would let them work on perfecting the craft she said she'd been promised by her spiritual guides. The one that would serve as a portal through space and time and help the Vrillians usher in the new Age of Aquarius where all of mankind would live in peace and prosperity thanks to the advanced technology she swore the advanced beings from Alderbaran had promised.

In the meantime, all funds and resources were coming from the Nazis, so it was best to appease them. She hoped the new version of the RFZ-2, with refined magnetic field impulse steering and electro-magnetic-gravity drive system, would satisfy them. I personally hoped the damn thing would fail just like the previous ones and the unpleasant men from Berlin would go back there and leave Maria and me to snuggle in peace.

And despite my hopes to the contrary, the H-Gerät machine did not explode or crash. But when it returned from its test flight, it was dented, scratched, and worn to the point where it appeared as though it had been traveling for a hundred years, though by our measurements it had been gone for only hour.

Everyone was puzzled by this, and I made the appropriate clucking noises with the rest of them but dismissed it in my mind as just another in the growing list of anomalies attached to our research.

I should have paid more attention.

* * * *

In 1938, Himmler personally assigned me to an expedition led by Dr. Franz Altheim and his research partner Erika Trautmann to the newly-sovereign Kingdom of Iraq, which was under increasing pressure to form an alliance with Germany. Thus, it was arranged for us to meet with local researchers and be driven to some recently discovered Parthian and Persian ruins in southern Iraq and Babylon. From there, the Baghdad team, myself included, went north to Assur where we met Sheikh Adjil el Yawar, a leader of the Shammar Bedouin tribe, who assigned us a guide to lead our team to their final major stop—the ruins of Hatra on the border of the ancient Roman and Persian empires. This is where I made the find that caused me to revise my skepticism of Maria and her visions from Aldebaran.

It was near dusk on the fifth day, and we had been digging in the southeast corner of the ruins, when one of the Bedouin diggers motioned me over to where he'd been digging. With much excited jabber, he pointed to a dusty basalt stela covered with pictograms and Sumerian cuneiform. I bent down and began to swish away the dust with a whiskbroom from my pack and noticed something strange as the markings and contours of the stela became revealed.

The first thing that struck me odd was how skillfully polished and precisely cut the edges and markings of the stela were. Right down to the cuneiform writing, the black, polished stone appeared as though it had been carved yesterday—and by a modern factory equipped with diamond cutting tools!

I called to Franz and Erika. "Come, quick! I think I've found something!"

When they arrived Erika exclaimed, "Franz, look. An ancient Sumerian tablet...but I've never seen one so large!"

"Or so finely carved." Franz whispered, dropping into the hole beside me. He ran his hands over the surface and frowned, puzzled. "What is this material?"

"Basalt," I said, but he shook his head.

"I don't think so, but..."

He took out a small rock hammer and chisel. At first he tapped lightly, and when it didn't leave a mark, harder. But there was not even a scratch on the surface.

"What are these pictograms?" asked Erika. "I don't recognize them from any of the artifacts we've uncovered here."

Our puzzlement increased. Franz pulled out a small magnifying glass and stared at the markings intently, then looked up in wonderment.

"That's because they are older than the Roman or Persian periods." He looked at us. "If I am correct, much older than you could imagine."

Utilizing additional diggers, it didn't take us long to uncover the entire stela and expose the markings on the other side. They were, if anything, even more remarkable. Most of the stela was taken up by an intricate and finely chiseled drawing running from left to right across the center. This consisted of concentric circles intersected by lines and angles with strange markings resembling some type of unknown mathematical formula.

But it was what we uncovered when the workmen finally wrestled the stela out of the pit with a winch and pulley that most excited the good doctor and his assistant. I was the first to notice it. While everyone else scrambled out of the pit and gathered around the stela, talking and gesturing, the gleam of something sticking out of the sand at the bottom caught my eye.

I jumped back down into the pit, and picking up one of the pocket whiskbrooms, carefully brushed away the sand. Fortunately, the object was embedded in the soft sand, otherwise it would have been squashed flat from the immense weight of the stela.

At first, I thought that had indeed been the case, because the face of the object was worn and flat although polished to an intense brilliance. But as I gently whisked away more of the surrounding sand, it appeared to be a large gold ring or pendant.

Initially, I dismissed the idea of its being a ring strictly due to the size of the object. The flat upper surface looked to be about 100mm by 50mm, or four inches long by almost two inches wide, and while carefully picking the artifact up, I realized what I thought had been a flat, polished, mirror-like surface really had finely etched designs on it. In fact, as the sun's rays lifted off the surface, each of the lines appeared to change color and reflect back at different angles. Turning it over I discovered I had also been wrong about dismissing the possibility that it was a ring. One half of the back of the flat surface was taken up with a continuous spiral of finely wrought gold made quite obviously to accept a finger, and in the center, where the knuckle would have fit, was a concave head of a lion sunk into the gold surface. But what kind of a finger could have ever worn such a strange, ring-like object? I held the thing up to my middle finger.

I do not have small hands, but whoever had worn this had fingers twice the length and breadth of my own.

Slowly, I climbed out of the hole and walked over to the doctor and his assistant who were on their knees; he with a magnifying glass and she with a notebook. He was reading each of the symbols as she reproduced it and made the appropriate notations on paper. He looked up as I approached.

"This is the most remarkable series of ancient Sumerian text I have ever come across." He smiled. "In addition to having the appearance of the first rudimentary example of proto-cuneiform, there is a duplicate text running below the early cuneiform of a style that I've never seen. If my suppositions are correct, I believe what we have found is a possible link with the root of cuneiform writing."

"And the markings on the stela?" I said pointing at the strange drawings.

"They appear to be some sort of astronomical observations or sky chart."

"Sky chart?"

They probably thought I was questioning their assumptions, but far from it. I was afraid it might confirm the uneasy feeling coming over me ever since we had uncovered the stela. However, assuming I was being skeptical, and that skepticism might find its way back to the Ahnenerbe and the

SS command structure, he felt compelled to qualify his statement.

"You know, of course, that all ancient civilizations from Babylon to Egypt were tireless observers of the heavens. They traced the orbits of all of the visible planets and constellations, even predicting the return flight of comets and other near-Earth objects many thousands of years into the future."

"Is that what these circles mean? They are the paths of planets or stars?"

"Yes, I believe so."

"Then what about these intersecting lines, and the ones with tiny circles and things looking like Norse ruins in the middle?"

He looked uneasy. "Those? Those, I must admit, give me pause. At first glance, and you must understand I have had only minutes to study this, they could be construed as various points in the sky that, for some reason, the ancients wanted to make particular and precise notation of their position in the cosmos."

"And what about these other lines?" I pointed to the hundreds of finely etched lines crisscrossing the concentric circles and their strange markings.

He shook his head. "I have several theories I am currently working on, but I don't feel comfortable discussing them as yet."

"But that is the whole purpose of this expedition, Herr Doctor. We are here to explore, discover, and propose bold, new theories to the origin of our sacred Aryan race."

The last line made me want to vomit, but I knew it would produce results. And it did.

"In that case… And please understand, this is only a working theory. Do you see how all of these lines run from this one large circle on the left of the drawing and intersect with the lines and tiny circles inside the larger group of concentric ones?"

I nodded.

"If I am correct, these appear to be direct lines running from various points on the Earth to planetary or even star systems with in other constellations."

I studied the lines. "Assuming that is the case, then wouldn't the lines be curved instead of straight, to show the orbit of how an extra-terrestrial object would have to travel to get to one of these systems?"

"No, and there is the crux of the mystery that makes this such an astounding discovery." He smiled. "There is a way lines like this could be shown to denote travel to another star system…if that travel was done beyond the speed of light using some sort of teleportation device."

"Then where would these transporting devices be found?"

"Ah, that is what makes this discovery so exciting!" Franz swept his hand in a circle as if to encompass the ruins sprawled before us on the parched plain. "In places like this— in Egypt, India, Mesopotamia, even the ancient cities of the Mayan and Aztec peoples—the structures found worldwide like the pyramids and the Sphinx, which have never fully been understood, could have been built as hubs or transportation centers to the stars!"

His eyes took on a dream-like glaze as he stared intently at the dark, polished surface, then slowly stood up and dusted off the knees of his trousers. "Now if only we could find some sort of evidence in this site to prove that it could have been inhabited by the progenitors of the early Aryan race."

I almost didn't show him, but I was in too deep, and the fever of discovery and answer to my many questions held too strong a grip back out now.

I opened my palm showed the doctor what I had found.

He stiffened, and then his eyes opened wide as he took the object and turned it over in his hands.

"Is this what I think it is?" he whispered.

I shrugged. "I'm hoping you can tell me."

He studied it for another moment and then looked up. "I think what you may have just found, Herr Sturmbannführer, could be the proof the Reichsführer has been searching for."

He held it up to the light to let the late afternoon sun play off the polished surface and turn the tiny lines to a deep blood red.

"I think what we are looking at is a ring worn by the race of god-like giants whose advanced technology and seed helped to create the first Aryans...the ancestors of the German people!"

That night, Herr Professor-Doctor Franz Altheim called me to his tent to show me a picture in a text he had with him. It was of a coin found at the end of the last century in a dig near Nineveh. On one side of the thick-looking coin was a raised lion's head, and on the reverse, a concave one, just like the sunken image on the underside of the ring I'd found.

"It is the same as the one in the object I found," I said to him. "What is the origin of this coin, Herr Doctor?"

"It is called the Lydian Lion and is made of electrum, a gold and silver alloy, and is likely the world's first wide-usage coin minted by King Alyattes of Sardis, Lydia, and Asia Minor around 610-600 BC."

"Then that dates the stela and the ring to that period too?"

He smiled and shook his head. "No, my friend. That is what makes this find so unique. Here, look at this." He picked up one of the many pot shards we'd uncovered at the site the previous week. "Do you know the period this is from?"

I shook my head. "No, Dr. Altheim, unlike you, I am not a trained archeologist, merely one of Himmler's clerks."

He looked at me oddly for a moment but then held up the shard and continued. "This is from the early Kingdom of the Upper Nile—before they were unified under the first Egyptian Pharaoh, which means it is more than 5000 years old, And since it was found on top of the sand above the stela, this means, my young friend, the stela is more than 5,000 years old. And I believe much, much older than that!"

Chapter Twenty-Four

"For Christ's sake, Max, don't stop there! What the fuck happened? Was it the ring of some E.T. or just more Nazi bullshit?"

He put his pipe down and chuckled. "Herr Chris, I am thinking that instead of computer and writing, you should maybe have become a lawyer or police, ja?"

"Sure, whatever. But answer my question. What happened?"

He sighed and finally nodded. "Ja. Of course. You need to have answers, natürlich."

He took a deep breath and resumed.

"Do you have any idea how old that stela was? Guess?"

But before I could say a word he held up his hand.

"Don't bother. Whatever you guess—however wild—you could not possibly guess close to what I believe the true age of the strange, black stela of 'rock' that was no rock."

"Max, you're a great storyteller, but I'm not up for guessing games. Just tell me how old the fucking thing was and let's all get the hell outta here. 'Cause sooner rather than later, those guys are gonna come here looking for us and—"

And, as if on cue, the telephone rang. First, it was the old pushbutton phone on the wall in the kitchen, and then Kat's cell, and then—mine.

Kat pulled out her cell phone, but I put my hand over hers and pushed it back towards her purse. "Don't answer it."

I didn't have to tell Max. He knew who it was, and I had a pretty good idea too, I just didn't know which collection of unpleasant fanatics were going to find us first. And I wasn't interested in finding out. I got up and tugged at Kat's hand.

"C'mon, time to roll." Grabbing my jacket I motioned to Max. "You too, old dude. Get your coat."

"But I haven't finished. Chris, Kat, there is more I must tell. More you must know if you are to have a hope of eluding all those who will be coming after you."

"Us! What about you? If you'll excuse the morbid analogy, it seems to me you'd be number one on their hit list."

He made no motion to move, merely shook his head. "They don't dare. They know I have too much information that could bring down all of their plans and turn their warped dreams to dust." He smiled and rose to get another match. "You two go on. I'll be—"

The bay window fronting on Beacon Street exploded inward in a shower of glass.

I heard, rather than saw, the bullet strike Max in the shoulder. He gasped and stumbled backwards. Kat screamed and we both ran towards him. He staggered and slumped towards the floor, but I got under one arm and Kat the other, and as gently as possible, we lowered him into a chair. The color drained rapidly from his face. He was going into shock.

"Kat, get me some towels, quick!" I opened his shirt collar and looked at his pupils. Not good. Kat came back with a bath towel, a facecloth, and a hand towel. I took the facecloth, folded it into quarters, and gave it back to Kat.

"Keep it pressed against the open wound." I took the hand towel and spread it diagonally over the facecloth. Then, taking my OTC, out-the-front, Italian stiletto, I zipped open the blade and began cutting the bath-towel into strips that I wound around the facecloth and the hand towel. Soon we had a tight bandage over his shoulder. The blood stopped seeping through the yellow and blue designs on the towels.

"Now, get me the bottle of schnapps on the sideboard."

She ran over, grabbed the bottle and a glass, and I poured half a tumbler full and put it to Max's lips.

"Come on, Max, drink this down." He did and a little color came back into his face. I nodded at Kat. "Call a cab." She took out her cell phone and began to dial.

"No," Max rasped, shaking his head. "No cabs. Unless...no—yes, call the cab. But it will not be for me. You two will be taking it. They won't dare risk another shot in this neighborhood."

"No! Uncle Max, what are you talking about? We need to get you to a hospital right now."

He winced and shifted in the chair. "Listen to me, both of you. I was wrong. They must be nearer to the completion of their project than I thought and have decided that what I know is unnecessary, or they simply feel it's too dangerous to let it fall into the hands of anyone else."

He tried to get up, but his knees buckled and he sank back into the cushion.

"The ones who fired the shot won't stop with this. When they find out I'm not dead, they'll come for me. And if they catch up with me, it's going to be very bad for anyone around me."

"What are you talking about?" Kat was equal parts angry and terrified. "I don't understand any of this." She made both hands into fists as if she was going to pummel the old man, but he reached out, and with surprising strength, grabbed her hands and pulled her until her face was close to his.

"You know how much I love you, little Katrina, but now I need you to do something for me."

"I'll do anything you want, if you just let me call a cab so we can get you to the hospital."

"No hospital. That's what they'll be expecting. They will survey every hospital in the area and most likely have operatives in each one of them."

"But why, Uncle Max?"

"Because they mean to have me—alive if possible, but if not, dead." He glanced up at me. "You, too, are in great danger."

"Jeez...tell me something I don't know. What they want from me is the flash drive, right?"

"That's one thing." Max nodded.

"What's the other?"

"To kill you."

"But why, if presumably, they get the flash drive?"

"Because they can't afford to take the chance that you have read what is on it." He drew a deep breath and grimaced. "You must keep one step ahead of them and never allow them to get you or the flash drive."

I had heard this song once too often and it wasn't improving with age.

"These are the same assholes who have been chasing me since Munich—right? The SS, who should be in their nineties and trading in their jackboots for some Depends?" My two cents were long overdue, and bullet hole or not, I was tired of Max's enigmatic answers.

He closed his eyes and I was afraid he'd passed out, but a moment later he opened them. "They are not affected by the passing of years...far from it. Which is why you can't delay. You must take Katrina and go. Now."

He reached into his pocket and pulled out a bright gold coin and a folded piece of paper and gave both to me.

"Take this coin to a dealer who is an old friend of mine. He has a shop in St. Petersburg, Florida. The address is on the piece of paper. He knows what the coin means and can tell you what must be done."

The buzzer for the downstairs door erupted with a long staccato burst making us all jump.

"Christ, they're here! And that means you're coming with us. Regardless of what you say, I'm not leaving you to those Nazi bastards. Who knows what they'll do." I turned to Kat. "C'mon. You grab one arm and I'll take the other."

"Leave him where is."

A raspy heavily accented voice spoke from the hall behind us before we could move. I glanced over my shoulder as Kat looked up, startled. Her grandmother stood watching us, her expression stern and her gaze steady from cold blue eyes.

"He is right. Hospitals can cause problems. I will take care of him."

Who knows how long she had been standing there silently, but I instantly assessed she was not a member of the Cry and Faint Club. She looked like she considered gunshots through the window all in a day's work.

She walked over and took the bandages out of Kat's hands and continued wrapping the torn strips over Max's shoulder and across his upper chest. "I will do this. I was a trained nurse in Germany."

Knowing almost zero about all things medical, I took her at her word, but that didn't solve our immediate problem.

"All right, but finish up quick. We've got to get out of here before Kammler's men get up here." I motioned to Kat. "Get his other arm and let's try to get him up and—"

"No!" He held up his hand. "No, it is not Kammler and his men. They would never have buzzed. They'd have kicked in the door like they did in the old days. No, the ones who will be up here in a very few moments will be from your government. They will take care of me and get me medical attention."

I wasn't sure if I trusted his line of reasoning, but he forced a smile.

"Believe me, in addition to finding you, they want to finish the line of questioning they started with me during Operation Paperclip at the end of the war when they were racing to bring the rest of Germany's rocket scientists to your country."

We heard footsteps on the stairs.

He waved his hand a slight smile wavering on his lips. "Please, don't worry. Life in the Third Reich taught us much about survival. He looked back at us as the smile faded and he closed his eyes. "Now, please—go."

* * * *

Max was right. It was the Feds and the Air Force, both. The grey-and-black cars were double parked when we slipped out a side service door and made our way down the alley and through the same back way we'd used what seemed to be a thousand years ago.

We decided against taking the T to the airport for fear of the cameras in the stations. Instead we took the Green Line Trolley, got off just before Kenmore Square, and hailed a cab. On the ride to Logan, I used my phone to buy two tickets to

Tampa/St. Pete on the next flight out. Between the credit card record for the flight and airport surveillance cameras, they'd be on to us soon. But we didn't have to disappear in Boston. Tampa/St. Pete was a big place and it would do nicely, thank you very much. All we had to do was reach it. Alive.

Once in the airport, we ducked into Brookstone and picked up two small carry-on suitcases and stuffed them with a couple of T-shirts and some toiletries purchased at one of the newsstand shops to complete our facade of being typical, young yuppie vacationers. And whether we projected that image, I don't know, but we did arrive safe, sound, and unmolested in Florida three hours later.

We took a cab to the address that Max had given us, which turned out to be a small shop behind a dingy glass window-front in a faded pink stucco building a half dozen blocks from the waterfront area of St. Petersburg.

I was peering through the glass at the meager display in the dark store when Kat noticed a small sign hung next to the door buzzer. It read: Gone to Lunch. Back in 1 hour (maybe). So please return then. Or not... A.G.

"Wow, this guy sure knows how to make his customers feel welcome." Kat laughed and I raised my eyebrows.

"Hey, don't look at me. This was your uncle's idea."

She cocked her head and put one soft finger to my lips. "Hush. Let's go somewhere and wait. Lunch strikes me as a good idea too."

I glanced at my watch: 2:30. "Might as well. Since it looks like this guy doesn't keep regular hours, no sense in going hungry while we wait."

We wandered on down the street towards the expanse of sparkling blue water that shimmered at the end of the gently sloping street. This eventually took us to a trendy, upscale, little waterfront district of shops, hotels, and sidewalk cafés. One on the corner had a dozen tables set out on the brick sidewalk beneath blue-and-white umbrellas. We went there and the waiter steered us to a table in a corner farthest away from the street but close enough to keep watch for nasty looking characters.

Seeing how we'd missed both breakfast and lunch, we decided on omelets; Western for me and spinach for her. I ordered a local Key West Ale to wash it down. Kat settled for mango green tea. While we waited, I ruminated over all of the strange events that had plagued me ever since I met Max.

Kat ran her hand over mine. "Not nice to daydream unless you invite me along."

"Sorry. I guess I was zoning out, or I would never be accused of paying insufficient attention to a hot looking girl."

She smiled back and then it struck me. Hot looking girl...wait! The crap didn't start with Max— it started the night I met Ria.

"Ria! Yes, it all started with her!"

Kat frowned. "Come again? Who?"

"Sorry. Guess I owe you an explanation of what stared this shit storm."

The omelets appeared and we ate them. I filled her in as best I could with all of the weird events leading up to last night.

When I got to the part about my brief, if intense, "meetings" with the elusive Ria, she was not about to let me skate over the salacious details of our romantic encounters.

"Did you sleep with her?" was the way she began her interrogation.

There was nothing I could say that had even the remotest chance of being believed, so I just nodded.

"How many times?"

"Hey, what's with the police grilling? I mean, c'mon, Kat. That's getting a little too personal, don't you think?"

She cocked her head to one side and placed a finger to her cheek as though evaluating my newfound propriety. "Ummm, nope. Not if I'm gonna fill the role of being the rebound girl."

"Rebound? Where do you get that? I would have to have had an actual relationship with Ria for that to happen, which I did not, by the way."

Kat tried to hold her skeptical expression, but my hurt, wounded, and unfairly accused face finally got to her and she giggled.

"Oh, stop. You look so pathetic, like your puppy-dog eyes are gonna fall out if you don't smile again."

"How's this?" I broke into a big grin and her giggles turned into a full-throated laugh. I leaned across the tiny table and gave her a long, slow, passionate kiss, with a little tongue thrown in for good measure.

When we broke apart, she put her lips next to my ear. "Hey, this could actually go someplace."

I kissed her again. "C'mon. Let's see if our mystery man decided to come back from his lunch."

Chapter Twenty-Five

When we got there, the shop was still closed, and after a pointless rattling of the doorknob, I leaned against the pink stucco storefront.

"Shit! How long does this asshole take for lunch anyway?"

"I don't know. Why don't you ask the asshole himself?"

I spun around and a short, bald man with an enormous belly straining against the buttons of a brightly colored Hawaiian shirt stood before me.

Oh crap!

"Ahhh...are you the owner here?"

"No, apparently I'm the 'asshole.'"

"Yeah, listen, sorry about that. We were here earlier and saw the sign and—"

But I was talking to empty space. The old man had unlocked the shop and was walking around behind the counter.

"Come in if you're coming. You're letting all the hot air in, and I provide enough of that myself. I can't afford any more."

We went in. The shop was dark and cool with a minimum of light filtering through the dusty glass front window. The glass of the display counter was equally dingy and held an eclectic mix of tarnished, largely Victorian estate jewelry, and several rows of old coins in individual plastic Lucite boxes.

Kat and I approached cautiously. Should we be circumspect or just blurt out why we came? Given my record over the past ten days, I chose circumspect.

I pulled the slip of paper with the address out of my wallet. "Hi. Are you Aron Gottlieb?"

"No. I'm his fat 'asshole' cousin from Cincinnati."

Oh man, this was not going to be easy.

I tried another tack. "Ohhkaaay....Do you know a Max Becker?"

He looked ready for another snarky comeback, but then narrowed his eyes suspiciously and asked, "Who?"

"Max Becker. Max from Boston, and before that, Munich. About six feet, 175 pounds, white hair, blue eyes...Max."

He had stiffened when I said "Munich," and now he stared at me warily and let a full minute go by before he finally said, "I don't know any Becker's, from Boston or Munich or anywhere." He gestured toward the door with his chin. "Don't let it hit you in the ass on the way out."

"OK, then. Fuck you very much and goodbye!" I stormed to the door. But Kat grabbed my hand.

"Major Maximilian von Buchholz," she said.

He looked up and pushed away the coins he had started sorting.

"He was not a major. He was never in the regular German army, the Wehrmacht. He was SS, and in the SS, the rank of major is called Sturmbanführer. I should know. I had to learn all of their ranks and quickly." He stared at Kat and me. "Do you know what the penalty was for not knowing an SS man's rank at Gross-Rosen?"

"You were there?" Kat asked softly.

He turned over his left arm. The skin was wrinkled and speckled with age spots, but there, in faded blue ink, was the concentration camp tattoo, still visible after seven decades.

"Oh, yes, I was there with all the rest of the 'chosen people.'" His lip curled in disgust. "And for the record, the penalty for not being able to come to attention and spout,

Jawohl, Herr Sturmbanfuerer if a so-called 'major' in the SS spoke to you, was a 9mm bullet from a Lugar Parabellum through your brain."

I didn't know what to say, so I stood there uncomfortably and replied, "Sorry."

Why in the hell Max had sent us on this wild goose chase? I mean, I know he was shot and all, but maybe he got confused saying he knew this guy. It didn't make sense. Why would he write down the address of someone he didn't know and then give us a coin to show him?

And then it hit me. Of course he knew Max, and that he was in the SS and his rank.

"Max told me to show you this and that you'd know what to do." I pulled out the coin and plunked it on the counter. "Which, by the way, I fervently hope you do, since neither of us has a clue."

Aron Gottlieb held a jewelers loupe to his eye and picked up the coin, turning it over and over in his hand and examining both sides, even the edges.

He flicked on a high-intensity gooseneck lamp and angled the coin allowing light to reflect off the inscribed surface and create a faint sliver of artificial gold sunlight glittering across the dark wall.

"Do you know what this is?" He asked without looking up or pausing in his scrutiny.

"No," Kat answered. "My great-uncle gave it to us along with your address and told us to come here. He said you would know what it meant."

He finally looked up, thought about it for a moment and finally said, "Come here. Both of you."

We did, and he laid the coin on a small piece of black velvet on the counter. He got out a large, musty smelling book with old black-and-white pictures of coins. He thumbed to a page and pointed to a coin. Our coin.

"Read what it says."

I did.

"'The Lydian Lion. Possibly the world's oldest coin. Lydian electrum trite (4.71g, 13 x 10 x 4mm) of a gold and silver alloy, minted by King Alyattes in Sardis, Lydia, Asia Minor (present-day Turkey), circa 610-600 BC.'"

I put the book down. "This is pretty much what Max already told us. We've got the world's oldest coin? It must be worth a bundle, right? Is that why he sent us here? To sell a rare coin? Couldn't he have done that anywhere?"

Aron shrugged. "Depends on the market and who's buying and who's selling, but that's not the point here."

"OK, I'll bite. What is the point? I could sure use one or two since I don't have any of my own."

He didn't answer but motioned us to come closer. "Do you see this?" He handed me the jeweler's loupe. "Right there, to the left of the lion's head."

I looked where he pointed, and sure enough, there was some sort of writing that looked vaguely like cuneiform writing, and then I noticed very faint lines and circles radiating from the crudely carved lion's head.

"Do you notice anything odd about the writing or the design marks?"

I looked closer. "Yes, it almost looks like there was once a complete pattern on the coin, but then someone stamped a lion's head right in the middle."

"Yes. Excellent!" He beamed, and then pointed the tip of his pen at the edges of the coin. "What else?"

I squinted along the edges of the coin and realization dawned. "The design. It looks like it should continue on past the coins edge."

"*Mazel tov*! Give the young man a cigar. That is exactly the case. Furthermore, my assumption is that this coin came from a much larger gold disk, perhaps as much as 200-300 centimeters in diameter, and back in the seventh century B.C., a king, probably Alyattes, had the original larger disc punched out into several coins and stamped to be used as his Lydian Lion coin."

"Meaning...." Kat said leaning forward to scrutinize the coin.

"The writing and marking from the original disk are older than the coin. And unless I miss my guess, far older than you could imagine."

"And how old would that be? I've got a pretty fertile imagination," I said.

For the first time, Aron smiled. "Would you believe possibly 10,000 or even 12,000 years old? I think what you have here, mein Kinder, could be made of gold mined in ancient Atlantis!"

I don't know how long we stood there stunned, but I do know I vacillated between wanting to believe the old man and wondering if I should reserve him a rubber room somewhere quiet and secure. Finally, I spoke.

"Atlantis? Really?"

Aron sighed. "All right, so you're a skeptic."

It was not a question.

"Uh, yeah, until I see some hard evidence that doesn't consist of cheesy videos on YouTube that have all been photo-shopped. Or using the same, murky, out-of-focus shots of bits of something at the bottom of the sea that could be the fabled towers of Atlantis and Mu, or the seaweed covered remains of a freighter that sank fifty years ago."

He clucked his tongue. "My, my, we do have a doubter, don't we?"

I shrugged and glanced over at Kat, who was looking as though she thought we were all crazy, which based our present situation was the safest bet.

"OK." He sighed. "You must have heard some pretty amazing things from our mutual friend Max to have made the journey all the here from?..."

"Boston." Kat supplied. "My great-uncle is staying with my gram and me up in Boston. Well, Brookline really."

"And you, my young skeptic." He glanced at me. "Just what is your relationship to Herr Sturmbannführer Maximilian von Buchholz, previously of the SS Anenherbe, who now calls himself Becker?"

"You have asked the number one question of the number one most-baffled asshole on this side of the Atlantic."

"Ah, I see you're one too." He smiled.

"No quarrel there. But my best answer to your question is that, somehow, I stumbled into the middle of a mystery wrapped in a riddle and baked in pre-heated oven for several millenniums into a piping hot enigma—to paraphrase Winston Churchill. And to be honest with you, I don't have the faintest clue as to what's going on outside of the fact that everyone I run across wants to kidnap, threaten, or kill me."

"Ah-hem...." Kat raised a pair of neatly trimmed eyebrows at me.

I made a small bow in her direction. "Present ravishing company excepted, of course."

She smiled prettily, and shifted her equally pretty little butt on the edge of the counter where she'd perched herself.

"And of course you'd like to know what is the connection of old Mr. Max from Germany to these schmucks who are after you, and, by the way, they won't stop until either they get you, or you—or them—are dead."

"There's a cheery thought. Gee, I feel better now."

Aron's face broke into a full grin. "I like you, kid. Are you sure you're not Jewish?"

"Not unless me Irish da' was foolin' around."

"How about your Irish ma?"

"Hey!"

"Sorry." He held up his hand and then leaned both elbows on the counter. "OK, which mystery would you like me to illuminate first: Max and the German occultists, the Nazi/Vrill secret projects and the Anunnaki, or how they are all connected to the legend of Atlantis?"

"Can't we sorta' combine them all and wrap the whole thing up in one, big, easy-to-understand package?"

"What fun is that?" He grinned and then sighed and turned serious. "Let me see if I can just hit the highlights here. Yes, I do know Max. I saw him for the first time in the work camp at Gross-Rosen, the day the doctors lined up all of us children on the parade field to select who they thought would be strong enough to last a few weeks at one of the slave labor projects the SS were operating in Upper Silesia.

"I had just passed my eleventh birthday and wasn't the fine, strapping mench you see in front of you today." He leaned forward and stage whispered, "Between you and me, I was kind of skinny." He gave a short, bitter laugh.

"At any rate, one of the camp quacks the Nazi's passed off as doctors was marking an 'L' for 'Links'—the traditional designation for those to be immediately gassed—next to our names on his chart. It meant we would be transferred to Auschwitz/Birkenau where we and all of the other weak Untermenchen would be sent down the Himmel Strause—the road to heaven—leading to the gas chambers and ovens. The SS guard had started to push my friend and I into the left-hand line, and my younger friend, he was only ten, somehow sensed what was going to happen and had started to cry. The SS guard slapped him in the face, and when it only made him cry harder, he raised his rifle butt and would have staved in his skull right there, when a voice came across the square like the crack of a whip. '*Achtune!*'

"The SS man turned slowly, and then seeing it was an officer, came swiftly to attention and crashed his heels together. '*Jawohl, Herr Sturnbanführer!*'"

Aron Gottlieb looked at Kat. "It was your uncle. He was tall, blond, blue eyed, handsome—a recruiting poster image of the Nordic ideal. Everyone on the square knew it, and he knew it too."

Chapter Twenty-Six

Gross-Rosen Concentration Camp, Upper Silesia, September 1943

"What are you doing with those two boys, soldier?"

I could see the sweat forming on the lip of the SS guard.

"I am escorting them to the Links line for transportation to Auschwitz, Herr Sturmbanführer."

"Why not put them to work?"

"The Herr Doctor has already classified them, sir."

Max took up the clipboard, glanced at my friend, then me. He placed a hand on my shoulder, and turning to the doctor said, "Hmmm...I think you have made a mistake here. What I see is a fine, strong lad, who is fully capable of working for the glory of the Fatherland."

The camp doctor bobbed his head up and down so violently, I thought it might snap off at the neck. The doctor quickly scribbled a notation and motioned for the guard to take me to the trucks bound for the work camps. But I could see my little friend, a young, Jewish, Polish boy named Dombrowski, being pushed to the crowd bound for the gas chambers, so, without thinking I threw myself at the feet of the tall officer.

"Please, sir, I beg you. My friend is really much stronger than he looks, and I know he would be a tireless worker. His father and uncle have been sent to the Buna Werke to labor for the Reich, and if you sent my friend Jerzy there, he would help them to produce twice as much for the glory of the German Victory!"

Max laughed, even though there were strict penalties, even for SS officers, to help a Jew.

"Well," he said, "I don't see how the Reich could pass up an opportunity to win the war from the Buna Werke. Send our hard working little friend to the *Buna*. And as for you, my silver tongued young imp, I think I know just the place where you may best serve the Reich."

The camp, SS Geheime Gruppe Glocke, consisted of a played-out mine the Nazis were expanding for use in their growing network of underground factories, built to shelter war production from the increasingly heavy Allied bombardment.

The prisoners, no surprise, were overworked and malnourished, but with a word from Herr Sturmbannführer Maximilian von Buchholz, I was given a comparatively easy job as runner and errand boy for the scientists working on the Bell project.

The Bell itself was about four meters high and five around. When not in "testing," it hung suspended from thick steel chains that also supported massive electrical cables. It was placed exactly in the center of a large, circular, cement structure that reminded me of the English Stonehenge but was really made of poured concrete and steel reinforcing rebar.

Normally, I would be running from the underground parts workshop in the mine up to the test area where the scientists worked. They would scribble out a note or call ahead, and the requested part would be waiting for me when I got there, and I would carry it back as fast as I could go.

It went on like that for about 14 months, and from time to time, I saw Max. Then, in late 1944 I saw him again, but this time he was with a beautiful woman. I was between twelve and thirteen—right at the point where a boy begins to notice girls, but this one was a woman not a girl. And she was the most beautiful creature I had ever seen.

* * * *

SS Geheime Gruppe Glocke, Wenceslaus Mine, Upper Silesia, November 1944

The first time I saw her, I was delivering some type of electronic tube to one of the scientists who was talking to her. I noticed how all of the scientists wanted to be wherever she was. But where she was, she was usually accompanied by Max, who I learned was her bodyguard and liaison between the Bell Project and the harsh realities of the SS. Apparently, Himmler and Hitler were so impressed by the information she provided the scientist that they committed enormous resources to making whatever she was learning from her trances into reality.

It was only years later when I uncovered a portion of what some of the whispered possibilities of the device were: from an interstellar space ship, to a time machine, to some sort of a teleportation device.

But the first day I saw her, if she had asked me to walk into the SS's machine guns, I would have gone, grinning all the way.

I don't know how long I stood there gaping at the vision in blue and grey with long, fair hair that flowed over her shoulders and down past her waist, but it was long enough for the scientist who was waiting for the part I carried to become angry. He strode over to me, snatched the component out of my hands, and gave me a brain-jarring clout on the side of my head.

I saw stars and my ears rang. The guard nearby started in my direction, the butt of his Schmeiser raised to accentuate the smack I had already received. I instinctively raised my hands and cowered, as I tried, hopelessly, to protect myself from another blow. He raised the steel machine pistol.

"Stop it!"

He paused with the gun in mid-air.

"What are doing to that child?" The voice belonged to the stunning lady with the long hair.

At first the guard tried to bluster it out, answering curtly, "This Jew brat has been negligent in his duty and must be punished."

The lovely creature walked over until she stood between me and the guard. "Negligent? Oh, please, can't you see he's only a boy?"

"That is no excuse. I am bringing him to the duty officer, and I'm sure he will send him to Auschwitz to go up the chimneys with all of the other sub-humans."

At this, her face paled and her lips became tight. "A child? You would do that to a child? You are lying to frighten him. That could not possibly be true. I will ask the Reichsführer himself." She looked around the enormous laboratory as if seeking something. "Where is your telephone? Please take me to one immediately."

Now it was the SS guard's turn to pale. He looked around franticly and spotted an Unterscharführer talking with another group of scientist on the other side of the chamber and walked swiftly over to him. I saw him point to us, and the

Unterscharführer looked in our direction and immediately yelled something at him, and then headed in our direction.

He stopped in front of the lady, clicked his heels and bowed deeply.

"Gnädige Fräulein, I am so sorry. That Dummkopf over there," he pointed at the guard who was now intently studying the floor, "made a mistake. He is new here. A Romanian conscript, and you know how stupid they are." He attempted a smile, which quickly became ingratiating. "Please, let me assure you that he has been spoken to and will have a lot of time to mull over his mistake on double shifts of midnight guard duty over the next several weeks. I hope you will forgive him, Fräulein Orsic, and agree there is no need to bother the Reichsführer with so trivial a matter."

She was gracious in victory. "Certainly, Unterscharführer. I am glad you have taken care of the situation." Then she bent down and looked at me. "What is your name, young man?"

"A-A-Aron, *Gnädige Fräulein,*" I stammered, whipping off my cap and bowing as low as my skinny legs would allow me. "*Danke, schöne Dame.* My name is Aron Gottlieb and I would gladly die for you."

Chapter Twenty-Seven

"And that, my young friends, is how I came to meet with the most important psychic medium in Germany who had the ear of both Himmler and Hitler. Maria Orsic, leading light of the Vril Society, and the woman widely believed to hold the key to unlimited power." He produced three mismatched glasses and a bottle of very old cognac from underneath the counter. The wise-cracking coin dealer, who had talked his way out of the gas chambers, filled the glasses and smiled. "Can you believe it? I was once a skinny kid who could run like the wind."

"But what's the rest of the story? What, exactly, was the mysterious 'Bell' and what happened to Maria after the war, and for that matter, Max?"

"Yes," Kat added, "and what does it all of have to do with those crazy people who are chasing us? I mean, how could they expect us to give them some kind of nebulous information we don't understand and don't even have?"

Aron glanced at me with one eyebrow slightly raised as if to say, *How are you gonna talk your way out of this one, pal?*

"Ummm... that's not entirely true, Kat."

Now it was her turn to raise an eyebrow at me. In fact, she raised her entire body off the counter where she'd been sitting and stood in front of me. She cocked her head and bit the inside of her lip.

"Please tell me you haven't been bull-shitting me and we haven't been running all over hell and back for some silly secret you could let them have and end all of this nonsense."

"Yeah, when you put it that way...but, there's more to it than just telling them what I know, which isn't much by the way. They want a flash drive your uncle gave me back in Germany. And for what it's worth, he was the one who said that no matter what happened, I couldn't let them get their hands on it."

"Yes, I remember he made reference to some great secret they wanted, but what exactly is the secret?"

I hesitated.

"I think I have a right to know since it's something that could get both of us killed," she said.

She, of course, had a point. I tried to pass the buck to Aron in hopes he might have something to add, but no luck. He just grinned and shook his head.

"Don't look at me kid. You're on your own for this one."

Oh, what the hell, I was getting tired of pretending to be the strong, silent type. I pulled up the leg of my jeans and slipped my left thumb down between the bootstrap and the lining (my latest hiding place) and pulled out a small rectangle about two inches long by a half inch wide, and slapped it on the counter.

"There. This is what this whole mess is all about. This dumb, fucking little piece of silicone."

Kat reached over and picked it up, turning it over in her hand. "This is what everyone wants?"

I nodded. "Well, technically not the actual flash-drive, of course, but what's on it."

"Which is?"

I don't know why, but I looked over at Aron as if asking for permission to spill the beans. And for the same inexplicable reason, he nodded, making me think he knew a lot more than he was letting on.

"From what your great-uncle told me, it consists of hundreds of pages of drawings, formulas, schematics, and translations from an obscure, ancient Sumerian language."

Kat shook her head, puzzled. "I don't get it. Drawings of what? And what makes them so valuable? Valuable enough to try to kill my Uncle Max and us?"

I opened my mouth to share the dozen half-baked theories I'd been kicking around and discarding ever since Max had given me the damn thing back in Munich, but Aron spoke first.

"It's the information translated by Sigrun and the 'beautiful lady' of my childhood, Maria Orsic. And according to everything I've been able to uncover over the last seventy years, these contain not only detailed plans of how to construct a means for interstellar contact, but actual records of these contacts, perhaps even meetings with otherworldly presences over the past century."

Suddenly, Aron's face twisted into a grimace of anger and sadness. "Meetings in which the secrets of the universe and the power to control them was given to a small group of gullible young women, who, in their naivety and childish belief in the goodness of all men, passed them on to the greatest concentration of evil the world has ever known: the Nazis."

"And now their descendants want it back." I turned to Aron. "You mentioned the name of your friend, a boy named Jerzy Dombroski. Do you happen to know what became of him... after the war?"

He thought for a moment. "I heard somewhere that, like me, he had come to America and had gotten a job as a teacher someplace up north. Why?"

"Professor Jerzy Dombroski of MIT," I whispered.

Now the incredible became credible, and the answers to questions I never asked came thick and fast.

I looked over at Kat, who was trying to look tough and unconcerned. She wasn't doing any better job of it than I was.

So many layers; So many twists and turns.

Fuck it.

"You know what, I'm rapidly coming to the conclusion that I really don't give a shit about keeping secret whatever rants and delusions are on this thing."

I picked up the flash drive and held it between my thumb and forefinger. "It's not worth putting any more lives at risk or getting me and Kat killed over some bogus secret from the last century. Screw it. As far as I'm concerned, they can have it. I hope it brings them as much crap as it's brought me."

I scooped up the drive, took Kat's hand, and she slid off the counter top. "Thanks for all your help, Aron, and if those clowns show up, tell 'em we're calling it quits."

Aron said nothing as we walked to the door.

"We'll be over at the Marriott," I said while trying to calculate how close I was to maxing out the limit on my poor abused Visa card.

"C'mon, Kat."

"Wait!"

He came around the counter. "Are you sure you really want to do this?"

I nodded. "Unless you can come up with a convincing alternative argument, which includes but is not limited to, granting us eternal life, youth, and let's say...oh, an even million in cash."

I smiled but he didn't.

"You might be surprised how the information on that drive could get you all of those things, and more. Much more."

"No, sorry, Aron, I'm not going for it anymore. Everyone keeps telling me that this stupid thing is the new Holy Grail. If it is, then someone else can have it. I'm officially laying down my sword and shield in favor of a cold beer, a hot chick," I winked at Kat who rolled her eyes, "and a nice, quiet day at the beach."

I put my hand on the doorknob, but Aron put his on my shoulder.

"All right. If you really don't care, then give me tonight with the drive, so I can satisfy myself that there's nothing on it that could help evil, or even deluded fanatics, to bring about any more misery on the world."

I hesitated, then dropped the drive into his open palm. "Have fun. We'll stop by tomorrow."

He nodded. "Thank you. I open at ten." He winked. "One of the benefits of owning your own business. The income stinks, but the hours are great."

We left the little shop and I caught a glimpse of his image, distorted by wavering vertical lines from the late afternoon sun slanting through dust-streaked window. They looked like bloodstained iron bars topped with rolls of barbed wire.

Chapter Twenty-Eight

We got a room at the Marriott and then went pub-crawling down by the waterfront. After a dozen oysters with crunchy French bread and bottle of overpriced Moët & Chandon, we both decided it was time to go back to the hotel and play "What Really Constitutes a Back Rub?"

I never realized how much danger turns a girl on. Either I had been dunked in a bathtub of Axe cologne or had become the next Ryan Gosling, because Kat had my shirt off and was working on my jeans before I could even get the chain lock in the door.

A half hour, and several interesting positions straight out of the *Kama Sutra* later, we were snuggling in post-coitus bliss and I was thinking un-typical thoughts such as: Hey, I might be ready for something long term here.

Normally thoughts like this disappeared within an hour or two of getting hot and sweaty between the sheets, but when we finally got through giggling about several mindless reality shows and turned off the tube, I still felt the same. And as Kat kissed me lightly and cuddled into my arms, I'll be damned if I wasn't looking forward to waking up to her bright eyes and more of the same.

Which was why what happened next was so fucking...well, the only way to describe it is the "fickle-finger-up-yours-pal" ironic.

I was still half-asleep when I felt Kat getting out of bed.

"Mmm, whazzup, babe? What time is it?" I glanced over at the alarm clock. "Shit, it's only eight o'clock. Way too early. C'mon, check out's not until ten."

She smiled and touched her forefinger to her lips and then to mine. "Close your eyes, sleepyhead. I'm gonna do a little shopping. After all, the only things I have here are what we picked up in the airport. I need some clothes and maybe a trip to Victoria's Secret for a couple of nighties and sexy underwear." She winked.

"Sold." I grinned back.

She finished buttoning her jeans and slung her purse over her shoulder. "I'll pick up a couple of lattes and some pastries, and if you're a good boy, maybe a little 'honey' before we check out."

I leaned up on one elbow and reached for her. "Maybe I need some 'honey' right now, you know, to give me 'sweet' dreams while I'm waiting."

But she pulled away laughing. "Down boy. You need to save your strength for later." And with a little "toodle-loo" wave of her fingertips, she was gone. I rolled over and closed my eyes.

* * * *

The blinds were drawn so I'm not sure when I woke and felt her in bed with me, but never one to look a gift horse in the mouth, I rolled over and pulled her close with a long, sexy kiss.

"Back early?" I smiled, pulling back and looking at her in the dim light. And then my eyes opened wide at the sight of who was in the bed with me.

The mysterious, enigmatic source of all of the confusion and danger that had been mine since the night I met her.

Ria.

The Girl with the Faraway Eyes

* * * *

You know how when things go wrong they do in the worst possible way and at the absolute worst possible time? Yeah, you got it.

If this had happened ten minutes…just ten minutes earlier, or even ten minutes later…but it didn't.

Now, you'll recall this wasn't the first time Ria had popped up in my bed out of, literally, nowhere. So this appearance shouldn't have surprised me, and in many ways, it didn't, but this was so-o-o-o not the time or place, and in that same instant, I surprised myself by realizing that, while she was fascinating, mysterious, and looking even hotter than usual, I really wasn't interested. Kat had taken her place in my fevered affections. All I could think of was how to get rid of Ria before Kat came back. And to be perfectly fair, that was Ria's reaction too.

"Whear bin ich und wer bist du?"

Where am I and who are you—was not what I was expecting, and then I noticed how, once again, she looked different than before. On her last appearance, she had looked young—fifteen or sixteen maybe, and frightened and confused. Now she was still young, with even a little touch of timorous girlish innocence, and certainly looked no more than eighteen or nineteen. And she was shocked, much more than today's average woman would be, at the sight of a naked man next to her. The lacy, long, frilly nightgown only added to the illusion that she had stepped off the cover of some nineteenth century English novel.

All this flashed through my brain in a few frenzied seconds as I pulled at her arm.

"Ria, c'mon, you've gotta get outta here before Kat—"

And of course, at that exact moment, the plastic key card slid in the lock.

You know the sick, panicked feeling you get in the seconds just prior to some horrible disaster you see coming down the pike but are unable to prevent?

Yeah, just like that.

My brain fluttered like a caged bird as Kat pushed open the door, stepped inside with a big smile that dropped off her face like a falling elevator. It might have been funny if the scene was playing out in a smart, frothy romantic comedy with a suave, sexy star instead of a tongue-tied idiot. Me.

She did the classic on-screen double take, eyes widening and mouth open in disbelief while she tried to take in the bizarre scene of her newfound boyfriend in the sack with some young and very attractive girl.

"You fucking bastard." She threw the cardboard box of coffee and pastries at me. Fortunately, the worst of the scalding coffee splashed all over the bed before reaching me, but it was a small comfort compared to the hurt on her face.

Without thinking, I jumped out of bed.

"It's not what it seems!" I babbled, which was, of course, one more nail in my coffin, seeing as how I was stark, freaking naked!

Between Kat shaking with anger and Ria shaking with horror at the sight of a naked man, body parts swinging back and forth, trying to say something that didn't sound like, "Yabba, yabba..." I caught a glimpse of myself in the mirror looking like the first-place winner on *America's Funniest Home Videos*. Unfortunately no one was laughing.

Kat stared at me and shook her head once. "You know what, Chris? Save your bullshit for someone else. Fuck you. I'm outta here."

She spun on her heel and let the door swing shut behind her.

I don't know how long I stood there trying to think of something I could have said if she hadn't walked out on me. Then it hit me.

"Damn!" I whispered to the face in the mirror staring back at me. "You've gone and done it haven't you? You've fallen in love with her."

Crap!

I pulled on my jeans and a T-shirt, and without even a backward glance to see if the perpetually-popping-up Ria was still there, I bolted barefoot out the door and down the hallway. Of the two elevators, one was at the top floor but the other had just hit the lobby. Shit! I ran to the fire exit and took the stairs two at a time.

By the time I'd gasped my way down six flights of stairs and stumbled into the lobby, Kat was nowhere in sight. With barely a pause, I ran past the front desk, and collective raised eyebrows at the sight of a shirtless, barefoot, desperate looking character streaking through their lobby.

The outer door hissed open then closed behind me. I turned my head franticly from side to side, and there, about a half a block up on the other side of the street, I saw her walking along, head down, arms hugging her chest and slouched in her own private misery. Misery caused by me.

"Kat!"

Either she didn't hear me over the traffic or chose not to. No matter. This was one girl I wasn't going to let walk out of my life.

I started jogging down the sidewalk, looking for an opening in the traffic to cross when a beige, nondescript rental car of indeterminate make, slowed on her side of the street.

Time stuck in molasses. Everything happened in slow motion like a waking dream in suspended animation. I think I called out, "No!" or, "Kat! Run!" Or something equally foolish and impotent, but it was over before I even had time to move.

One minute she was a sweet silhouette on the other side of the street, and in the next, the car had slowed, the door opened, and a pair of strong arms grabbed her, pulling her into the car.

The car and Kat were gone, and I was left standing in my bare feet, staring down at the empty sidewalk.

Chapter Twenty-Nine

I don't recall how long I stood there, frozen to the spot, but finally the volume of puzzled stares I was collecting snapped me out of my bleak reverie, and fifteen minutes later, I'd checked out of the hotel and was standing in front of Aron Gottleib's dusty store window.

He let me in right away, and under his gently probing but germane questioning, I told him about the whole sorry mess.

"What the fuck should I do? I am fresh out of ideas, which is probably a good thing since each decision I make turns out worse than the last."

"I won't insult your intelligence by telling you things are not as bad as they seem, because they are—and very possibly a whole lot worse. But there is something you can do about it."

"What?"

He shifted uncomfortably in his worn, leather armchair behind the counter.

"You're not gonna like it."

"C'mon, Aron, I'm looking for some straws to clutch at. I'll take whatever you've got."

"OK, then here it is. Don't bother looking for Kat. They'll never let you find her, and even if you got close, they'd kill her before you could get to her."

I slammed my hand down on the counter. "Then what the fuck am I supposed to do? Why did they kidnap her in the first place?"

"They want to trade."

"Fine with me! I already said I'm willing to give them the flash drive."

"And from what I saw last night of what's already available on the Internet, they've probably decided that's just a down payment."

"Damn it, Aron, that's all I've got. What more do they think I have?"

"What I'm about to tell you."

"Huh?"

He got up and motioned me to follow him back to his small office at the rear of the store. When we got there, he pointed to a beat-up, wooden folding chair, motioning me to sit. He sat down behind the desk and opened an old coffee-table-sized book, flipping through several musty pages interspersed with old-fashioned black-and-white plates of ancient pottery and jewelry. Finally, he found the page he wanted, turned the book around, and pushed it towards me.

"This photo was taken in 1938 during a Nazi Ahnenerbe expedition to the lands of the former Mesopotamia. Do you know what this is?"

I studied the faded photos on both open pages, unsure of what I was supposed to be looking for.

Aron pointed to the picture in the upper right-hand corner of a hand, holding a spiral of twisted gold about an inch and half wide by five to six inches long, judging by the hand in the picture.

"The hand is there to give the object scale," Aron said as if reading my mind. "And the hand holding the object belongs to none other than Herr Sturmbanfurher Maximillion von Buchholz, the man who saved my life, and whom you know as Max Becker."

"The story," I said softly, recalling what Max had told Kat and me about finding the stela and what he had thought was some sort of an oversized ring.

Aron nodded. "He told you about it. Good. That saves me time and that's something rapidly becoming in short supply."

I breathed out heavily. "If time is so fucking short, then why are we wasting it talking about some archeological expedition from the last century instead of concentrating on finding something to help us get Kat back?"

"Because," he said, stabbing his forefinger down onto the picture, "This is the price of Kat's life."

Over the next hour, Aron filled in the missing pieces of the Ahnenerbe mission Max had been a part of. He told me that after returning to Berlin, Himmler had the mysterious stela taken to Wewelsburg, the ancient German castle he was turning into the spiritual and corporeal center of National Socialism and the SS.

"No one knows what happened to it after it was taken to the castle. There are all kinds of rumors from it being set into the wall in a secret chamber, to being used as a sacrificial alter stone in the sacred crypt under the castle. However, photographs of the stela were sent to a dozen of the great universities with instructions to translate them. Though most of the archeologists and linguists agreed that it was some form of proto-Sumerian, they were unable to translate the writing until Himmler personally directed Max to bring it to Maria Orsic. Supposedly, she and Sigrun went into a waking trance lasting five hours, and when they finally came out of it, they had not only translated the writing, but had also transcribed the rules for a hither-to unknown language. Himmler was delighted and excited by this revelation, and declared it to be undoubtedly the lost language of the ancient Anunnaki, and thus must contain secret messages about their superior technology for their descendants, the Aryans. Himmler ordered everyone connected with the Vril project to redouble their efforts to bring the objects, described by the ladies of the Vril Damen, into production. These would form the core of Hitler's Wunder Waffen project."

"And was the thing you saw at the mine site where you first met Maria, one of those objects?"

Aron paused, took a sip from a glass of cold tea and nodded. "And once, when I deliberately walked close to her and two of the scientists standing in front of the Bell, I heard her arguing that if they tried to put a canon and other weapons on the Bell, it would cause the machine to shake itself apart and possibly go tumbling through both space and time, exactly like what happened with the first Hanbrau saucer craft."

"Saucer craft?" I broke in. "As in UFOs?"

"Yes. I read after the war that one of the early tests of the Vril science had been with disc aircraft, and in one instance, the test craft returned to the airfield less than an hour after take-off but was so pitted and worn, it looked as though it had been traveling for hundreds of years. Which, according to Einstein, is exactly what would happen if you exceed the speed of light."

"But obviously they never perfected this technology because we never fought flying saucers during WWII, and last time I checked, there were no Nazis on the moon."

"Don't be too sure. Have you ever heard of the Foo Fighters? Glowing discs that moved at incredible speed encountered by our bomber crews over Germany?"

I shook my head. "If they did have all this advanced technology, why did they lose the war? And once they did, why didn't Himmler and Goring and Hitler, and all the rest of those guys, just escape to the stars?"

"Who says they didn't?"

"Aww, c'mon, don't give me that old shit about Hitler escaping to the Brazilian jungle or hiding out on Mars."

"They have never proved conclusively that the burnt body found in the ashes of the Reich Chancellery was Hitler."

I stared to speak but he waved me off. "But that's not really what I'm talking about. I do not think Hitler ever availed himself of the Vril technology. By the time he realized the war was lost, it was too late to escape from the bunker in Berlin. No, I think others used the strange, bell-shaped object I saw at the mine site in Upper Silesia."

His gaze locked with mine and there was no humor or warmth in them. "I believe several people used the Die Glocke, the bell, to escape the crumbling chaos of the Third Reich. One was Max, the second his lover Maria Orsic, and the third..." He drew a deep breath and spoke with anger undimmed after seventy years, "was General Dr. Ing. Heinz Friedrich Karl Franz Kammler, designer of the entire concentration camp system and the man who now has Katrina."

Chapter Thirty

Somehow, I wasn't surprised. All of the tiny, jagged pieces of this puzzle that had floated aimlessly through my life had been coalescing around these possibilities, and this was the only way they could all add up.

"So then, this Kammler guy and his goons who've been chasing me, took a ride in this 'Bell' thing at the end of the war, and went somewhere at light speed and came back having barely aged at all?"

"That would be my best guess."

"But if it were true, then why would they need the flash drive and resort to kidnapping Kat to get it? They must have all the whiz-bang technology they could want if they can zip around the solar system at light speed?"

"I told you. The only reason they want the flash drive is to make sure no one else will be able to access its information, which is essential to interpreting all of the other disconnected information about Vril technology and its wonders. But that's not all they want. They need the key."

"Key?" I looked up. My mind spun in circles like a mouse in a cage. All I could think of was Kat. Kat and a key. I heard again the sound of her key card clicking in the hotel door as I froze in confusion. Key...locks.

"Why the fuck didn't I lock the damn door the minute I discovered Ria in my bed?" I muttered.

"Ria? Bed?" Aron frowned. "You told me nothing of this. You picked up a girl and took her back to the same bed you shared with Sweet Katrina? No wonder she left the hotel. You're lucky she didn't break a lamp over your head."

"She tried." I sighed. "But, hang on a sec, you've got it all wrong. I didn't pick Ria up, she just keeps showing up in my life, anywhere and anytime. And I'm beginning to think she can't control it any more than I want it."

Aron looked thoughtful and asked quietly, "Describe her please, and more importantly, is there anything different about her each time she appears to you?"

I did the best I could, though it wasn't easy. "And yeah, every time she has on different clothes from different eras, different hairstyles, and the weirdest thing of all, she looks like she's different ages."

Aron leaned back in chair. "Ah...then she has what they are looking for, or at the very least, knows where it is. And since they have obviously been unable to get their hands on her, they are trying to get to those who have contact with her, like you and Max. Thus, the kidnapping of Katrina serves a dual purpose. She is your lover, and Max's grand-niece." He stroked his chin. "Yes, they will most certainly offer you a trade. The girl for the key."

There it was again. "Hold on, what the hell is this 'key?'"

But Aron wasn't listening. He stared over my shoulder, past the long counter, and through the dirty window. I turned my head just in time to catch a glimpse of the same nondescript car that had taken Kat, pulling away from the curb.

"Shit! That's them! The same fuckers who took Kat!"

I got up but Aron grabbed my arm. "Don't! Even if you could catch them, they'd have you in the trunk before you could touch the door handle. Besides, they don't have her in the car. She's stashed somewhere while they wait for you to come across with the key."

"Key? For the last time, what's with this fuckin' key you keep talking about? What is it? Why is it so goddamn important, and how the hell do you know that's what they want?"

Aron sighed and turned the computer screen on his desk around so I could see what he'd been looking at. "I received this just before you walked in."

I looked down at the screen. It was an email.

Herr Gottlieb.

You know who we are and what we want, so you will please tell the young man when he comes to see you, and he will, that if he wishes to see his lady love again, he will give to you the key, or its location, by no later than 3pm today. H.F.K."

"Kammler?"

Aron nodded. "Yes. And now it's time to leave. They will be back soon." He glanced up at the clock. It read 2:42. Eighteen minutes left.

"I'm not going anywhere 'til I get Kat." I sat back down.

"You must. You don't have the key. If you do succeed in convincing them that you don't have it, then you'll be of no further use to them and they'll most likely kill you and Katrina. So, you must keep clear until you can get your hands on the key."

"And how can I do that if I don't know where it is? I don't even know what the fuck it is!"

He picked up a pencil and began to sketch out a long, cylindrical object. "Its purpose is essentially two-fold, it is..."

His words trailed off at the sound of a car pulling up in front of the shop.

"They're early. How very un-German of them." His tone was fatalistic with a tinge of irony. Then he got up quickly and moved towards the back storeroom. "You must leave. Quickly, before one of them has a chance to get around back and cover the alley." He unlocked the back door.

"Wait! What about the key thing. You didn't finish telling me."

"No time but—" He walked back to the computer. "Your email address?"

I gave it to him. "Why?"

He typed it in and pressed send. "I've forwarded the research I've been doing, along with the address of where I believe it is."

We heard the sound of a car door opening, followed by another, and we could see the figures of two stocky men heading for the front door.

"Go!" he ordered.

"What about you? What are you gonna do if they decide they want to make you talk?"

He smiled and pulled a drop cloth from several boxes stacked in the corner revealing a jumble of army surplus weapons. Everything from a model 1911 Colt .45, to grenades, a Thompson machine gun...and even something that looked like a land mine!

"Don't worry about me." He grinned. "I sampled National Socialism hospitality in my youth and have no desire to repeat the process." He opened the back door and pushed me out.

"Find somewhere quiet and dark, a bar maybe, where you can spend the next few hours and read what I have sent you.

Then come back here at six when I close up and I'll fill in the missing pieces."

I nodded, still more confused than enlightened.

He winked. "Geh mit Gott," and locked the door.

Somehow I doubted God had much interest in going anywhere with me.

* * * *

I found a quiet table next to the window in a fern bar down by the waterfront and ordered a Key West Ale. Since my breakfast had been thrown all over me and my bed seven hours ago, I ordered a cheeseburger.

I tried to read what Aron had emailed me, but I couldn't open the attachment on my cell phone and the email itself didn't tell me much. Just the last part:

Now that you know as much as I do about the 'key', show this picture to an antique dealer named Marcel Thibodeaux in Paris. He has a showroom on the Rue St. Germaine, 'M. Thibodeaux - Antiquités Beaux', not far from the Luxemburg Gardens. There were many refugees, on both sides, who sold him things in the aftermath of war. Some selling what little they had saved from the collection of Nazi thieves who'd stolen them, others, those same Nazi thieves who had done the stealing. It made no difference to Marcel. He was an equal opportunity opportunist, making money off the desperate, whether they were trying to pick up the shattered pieces of their old lives, or trying to start another one with a new identity in a place with no extradition treaties. Marcel helped them all while helping himself.

It has long been rumored that sometime during the early fall of 1945, a former, high-placed member of the SS Ahnenerbe came to see Marcel with several museum quality pieces he swore had been part of Himmler's personal collection at Wewelsburg, where he'd been stationed as 'curator'. Though, when the Mossad caught up with him in Paraguay five years later, they pointed out to Marcel that before Himmler died, the bulk of his duties at the SS castle consisted of assigning the prisoners who were going to be worked to death on the castle construction projects. However, they never found any of the so-called 'items of power' in his possession, and they have never turned up anywhere in the museum or art world. So, it must be assumed that Marcel still has them or at least knows where they are.

I scrolled down to the photo he'd sent as a jpeg, and it came up clear and bright on my iPhone. As I suspected, it was a picture of the unusually large spiral ring, laid out on a black velvet cloth in some sort of unidentified display. I went back to the text.

But you must hurry. Not only because our enemies will be hot on your trail, but also because Marcel is well into his nineties, and the clock is pursuing him with as much vigor as those who are pursuing you.

Auf Wiedersehen und viel Glück, mein Freund.

PS... I think I can buy you some breathing room with the little 'Willkommens' party I've prepared for them. Ha!

I re-read the last sentence with an increasingly sick feeling in the pit of my stomach. I had my suspicions what sort of a "party" the former camp inmate was planning for those who'd stolen his childhood.

I left a twenty on the table and headed back up towards his shop at a fast trot.

Two blocks away, a flash, followed by a vibration through the sidewalk and an ear-splitting explosion tripped car alarms up and down the street. Turning the corner, I saw flames and smoke shooting out of the shattered storefront window that had once been Aron's shop. The cops were already there, and a fire truck came screeching to a halt with fireman jumping down and unrolling hoses.

I was too late.

I approached as close as the police with yellow tape in their hands would allow and caught a glimpse of two bodies being zipped into separate plastic body bags. One I could tell from the large, gold Star of David worn around his neck, was Aron. The other stocky figure apparently had no identification or personal affects until the medical examiner turned him over on his back and began examining him. He stopped and pointed with his pen to some dark marks on the inside of his upper arm. The cop zipping up the body bag shrugged, but I saw it, and because of Max, I knew what it was.

The man's blood type tattooed under twin lightning runes proclaimed him a former storm trooper of the SS.

I backed away before they started wondering why I was staring so hard and walked to the next block and hailed a cab.

Fortunately, spending much time in Europe had put me in the habit of carrying my passport at all times. Catching a flight to France would not be a problem. Although my heart wanted to stay here and keep looking for Kat, my head told me Kammler and the remainder of his crew wouldn't be far behind me. And as long as they believed I had something to trade, they'd have Kat handy. I just had to make sure that when they showed up, I really did have something to trade. One way or another, I swore to myself, I would.

Chapter Thirty-One

"Excusez-moi, monsieur, où puis-je obtenir le métro pour Paris?"

The only response from the bored clerk manning the only open window in the Charles De Gaulle Airport entrance to the Metro, was a sneer at my execrable schoolboy French accent. Oh, I had a fair command of French vocabulary and conjugations, but I'd never been able to master the slightly nasal, world-weary lilt the French have perfected to convince the rest of the world they're doing them a favor by talking to them.

Finally, out of pity or in an effort to get the line forming behind me moving again, an attractive coed in a long coat and short skirt tapped me on the shoulder and said in better English than my French, "Down those stairs and follow the signs to the platform."

I thanked her and took my leave of the clerk who looked annoyed with the girl for spoiling his sport of tormenting the American tourist. Following the girl's instructions, I slung my backpack over my right shoulder and clomped down the stairs.

Although I'd week-ended several times in France while struggling through my ill-fated software training in Munich, I'd been with friends who were far more fluent in all the languages of multicultural Europe than I. Most of the time, I'd been content to sip my Bordeaux and let them chat up the locals. Besides, the average European had it all over the average American when it came to being multi-lingual and could easily converse in three or four languages without blinking an eye. Hell, the majority of Europeans spoke better English than I and my fellow countrymen.

As I walked onto the multi-track cement platform, there was a muted clatter, a hiss of doors opening, and the Metro train pulled up. I started to get in and then noticed another train pulling in on the other side of the platform was attracting a stampede while the forlorn, empty one I was about to board had few takers.

Hmmm…

Both trains were getting ready to close the doors. I looked around frantically for some indicator that might, by some miracle, tell me where the hell the damn thing was headed!

And then, trotting towards the open door of the train behind me, I spied the girl with the long coat and short skirt. When in doubt, always choose attractive ladies over solitary means of transportation. She ran up to the closing door. I followed her shouting, "Excuse me—Paris?"

Tossing her scarf over her shoulder, she gave a backward glance and nodded.

"Oui."

I jumped through the closing door—and almost made it. That is to say I made it, but my backpack had other ideas and became lodged between the closing doors. This precipitated a series of squawking buzzers and bells until I was able to wrench the pack fully inside the car.

A guy with the skinniest skintight jeans I'd ever seen on a male, turned to his companion, and rolling his eyes in my direction, let go a string of rapid-fire Gallic commentary on my antecedents, who probably found walking and chewing gum simultaneously as difficult as I did entering a subway door. His partner twirled his long scarf and responded with the obligatory sneer eliciting the amused contempt of the group around him at the clueless foreigner.

I debated with tying the long scarf around his neck to one of the overhead luggage racks, but in the end decided I had all the trouble I could handle. It turned out I had a champion in the form of the chic-looking young woman whose age, I realized at second glance, I'd misjudged.

She turned to the two men, and in equally rapid-fire, beautifully accented French, told them not-terribly-attractive young men in frilly scarves and too-tight jeans struggling with their gender identification should look to their own glass houses before chucking stones at hapless tourists.

At least one of them had the decency to get red in the face before turning a cold, scarf-covered shoulder to her. I, on the other hand, having never been rescued by a damsel not in distress, I gave her a big grin.

"Merci beaucoup, belle demoiselle. Mon accent pue mais merci d'être venu à mon secours." Which, roughly translated, means, "Thank you, beautiful lady. My accent stinks but thank you for coming to my rescue."

She smiled prettily and laughed while regarding me from under long, black eyelashes that matched her pixie cut short black hair.

"You are most welcome, monsieur, I was honored to be your 'rescuer,' and besides, your accent is really not that bad." She tossed a disdainful glance in their direction. "They are, in truth, a couple of third-year students at the Sorbonne who themselves probably arrived from the provinces a few years ago with accents worse than yours."

Then she realized how that had come out and giggled. "Oh, forgive me. I really didn't mean to imply your accent was bad."

"No problem. I've been laughed at for worse and more often."

She giggled again. "Oui, you have taken your share of abuse since you arrived in La Belle France."

"All in a day's work for the Ugly American stereotypical tourist."

Her smile hovered between sympathy and interest, so I leaned closer. "Now if you could recommend a decent hotel somewhere around the Rue St. Germaine that might be able to comprehend my Boston/Irish accent..."

She looked up from under long lashes while momentarily brushing against me as the train tilted into a turn. "I think I might be able to help."

"What's your name?"

"Celeste."

"And your number?"

Raised eyebrows. "My, my, you are inquisitive."

"How else will I be able to thank you other than by buying you dinner? I can't very well come to get you without a phone number or at least an address."

I may have been in France to find Kat, but I was also in desperate need of someone familiar with Paris and the nuances of the French language far better than I. And damn me for noticing, but yes—she was cute.

She put one silver-painted nail alongside her cheek as if weighing the possibilities of me being an ax murderer or serial killer. Apparently I came up neither, because as the train pulled into the station announcing itself as the place to disembark for the Eiffel Tower, she pointed to the big poster on the station wall highlighting the four massive legs and tower entrances. She kissed the tip of the same finger and brushed it by my cheek.

"Meet me at the south entrance, eight o'clock."

She stepped off the train and was swallowed up by the crowd.

I pulled out my cell and typed in 8pm Eiffel, along with the name of the hotel she'd given located off the Luxembourg Gardens, and then I started checking the map on the inner wall of the train to make sure I got off at the right stop.

A few minutes later, we pulled into St. Germaine and I began walking across the park. It was a beautiful day filled with joggers, cyclists, kids, and old people sitting in the afternoon sunshine.

I was feeling good and started to whistle an old Beatles tune, "Here Comes the Sun." Things were looking up. I'd gotten here in one piece, had a place to stay, and now the company of a pretty girl for dinner.

And that's when it hit me. I stopped right in the middle of the gravel path. What the fuck was I thinking? I wasn't here to sample fine food, good hotels, and attractive companionship. I was here to save the life of the girl I'd just decided I loved. The tune died on my lips and I walked, slower now but with deliberation, to the other side of the park.

* * * *

I checked into the appropriately named Luxemburg Park Hotel, and it was as nice as Celeste said it was.

Celeste. Damn. I considered calling her to beg off dinner, but of course I didn't have her number. Damn! And I would be a total shit if I repaid her help by standing her up and leaving her waiting at the Eiffel Tower. No choice. I'd go there, buy her a drink, and then plead jet lag. Besides, I still needed a guide. Maybe I could ask her to help me without getting emotionally involved.

Ha! It's amazing the way we fool ourselves, isn't it?

It was still nice out and I decided to walk to the Eiffel Tower. It turned out to be twice as far as it looked on the gaily-colored tourist map with a big cartoon image of the tower bestriding Paris like some sort of steel-skeleton Godzilla. But I'd been cooped up in a 727 for close to nine hours and needed the exercise. Besides, it gave me plenty of time to continually check my cell for any texts or emails that may have come in offering me a trade for Kat.

Nothing.

But each time I checked, I also scrolled through the half dozen pics I'd taken of Kat on our first date, including a selfie in which we both looked foolishly, happily infatuated and blissfully ignorant of the shit-storm to come.

By the time I got to the Champs de Mars it was still early. I bought an overpriced Orangina from a street vendor and plopped down on a bench to wait.

Around quarter to eight I wandered over to see if she'd arrived. Nope. By five past, I was wondering if I got the location wrong and began to make a circuit of the other three massive legs of the colossal structure, but nothing. It was inching towards 8:30. I mentally shrugged and decided the Fates had finally chosen wisely, leaving me and the stunning brunette to remain forever "strangers on a train."

I saw a sidewalk café on the street heading towards Les Invalides, and according to the cartoon map, eventually back up to St. Germaine. I decided to head there for a long overdue dinner. I had only gone a few dozen steps when I heard a shout.

"Hé, où allez-vous?"

I turned and there she was. To the long leather coat she'd added an even shorter skirt and a beret, and unfortunately, she looked even hotter than I remembered. Damn.

She walked briskly towards me, a slight swaying of trim hips and an enigmatic smile. Stopping in front of me she cocked her head quizzically.

"Où allez-vous? Were you going to stand me up?"

"Where am I going? Was I standing you up? If you'll pardon moi, fair lady, you're the one who's a half hour late."

Her smoky, dark eyes grew wide. "Me, certainement pas!" She pulled up her left sleeve, revealing a diamond-studded watch on an intricate, handcrafted, gold bracelet. Someone in her life was taking very good care of her.

"There," she said triumphantly, "eight-thirty-five. I was right on time."

"Huh? One of us is living in another time zone. What time do you think you told me?"

"Eight-thirty obviously, mon cher," She pulled out her compact and reapplied a dark red lipstick to lips that were looking far too kissable with each passing moment.

She finished, closed the compact with a click and took my arm. "But I forgive you for getting the time wrong, chéri. You probably have a lot on your mind, but it's nothing a merveilleux dinner and Celeste can't cure."

We walked down the Champs de Mars, through lengthening shadows towards the twinkling lights stretching up the long boulevard ahead. Did I really get the time wrong? Must have, but...

"And since we will certainly be making sparkling dinner conversation, I must have something to call you other than, 'chéri,' oui?"

"Yeah, oui, absolutely. It's Chris. Chris Brennan. Pure Boston Irish, one generation outta Southie. College grad, decent hockey player, and all round 'wicked pissa' kid." I replied letting my full-blown Boston colloquial accent take over.

That stopped her cold, as it always did when speaking with anyone outside of a ten-mile radius of Boston and the nearly unintelligible flat A-sound we Boston locals gave words ending in R. And try translating that into any other language—including English!

She laughed. "I don't even pretend to understand what you just said, chéri, Christophe, but I like your name. It suits you."

"My parents thank you. And, if I recall correctly, Celeste means 'heavenly,' right?"

"Bravo, yes, though perhaps all would not agree."

"They'd have to be pretty picky if they didn't. What about the last name?"

"It comes from old French-Norman nobility, mostly impoverished now, sadly. Sainte-d'Aignau. Celeste Christiana Sainte-d'Aignau."

* * * *

She found us a fairly quiet table at a trendy little bistro along the Avenue de la Bourdonnais, where, over a plate of escargot and bottle of Cabernet, we proceeded to play Twenty Questions followed by only nineteen answers.

In addition to being a stone-cold fox, Celeste was witty, clever, and funny, with a worldly panache that belied her ingénue image and was at odds with the knowing look hiding behind her eyes. I noticed, during our game of jockeying for the most amount of information without giving much away, she always emerged on top.

I knew what I wanted. Someone with an insider's knowledge who could help me get around Paris and provide accurate translation when my limited French wouldn't suffice, which I guessed would be frequently.

On the other hand, I remained clueless as to what Celeste was in it for. I mean, while I was certainly not a "player" in the classic sense of the word, I knew when a woman was in the process of coming on to me, and believe me, it was not all that often. I guess what disturbed me the most was how good she was at it. Had I not spent the past two weeks tangled up in treachery, murder, and mystery—not to mention being in love with someone else—I would have plunged headfirst into helpless infatuation with her. As it was, despite my host of red flags, I found it difficult not to suggest that we adjourn to somewhere more quiet and...private.

She must have sensed this and upped the percentage of erotic double-entendre, making it hard to keep my mind out of the gutter and on the reason I was in Paris in the first place.

"I guess I was wrong about you."

"Really?" She blew a lungful of cigarette smoke towards the ceiling and regarded me through dark shadowed eyes. "In what way?"

"When I first saw you out at the airport, I thought you were a school girl."

She smiled over the edge of her wine glass. "Oh, is that your style? You like to pick up schoolgirls? Or perhaps you like your women to wear little plaid skirts and frilly ankle socks."

"No. At least not since high school."

As if to prove me a liar, she gave a very schoolgirl-like giggle, which made it hard not to fantasize about the very scenario she'd described—and she knew it.

Determined to take charge of keeping this as romantically unencumbered as possible, I finally said, "Hey, do you happen to know where this is?"

I pushed the piece of paper across the small table with the address Aron had given me. She glanced down without picking it up.

"Why? Is he a friend of yours?"

"Ah, you know it's a he?"

"Who wouldn't, chéri? I'm looking at shop with the name of Marcel Thibodeaux."

"But it doesn't say Marcel, it says: M. Thibodeaux - Antiquités Beaux. "

Gotcha.

She threw me a perfect little Gallic shrug accompanied by a most alluring pout. "Marcel is an old and very respected dealer in Paris. No mystery." Now the pout deepened and cozied up to just the right touch of hurt.

"I'm beginning to think perhaps this date was a mistake, Christophe. I don't think you like me."

Oops...

"No, that's not it at all." The real problem was that I did like her...way too much. "I guess I'm just tired and jumpy after everything and what I need to do here and..."

I let the rest of the sentence trail off as I realized how tired I really was and what little I knew compared to the mountain of what I didn't.

She leaned across the tiny table and took my hand.

"Then please, let me help."

Chapter Thirty-Two

It turned out not only had Celeste heard of M. Thibodeaux - Antiquités Beaux, she had some very distant family ties through the bewildering lines of inbred nobility threading across Europe.

The next morning, while I sipped my cappuccino in the sunny little breakfast room off the lobby of the Luxemburg Park Hotel, my cell rang.

"Bon jour, Christophe. Are you up and about?"

"About as up as I ever get. Why?"

"Because I have an appointment for us at 11 a.m. at Thibodeaux's shop."

"Us?"

"*Oui*, chéri. The only way I could get Marcel's son to agree to allow us to see his father was by calling in a few family favors."

"Family favors?" I realized I was beginning to sound like a parrot in an echo chamber, repeating every word she said, but I couldn't help it. Confusion had settled into my brain for such a long stay I was beginning to doubt I could find the door without a roadmap and a guide.

"I'll explain more when we meet, but for now, meet me in a half hour in front of the shop. Au revoir."

She rang off and I sat, as if waiting for some additional information from the smart phone, which, in truth, was almost as dumb as I was. I got up and walked the eight blocks to the address on Rue St. Germaine.

This time she was already standing in front of the shop when I arrived and gave me a sweet smile. Today she dressed in a sweater, mid-length skirt, and long scarf. Her eyes were bright and guileless, cheeks rosy, and lips tinted a modest baby pink. The entire package reminded me again of a precocious college-age ingénue.

Her behavior was likewise demure. No dark-eyed, smoky looks or lingering touch of hands, merely a quick press of my arm sans embrace, providing the bare minimum of the Gallic way of greeting.

We walked through the heavy brass-trimmed door.

"Old Marcel has become something of a curmudgeon over the past few years, but young Marcel is pleasant enough, and just between you and me, he's a bit amoureux de moi."

"Who wouldn't be enamored with you?" I whispered back.

"You?"

I looked for raised eyebrows and tongue-in-cheek, but the look she flashed me was open and quizzical. More puzzles that I didn't need.

The shop was lit with a variety of Tiffany lamps I had no doubt were all originals, and polished display cases filled with museum-quality pieces without price tags. In other words, if you had to ask, then you must have wandered into the wrong shop.

Celeste walked confidently toward the back of the store and knocked on a partially open cherry-wood door.

"Entrer," a male voice called out.

We walked in to see a well-dressed middle-age man in a blue blazer with some heraldic crest on the pocket. Sitting behind a massive walnut desk, probably several hundred years old, was a wizened, little, old man who looked as though he and the desk could have been contemporaries.

The middle-aged man came over and warmly embraced Celeste with what he considered a fraternal embrace, but I could see the lust behind his eyes. She was right; he did fancy her. The old man didn't say a word, but the bright little eyes sunk in the wizened face, missed nothing.

Celeste slipped gracefully out of the embrace, rounded the desk, and gave the old man a kiss on the cheek. I caught the look the old man flashed the younger man, obviously his son, and it reinforced my first impression; Marcel the Elder was a man who liked to win in every arena, regardless of age.

Celeste straightened up. "Comment ça va, Oncle? You are looking very well."

"And you are a charming little liar with more allure than any woman has a right to. Just like your mother."

I caught the briefest look flash between them at that last sentence, but it was gone before I could figure out what it was. She sat on the side of the wide desk and spoke.

"As I mentioned to Marcel, Oncle, I have a friend, Monsieur Christophe, who is in dire need of your help and advice."

For the first time, the keen eyes focused on me, measuring me and most likely coming up short. Finally he spoke.

"And how does this Américain think the shop of Thibodeaux can help him?"

His voice was cracked and raspy but sharp as a whip. I guessed this was the way he'd started thousands of negotiations, knowing that in the end, he would wind up besting the person on the other side of the desk. How much should I tell him? Every instinct screamed: as little as possible!

"Do you know a man named Aron Gottlieb, Maximillion von Buchholz, or Hanz Kammler?"

I don't really know why I blurted it out rather than setting it up carefully and dancing around the subject. Maybe I'd just had it with all of the layers of lies, obscuration, and bullshit. Or maybe, just maybe, I was hoping to generate some sort of reaction from the lizard-faced nonagenarian on the other side of the desk.

If so, I was disappointed, because the old man never moved and his expression never changed, except...for a split second a flicker behind the hooded eyes when I said the name Kammler.

I quickly glanced around the room. His son looked at me with an expression wavering between puzzlement and irritation, no doubt from his dawning realization that I was neither seller or buyer, which left only his most useless category: someone who wanted something for nothing. I had to change his impression if I didn't want to be shown the door. I pulled out my iPhone and put it down on the desk.

"This is what I'm looking for."

The old man slowly turned the phone around until he could see the picture. He stared at it, but he sat too far down in the chair with his head bent for me to tell if he recognized what I put in front of him. Marcel Junior walked around and stood behind his father.

"And precisely what is it we're looking at? Is this something you wish to purchase? I can tell you it is not in our shop, nor am I familiar with it. We could undertake a commission to find it, for a fee of course. You will have to give us some background on its bona-fides and last known whereabouts."

The old man said nothing. I could tell he was waiting for me to spill more of the beans. What could I tell without giving too much away? Surely the father knew what it was. From what Aron told me, he most likely knew where it was or who had it.

Oddly enough it was the girl, who remained an enigma to me, who came to the rescue. She walked around the desk and stood on the other side of the old man.

"Oh, mon chére Oncle, my friend Christophe is truly at his wits end. He represents a wealthy American client who, for tax reasons, does not wish to go through the normal channels to acquire this object, and my pauvre ami has been searching all over Europe for this piece with no luck."

She looked over at me with those innocent eyes. "That is correct, n'est-ce pas, Chéri?"

She was good. I had to keep reminding myself that if she could do it to them, she could do it to me.

"Yup, that just about sums it up."

"And if monsieur could share with us what your employer is prepared to pay...?"

Sonny-Boy was definitely interested now. I shook my head and shrugged.

"Sorry. My employer was very adamant about that. No discussion of price until the object is located. But I can assure you," I hoped my smile didn't look as phony as it was, "he is willing to pay top dollar."

"Of course," replied Marcel the Younger with a slight bow. "What is it?"

The raspy voice came from the wizened figure still bent over the image on my smart phone.

I shrugged again. "I'm sorry. I'm really not at liberty to say any more."

"Not at liberty or don't know?"

He didn't pull any punches.

"Take your pick." I took the phone back and started to put it in my pocket, but he held up one age-spotted hand, then gestured to his son and pointed to a large leather-bound book on the shelf behind him. His son retrieved the book and the old man took it and began flipping through the pages until he came to one with pictures on one side and text on the other. He stabbed a gnarled finger on a black-and-white photo next to a faded color one. "Is that it? The same image on your phone?"

I bent down to look and smelled his old-man smell of mothballs, tobacco and expensive cologne.

"Looks like it." It was a washed-out, tinted copy of the same black-and-white picture Aron had sent me. This color one I'd never seen before. "You know where is then?"

He made a sound that might have been a laugh forty years ago.

"I know where it was. This picture was taken before the war when it was on display in the Berlin Museum. Shortly after, it was removed from the display on ancient Mesopotamia and was rumored to have become a part of Himmler's private collection."

His information tallied with what Aron had told me.

"Where did it end up after the war, and where is it now?" I pressed him, remembering that Aron said old Marcel had bought it from a fleeing Nazi, but also knowing Marcel wouldn't answer unless it suited his purpose.

And he didn't. Not really.

"Well, as I'm sure your employer knows, it is not on display in any museum. Therefore, I would imagine it is in the hands of some private collector."

His expression was bland but his eyes were watchful. He was doing the same thing I did. He was checking my reaction.

I responded as evenly as I could. "And do you happen to know who this 'private collector' might be?"

"Perhaps."

He leaned back and briefly closed his eyes. When he opened them again they were blank. "And now you must forgive me, but I am an old man and I need my lunch followed by a long nap." He waved us away towards the door, but as I turned away he said, "Come back tomorrow at 5:30 just before we close. Perhaps we'll have some information for you."

I nodded and held the door for Celeste, and before it closed, she looked back at the old man and blew him a kiss.

Chapter Thirty-Three

I spent most of the next day moping around the streets and cafés on the Left Bank while waiting for someone to contact me about something—anything. Ironically, it was the guys who had chased me across two continents I now found myself waiting to hear from. They had Kat, and they wanted something from me, or Max, or both of us. I only hoped that when they finally made up their minds, whether it was the flash drive or the mysterious "key," whatever the hell that really turned out to be, I'd have it.

I wanted to stop brooding and go see some mindless tourist sites like Nôtre Dame, the Louvre, or even throw pebbles off the Pont Neuf; anything to take my mind off it. But it was no good. Every time I tried to focus on something else, Kat's sweet face formed before my eyes. Even worse, sometimes, as I was drifting off into a daydream, another face hovered just outside the gate of the place where we keep those warm memories. Celeste.

By the time 5 p.m. rolled around, I'd gone through three or four draft beers and was almost wishing I smoked, partially out of boredom and partially because I was in a mood to blow smoke into someone else's face for a change.

It was only a few blocks to Thibodeaux's, so I walked and got there at about twenty past. The appointment was for 5:30, but I didn't feel like waiting. I went toward the offices at the back of the store and the door that read: M. Thibodeaux – Private. I pushed it open and froze.

Leaning against the ornate wooden desk was Celeste. She had her back to me and hadn't heard me come in. But the old man had and gave me a knowing, thin-lipped smile. He also continued doing what had brought me to a dead stop torn between anger and disgust. She leaned on the desk next to him, both hands gripped tightly on the desktop while his parchment-like hand traced lazy circles up and down her thigh. He squeezed the soft flesh at the top of her stockings.

"No," she whispered.

I don't know how long I stood there. Probably no more than a minute, but it felt like an hour. Finally, I heard Celeste whisper in a hoarse voice thick with shame and pleading.

"Please, Oncle Marcel, please don't. No more, please."

That broke the spell of my indecision.

"Hey, Marcel, you old perv. Didn't you hear her? Knock it off!"

It probably wasn't the best way of getting the old goat to help me, but it was either that or pound the crap out of an nonagenarian. The hand and his smile stayed right where they were, but Celeste whirled around and turned bright crimson.

"How long have you been...what did you see? I mean, *think* you saw? Whatever it was, it is not what you think. I was only—I mean, my oncle and I were just talking and—"

She ran out of words. I walked over to the desk and sat down in the chair. I wasn't interested in signing on to some pleasant fiction of pretending to buy her lies. We all knew what was going on, and the question "why" would have to wait for later. Right now, I was there for answers.

While Celeste searched for an explanation that didn't exist, the old man regarded me with a mixture of amusement and contempt.

"You have much to say for a man who approaches me as a supplicant."

"First of all, in case you've forgotten, I'm the fucking client here. I mean, my employer is." We both knew that was a lie, and he'd decided to let me know it too.

"I know all about Aron the Jew who is no more." The eyes narrowed until he looked more like a rattlesnake than a man—probably a good analogy. "I did business with many of his tribe before the war." The snake eyes sparkled. "You know how it is always said that the Jews made good business, but then, with the specter of the Third Reich at their shoulder, they had to take what they could get. And what they got was me."

His eyes rose to the ceiling as he recalled. "I bought the best of old Europe's art, literature, fine wines, and property. At the beginning of the war it was the desperate Jews who came to me, and at the end of the war it was the Nazis."

He leaned forward in his chair. "They lost. All of them. And I won—everything." His breathing was labored and I could see his chest rising and falling like a runner's. Suddenly he stopped, took a ragged breath, and sat back.

"Yes, I won everything. Everything except one thing. Just one. The most important thing." He turned and stared at Celeste as if his gaze could burn her to cinders. "But I will have that one thing, n'est pas, ma belle Celeste?"

Her blush of humiliation turned into pale fear. She looked at me with frightened, pleading eyes, as if somehow I could liberate her from chains I couldn't see or understand. Somehow, in some sick way, this obscene, old man had a hold on her, and she was asking me for help I didn't know how to give.

He glared at me defiantly. This was some kind of a contest to him.

Without breaking his eyes from mine he said, "Celeste, come here and...sit on my lap."

There were tears of shame in her eyes as she shook her head. "No, Marcel, I won't. No more. I am not your whore."

He laughed. "You don't tell me what you are not. You are whatever I say you are. And that is, yes, a whore." He reached out a closed, claw-like hand around her wrist. "My whore. Just like when you were a little girl whose parents left with her 'kindly, old Oncle Marcel.'" His yellowed fingernails pressed into her wrist drawing thin lines of red that oozed from her skin. "Do you remember all the secret, grown-up games we used to play, chérie?"

That broke her. He had meant it to. She put her face into both hands and sobbed the sorrow of the doomed and damned; the ones who have been abused to the point that they can never, will never, break away from their tormentors.

And that was what the old bastard wanted me to see. He had total control over this girl and could make her do whatever he wanted, regardless of how sick or demeaning.

Still watching me with amused contempt, he spoke without raising his voice. "And now, ma petite fille douce, you will remove your blouse and skirt so you can show our friend all of the talented things you used to do for me when you were a little girl."

With dead and defeated eyes she turned her back to me and began unbuttoning her blouse.

I lost it.

I forgot about Kammler, I forgot about Max, the Bell, Ria, the key...and even Kat. All I could think about was smashing the sneering face in front of me to a bloody pulp.

He saw it too, but he was ready. He stabbed down the brass button beside the phone.

"Marcel, Jacques, Stephen, come in here, immédiatement."

Almost as if they'd been waiting for his call, the back door burst open and his son flanked by two huge bruisers burst into the room.

I was dead meat and thought with surprising calm, *That's what you get for trying to play Galahad, asshole.*

I had nothing to fight with and nowhere to run. So this was the way it ended: getting the livin' shit kicked out of me in a back room in Paris. Sorry, Kat. And sorry, Celeste, too. Next time choose a guy who's more like Bruce Willis or James Bond.

I shrugged at Celeste and put on my best tough-guy face, prepared to give the best account I could while they were beating the crap out of me.

The two goons moved toward me but suddenly...

The sound of an open palm striking dried old flesh.

"Cochon! You pig! Know this. You have had your way with me for years, but if you harm him, I will cut off your parts while you sleep and choke you with them!"

The old man stared at her, and for the first time I noticed a glimmer of fear on his face. "You wouldn't dare." He blustered, but I could tell that deep down he knew she meant every word she said.

The two men looked around for instructions. His son nodded, but his father held up his palm and shook his head.

"This is what you want, Celeste? This?" He pointed at me with contempt.

"Yes." Her voice came out in a whisper but it dropped like a stone in the quiet room.

He shrunk like a punctured balloon. Whatever hold he'd had on her for so long, was broken, at least for now.

"Go." He pointed at the door and she moved towards me. "Wait!" His eyes glittered with one last malicious thrust. He pointed at Celeste. "I hope my little slut is worth it, because you've just forfeited what you seek and the girl you love will now not be saved."

The sneer was back in control and he was going to deny me...wait...

How did the old bastard know I'm looking for Kat?

"'Girl I love?' I didn't say anything about a girl. What makes you think I—"

He held up one liver-spotted, yellow hand. "Please, don't make yourself look more foolish than you already appear. There is nothing that goes on in the unseen world of Paris I do not know about." The sneer deepened to malicious contempt. "But now, you never will."

I tried to think of something brave and cool to say, but I had the sickening feeling the old bastard was right. I'd blown it.

The pair of heavies pushed us toward the door and shoved us outside. It closed behind us, and the click of the lock confirmed that I had well and truly fucked it up.

Chapter Thirty-Four

"Christophe?"

I kept walking.

"Chris!"

The staccato sound of high heels on the sidewalk rushed up behind me. I continued walking until I felt a hand on my shoulder. I spun around.

"What!"

She stood in front of me, tears rolling down her cheeks and streaking her mascara. "I'm so sorry. You have lost your chance to get what you were seeking, and it's all because of me."

I couldn't argue there. I turned back and resumed walking.

This time she moved ahead and planted herself squarely in front of me. "And because of that, I am willing to do whatever is necessary to help you regain that information. Even…" She took a deep breath and swallowed hard. "Even if it means submitting to my oncle, again."

She looked at me for some reaction: gratitude, disgust, indifference? I don't know. I really didn't want to think about any of it any more.

"Look, Celeste, I don't know what perverted shit you've got going on between you and your so-called uncle. I don't really want to know. But let's get one thing straight: you don't owe me anything. I don't like your uncle or whoever the hell he really is, and I probably would have gotten pissy with him even without him putting his hands all over you. If I helped you out, fine. You helped me, or tried to anyway, and I reciprocated. We're even."

An early evening wind gusted down the street and I turned up the collar of my old leather jacket. Celeste shivered but left the long coat unbuttoned.

"If you'll excuse me, I've got a kidnapped girlfriend to find, some refugees from the Third Reich to confound, all preceded by some serious drinking. Bon soir to you, Mademoiselle, and I hope you have a nice life."

I didn't wait for her reaction. She could either like it or lump it, as they used to say, and at that moment, I didn't care which one she chose.

I had only walked a few steps when the sounds of crying behind me turn into sobs.

Don't turn around. Don't turn around! I kept repeating to myself, but it was no good. Despite all my right-brain advice, I couldn't leave her crying on the street corner. I turned around, walked the three steps back to her, and she threw herself into my arms, her breath coming in ragged sobs.

"Merci, Christophe, thank you, thank you."

We walked a few steps with her clutching my arm like a life preserver, which is probably what it was for her. Soon we found ourselves in front of a small neighborhood brasserie.

"C'mon," I said. "Let's open a bottle of something and you can talk if you want to."

And she did want to.

She was ripe for a catharsis and I was there. For the next two hours she walked back down the alleyways of her life and I tried to make sense of stuff I'd only read about. Stuff like impoverished aristocrats who couldn't give up the trappings of faded wealth and power, Euro-trash ennui, laissez-faire parenting, and twisted pleasure.

"I suppose it started long before I was even aware of it, when I was a little girl, eight or nine. Back then, my dear 'Oncle Marcel' was a frequent visitor to the crumbling chateaux that used to be the Sainte-d'Aignau seat of power. By the time my father had inherited it, the only thing left of the once-great name was a rundown pile of bricks and mortar and debts.

"I am not saying my parents formally approved of Marcel's wandering fingers every time I sat on his lap to accept the candy, and later jewelry, he brought me whenever he came to visit. But what I do know was that by the time I had reached puberty, I no longer wished to accept Oncle Marcel's presents, or even be around when he visited. However, he always insisted I be there. I can't say for certain if my parents knew about what went on. Even if they suspected, they did nothing. They were too dependent on their distant relative for money and invitations to the best parties and smartest social set.

"By the time I went off to a girls' boarding school, all I could feel about my parents was resentment and betrayal, but mostly relief because, except for summers and holidays, I didn't have to see them or my hideous 'Oncle Marcel.'" She smiled grimly and took a long drink of wine. "But I should have known even at that young age I could never truly escape him." She shuddered. "I still needed someone to pay my tuition, room, board, and clothing, and it certainly was not going to be my parents." She stared down at the tabletop and closed her eyes tightly. "But the one great lesson I learned, well before my eighteenth birthday, was that nothing in life is free." She opened her eyes and stared through me, her expression blank. "Everything comes with a price. Everything."

* * * *

By the time we finished the bottle it was after midnight. She asked me if I'd walk her home. Why not? I had nothing worth robbing, and it might even feel good to hit someone or something. But there were no incidents, and fifteen minutes later we arrived at a fashionable, six-story building of flats. She turned the key in the lock.

"Will you come in?" And when I hesitated she added quickly. "Just to make sure Marcel has not sent anyone to bring me to him."

"Sure, no problem."

But after I'd given the flat a cursory check and turned to go, she stood in front of the door.

"I don't know how to thank you, Christophe, for listening and everything else you've done for me tonight, but I have one last favor to ask of you."

I sighed. "What?"

"Please...make love to me."

* * * *

Here's where I could wax poetic about how frail and fickle the human heart is, but to spare us all a lot of extraneous bullshit, I'll leave it at this: we screwed our brains out.

Now, this is not to say that I didn't find myself more than just a bit in love with her before, during, and after. But in retrospect, I suspect it was one of the never-ending self-image make-over attempts to assuage my guilt and make myself feel less of a cheating horn-dog and more like a Galahad, bringing comfort to the bereft and hurting.

Right.

For her part, Celeste woke me with a smile, coffee, and nothing else.

"*Bon matin, Monsieur* Sleepy-head."

"And a boney Martin to you too, sweet thing."

I yawned and sat up as she handed me the coffee in a big yellow mug with hand painted flowers intertwined around the rim. The coffee was hot and strong and would have been absolutely perfect had I not been feeling just a tad guilty for cheating on Kat. Even though, as I tried to rationalize, we had never come to any kind of exclusive agreement. The conscious part of my brain, where we store our excuses and self-delusion, was perfectly content with that explanation. But my subconscious wasn't buying it and was making it increasingly uncomfortable to stay lounging around in her bed. I got up and figured I'd better get dressed and go before she started asking uncomfortable questions like—

"Christophe? May I ask you something?"

Too late.

"Ahh, can we save it for later? I really need to get going, here."

She continued as though she hadn't heard me.

"It's about last night."

Isn't it always?

"Despite what I told you about all of the encounters with my horrid uncle, I am not someone who easily sleeps around."

I said nothing, concentrating on looking as non-judgmental as possible, but she mistook my bland expression for skepticism and quickly continued.

"In other words, in spite of my childhood, or maybe because of it, I am no coquette. You know. What you Americans call a 'slut.'"

"Hey, no argument here. I think you rock."

She smiled. "I'm glad, and I hope you don't think I am being too forward or trying to put words in your mouth."

I didn't like where this was going.

"So, I guess I will simply ask you." She took a deep breath. "Do you love me? Because I think I am falling in love with you."

Crap.

I took a sip of coffee to give me time to think. I was pretty sure it wasn't love, but then again, it wasn't only lust either. I took another sip and looked at her. A definite fox, no argument there, but love?

"Look, Celeste, last night was great, but I'm really involved with someone else. Like I told you, she's the main reason I'm here in the first place."

She smiled sadly. "And so we have merely la hook-up, oui?

I shrugged. "Look, I never said—"

She sat down on the bed and kissed me into silence. "Shush, you're right. No promises, no commitments. Just whatever the moment brings us."

* * * *

Yes, I enjoyed it. And yes, I felt guilty, but what could I do? What would you do?

To be honest, the more I was with Celeste, the more I started to think that maybe, despite my best intentions, perhaps I was falling in love with her. Think of it. Six months ago, I was a horny, lonely bachelor. Now, I was in love with two girls. No, make that three if you count the continually appearing-and-disappearing Ria.

But at the end of the day, I was here for Kat, and that meant I had to figure out how I was gonna get that old bastard Marcel to help me locate the key.

It was Celeste who finally came up with the answer.

But in the meantime, proving once again not only is the "spirit willing but the flesh weak," I discovered that, in my case, the spirit was wishy-washy and the flesh downright enthusiastic at the prospect of another round of bedroom Olympics with Celeste. Thus late afternoon found me in the spot I'd awakened in the morning.

Celeste lay next to me, one silver-painted fingernail tracing lazy circles on my chest.

"I know you won't say you love me, Christophe, and I understand why. But I think secretly, deep down in here you do, maybe a little?" Her finger rested on my heart.

I shrugged. "Maybe even more than a little."

That earned me a long, passionate kiss, which I'm not complaining about, but it wasn't why I said it. I said it because it was, unfortunately, true. Unfortunate because my heart, supposing I still had much of one left, was centered on Kat. But my body, that easily distracted thing, was becoming more and more captivated with the lovely Celeste.

Almost as if she could sense this and wanted to ensnare my soul and the corporal parts of my anatomy, she sat up.

"I've been thinking, and I am more convinced than ever that the only hope we have of obtaining what you seek is to get Marcel to tell me."

"Ah, I don't know… I mean, from what you told me and what I've seen, there is no way I could let you go back to being a pervert's plaything."

She hugged her knees and regarded me with a fatalistic expression. "Why not? What else could he do to me that he has not done before? At least now, I am prepared for it and no longer blame myself for being the object of his lust."

I shook my head. "That's pretty fuckin' bleak."

"As is most of life, n'est ce pas?"

"I can't ask you to do it." I repeated for the tenth time in as many hours. But truth be told, each time I said it, I became less adamant…because she was right. It was the only way.

"But how will you do it? After last night when you threatened him and walked out with me, he'll think you're bullshitting him to get information."

"I will use the twin motives he understand best: hatred and revenge."

"Huh?"

"I will tell him you told me you loved me, so I went off with you, but after you had used me for a while as your plaything, you discarded me with scorn. He will understand that. Then when I tell him I want to get even with you and make you suffer, he'll be only too glad to give me whatever I ask for to help me do this."

"And that is?"

"The whereabouts of the mysterious key, which I will tell him I want to use to torment you with by promising it to you, and then force you to corrupt yourself and your beliefs to get it."

"Wow. Old Mr. Machiavelli has nothing on you."

She grinned mischievously. "A girl learns a thing or two along the way."

"OK. When do we put this grand plan into action?"

She snuggled back down against me. "We have already begun. Old Marcel will have his spies watching the building. When we don't leave the apartment for several days, he will know what is happening."

She moved closer until her lips brushed mine and whispered, "All you have to do, my bel homme, is make love to me."

Ummm, yup. I could handle that.

* * * *

And that was where we stayed for the next two days, interrupted only by two quick trips for refreshments when Celeste noticed that Marcel's creeps had taken a café break.

One of the great advantages of being with someone who has not only intimate knowledge of your body but of the local environs as well, is you wind up at the places those in-the-know love best. The first of our little forays, "to keep our strength up," as she put it, was to an incredible place on the Rue Bonaparte called, Pierre Herme, a place selling nothing but cookies! Well, macaroons to be precise, but you'd have thought they were all baked with gold leaf judging by the clamoring crowds waving Euros around the cases filled with round cookies in every pastel color you could think of. Not being much a cookie aficionado, I didn't really get it. I asked Celeste what the big deal was.

"Mmmm, chéri, they are so heavenly, they are almost better than sex." Seeing my skeptical expression, she squeezed my hand and giggled. "Almost."

We got a bag full of little round biscuits with exotic names like, Infiniment Prailine, Noisette, and Huile D'Olive a La Madrarine. And while they didn't even come in a close second to sex, I gotta admit they weren't bad.

Our next stop almost lived up to the hype and upscale surroundings. A candy store, or to be more precise, a chocolate shop called Patrick Roger, who apparently styled himself as an Artist et Artisan du Gout, which loosely translated means the guy is a craftsman of good taste. Okaaaay... On the other hand, he made damn fine chocolate that was both obscenely expensive but good to the same degree, and labeled it with enticing names only the French could come up with such as Audace, Vanuatu, and Jacarepagus. Whew!

The third night together, our chocolate and sex-filled idyll came to an abrupt end. I was awakened by Celeste's hand on my shoulder.

"Christophe, wake up!"

"Huh? Whazzup?" I looked at the alarm clock: 3 a.m. "Damn, it's the middle of the fucking night!"

She thrust a plain envelope into my hand.

"I heard a noise at the door, and when I went to check, I found this had been pushed under it."

Still half asleep, I tore it open. I had to read it through a few times before it registered, and when I did, I wished I hadn't.

Been having fun? It's time for you to end your carnal interlude and decide if you want your girlfriend back or if you want her back in pieces—a little at a time.

If not, you will bring us the item in question by no later than 10pm on Friday. Take an outdoor table at the Café Deux Magots at Place Saint-Germain des Prés. You will be contacted.

I turned the letter over several times, but that was it—nothing on the other side. No watermarks or handy hotel return addresses to make my life as the eternal chump a little fairer.

"You say you got up and found this pushed under the door?"

A nod.

"But you also said you heard a noise. Did you open the door and check the hallway?"

Vigorous shake of the head. "I was too frightened, Christophe. That's why I woke you."

I nodded absently. Couldn't blame her. She sat down on the bed next to me and put her arms around me.

"I know you are afraid for your girlfriend and must concentrate on freeing her." She looked down at the floor. "And if I am to be completely honest, I must tell you that part of me wishes you did not love her so much, and then you could maybe love me a little."

She raised her head and looked at me. Her eyes wet with tears. "But know this, I will do everything in my power to help you save her." She swallowed hard. There was pain in her eyes but it was said with great determination. "Even if it means giving up everything. Including my life."

Shit, what could I say? I pulled her close and held her until we both drifted into an uneasy sleep.

* * * *

She left for the antique shop at 8 a.m. saying she wanted to see old Marcel before his son arrived at 9 a.m. I couldn't stand waiting around her apartment and decided it would be a good time to visit my unused hotel room I was still paying for. I almost checked out. After all, I was practically living with Celeste. But halfway through packing my single bag, I paused. It might be a good idea to have somewhere to take Kat when I got her back. She'd probably want a shower and a place to rest and change and...

Yeah, I was taking a lot for granted. Worse still, I wasn't prepared to think about how I was going to kick my Celeste habit once I had Kat back in my life. And naturally, that nasty little bugger of rationalization kept whispering in my ear, *Hey, who says you have to give her up? What Kat doesn't know won't bother her.*

Not a good way to go into a plan that was gonna take all my wits and the full remains of my A.D.D. addled attention to detail.

But I was getting ahead of events and myself. Before concerning myself with love triangles, I needed to concentrate on what I hoped would be a straight line to getting Kat back safe and sound.

I left everything the way it was and walked slowly to the outdoor café in the Luxemburg Gardens where Celeste and I had chosen to meet after her tête à tête with Marcel. And I found myself hoping, for my sake as much as hers, Marcel would limit his discussion to head-to-head rather than letting his sticky fingers do the walking. Was I getting jealous? I answered with big mental, *No!* But I was no longer sure.

Between dueling visions of Kat and Celeste, I was in a fine state of anxiety by the time Celeste showed up around 11:30.

"Well?" Were the first apprehensive words out of my mouth.

She placed her purse on the wire table and took out a cigarette. After lighting it and drawing in a deep lungful of smoke, she looked at me with a small, weary smile.

"It's done."

"What's done? You? Me? The possibility of getting our hands on the key or ever seeing Kat alive again?"

Shaking her head she took another deep drag. "No, nothing like that. I simply meant it is done between me and Marcel." She closed her eyes. "I am back in his...good graces."

She almost spat the last words. I could only guess what that accomplishment must have cost her in dignity and God knows what else.

I cleared my throat. "Look, Celeste, I hope you didn't have to...you know...on account of me..."

She smiled the sad smile again. "What is the expressions you Americans use all the time? 'Don't ask, don't tell.'"

She stubbed her cigarette out and got up holding out her hand to me. "Come. Dear 'Oncle' Marcel wants to give us both the details in locating the key in person. No doubt he wishes to gloat to you about having me back under his thumb, but no matter, what is done is done. We must claim our reward and damn the consequences, eh, chéri?"

As I fell into step along side of her and we exited the park, I continued to wonder if the consequences were just beginning.

Chapter Thirty-Five

By the time we arrived at the shop, the two smirking assistants/goons/bodyguards informed us with great pleasure that Marcel had already eaten his lunch and was now having his afternoon nap and we should come back in an hour. We walked across the street where I had two cognacs in quick succession before Celeste waved off the waiter.

"Please, Christophe, I know you are upset, but you must be prepared to keep your feelings restrained when talking to Marcel. Please, *ma chéri*, try to allow me to do the talking. Instead of allowing Marcel to goad you, think of the reward when we find your darling."

I nodded, but the price we were paying might be too damn high and might be paid by the wrong person.

It was almost two by the time we were finally seated in the stale-smelling office. I sat there in front of the desk while Marcel studied our faces, trying to see how deeply he could humiliate us before he finally paid off on his side of the bargain. I tried to keep my features calm and concentrate on unclenching my jaw so it didn't look as though I was about to leap from my chair and rip out his scrawny, mottled neck with my teeth. The thought was appealing, however.

With a satisfied smirk, he picked up the folder from his desk and began to read from his notes.

"One morning in late 1945, I opened my old shop on the Rue Danton; not as large or fashionable as what you see around you." He raised a hand to indicate the opulent surroundings. "But then, I had just started to appreciate the many benefits that could be had by doing business with all types of clients."

"Yeah, you told us already. You were an equal opportunity crook."

Celeste pinched my leg and shot me a look, but Marcel was feeling generous in victory.

"Crook? Certainly not, *monsieur*. Like all other good businessmen, I merely was providing a very necessary service. Only after the war, it was the Bosche who were coming to me hat in hand to sell their artworks."

"Which they had plundered from all over Europe." I deadpanned, earning me another stricken look from Celeste. But I couldn't help it, I was barely holding it together.

He shrugged. "That, of course, was not my concern, as long as they could show me some sort of document which proved ownership." He smiled. "And before you bother to say it, yes, many of those documents were probably forged or coerced from their former owners in the Nazi death camps." His smile got wider. "But as I said, that was not my concern. On this particular morning, when I came to open the shop, there was a man waiting for me in the doorway. He was a short, squat, rather brutal looking man, who appeared to have been someone very prosperous under the Nazis. But the way his clothes hung off his stocky frame, I guessed he was not doing well any more. And of course, he had something to sell. When I sat him in my office and gave him a cup of coffee, which he drank in one gulp, he unwrapped a small package about 12 centimeters by 25, consisting of what looked to me like a black velvet cloth typically used to display objects at high end jewelers or museums.

"As soon as I saw it, I knew it was valuable. It was the same object that is in your picture and those two photographs I showed you. I also knew it had come from the pre-war Ancient Sumerian collection in the Berlin Museum that had been expropriated by Himmler. I was also sure the man who wanted to sell it to me had probably stolen it from Himmler after he committed suicide at the end of the war.

"I told him all of this. And that I was sorry, but as the item was most probably stolen from a museum collection, it was something the art history unit of the US Army would be coming after, and I could not take the chance and must bid him a good day. He was quite put out and desperate to raise money for a Vatican passport to South America, so he named a laughably small price for the object."

Marcel sighed, and for the first time, looked genuinely sad. "I was, regrettably, very ambitious and rather too greedy in those days. I was sure that given twenty-four hours to let him stew, I could pick the object up for half the sum he had named. So I told him to return in twenty-four hours and I would give him my final decision on the price I would pay. What I did not know, was that I was not the only dealer whose name he had been given.

"When he failed to return the next day, I sent word to some of my contacts to discover his whereabouts. Two days later, they did. Apparently, after he left me, he had gone to a shop owned by a well-respected and knowledgeable dealer before and during the war who did not like the Nazis and refused to buy the art they stole from the Jews they deported to the camps. His actions raised ire in the wrong places, and one of them turned him in to the Gestopo for being a *mischling*, having Jewish blood, and he died in a camp. Unfortunately, they did not include his daughter in the deportation and she survived the war and took over his shop. She naturally hated all Nazis, and even more, those who did business with them."

"Like you," I said.

"Yes." He nodded. "Like me. In any event, she was determined to wreak vengeance upon me and tried to do it by out-bidding me on every piece that came on the legitimate market. But I never thought in my wildest dreams she hated me so much that she would out bid me for a piece of Nazi plunder. But she did.

"When I discovered the wretched little man had sold her the Sumerian 'key,' I went to see her and offered her what I thought would be a handsome profit. Fool that I was, I should have realized vengeance was more important to her than money. She nearly spat in my face and ordered me from her shop.

"So I did what I usually did when confronted by someone who was not prepared to be reasonable. I sent my associates, the fathers of these two," he pointed to his two goons, "to convince the young lady to see reason. Unfortunately, she did not, and her recalcitrant attitude put my associates in a bad mood. They put her in the hospital where a few months later, she died. But before she did, she sent word to me that she had made a bequest to the Louvre of much of her stock, including the 'key,' where it would be under the same guards who protected the most precious art treasures in the world. I have spent the past sixty-eight years trying, unsuccessfully, to get my hands on it."

Shadows of anger and frustrations crossed his face, but then he smiled wider than before. "But now, because I am a man of my word and I promised my dear Celeste to set you on the path to acquiring the piece, I invite you to go to the Louvre and politely ask them to put it into your virtuous hands."

He laughed and motioned for his flunkies to show us the door.

As the door clicked closed behind us, I heard him call out, "*Bonne chance, mes enfants.*"

* * * *

Back at my hotel, we took a small marble-topped table in the dimly lit walnut paneled bar.

"I confess," I said to Celeste. "I've hit a brick wall. Maybe I should pack it in, fly to Boston, and try and see if I can pick up any trace of the only person who can guide me through this hopeless maze of blind alleys and enigmas. Max."

"Don't give up." She told me, giving my hand a squeeze.

"In less than twenty-four hours, unless I can come up with some ancient piece of bling that rests alongside some of the most closely guarded items in the world, those bastards are going to start chopping pieces off of Kat. Even if by some miracle I could manage to get my hands on it, I don't even know what it is or why so many people are willing to kill for it."

"I can't help you with that, *mon couer*, but I think there is a way we can find out."

"How? Walk in the Louvre and say, 'Hi. You've got a stolen art treasure we'd like to steal back, and oh, if it's not too much trouble, could you tell us all about it?'"

The corner of her mouth turned up slightly. "*Oui, chéri,* that is exactly what I am saying."

So color me surprised. How the hell was she gonna pull that off? Of course, if I'd thought about it, I'd have realized right away that, this being France and the world being such as it is, there was only one way.

"Celeste, you don't have to do this you know."

"Yes I do. You already said no other path is open to us, and you must have it to trade for your *petite amie, n'est ce pas*?"

"Yeah, but you've already had to do this once."

She leaned over and kissed me on the cheek. "Then I should be getting quite good at by now, *oui*?"

We walked on toward the Louvre in silence. I couldn't think of anything else to say and she couldn't think of anything else to do to get what I needed in the short time we had left.

I turned my coat collar against the damp mist blowing in off the Seine and watched her out of the corner of my eye. Christ, how many girls would make themselves a whore to get their lover something that would save his girlfriend—her rival?

That, of course, was the plan she'd come up with. She was going to use her body again to bail out my useless ass. She knew a curator her lecherous old uncle had introduced her to, and based on the way he'd drooled over her, she was certain, given the opportunity of spending a little one-on-one time with her in return for letting her "borrow" one of the pieces that was probably gathering dust in some storeroom, it would be no contest.

I was grateful and guilty in equal measures. No, make that mostly guilty, which was rapidly becoming my default setting. Twice she'd had to fuck fossils in as many days, but what could I do? The only other option was letting Kat get cut into small chunks by sadists. But I was gonna come out of this thing owing Celeste big time. And not only that, I was starting to believe if I'd never met Kat, the girl walking beside me, one hand wrapped around mine, might have been The One.

When we got to the Louvre, a guard met us at the entrance of the big glass pyramid and led us through a dizzying maze of corridors and exhibit halls until we came to a series of offices off to themselves in quiet wing.

The guard knocked on one marked H. Merchant, Directeur: Antiquités Sumériens.

"*Entrer.*"

To say that the director of the Sumerian department was a "large man" was to short change plus sizes everywhere. He must have weighed close to three-fifty, and when he tried to pull himself out of the chair to stand to welcome us, and he ended by panting like he'd run a marathon. Celeste smiled prettily and beamed when he kissed her hand like some portly knight of old.

"Welcome, welcome *ma chérie*, so nice to see you again. And how is your charming *oncle*?"

That's when I knew he was a perv too... "charming uncle" my ass.

Celeste kept up the pretense, and after a few minutes of mindless pleasantries during which his eyes never left her boobs, we finally settled down to business—at least ours.

"So," he said, gesturing to a large, plain, wooden box on his desk, "you wish to know about this piece we acquired at the end of the war?"

"*Oui*, Monsieur Director, my friend and I are collaborating on an article for *le Monde* and wish to know anything about this unusual object that you could tell us. There seems to be very little about it from the German archives from the mid-thirties."

"Understandable." He nodded. "Most of the archives were destroyed in the Allied bombings of '44 and '45, and from what has been rumored, the ones who knew most about this, perished during the fighting."

"So there's nothing you can tell us?" He wasn't pleased by my interruption and let me know it.

"I didn't say that, young man, and if you would let me continue, I was about to tell you what we do know."

I shut up.

He opened the box and removed a cloth wrapping revealing a clear plastic tube. He popped one end open with his thumbnail and carefully lifted out the object I'd seen only in pictures until now. It was as described, but somehow looked bigger sitting in front of us. And while it looked like a ring, it wouldn't have fit any finger I'd ever seen. It was as long as my hand.

"Monsieur Director..."

"Please, Mademoiselle, it's Henri, and may I call you Celeste?"

She smiled at him and went on. "I was wondering, Henri, what do you suppose this could have been made for? It looks like a ring, but it is too long, and is likewise too narrow to fit on the wrist as a bracelet."

"Ah, but you are closer than you know, *chérie*. According to the few documents that were made public when it was discovered on a Nazi state-sponsored dig, at least two of the archeologists claimed it was a ring of great power worn by the old race god-men who purportedly brought civilization to Sumer."

Max and Aron had told me this too. But there were a few things bothering me about Henri's explanation.

"But if that's true," I said, "then wouldn't they have had to have been well over ten feet tall to have a finger like that?"

"According to an Osteopath and forensic pathologist, close to three meters."

I whistled. "And you said 'ring of power.' Unless it was owned by Frodo Baggins, what could it have been used for?"

He didn't dignify my Tolkien pop-culture reference with an acknowledgement but said, "Again, monsieur, I can only repeat what the German documents claimed; that these superior beings were not of this world and had been coming to Earth for thousands, perhaps millions of years. They had taken an interest in mankind, and according to some speculations, they had even used some of their genetic material to created hybrid humans, of which we are the result, and were doling out to our ancestors such bits of their technology as they felt was appropriate and safe."

"But what about the ring?"

He drummed his fingers on the desktop. "I was coming to that if you'll allow me to continue. Hmmm, where was I? Ah, yes, the ring. It was purportedly to be, in reality, one of the devices the Anunnaki used to communicate with their miraculous technology and with each other."

"And how did that work?"

"Based on Mademoiselle's comments on the phone, I anticipated you would ask. Let me call your attention to the black stone on the table."

He indicated a dull black stela about three feet by four feet, resting on a wide Empire-style table. It was covered with cuneiform writing and strange drawings. I recognized it from somewhere, but where? Then it came to me.

"Max!"

"Pardon, monsieur?"

"Nothing, I just meant that thing looks like it's cool...to the max."

He looked at me strangely, obviously not buying it but not interested enough to pursue it. Celeste, on the other hand, looked at me as though she'd like a long and detailed explanation, which I wasn't prepared to give, especially not here. I tried to recall if any of our bedroom chats had included Max's role in my current mess, and while I was sure I'd mentioned him, I was equally certain that I'd never touched on anything connected to Max's participation in finding the stela. But from the way she cocked her head and looked at me. I was also sure that when we got out of here, she was going to ask.

"This artifact was apparently uncovered with the Anunnaki Ring, as some of the more fanciful members of the Anenherbe and Vril Society took to calling the spiral shaped relic," he said.

"Has the stela been translated?"

"Some of it, which is to say the portions that were written in the Sumerian language. The other parts are some sort of pre-language pictograms which have baffled our best linguists and philologists."

"So nobody really knows what it says?"

"I didn't say that, young man. A translation came to us when the piece was donated to us after the war. However, after careful scrutiny it was discovered that the translation of the protolanguage and cryptograms were done by a group of

German clairvoyants; the same group of women who claimed to be in psychic communication with the god-race of the ancient Sumerians, the Anunnaki. Ridiculous, of course, nothing but Nazi claptrap."

At this point I wasn't so sure anymore. "Just for the hell of it, do you have the translation the ladies worked out for Himmler?"

He snorted in place of a laugh but finally shuffled through a stack of papers on his desk and handed me one.

"It's a copy of the original documents that came with the items when Madame Frontenac donated the objects to us."

I started to read it but he waved his hand. "Please, monsieur, the hour grows late and other matters need my attention. You may keep that copy and examine the translation at your leisure."

I nodded, folded the two pages, and stuffed them into my jacket.

"And now..." He leaned back, looked meaningfully at Celeste, and put his hand on the desk. He made a tent of his sausage-like fingers and smiled at her with what I'm sure he thought was a debonair expression. "I believe you mentioned when you phoned that you wished to have a 'private' discussion about the possibility of borrowing the Sumerian ring. Is that correct, Mademoiselle Celeste?"

She stared straight ahead and nodded.

"Well then, monsieur." He motioned to me. "Perhaps you'd be so kind as to wait outside while Mademoiselle Celeste and I go over the details of how best to insure the safety of museum property." He pointed to the door. "We have an excellent exhibit in the next gallery of Mesopotamian artifacts from Ur which you might find interesting."

I wanted to smack the smirk off his fat face, but I had to play my part, so I got up, opened the door, and stepped outside.

For five eternal minutes I stood in the dim, silent gallery staring at the same clay pot and then suddenly, something snapped. I'd had it—really had it. I started back down the hall ready in one flash of anger to blow it all.

I gently eased the door open and saw him with his pants down around his ankles, both flabby arms enveloping Celeste's slight form.

"Hey, Slim, smile." I called, pulled out my phone, and snapped the picture.

He turned and my cell camera flashed again as he grabbed for his pants, but it was too late. I held up the cell, and with my finger scrolled the image open. I held it up to him. "Nice likeness, don't you think?"

He turned beet red.

"Both of you," he blustered, "leave this instant. The artifact stays here!"

I shook my head. "Nope, it goes with us. Fact is, the way I see it, you've just made us a gift of it."

"Why, I'll never allow you to take—"

"Or, I can click 'Send' and post this lovely shot of your fat ass to a hundred emails, web sites, and Twitter accounts." I held my thumb poised over the cell screen.

The color drained from his face. "Take it."

I held my hand out to Celeste and we left his office.

Chapter Thirty-Six

"Once again you come to my rescue, *mon amour*." She stood on tiptoes, kissed my cheek, and then giggled. "And in such a perfect way, *très amusant*. Serves him right, the fat fool." She wrapped both arms around my left one and leaned her head against my shoulder as we walked back over the Pont Neuf toward Saint-Michel.

We passed a small brassier.

"Coffee, wine...me?"

But before I could ask her for a double helping of the later, she pulled me through the frosted glass door and into the warm, smoke-laden air that smelled of onion soup, warm bread, and café au lait.

"Mmmm, it smells so nice in here, it's making me hungry. How about you, *mon coeur*?"

"Sure, I could eat something."

"Something" turned out to be one of my favorite peasant meals of onion soup, Camembert cheese, and a baguette of fresh baked artesian bread, all washed down with a bottle of very decent Cote de Rhone.

While we ate, we unwrapped the Sumerian ring, which apparently some called "the key," along with the Xerox copies of the translation, and started to read.

After a half hour of puzzling over the obscure references to star entities, the constellation Taurus, and the Aldebaran system, we were more confused than ever. Especially since I was trying to figure out where all the business of the "key" came in. All I could find was a reference that the tablet provided to more detailed instructions on how to use the key to contact the Anunnaki and access their technology. With more hope than was prudent, given my track record of lucky breaks, I read down to the bottom of the page:

...the high priest or one of the chosen ones who has been initiated into the rites of Aldebaran must take the key and place it... (continued on page 3).

I sat blinking at the table, foolishly holding one piece of paper in each hand. There was no page 3.

* * * *

And then it was time to go and make the hand-off to the bad guys.

I told Celeste, and of course she insisted on coming, but for some reason I said no.

"Why? I want to come and help in every way I can."

"Then stay here in case anything goes wrong. Besides, I think they want me to come alone."

"What makes you think so? They didn't say that in their note."

"Maybe not, but I kinda' got a feeling."

Truth was, she was right, but I felt this was something I needed to go solo on.

Celeste wasn't happy about it. Her eyes narrowed and I could see her struggle with herself not to say more. Finally, she bit the inside of her lip and forced a smile.

"Very well, Christophe. I will wait for you at my flat, but you must promise to call me the moment you've made the exchange."

"Of course."

We left the brasserie, and at the corner, headed in separate directions. There was no goodbye kiss.

* * * *

When I got to Deux Magot, it was crowded, but the weather was somewhat chilly for outdoors. I had no problem finding an outdoor table on the Saint-Germain side of the café where I had a good view of three sides of the intersection.

However, by the time I'd checked out the Rue Bonaparte side of the street and turned back, there was a man sitting at my table.

He didn't say anything. He didn't need to. I knew who he was. I recognized him as one of Kammler's thugs. He was of medium height and build and wore an old 1950's vintage, olive-colored raincoat that went with his buzz cut. But under the outward banality, evil radiated off him like the heat of those dark ovens had, day and night, in the SS death camps.

He wasted no time on introductions or anything else. "You have it?"

"That depends. Where is Kat?"

He shrugged. "You do not expect me to carry her here to this table like some sort of package, do you?"

"Then you don't get my 'package' until you bring yours."

His cold, barracuda eyes stared back at me. "In that case, we'll be happy to send her back to you. Which piece would you like first? Fingers, nose, eyes, tongue?"

The expression never changed. He meant what he said. The SS had no regard for human life. I suspected most of them were sociopathic sadists and I doubted seven decades had improved their inclination.

I tried not to let defeat show on my face, but it didn't matter. They knew I cared and they didn't. They had me.

"All right, but before I hand it over, I want to at least see that Kat's OK."

"How do you propose we do that? I told you she's not with me."

"You've got a cell, I'm sure. Call her. Better yet, have your buddies call my phone and put her on face time so I can see her."

He gave me another fish-eye stare and then pulled out his cell and dialed. He said something in rapid fire German, too fast for me to understand, with a guttural accent. He grunted, "*Ja*," then passed the phone to me.

"Hey, I said to put her on my phone."

"You're wasting the little time you have. Talk."

I was about argue some more, but suddenly Kat was on the screen.

"Kat! Are you all right?"

Her face was drawn, and she had deep dark circles under her eyes, unkempt hair, and I could tell she'd been crying, but she still looked beautiful. She tried to put on a brave face. "Yes. Oh God it's so good to see you. Are you OK?"

"Shit yeah. Listen, don't worry about me and don't worry about anything else either, 'cause I'm gonna get you out of there," I said with a confidence I didn't feel. "Are they taking care of you? I mean are you getting enough food and water and—"

"Chris?"

"Yeah, Kat. What can I do?"

"About the hotel and that girl and ... Well...I'm sorry. I mean, I didn't even give you a chance to talk and—" There was a catch in her throat. She was trying to hold back the tears. "And even if you were doing something with that girl, well, I don't own you. It's not like we have an exclusive thing. I mean it would be great if we did because... Oh Chris, I love you!" Tears rolled down her cheeks. "And I miss you so much! Oh please come and find me. I'm—"

The phone went dark and it was plucked from my fingers.

"All right, now you've seen her. Hand it over and we'll deliver her to this corner within an hour."

My heart sank. An hour? That meant they weren't even in Paris. Unless...they could be right around the corner and making me think they were farther away. But either way, I was going to have to give them what they asked for. Once I had Kat back, I was gonna chuck this whole damn thing, go back to Boston with her, and ask her if she'd like to share my roach-infested apartment on an "exclusive" basis.

I reached inside my jacket and placed the bundle in front of him. He unwrapped it to see the twisted, yellow cylinder. His flat expression turned into a frown. He felt the folds of the cloth.

"Where's the rest of it?"

"The rest of it? The rest of what? That's everything I've got. Your boss asked for the key doo-hickey, and this is it. What more could there be?"

He leaned towards me. His breath smelled of onions and stale beer. "The object that the key fits. They go together. One is useless without the other."

He dialed the phone again and spoke in sharp, angry bursts of guttural German again. I could hear a voice rising on the other end and he shoved the phone into my hands. It was the one who ran whatever game was being played.

"Are you Kammler?"

He didn't bother to answer.

"Ernst tells me you have come up short on our exchange."

"I don't know what the fuck you're talking about. You asked for the key gizmo and I got it."

"You didn't get the lock the key fits."

"Oh, for Christ's sake! What the hell is it?"

"The box of Queen Paubi, you fool. The one she sent to Bunefer!" There was a brief silence. Then, "On the off chance that Herr von Buchholz really didn't tell you, it is a box shaped like a half moon. It was mentioned in the translation of the stela he found with the ring. I understand you had a translation you obtained with the ring."

Shit. "Yeah, but it was missing the page explaining what it is or where or—"

"Enough. The problem is yours to solve, not mine. But remember, my patience is not endless. If you can't procure it, then I must eliminate our hostage and begin the search anew. It's now 10:30. You have twenty-four hours."

The screen went blank.

I looked up and the man called Ernst said, "I come for the box tomorrow, and if you don't have it, you may look for what will be left of the girl in the Seine."

* * * *

I don't remember the walk back to my hotel, but when I'd walked a few blocks, my phone rang. I ripped it out of my pocket hoping it was Kat. But it was Celeste.

"Christophe? Is everything all right? Did they meet you? Did you get your lover back?"

"No, yes and no. I don't know what the fuck is happening anymore."

"Where are you?"

I read the street name.

"You're only two blocks away. Come to me. Maybe I can find a way to help. I'll be waiting at the door."

* * * *

She met me at the door and threw herself into my arms. "*Mon pauvre*, Christophe. How could they do that to you? Build your hopes up only to snatch away your sweet Katrina at the last moment."

I said nothing. I was numb. She tried everything to get through to me, including the one thing that normally could always break through whatever ennui happened to be bogging down my passions: sex. But this time it didn't work. Maybe it was because I'd seen and spoken to Kat, but those few minutes shared on a couple of inches of screen brought me back to where I started. She was something special.

Celeste finally broke her embrace when she saw I wasn't responding and sighed. "You're upset, I know, I only wish there was something I could do."

I tried to smile. "Yeah, I know, and I appreciate it, really. But I'm just sort of out there in my own private ozone."

"How about a cup of tea? I've got some really nice yerba mate tea which always helps perk me up."

OK, sure. I could probably use it."

She went to the kitchen and I felt my cell buzz. Still hoping against rational thought that it could be Kat or her kidnappers, I fumbled it on and saw I had a text. I clicked message and read:

I know what has happened and I believe I know the object they want. I am going to send you an email explaining what it is and where I believe it can be found. Make sure you are alone when you read it and delete it as soon as you have. Do not make any copies, forward it, or speak about it in any way. I also know you have a million questions, not the least of which concerns me. All will be explained as soon as practically possible. In the meantime, keep a watchful eye and don't believe everything you see. All is not as it seems.

 And that wasn't even the most puzzling part...
The name of the sender was Max!
I quickly texted back:

Max – where are you? What happened? Did you get to a hospital? Are you still in Boston? Do you know Kat has been kidnapped and I'm in Paris? Is that what you mean when you say you know what's happened? And most of all, what the bloody fuck is this all about?!

All good questions. Unfortunately, I received no reply. Celeste returned with my tea.

She watched my clumsy thumbs press send again and looked down at the screen.

"Did you get a text message, *chéri?*"

"Yeah," I grunted. And when no text came back from Max, I stuffed the iPhone back into my jacket.

"Who was it?"

I opened my mouth to tell her, but because of the underlying message in the text, I held back."

"No biggie. Just a guy I did some work for in Boston, asking me about another freelance job."

I could tell she didn't believe me any more than I did, but what could she do? Call me a liar, even though I was, and I wasn't quite sure why? But Max, who was probably the only one who could help me now, had said to expect an email and be alone while I read it. I took the tea and drank it down in two scorching swallows.

"Thanks, Celeste. I'm gonna get rolling. I'm really fuckin' beat, so I'm gonna go back to the hotel and crash for a while."

"Silly." She wrapped her arms around me and began to gently steer me towards the bedroom. "*Ma pauvre petit*, you do look *très fatigué*, but you don't need to go back to a lonely hotel room. I will take care of you right here."

She kissed me with lips filled with promise, but I gently took her hands and held them instead of returning the kiss.

"Thanks, babe, but I gotta go rest my weary, cobweb-filled brain, and I'm afraid you might be a distraction...although a sweet one."

My words had been intended to take the sting out of my turning her down, and she tried to accept them in the same spirit, but her eyes told a different story. She was hurt and...something else.

But I was too tired and worried to say anymore. I really did intend to zonk out for a few hours at the hotel. Just as soon as I read the promised email.

I kissed her on the forehead. "I'll be back soon. Promise."

I left her standing in the doorway, both of us wondering if it was true.

When I got back to the hotel, the first thing I did was to check my email. Sure enough, I had an email, but it didn't come from an individual, private account address. It came from the Boston Public Library, obviously one of the public computers, but all it contained was a link to an encoded PDF. I was pissed, as well as frustrated. Why the hell did he send me an attachment I couldn't open? And then I remembered our last conversation about the Bell and the Vril; a phrase that was used as a coded recognition signal between members: "All that was will be again."

I clicked the link, and where it said "password," I typed in: ATWWBA, and poof! The attachment opened and I began to read.

Chapter Thirty-Seven

I know you are angry, confused, and frustrated, my *jungen Freund*, and I don't blame you. But something is at stake here that is of even greater importance than you or our dear Katrina.

The future of humanity.

As you must have deduced by now, there is an object that goes with the spiral cylinder ring Kammler refers to as a 'key'. Because key it is. Used properly and with the correct 'lock', it can open doors unimagined by any human.

But what is it, you ask? I can tell you what it looks like and what others have thought it was for thousands of years.

It's not large. It was crafted in the shape of a cosmetic box; only 3.5 by 6.4 cm in a semi-circular shape, made of silver, inlaid with lapis lazuli.

According to the legends and the translations on the stela, the wise fathers of the Anunnaki created a special device for Queen Puabi of Ur. And legend has it that they made it in the shape of one of the small boxes women of high station used to keep kohl, a black pigment used to highlight the eyes. The half-moon shaped box showed a lion attacking a goat carved in silver on the lid.

Puabi was thought to have been both an independent queen and high priestess, responsible for communicating the instructions of the Anunnaki lords to their mortal subjects. In some unknown way, when a spiral cylinder bearing the name of the gods was inserted into an opening within the box itself, it would enable the user to enter the 'Portal of the Gods' where they would see their wonders and receive instructions.

Also found in the same Tomb of Puabi, among the many grave goods, was a bowl, and this bowl sent Himmler and the Ahnenerbe into paroxysms of delight. Because painted at the bottom was an image that resembled a continent with fish swimming around it, which could have been either the North or South Pole, or as the Thulists suggested, the lost continent of Atlantis or Hyperboria. But the thing that appeared to prove all of the Nazi theories correct was painted on the image of an ancient continent, thought to be the original homeland of the Aryan race—a large swastika.

The original box itself, the purported Anunnaki communication device found in Puabi's tomb, had been badly cracked sometime in antiquity, and if it had ever functioned as conduit, it certainly did not now.

However, one of the most exciting discoveries from the translation of the stela we had uncovered with the ring, was the text of a letter from Queen Puabi, priestess of Ur and confidant of the Anunnaki, to her fellow queen and likewise priestess in Egypt, Bunefer. In this letter, she tells the Egyptian Priestess-Queen Bunefer, that the great Anunnaki have caused to be made a duplicate box so both Queen Paubi and Queen Bunefer may communicate with each other and behold the wonders of the gods together, and thus bring their instructions to their respective peoples. And according to the text of the stela, the two women used them to call down the gods who performed many miracles for both the Sumerian and Egyptian peoples, particularly in the creation of temples, cities, and massive stone monuments.

As was the custom of their day, both women were buried with all of their possessions to help them in the afterlife, and there it was assumed they rested for centuries. In Puabi's case, this turned out to be true. When Queen Puabi's tomb was discovered by British archeologist Leonard Wooley back in the mid-twenties, amid the treasures was indeed the lion-headed box. But as previously mentioned, it was badly damaged, so even if someone had wanted to put the legends to the test, it would have been impossible. Until a curious scholar noticed that the tomb inventory of High Priestess-Queen Bunefer listed an object that sounded identical to the cosmetic box of Queen Puabi of Ur. But this one could not be tested either, because Bunefer's tomb had been plundered in antiquity and stripped of all objects of value.

That, however, did not satisfy me. In light of what was going on between Maria and the Thulists, I felt there had to be something to the legends. So upon my return to Germany after our dig around the burial sites of Ur, I convinced Himmler to allow me to use the full resources of the Reich and the Ahnenerbe to see if I could locate the whereabouts of the second 'god-box', as one of the hieroglyphs had titled it.

And with those extensive resources, I did.

I discovered that, centuries after it was plundered from Bunefer's Tomb, it turned up in ancient Canaan and was presented by a holy man to King Solomon, who may have used it in building the First Temple.

Four hundred years later, during the siege of Jerusalem by the forces of King Nebuchadnezzar, it was apparently hidden, with much of the other treasure, under the site of the First Temple. There it rested until it was discovered after Jerusalem fell to the Crusaders in 1099. Some twenty years later it came into to the hands of the Knights Templar when they made the Temple Mount the headquarters of their new order.

But over the next century, the Templars began to fall out of favor with the papacy and the kings of France, and sometime during the first quarter of the thirteenth century, the Templars decided to take much of their gold and sacred treasures to the Cathars for safekeeping. The Cathars lived in the Languedoc region of France and practiced a simple form of Christianity whose independent spirit matched the Templars' own. The Templars, who correctly foresaw their own persecution at the hands of the church, unfortunately did not foresee the even worse one that befell the Cathars. The papacy and kings of France, fearing the less worldly and materialist lifestyle of the Cathars, decided they must be wiped out. Thus began a bloody campaign of fire and sword that ground down the Cathar towns and strongholds. It was said that after the massacre of 20,000 men, woman, and children at Beziers, the river ran red with blood.

By March of 1244, the last refuge of the Cathars, the great mountaintop fortress of Montsegur, was enduring a siege, which had dragged on for ten months. On the night of March 16th, just before the final capitulation and slaughter of the last of Montsegur's defenders, four men, accompanied by a guide, were lowered down the sheer, but unguarded, cliff face and escaped with the bulk of the Cathar treasure. Among those riches was the millennia's-old box.

From there until the end of the eighteen century, the trail goes cold. Then, in 1785, when the French queen, Marie Antoinette, was settling into her new Petite Trianon Domain Estate her husband Louis had given her in 1774 as her own little, private realm on the grounds of Versailles, a purveyor of cosmetics, hoping to curry favor, gave her an unusual little powder box.

It was reported that she commented on the silver lion on the lid. I believe it was the same cosmetic box given to Queen Bunefer by the Anunnaki Priestess-Queen Punabi.

It goes missing again during the French Revolution until it finally surfaced in a Paris antique shop in 1930. In 1937, a German researcher, Otto Rahn, who was connected with Himmler and the Ahnenerbe, was doing research in the Languedoc region on lost Cathar relics of interest to the Third Reich. He got wind of it and tried to buy it. However, the owner of the shop had Jewish blood and no love for the Nazis, so he told him no. But as soon as the Germans marched into France in 1940, the antiquities dealer knew the SS and Gestapo would be at his doorstep. So, in a flash of genius, he decided to hide the piece in the last place they'd ever think of looking for it.

In plain sight.

He took it to the Palace of Marie Antoinette who had once owned the box, and had it listed on her inventory of household items prior to the Revolution. There, after slipping away from a guided tour, he placed it on her vanity table with all of her other cosmetics. But to make sure it stayed innocuous, he'd had a pink lace cover made for it and filled the inside with face powder. Soon after, the Nazis sent him to a death camp, but they never found the box. I believe you already have heard about him and his daughter. They were the same ones who wound up with the ring and stela we discovered on the dig in Ur. And just as they'd done with the box, they put the cylinder ring and stela out of the reach of the Nazi's at the Louvre.

I know you have managed to obtain both of those items, or in the case of the stela, a translation. But now you are in the greatest danger of all because Kammler knows you have them and you'll do everything possible to obtain the box and save Katrina.

And be assured that I am likewise working from my end to secure her release and safe return, but I must be careful of letting them see me for reasons I cannot go into in something like an email. But I am aware of what is going on and will soon be closer than you know. So keep on with your battle, and I will contact you as soon as possible.

Max

P.S. Memorize what you need then delete it. Do NOT, under any circumstances, print this, and do not mention its contents to anyone. ANYONE!

Chapter Thirty-Eight

If Max had been there, I would have said, "OK, OK. I get the friggin' picture."

But he wasn't, so I hit delete. I grabbed my jacket and started off for...where?

In the back of my mind I intended to race off to Versailles without even stopping to consider it was still the middle of the friggin' night. And while I knew it was a popular tourist destination, I'd never been there. Hell, I didn't even know which Metro to take. Once I got there, how was I going to get access to wherever the queen kept her cosmetics before she got her last haircut from Madame Guillotine? I needed help. And in Paris, aside from those who wanted to kill and/or make life generally difficult for me, that left only Celeste.

I got to her building in five minutes and rang the buzzer. A minute, then two passed, and nothing. Probably asleep, I thought. Or, she could even be shacked up with some other guy. I certainly had no claims on her.

I gave the button one more stab then turned down the stairs, but as I reached for the door handle, the lobby speaker buzzed. I hurried back up in time to hear a sleepy voice.

"*Qui est là?*"

"Celeste, it's me, Chris."

She didn't even ask what the hell I was doing at her door in the small hours of the morning, she buzzed me up and was waiting at her door with a kiss when I got there.

"Ummm, I'm glad you came. I've missed you." She nuzzled my chest and kissed me again. "Do want coffee or anything?"

"No, thanks, all I need is your help."

"Of course, I'll do anything I can."

I began to explain needing to get out to Versailles ASAP, but when I got to the part about what I was looking for and why, I kept seeing Max's words about not telling anyone under any circumstances. Do you suppose he meant I shouldn't even ask Celeste to come with me? No, I decided. If he meant that, he would have said so directly.

Still...I continued to have the nagging little canker of doubt, even as we boarded the early morning Metro out to Versailles.

* * * *

The sun was fully up by the time we arrived, but the grounds and palace weren't open yet, so we stopped in a small sidewalk café for pastry and coffee.

Celeste sipped hers and nibbled at the croissant with her perfect front teeth while I wolfed mine down and held up my finger to the waiter for a refill on both.

"So, *chéri*, what exactly are we looking for in Versailles?"

"Not exactly sure," I lied. "I guess it'll be a case of, 'I'll know it when I see it.'"

She looked at me skeptically but let it slide and looked at her watch instead. "I think they'll be open now."

We paid and left. Ten minutes later, we stood in front of the gilded gates of the palace that was once home to a dynasty of kings before bloody revolution shortened their tenancy by mob justice, along with their personal, royal stature by removing their heads.

We walked through the gates, trying to keep ahead of a busload of Japanese tourists swarming into the courtyard.

Fortunately, they reinforced that peculiar Asian trait of taking millions of pictures of every detail of every place they ever went. This allowed us to make it to the ticket window before the bus rush. Soon, we were entering a dim hallway and blinking the bright sunlight out of our eyes as we proceeded deeper into the opulent chateau.

I opened the tourist map of the estate but wasn't sure if I should drag Celeste out the back door and towards the Queen's chateau a mile away. I needed to buy myself more time to try to make a moderately intelligent decision.

"C'mon," I said, "let's go see the Hall of Mirrors."

We did, only moving out when the human tidal wave of tourists entered at the opposite end of the long hallway. It provided a good segue for leaving.

"It's getting too crowded in here to find anything. Maybe I'll recognize something if we come back a little later." I pulled the brochure out of my back pocket and pretended to study it. "Hey, let's try the Queen's Palace. It's probably not as packed and maybe we'll find something there."

I hated lying to her and was about ready to spill the whole thing, when, while heading down the stairs, I bumped into a man coming up the other way.

"Sorry," I mumbled automatically and went down two more stairs before my brain caught up with my feet. I'd seen that guy somewhere before. I turned around and caught a glimpse of him and his companion as they were lost in the crowd. I knew him, and maybe his friend too, from somewhere, but where? He was probably one of the legions of people who signed up to ensure my life would stay filled with crap 'til the end of my days. Well, he'd have to get in line. In the meantime, Celeste and I exited the main palace and found ourselves staring down across the long, ornamental lake resembling some sort of gigantic swimming pool.

I pulled out the brochure and map again and pointed to the distant trees. "It looks like her palace must be over there."

She nodded. "*Oui*. The last time I was here, I was a skinny schoolgirl on a class trip, but I do recall it being over there."

I smiled and we started down the gravel path. "Hard to picture you as a skinny schoolgirl."

She grabbed my arm and giggled. "I wasn't always devastatingly beautiful, *chéri*."

"Like I said, hard to believe."

She smiled back and rested her head on my shoulder and we walked on in silence while I tried to figure out when would be the best time to let her know what I was looking for. I wasn't quite certain I'd know it when I saw it, so I really needed another pair of eyes for the hunt.

When we finally got to the pink marble palace the king had built, (poor old Louis the XVI who'd never have a Seventeenth succeed him) the crowd had dissipated to almost zero. We had no trouble having the place almost to ourselves.

I pointed to the guidebook. "Here's where we want to go. The Queen's bedroom."

"*Certainement.*"

We headed across the courtyard.

"Can you tell me what you are looking for? It is *très difficile, chéri*, to help you find something when I don't what it is."

We entered the French doors off the garden and into a lavishly decorated set of rooms staged to display ornate tables and gilded chairs. Finally, there was the luxurious boudoir of Marie Antoinette. It was time.

"It's some sort of a cosmetic box wrapped up in a pink lace doily and may be filled with powder."

Her eyes sparkled as though that meant something to her.

"Have you ever seen anything here like it before?"

"Not that I recall." She shrugged.

She didn't elaborate and I wanted to get in and out as quickly as possible. After checking that there was no one in sight, I unsnapped the velvet rope and we stepped carefully into the bedchamber.

Celeste made straight for a small table sitting in the shadows at the other end of the room and peered intently at the items arranged there. After a few moments, she picked something up and held it out to me. "Could this be it?"

It was.

It was exactly as Max had described it, but to make sure, I forced up the sticky lid until I could see the substance inside: a dry cake of a cracked, yellow material that long ago might have been face powder. I tried to get under the dry, cement-like powder to see what the inside of the box really looked like, but it was congealed solid.

"*Que faitez-vous, monsieur?*"

Well I certainly knew what I was doing, but I had a feeling an answer of, "Stealing one of your exhibits," wasn't going to cut it.

"Uhhh, just showing this to my girlfriend."

Before he hit me with the French equivalent of "bull shit," Celeste broke in.

"It's all my fault, monsieur. I was curious so I asked him to get it so I could look inside."

"That is no excuse, Mademoiselle. I must ask you to come with me."

"I don't think that will be necessary," said the voice of a figure walking up the corridor from the opposite direction.

"And who are you, monsieur?"

My thoughts exactly.

The man, actually two men, stepped up to the security guard and flashed an ID.

"You can check this with Interpol if you like."

I stared. It was the man I'd bumped into on the stairs. Now I recognized him from Boston, no—Cambridge. MIT to be precise. The Air Force colonel and the professor. Another wheel had turned.

Chapter Thirty-Nine

Several minutes passed as the guard used his walkie-talkie to check their credentials with someone, presumably his shift captain, while his eyes continuously flitted back and forth between us and the two men in front of him. It was clear he had his doubts with all of us, but soon the two-way radio crackled and he said, "*Oui*" a few times and handed back to the colonel and professor their ID's. That left only us, and I had a feeling our story wasn't going down as well.

He marched over to us.

"*Remettre ça,*" he said gruffly tell Celeste, which she promptly did, putting the lace-covered box back in the dust outline matching the exact spot where it had probably sat since WWII when the doomed antique dealer had placed it there.

He said in heavily accented English to the colonel and the professor, "I have been informed that your papers have been co-signed by Interpol giving you jurisdiction." He stepped back, and with a curt nod of his head, disappeared back down the long corridor.

"Colonel, Professor," I said. "Nice meeting you again. To what dubious honor do I owe this visit?"

The colonel continued to maintain his unwavering expression of humorless competence. The professor continued to look pissed at the world.

"Since you decided not to return from our last meeting, we came to you," the colonel replied.

"Great. There are some chairs and a rather rare and uncomfortable looking couch right here." I swept my arm around the room. "Shall we sit? Who knows? If the topic follows the genuinely weird theme of our last conversation, maybe we'll get the ghost of Marie Antoinette to drop by."

"No, that's not the Marie we're interested in. But I think you do know the one whom we are interested in, and this time, you're not going anywhere until you tell us."

Like I didn't know.

"Look guys, I skipped out on you before because: one, I didn't have the info you wanted," (which of course wasn't quite true) "And two, there was a bunch of guys trying to put a bullet through my head, and as far as I know, they still are."

"Well, as of this moment you are under the protection of the Air Force, CIA, Homeland Security, and the United States government." He stood at semi-attention while he waited for me to become duly impressed, which I was not and did not.

"Great, except for the fact that the guys after me have been practicing double dealing and murder since before any of us were born, and they had no trouble snatching Kat in broad daylight. So you'll excuse me if I don't do cartwheels."

The professor looked at me with disgust. "Oh, for Christ's sake, Colonel, just put the cuffs on him."

That didn't sound like fun, but apparently the colonel's fuse wasn't quite as short as the perpetually pissed professor.

"No, thanks. I've got my ass to protect and I don't want to hurt your feelings or anything, but I trust me to do a better job of it than you two. Besides, I've got my friend to think of. She's in danger too."

For the first time, they really looked at Celeste, and when neither tongue hung out, it made me wonder if the pair weren't spending too much time together.

The colonel shrugged. "She's of course welcome to come along if she'd like our protection."

I glanced at Céleste but she shook her head. "*Merci*, but I only wish to go home. I don't really understand any of this."

"There is no reason why you should. We have a car waiting outside and we'll drop you at your flat on the way to the American Embassy. And then I must inform you that you are enjoined to keep silent about everything you've heard and seen concerning this topic."

Celeste didn't answer, merely gave a slight nod and kept her eyes on the floor as we wound our way back through the entrance and to the waiting car beyond.

The ride back to Paris was uneventful and silent. It wasn't until we were about half a click from Celeste's flat when I finally spoke.

"Look, I really don't care if I spend the next three hours playing Twenty Questions with you guys, but I'm on a friggin' deadline here. If I don't get those guys what they're after, they're gonna start cutting up Kat. So pretend you actually give a shit and turn this thing back around to Versailles so I can get them their doo-hicky."

The colonel, who was sitting in the front seat next to the driver, turned around. "Good point. Let's talk about what they asked you to get. Please describe it for me. In great detail."

I thought of a few choice remarks, but Celeste, who was sitting on my right, slipped her hand into my jacket pocket. When she removed, it there was something hard and cold in its place. I ran my fingers over the contours. It was a gun, a small, automatic pistol, and I didn't have to think about what I needed to do with it.

"Stop the car right now."

I reached over, grabbed the professor sitting next to me and held the pistol against his left temple. I thumbed the hammer back. "I don't wanna do this, but I'm gonna save Kat one way or another. If you're not gonna help, then stay the fuck away from me. Pull over." I pushed the pistol harder against his head. "Now!"

The car pulled over and the colonel, looking unflappable as usual, watched the barrel of my pistol.

"You don't understand. If you do find the object they refer to as the 'key,' they will be able to activate a device every world power has been seeking since the end of the Second World War. It is one of the crucial technologies we were trying to acquire when we began Operation Paperclip, the operation to smuggle Nazi rocket scientists into the country before the Soviets could get their hands on them. The technology your friend Max and his girlfriend Maria and her group were involved with, was probably more important than all of the rocketry and UFO technologies combined."

I was momentarily torn between wanting to get the hell out of the car and wanting to hear more from people who obviously knew more than I did.

"So in all those years you've never found this 'critical technology?'"

"Once. Back in 1965, the evening of December 9, in Kecksburg, Pennsylvania, the 'Bell,' or as the local newspaper dubbed it, the 'Kecksburg Acorn,' appeared or crashed in a heavily wooded area. We were able to get it before too many people got a good look at it."

"OK, I'll bite. So what happened to it? Do you still have it?"

"No. We took it back to Wright Patterson Air Force Base, but thirty-six hours later, right in the middle of an experiment

Professor Dombroski and his team were performing in an attempt to open it, the Bell suddenly disappeared and we've never seen it again."

"Well, tell you what. If I stumble across it while I'm looking for Kat, I'll let you know."

"Don't be stupid. Once they get their hands on the objects necessary to access the Bell, they'll have no reason to keep you or your girlfriend around." Suddenly he looked at me and then at Celeste as though seeing her for the first time. "Or maybe I'm wrong. Maybe the kidnapped girl doesn't figure into the equation at all anymore. Maybe you want the Bell for yourself and whoever your new girlfriend is." He stared at Celeste.

When I didn't answer, he gestured at her. "Is that who you are? Are you the new girlfriend?"

"She's a friend, Colonel. She's helping me, which is a whole lot more than you or my government has done."

He ignored me and stared more intently at Celeste. "Don't I know you?"

"I doubt it." She answered sharply. "I've never spent much time around *batteurs de papier du gouvernement*, and have no desire to start now."

She pulled out a cigarette and lit it. I noticed her hands were shaking. Well no wonder. I was mad too and seconded her feeling about "government paper pushers."

The professor, who up until now had been silent, pushed the barrel of the pistol aside and stared at Celeste even more intently than the colonel had. I pushed the barrel back up to his face. "What's your problem?"

"It's coming back to me now." He smiled–not a pleasant smile. "Yes, the way it sometimes does. In little pieces like a tiny jigsaw puzzle a bad-tempered child throws to the floor, and—when after so long staring at it—another piece suddenly falls into place."

Celeste took another drag from her cigarette and scowled before her expression morphed into unease.

"Christophe, please let's go now. Quickly. I don't trust these people. Who knows what kind of a *trahir*, double cross, they are planning."

"Can't argue there." I pulled the pistol back from the professor's head but kept it pointed in his general direction as Celeste opened the door and I backed out behind her.

"Look, I'm only gonna say this once more. I'm going to do everything in my power to save Kat, and if it means giving them a million 'keys' to some cosmic skyhook, then so be it. And once she's safe, presuming I can pull that off, I'll be glad to tell you anything I learn...assuming there is really anything to learn, and the whole bunch of you haven't been chasing some Indiana Jones-type fantasy for the past seven decades."

The colonel opened his mouth to speak but Dombroski shook his head, and after a brief hesitation, the colonel tapped the driver and they pulled out into the traffic.

I must have looked like the kid who's just opened his stocking to find a big lump of crap-coated coal. Celeste squeezed my arm.

"C'mon, *chéri*, it's not that bad."

"Not that bad? How the fuck could it be any worse? After all this time spent running around hell's half acre, we're no closer than when we started. We still don't have that box thing. The time is up tonight, and even if we could get close again, which you know we can't now, we'd never have enough time to make it out to Versailles and back for the exchange at Deux Magots."

She gave me a cat-and-canary smile.

"What makes you think we don't have the box, *mon ami*?"

* * * *

I wasn't sure if the colonel would be changing his mind and come after us with reinforcements. Therefore, we took the long way to Celeste's flat, ducking down alleyways and cutting through shops, but as far as I could tell, we weren't being followed. However, given the sad state of my attempts to accomplish something of value out of the current mess, I doubted anyone felt I was worth following.

To say I was depressed was putting it mildly. It must have showed, because after pulling down the blinds, Celeste came over and gave me a big, consoling, kiss. But when I didn't respond, she stepped back and regarded me with a pretty pout.

"Hmm, I must be losing my touch, *chéri*."

"Not you. Just me feeling as useless as tits on a bull."

"Oh, *mon pauvre taureau*. Now we can't have that."

She opened up her pocketbook and pulled out something that glinted silver and blue and held it in her open palm.

I had forgotten her comment about the box. Could it be…?

It was a glimmering silver box inlaid with deep blue lapis lazuli, and then I saw the raised silver lion on the lid.

"The box! How the hell did you get it? I mean, how could you smuggle it out under their noses? Wouldn't the guard have noticed it was missing even before we left the building?"

Her smile turned into a grin. "A woman's wiles perhaps? *Non*, nothing so complicated, *chéri*, just what an American told me once is called the old 'switcheroo.'"

"Huh?"

"Simple. While all the rest of you were yelling at each other, I slipped the box out of the pink lace covering."

"Yeah, but they would have noticed if the damn thing was just an empty cloth cover."

"But it wasn't empty."

She saw my confusion and giggled. "It covered a cosmetic box for eye shadow, *n'est ca pas*? Well, it still does. I just substituted my eye shadow box for this one. An almost perfect fit into the cover, *et volià*, no one the wiser."

I whistled. "You are one hell of a girl, Celeste." I hugged her.

She smiled again and pressed her forehead on my chest so I couldn't see her face. "Well, if I cannot be the one you love, then I will settle for that."

I thought I heard something catch in her throat, but she pulled away and wiped her eyes with the back of her hand. When she turned back, she was all smiles.

"And now we can arrange to make the exchange. Did they give you a number to call them?"

I shook my head. "No, just to be at Deux Magots tonight with the box. But before we meet them, let's take a look at this little gizmo and see what the hell makes it so damn important."

I opened the lid and we peered inside. There was a dark cake of residue that could have been eye shadow or some type of powder, but now it had the consistency of sun-dried brick. I flicked out my OTF knife and pried the small block of remains out and stared at the bottom. Nothing.

What the hell? Was this what the fuss was all about? An old, empty box?

Celeste's cell phone rang.

"*Oui?*"

I watched her expression change from curiosity, to anger, and finally to resignation.

"Who is it?" I mouthed, but she only shook her head.

Moments later she said in a dull, flat voice, "*Oui, je serai là—quinze minutes,*" and rang off.

"And exactly where are you going to be in fifteen minutes?" But I was afraid I already knew the answer.

She didn't meet my eyes. "Marcel's."

"Why? Why, Celeste?"

"He said he thinks he can get Kammler to meet us at his office."

"How?"

"You know what kind of a man Marcel was during the war and after. He has done business with Kammler in the past and the man trusts him; at least when they have a shared interest. As you Americans say, 'honor among thieves.'"

"Yeah?" I snorted. "Well, even if it's true, we don't need that old perv as a middle-man. We'll go to Deux Magots and wait 'til they show up."

"But will they have your girlfriend with them when they come for the box?"

"No, probably not, but they said as soon as they had the box and everything they'd arrange for—I mean bring her to..."

Yeah, it sounded lame to me too.

"You're right. I should have told them not to show up without Kat, but what would I do if they said no? I mean, even if I could find a way to get in touch with them, they aren't going to bring her to the meeting just because I ask them."

"No, but they will if Marcel does."

"And he would because...?"

"You know why."

I joined her in staring at the floor. "Celeste, I..."

"I know." She kissed me with a little half smile, then grabbed her purse and slipped on her leather jacket. She was halfway to the door when she turned.

"Oh, while I'm thinking of it, you better give it back to me."

"What?"

She pointed to my jacket pocket. "My pistol."

"Oh... yeah, sure." I pulled it out. "Any chance you might use it on Marcel?"

She gave me a weary grin. "Who knows, maybe someday."

As I reversed my grip and held it out to her I noticed for the first time that it was engraved. The barrel had something engraved in a heavy, old-fashioned Gothic script. German. *Die Sterne sind Deutsch.* And on the gold inlaid ivory grip was the word: *Siggy.*

I was puzzling over the inscription when she took it out of my hand. I raised my eyebrows in question and she shrugged. "Nothing but an old pistol I picked up in a second-hand shop."

She kissed me on the cheek and left.

I stood there trying to picture the ornate, little automatic and the strange inscription in my mind as I walked to the window.

I saw her trot down the steps and cut diagonally across the street. She began to walk briskly to the corner. I was about to turn away when she suddenly stopped in front of two people standing there, almost as if they had been waiting for her. It was a man and a woman, and while I couldn't make out their faces from this distance, I felt that I'd seen them before. The woman was about Celeste's height with a beret covering blond hair, but the strangest thing was that her companion, the man, was wearing a hat. Not just any hat mind you, a frigging fedora hat a la Humphrey Bogart. I shook my head. Well that was Paris for you. Probably in a few months, all the cool guys in NYC and LA would be wearing them too.

When I looked back, the corner was empty.

Chapter Forty

An hour later, tired of pacing and having balled up and shot all of her cute, little cocktail napkins into the wastebasket, I was putting on my jacket to go to Marcel's regardless of what might be happening there, when the door opened.

"*C'est fait.* It's done." Celeste brushed by me and slumped down on the couch and closed her eyes.

I didn't want to ask the question we both didn't want to discuss, so instead I asked, "What time?"

"In one hour. The shop will be closed by then."

"And they're bringing Kat?"

"Yes. I told Marcel that was a must or no deal—on anything."

Her voice cracked on the last syllable and I could only guess what that concession must have cost her.

"Thanks."

It sounded totally inadequate to me too, which is why I almost didn't have the heart to ask her the next question.

"Who were those people on the corner?"

Her eyes flew open. "People? What are you talking about?"

"I was watching out the window, and I saw you stop and talk to two people, a guy and a girl, at the end of the street. I really couldn't see their faces, but they looked familiar to me. I'm trying to figure out where I've seen them. Are they friends of yours?"

I could almost see her thoughts racing behind her eyes.

"Friends? *Oui*, yes, they are old friends of mine I haven't seen for a while. I had forgotten all about them, that's why your question surprised me."

"Have I met them?"

"No, I don't believe so."

"And they walked with you to Marcel's?"

"Why do you ask?"

"Because after speaking for a few minutes you all walked off together."

She stood up and put her hands on her hips. "*Qu'est-ce qui se passe*? What's your problem? I put myself through *beaucoup merde* for you, and this is what I get?"

Then the tears started. I was a bastard. But I was a curious bastard. I put my arms around her.

"Look, I'm sorry if it sounds like I was giving you the third degree, but it's just that there's so much going on I don't know about or where anything fits in."

She gave me the little sad smile again and hugged me tighter. "And I'm sorry, too, for snapping at you. I know how worried you must be."

She gave me a long, lingering kiss half way between "poor baby" and "let's get it on!" But for once, I wasn't in the mood for either. My adrenalin had kicked up another notch and I was ready to rumble. I took a step back and pulled on my leather jacket.

"C'mon, let's get this thing done."

She nodded and gathered up her purse.

I pointed to it. "We're going to need some back-up while we're with these guys. Do you still have the gun in there?"

"*Oui*." She opened the purse and I could see the barrel of the automatic poking up between a mound of lipsticks and wadded up Kleenex.

I paused with my hand on the doorknob. "You know, while I was waiting for you, I was trying to keep my mind occupied, so I did a Google search on that second-hand pistol of yours. And do you know what I found?"

Her expression was unreadable.

"I think you might have something really valuable. It turns out that the closest match I could find for your gun was a Walther PPK 7.65mm that was manufactured as what is called a Presentation Gun—a gun specially made and engraved for an important person. So, do you have any idea who was given a pistol, similar to yours, by the director of the Walther gun-works himself?"

She shrugged. "As I told you, I bought it at a second hand shop. I only picked that one because it was inexpensive and I rather liked all of the baroque decoration on it."

"Well then, I may be delivering you good news. Because the one I found that's a dead ringer for yours happens to be the Presentation Pistol that was given to Adolph Hitler."

She turned pale. "Oh, my God. I had no idea. I must get rid of it immediately."

"Hey, I didn't say yours was Hitler's gun. All we know is that it was given to someone named Siggy. But once this is all over, if we can find out who Siggy is, you could have a very valuable antique on your hands. In the meantime, I think we should keep it for protection. If you really don't want to carry it around, I'll take it."

She thought for a moment and shook her head. "Thank you, but it's all right. I'll just keep it in my purse and hope we never have to use it."

"I wouldn't want to take that to the bank, so keep it close."

I opened the door and we went to find out who was playing it straight and who was dealing off the bottom of the deck.

* * * *

By the time we got to the antique shop, the day had devolved into the deepening dusk that stimulates Parisian's to start wandering into the bistro's and cafes in search of wine, cheese, and conversation.

The shop was dark with a "Closed" sign on the door, but it wasn't locked. Celeste opened it and walked toward the back office where one of the bodyguard/associates stood waiting with folded arms. He opened the door to the office but immediately pointed to the bookcase at the far end where we all paused. I raised my eyebrows, but Celeste either didn't see it or ignored me. He reached into the bookcase. I heard a soft click and the bookcase swung inward revealing a dark passageway. He flicked a light-switch and motioned for us to follow him.

The passage ended in a flight of winding stone steps leading down to a narrow corridor with an ironbound door at the end. He rapped his knuckles once, it opened, and we stepped into a cavernous room made of old brick and rough stones, topped by a barrel-vaulted ceiling stretching higher than the dim light could illuminate.

I almost expected to see the Phantom of the Opera step out of the shadows and swirl his cloak in our direction, but no such luck. All I could see was malevolent old Marcel and his odious son seated at the far end of a massive sixteenth century-style oak table.

"Welcome, young paladin," he greeted me with amused mockery.

"What the hell is this place?" I asked, trying to take everything in.

"Well, what it used to be, when a townhouse stood on this site, was a wine cellar that did double duty as a repository for smuggled goods and a handy place to stash young girls from the country until they could be sold to the local brothels."

"Figures. It's the perfect spot for you. All the right atmosphere."

He laughed. "I can't say that I like you, young man, but you do amuse me."

"Oh, be still my heart. Unfortunately, I can't return the compliment. I don't like you nor do you amuse me."

He made a sound which might have been a chuckle or cough. I couldn't tell which, nor did I care.

"OK, let's get on with this. Where is Kat?"

"Do you have the box with you?"

"You know I do. Stop playing games. But you're not gonna see it until I see Kat."

"You're in no position to argue. You'll see her only after I've authenticated the box and delivered it to my clients."

My anger increased. "Don't feed me that bullshit. The Nazi wannabes were supposed to be here and they were supposed have Kat with them."

"Unfortunately, they had other business and could not be here tonight, so they have authorized me to act as their general factotum."

I wasn't sure of much anymore, but one thing I was sure of was that, after all this time and hassle, those guys were not about to turn this deal over to anyone. They were somewhere close, very close...and so was Kat.

"OK, you want to see the box? No problem."

I pulled the bundle from my jacket and unwrapped the piece of bubble wrap I'd placed around it. I set it down on the far end of the table and watched as Marcel strained forward, trying to rise to see it better.

"Bring it to me." He snapped at his son.

But before he could move, I picked it up and held it over the rough stone floor. "No deal. Either you produce Kat or I drop this thing and stomp it to dust." And I was just about angry enough to do it too.

Marcel looked like he was about to burst a blood vessel and pointed his bony finger at Celeste.

"Bring me the box, immediately!"

She shrugged disinterestedly. "I think this time you must accept that someone else is in control, Marcel. My advice to you is to give him the girl."

He made a sound like an ancient billy-goat choking on tin cans, but finally nodded and flipped a switch on the table which illuminated the far end of the cellar.

I heard muffled sounds and started towards it as my eyes adjusted to the brighter light. I saw a petite figure tied to a chair, her mouth covered by silver duct tape.

Kat.

"The box!" snapped Marcel.

I turned around and handed it to Celeste. "I think this would be a good time to pull out that pistol."

She nodded and removed it from her purse, holding it in her right hand as I put the box into her left.

A few seconds later, I was kneeling in front of Kat, my OTF knife slashing the ropes. I peeled away the duct tape as gently as I could, and then she was in my arms, crying and hugging me as the anguish of her captivity broke over her.

But it was short-lived. A none-too-gentle kick to my back brought me around, and I looked up into the dead, flat, black eyes of one of Kat's captors. It was the man behind the goon who finally spoke in heavily accented English.

"Step back. You may reminisce with your lady friend as soon as we have authenticated the box."

He stepped out of the shadows and right away I knew it was "him." The guy—the overseer of slave labor and administrator of the death camps, SS Gruppenführer and General Waffen SS, Dr. Ing Hans Kammler.

I'd seen his picture online when I'd Googled him and had wondered how such a bland-looking man could have been responsible for so much misery. But now, up close, I understood.

They say the eyes are the windows of the soul. Well, if this is true, then most of the time dark shades were pulled down over his "windows," except for occasional, brief flashes indicating that behind the windows no one was home. Or what lived there was pure, unadulterated evil.

His thin lips compressed in a perpetual sneer of contempt. His eyes were what my dear old granny would have described as "beady," and set close together, giving him an almost cross-eyed look.

Regardless, he looked like what he was: a mean, stone-cold killer.

"*Gibes mir.*" He held out his hand, rock steady, no trace of nerves or excitement. "Place the box in my hand immediately or I will instruct Ernst to cut the girls throat."

The goon standing behind Kat flicked open a nine inch Italian stiletto and held the tip about an inch behind Kat's right earlobe.

Oh fuck it. I didn't really want the damn thing to begin with. I leaned forward, but before I could hand it off, something hit the tabletop with a "smack." I glanced around and saw it came from Marcel. The gold-topped cane clutched tightly in his right hand had slapped the table.

"You're forgetting one very important thing, Hans."

Kammler's expression didn't change nor did his hand waver, but he turned his head and locked eyes with the old man. "And what is that, Herr Thibodeaux?"

"That the first claim on the box, and what it will lead to, is mine."

"I am aware of no such arrangement."

But I noticed the faintest waver in his hand.

"Really? Then, as they say in court, 'let me submit the following document as exhibit A.'"

He produced a folded letter and used the tip of his cane to push it down the table to Kammler, who picked it up and quickly scanned it before making a small sound of dismissal.

"Surely you do not expect a casual letter from seventy years ago constitutes some sort of legal agreement?"

"According to the bargain we made the night you came to me with a fantastic tale and promises of power and immortality, it does. I kept my part of our arrangement. You got your false papers and escaped the Allied arrest warrant, which kept you from joining Ribbentrop, Keitel, and Kaltenbrunner at the end of the hangman's noose."

"That would never have happened and you know it!" Kammler snapped, momentarily losing his stony control. "I was far too valuable to the Americans. Why do you think my name never appeared on the docket at the Nuremberg Trails?"

"You promised them much when you wormed your way into the American's confidence during Operation Paperclip, but when it came time to deliver, what then? Is that why you've topped their list of wanted war criminals for the past seventy years?"

Kammler fixed the old man with an icy stare. "Be careful, Marcel. I am not the only one who cannot afford to be placed under the lens of scrutiny."

The old man's mouth opened, but then he seemed to think better of it and compressed his lips into a thin, tight line.

"Enough of this nonsense." Kammler snapped turning back to me. "Herr Brennan. The box."

I took the hand of the one called Ernst and pushed it away from Kat's throat. At first, he didn't budge, but Kammler nodded. Ernst sneered contemptuously and took a step back.

"Now you." Kammler said. I placed the box in front of him and backed away holding Kat tight.

As we moved to the other side of the table, Kamler was breathing heavily.

"*Ich habe so lange gewartet.* I have waited so long...so long."

Marcel was also breathing heavily, and his face was beet red like he was about to have a stroke, which, from my perspective, would have been a nice treat.

Kammler took out a pocketknife and flipped the remainder of dried powder out, walked to the center of the huge cellar, and placed the box on the floor.

"Klaus, bring me the key."

The other forbidding-looking ex-storm trooper handed him the cylinder-shaped ring they'd extorted from me...was it only a day ago? Kammler removed the lid from the box and placed the twisted, cuneiform-inscribed circular coil upright in it. The gold spiral ring was so much taller than the box, I expected the whole thing to topple over, but it stayed upright and began to glow.

Everyone took a step backwards.

The air crackled with static electricity and from somewhere a cold breeze stirred. Kat squeezed my arm.

"Chris, let's get out of here. I don't trust any of them. Especially not with whatever this thing is. Maybe we can slip out while everyone is watching it." She glanced at the glowing device and gave a small shudder. "I don't know what it's going do, but I think we'd be a lot better off not being here when it does."

I couldn't blame her. I felt the same way too, but despite Kat's instinct for the ever-increasing chance of impending disaster, I wanted to stay. No, I *had* to stay. I'd been chased halfway around the world, shot at, beat-up, and made everybody's favorite target, and now, by God, I was about to find out what the fuck it had all been about. I wasn't going anywhere.

By now the box and ring had grown brighter while the room had grown dimmer; almost as if the objects were sucking in the light.

And that's exactly what they were doing; drawing in light and air and pulsing with an increasingly brilliant glow running the spectrum from crimson, electric yellows and orange, down to cold cobalt blue. Every few seconds it would appear as if everything was about to wink out, when suddenly, a huge pulse of energy would burst and the cycle would begin again.

Faintly at first, but with increasing strength, an object, wavering in the center of the pulsing power, appeared. Like the ring, it was bright gold in color and shaped like...

A bell.

Chapter Forty-One

This was it. *Die Glocke*—the Bell. The device the Nazis had lavished so much time and treasure and blood upon.

It was clearly visible now. The polished surface was ringed with pictograms and ancient cuneiform writing like the ones on the stela. And dominating the object, glowing blood-red, right in the center, was the twisted cross the Nazi's called "*der Hakenkreuz*," the ancient symbol of good fortune, but they warped into one of terror. The Swastika.

The bell-shaped object hung in the center of the room, nine or ten feet tall and about fifteen feet in diameter. If this was some sort of a Nazi rocket or flying saucer, where was the room for the crew? It only looked big enough for three, maybe four people to fit inside. But the rest of the crowd watching it was unconcerned. They all gazed at it as though it was Santa's sleigh come to take them to Lollipop Land.

Marcel's face was slicked with sweat, his mouth wide open in an effort to suck in enough oxygen, while Kammler gazed with fulfilled satisfaction. But the strangest reaction came from Celeste. Her rapt gaze was as though she beheld a vision of the Virgin Mary.

I had no time to consider this further because Klammer broke his rare smile with a business-like, "And so, Klaus, get the instructions and begin reading them to me."

He moved closer to the Bell until he was almost underneath the rim. One of his men opened a three ring binder and began to read in a mixture of German and some strange, guttural language that sounded like a combination of German and an ancient Semitic tongue.

He walked to the edge of the Bell and reached up with both hands. Blue electric sparks danced around them as he began to chant in the unknown language. The Bell began to oscillate and the barely audible hum became louder.

"Klaus, Ernst," he said, his voice strained and hoarse. "Be ready to move within *Die Glocke's* perimeter when I give the command."

The two men nodded and started to move closer.

"No!"

A fist smacked the table all heads turned. It was Marcel. He had risen out of his chair and was moving towards the Bell with uncertain steps.

"*Mon père,*" his son said, "you must sit back down. Your heart will not stand this strain."

But the old man shook off his hand. "You fool, you understand nothing. I have waited for this device for more than seventy years." He pointed a shaking finger at the Germans. "These spawns of Satan cheated me out of what should have been mine seventy years ago, but they will not do it again." He pulled a mean-looking Glock automatic from his pocket. "Step away from the portal to immortality."

What...? This was a new one. "Portal to immortality?"

Kammler didn't even stop what he was doing. "Klaus, take the gun away from the ridiculous old fool. If he resists, shoot him."

Marcel's son and his bodyguards pulled out their pistols. It looked like we were about to experience the Gunfight at the O.K. Corral in a Paris cellar.

"Remember what you said about making tracks?" I whispered in Kat's ear. "I think now's the time."

We started edging towards the door.

We were almost there when the click of a latch opening and the slight rush of clean air into the static-charged room. A voice behind me said, "No one is shooting anyone... that is, unless we do."

It was a voice I hadn't been anxious to hear in the past, but now...well you know what they say about any port in a storm. I turned and confirmed... Yup, our friends from the "Project Spook" division of the US Air Force.

The colonel was dressed in the same uniform as when we last parted company, but now he was accompanied by not only the always-annoyed professor, but a trio of CIA-types with military haircuts and bad suits. They both had drawn the good old USA standby—Colt model 1911 .45 automatics—perfect for splattering brains in close quarters.

"All right," The colonel continued in a pleasant, almost convivial tone, "if everyone will kindly lay their firearms on the floor in front of them we can begin to wrap this operation up."

He turned to Kammler. "Hmm, yes and speaking of, 'operation.' Do you remember Operation Paperclip, Mr. Kammler? We kept our part of the bargain. We got you to the US with a new passport and identity, got the war crime charges put in abeyance, and gave you a good job. All you had to do was to show us how to access and use the Bell."

The colonel stood looking at Kammler with a deceptively mild expression, but there was steel underneath the soft words. "And what did you do, Herr General Dr Ing. Hans Friedrich Karl Franz Kammler? You, in a word, 'fucked us over.'"

Kammler opened his mouth as if to speak and then apparently thought better of it. He stiffened to attention, with what I'm sure he thought was the pose of a brave warrior of the Third Reich.

In the meantime, old Marcel, who had been witnessing the confrontation, motioned to his son who helped him back to his chair. He sat down heavily and stared at the still glowing, oscillating Bell like a passenger on the *Titanic* gazing at the last lifeboat pulling away from the doomed ship.

The colonel motioned for the three Black Ops-types to pick up the guns and walked over to Kammler.

"Well, better late than never I guess. Why don't we pick up where you left off with my predecessors in 1946. Show us how you work this thing."

That's when I spoke up. I was real tired of being a passenger on the Fuck You Express. The cosmos owed me and Kat some answers.

"Hey, Colonel, I know we never did bond back in Boston or here, but I'd still really like to know just what the hell is going on and what we almost got killed for. What does the Bell do and why is everyone willing to die for it?"

The colonel turned to Kammler. "Do you want to explain it to him?"

But all he got for his pains was the SS general stiffening even more, if that was possible.

"Fucking Germans." The colonel shook his head and sighed. "Look kid, we've got all kinds of stuff to do to some really nasty people, so let me give you the condensed version, and then I suggest you take your girlfriend outta here, find a café, get drunk on a good bottle of wine, and screw your brains out. But that's just me."

He motioned to the CIA boys who moved to Kammler's men and began putting plastic tie restraints on their wrists.

"As I'm sure you know by now, the Nazi Bell was one of the hundreds of potential super weapons dear old Adolph was convinced were going to win the war for him. There were literally hundreds of these '*wunderwaffen*' sites scattered all across the occupied territories. This one was in Upper Silesia in what became East Germany during the Cold War, but back at the end of WWII, it was a facility for the development and testing of a device the *Vrillian Damnen*, particularly one Maria Orsic, claimed they received directly from the god-race from the star system Alderbaran.

"This 'god-race' became known as the Anunnaki and are mentioned in the early records of almost every ancient civilization; from Samaria to Egypt, to the Mayans, Toltecs and Incas as well as the early peoples in India and Asia. In every case, these and hundreds of other budding civilizations, received help and knowledge from the mysterious Anunnaki whom they also referred to as the 'Star People.' This race of advanced extraterrestrials facilitated a great, and otherwise unexplainable, leap forward in technology and development at the dawn of history. And again, according to legends backed up by some recent archeological discoveries, they taught the early societies writing, astronomy, mathematics, and advanced construction in stone that we have not been able to replicate even with today's modern tools and technology.

"According to the legends and descriptions from psychics such as Maria and her fellow clairvoyants, the Anunnaki were tall; well over ten feet, and perfectly formed in every physical way. Which, of course, meant that their image was tailor-made for the budding National Socialists to set them up as the fathers of the Aryan race."

Despite the uncomfortable feeling that I should be getting Kat and myself out of the place while the getting was good, I couldn't resist asking.

"If these super E. T.'s were so friggin' smart, why the hell did they choose to give their technology to a bunch of murderous assholes like the Nazis?"

"Good question. And one we've wanted an answer to for the last 75 years. And as far as I know, there are only a few people who could answer it: Maria Orsic, and a few of her Vrillian, such as Gudrun and Sigrun."

Something flashed big, red warning lights at the back of my brain, but before I could pin it down, the colonel had resumed and it flittered away.

"We didn't really have any effective, organized agencies for foreign intelligence before the creation of the OSS, Office of Strategic Services, at the outset of the Second World War, so the warnings and rumors of fantastic, new technologies being developed by the Third Reich went largely uninvestigated and unheeded. Thus, we were forced to scramble and play catch-up as the war progressed. Quite frankly, if it had lasted another year, and Hitler had a chance to bring his jet planes and V2 rockets into play, things might have turned out very differently."

"But it doesn't answer my question, Colonel. How come the Nazis wound up being the only ones who got clued in to all those wonders?"

"Because they were the only ones who had the Vrillian. We've been trying to track them down since 1945 when they all vanished. It's also the reason why we've been forced to do business with Hans and the Kraut Twins over there." He jerked his thumb in Kammler's direction. "They promised they'd bring us the 'Ladies of the Vril,' or at the very least, their technology. But by the time we realized they had neither, they'd bolted on us and left the Department with a very large open file that has been the nemesis of several generations of intelligence officers, until the damn thing landed on my desk." He shook his head in disgust. "I became determined not to retire with my gold watch until the blue file marked 'Open' was officially closed. Fortunately, I found someone who was a kid in the concentration camps and had seen our pal Kammler in the flesh and in his element as he picked out victims to work to death at the mine site where the Bell was being developed. And thanks to Professor Dombrowski, who had worked with Simon Wiesenthal after the war to uncover the rat's nests of former Nazis, about five years ago we turned up a sighting of Kammler and have been tracking him ever since.

"Not only that, but we have reason to believe he or some of his fellow Knights of the Black Sun, another of the early twentieth century German occult groups, did manage to physically access some advanced alien technology."

All this time, Kammler had been staring straight ahead as the government operatives finished securing his wrists with the plastic ties, but at the colonel's last words a tic began to pulse under his right eye.

The colonel turned back to me. "I'm sure you are familiar with all the stories about alien abductions."

"Sure, you can't turn on the TV without seeing another program about those little grey buggers sticking a probe up someone's ass. Strikes me that they must be a bunch of space pervs."

That earned me a roll of the eyes from Kat, but at least it meant she was feeling more herself.

As usual, the colonel ignored my sophomoric sense of humor and continued.

"Well, you may also remember one of the early cases back in the 60s? One Betty and Barney Hill, who were returning to their New Hampshire home one evening when they claim they were abducted and subjected to hideous experiments."

"Ah, vaguely. UFO's are not my thing. At least they didn't use to be."

"Well, what you may not know, is that when investigators placed them under hypnosis separately, they both claimed the aliens they encountered looked like Nazis in SS uniforms."

He was speaking to me but staring at Kammler, whose stoic demeanor had now turned decidedly uneasy.

Seeing his words were having the desired effect, the colonel began walking slowly to the other end of the table. Still eyeballing Kammler, he resumed.

"And while you're pondering how the SS showed up as UFOs, I should mention that, despite our best efforts to pick up the trail of guys like Kammler and his buddies, it was like they'd vanished from the earth." He stopped directly in front of Kammler and leaned his face close to his. "Where do you suppose they were all that time? Any thoughts you'd like to share on it, Hans?"

Kammler's jaw quivered but he clamped it tightly shut as though struggling to prevent unruly words from escaping his mouth.

"I guess you and your rat pack were too ashamed of what you'd done to slither out from whatever wet rock you'd crawled under."

The colonel's last sentence proved too much for him.

"*Scheiße amerikanischen!*" He snarled. "You will never have the ability to comprehend the grand vision of our Führer, and the dedication unto death we of the SS have to see his vision made reality, regardless of the cost or how long it takes!"

The colonel put his hands behind his back. "So then you did figure out how to control the Bell?"

Kammler hesitated before spitting out a defiant, "*Ja*, we are the soldiers of the SS. We could not fail!"

The colonel nodded and walked back to our end of the table, calling out over his shoulder. "Who showed you?"

"What do you mean? I am a degreed engineer. I have knowledge of these things."

The colonel stopped and looked back. "Not according to all of the records we captured. They indicated that when you were in the process of closing down the whole operation in the spring of '45, you still didn't know how to control the Bell."

"Your information is incorrect. We had a large team of our most gifted scientists working to complete the final stage of the project."

"Another lie. Because if you were that close, you would have taken the scientists with you when you fled. But you didn't, because they were nowhere near completion. This is why you had them all machine-gunned at the site in Upper Silesia, so they couldn't resume their work in Allied hands. In the end, you couldn't use the Bell to escape into time and space as you had planned."

But Kammler had decided to go back to being a clam and kept his jaws tightly shut.

That didn't stop the colonel.

"However, someone did use the Bell to abandon the Third Reich and all of its nasty problems and nastier consequences coming on the heels on the Red Army." He suddenly turned, and like a prosecutor at a murder trial, fired his next words at Kammler. "And that person, or persons, was Maria Orsic, her boyfriend, and two members of the Vrillian!"

I heard a sharp intake of breath from one of our group standing at the head of the table. I turned my head to the left and saw Celeste, while keeping her features expressionless and controlled, had turned pale. But the colonel wasn't finished.

"We've been tracing the whereabouts of that group too. It's become apparent that the use of the Bell has some other unusual benefits as well." He glanced around the table before returning his gaze to Kammler. "For instance, it prevents you from aging."

The colonel continued to stare at Kammler but added softly, "Isn't that right Miss Celeste? Or perhaps you would prefer me to use the name you were born with. Sigrun."

We all turned to look at Celeste, me with confusion and disbelief. I started to tell the colonel he was crazy. But something stopped me. I guess it was the engraved Walther PPK she now held in her hand.

Chapter Forty-Two

I stared at the ornate pistol and the little flash of insight that had eluded me came flooding back and hit me right between the eyes. "The gun," I said. "It has a name on it–your name. Siggy. Sigrun. And it's a perfect mate of the famous one Walther himself presented to…"

"Adolph Hitler. *Ja*, that is correct." The lilting French accent had been replaced by a harsher German one. "The Führer liked his PPK so much, he had Fritz Walther make others for a few of his most admired friends, one of whom was the medium who had first introduced him to the Anunnaki and the concept of using their technology to help Germany win the war with wonder weapons."

One by one all those odd little pieces floating around my brain were starting to fall into place.

"The inscription on the barrel," I murmured to no one in particular, "'*Die Sterne sind Deutsch.*' I should have guessed who would own a pistol inscribed with 'The Stars are German.'"

She moved closer to me and I could smell her perfume. It still smelled of desire, except now it was mixed with something else. Deceit.

"Ah, but you were in love, *mon cœur l'amour, n'est-ce pas?* And we all know which head does the thinking for a young man in love." She blew me a kiss and winked. "Don't look so glum, *mon beau amant.* I was always quite fond of you, perhaps even a little in love."

"Thanks for nothin'."

She made a little-girl pouty face, sighed, and then turned back to the group.

"Where was I? Ah, yes, the Vril technology. Unfortunately, by the time Germany had started to produce the first of these weapons, two things had come to pass: Germany had run out of time, and the powers beyond the stars had become, shall we say—disillusioned—with the sometimes-brutal necessities we had been forced to adopt to help us achieve our goals. So, by the end of the war, they had withdrawn their support and left us with only the most basic of their wonders, such as the jet engine and V weapons rockets—along with one other, perhaps overlooked, working example of their miraculous technology, *Die Glocke*, the Bell—and the one person whom they had taken fully into their confidence and entrusted with the secrets of successfully operating the Bell." She smiled sardonically at Kammler. "Something you were never quite able to master, eh, Hans?"

She turned back to me. "And yes, that person was Maria, the girl you know as Ria. The best of us and leader of the Vril Society, Maria Orsic."

While my poor fogged brain struggled to digest everything, Celeste glanced over at Marcel. "And since this appears to be the time and place for sharing long-held secrets, I afraid I must tell you, Marcel, that the Bell only halts the aging process. It cannot reverse it."

"No! You promised! You promised me a return to youth and vitality!"

"I lied."

The old man who had been standing, leaning heavily on the table, collapsed back into his chair like deflated balloon figure, folding in upon itself. His face turned chalk white except for twin spots of blotchy red on each cheek giving him the look an antique, discarded Harlequin clown.

"How...how could you? All these years we have been together, while I adored you, worshiped you, gave you everything you wanted, even love."

The arrogant contempt with which he'd regarded the world was crumbling away, leaving nothing but the decayed shell of a broken old man. While most of me felt glad he was getting what was probably richly deserved, I couldn't help but feeling there was also a kind of cosmic justice at work for someone who'd had lied, cheated, and screwed over everyone around him getting paid back in his own coin—and by the only one he trusted. Way to go Karma. What goes around comes around.

"You have betrayed me, Sigrun. Me, your lover, your protector...your husband."

What????? Cosmic Justice jumped to a whole new level.

"Wait a minute... you two are *married*? What the fuck? I feel like my head is gonna explode. He's gotta be in his nineties while you're..."

"One hundred and fifteen years old, let's see...this September."

My mouth must have been hanging open wide enough to drive a semi-trailer

"You're married to him. Oh, my God, that's why you let him paw at you!"

"One reason, my gallant *amant,* and a very small one too."

"You used me!" Now Cosmic Justice had hooked up with personal irony, and I painfully aware that I was sounding like poor, deceived Marcel. I saw Kat look at me funny. I was gonna have some serious explaining to do.

"Of course, *chéri*, it is what I do, and I've had more than a century to perfect it. But now, as amusing as all of this catharsis has been, I do have other pressing matters. And for that, *mon beau ami*, I am sorry to say that I must deprive you of your paramour."

"What the fuck are you talking about?" I put both arms protectively around Kat.

"Come now, *ma chéri*. Don't be *difficile*. There is only one person who can provide me with the information I need—the information on how to program the Bell to move through dimensional time and space. Not just the a few parallel universes that my limited understanding can access, but literally anywhere. Unfortunately for both of you, the only thing that could persuade her to help me is this lovely young mademoiselle you are guarding so sweetly, if somewhat possessively."

Possessive or not, I kept my arms wound tightly around Kat. "And who is that?"

She laughed. "Oh, come now. Surely you must have guessed. Why, this is just delicious. She is another of your lovers. Your Ria. Maria Orsic herself."

I saw Kat's eyes widen. My explanations were going to have to go way beyond "serious."

Celeste pointed the barrel of her Walther at Kammler and the government men who were guarding them. "Cut them loose." They didn't move. "Right now or I start shooting, beginning with these two." She pointed at me but whispered in my ear, "Don't worry, *chéri*, I would never kill someone who pleased me so well between the sheets...unless he failed to do exactly as I say."

She pointed her gun at the end of the table again. "I said now!"

Everyone looked to the colonel who finally nodded, and the CIA-types snipped the plastic wrist cuffs off Kammler and his two thugs.

"And now, Herr General, if you would like a lift to a more welcoming environment for you and your men, I'll be happy to drop you off on our way to meet up with some old friends."

Kammler hesitated as though considering if there was a better option, which he obviously decided there was not because he nodded, clicked his heels in the best Teutonic tradition, and bowed.

"*Danke gnädige, Frau.*" He motioned for his men to follow him to the Bell.

Marcel, who had been slumped in his chair, trying to come to grips with his shattered dreams of eternal youth, snapped his head up.

"No! You cannot leave here without me. I had a bargain—with both of you. Do you want me to give evidence of the number of Frenchmen you sent to the camps or personally condemned to death during the war?"

Celeste/Sigrun, glanced at him contemptuously. "You will say nothing, Marcel, for if you did, it would very quickly come to light about your own part in those arrests that resulted from informants and betrayal. Your betrayal, Marcel."

She looked around the room with sardonic amusement. "You see, most of France knows Marcel Thibodeaux as a brave and selfless member of the Resistance during the war. But General Kammler and I know what his real role was during the war. He was not, as he claimed, a Captain in the Free

French Army and the Resistance, he was a collaborator and a traitor."

"You lie." Marcel tried to shout but it came out as a plaintive croak.

"For your sake I wish I were." She turned back to me. "Oh, he was a captain all right. But not in the French Army or the Resistance; that was his cover. He was actually a captain in a rather brutal and pitiless fascist-inspired organization called the Milice. The Milice was a Nazi-encouraged French paramilitary force created by the Vichy collaborators and organized to fight against the Resistance. Our brave Marcel would attend Resistance meetings and then report the details of their plans to his handler." She pointed her gun. "A high placed member of the SS...one General Dr. Hans Kammler."

Marcel held his head in his hands. "*Non*, no, you lie. I was a hero. All of France knows that. I was decorated by de Gaulle himself."

She chuckled. "Had de Gaulle known your true role, he would have pinned the medal to your chest with the point of a bayonet."

She sighed and shook her head. "And after all of these years of believing what you wanted to, all of your grandiose fantasies have come to nothing, and you will stay here, a wicked old man with nothing to look forward to except disgrace and death."

"Please, Celeste—Sigrun—do not abandon me. Take me with you." He clasped his hands, pleading. "After all, I am still your husband."

She smiled mockingly. "Ah, yes. How the bad decisions of our youth continue to haunt us. Oh, very well." She motioned to Kammler. "Hans, have your men bring him. Perhaps he'll find a welcome where you are going."

Kammler's men helped him out of his chair and began moving towards the Bell.

And that was when the professor and former concentration camp victim of Nazi genocide, Jerzy Dombroski, completely lost it.

In a split second, he yanked the colonel's 9mm Sig Sauer M11 and began waving it at Kammler.

"You aren't going to cheat justice this time, you Nazi son of bitch!"

Three wild shots rang out and one caught Marcel square in his skinny chest. As he slumped backwards, coughing blood, one of the SS men pulled a thin throwing knife from a concealed leg strap and whipped it at the professor. It hit him in the stomach and he doubled over, but he raised the pistol and shot the man in the throat. He loosed two more shots at Kammler as the CIA men circled to tackle him.

"Time to go," Celeste said with the barest hint of a derisive twist to her lovely red lips, and pushed the Walther into Kat's back, forcing her under the lip of the glowing Bell.

I hesitated. The hell with it; I wasn't going to let Kat go this time. I took a deep breath and ducked under the bright, pulsating rim.

Chapter Forty-Three

When my eyes fully adjusted to light, I was amazed to see that we were standing in an enormous hall with a fifty-foot ceiling supported by what looked like graceful marble columns, which kept shifting through all of the colors in the spectrum. The entire room, if that's what it was, kept shimmering and changing in shape and color.

Music that sounded vaguely familiar emanated from somewhere, though I couldn't place it. Likewise, the scents on a gentle breeze from nowhere and everywhere were a constantly shifting amalgamation of fondly remembered moments of my life. The cake my mom baked for me on my eighth birthday, the smell of burning leaves and jack o' lanterns from a childhood Halloween, the smell of perfume on the first girl I told, "I love you," my freshman year of high school.

"That's right. This craft picks memories out of your brain and matches them."

I whirled around. Celeste, or rather, Sigrun, stood about ten feet away, but the gun was gone and she was smiling, dreamily.

Upon seeing me, Kat ran and threw her arms around me.

Sigrun was completely unconcerned, as if in some way she had come home to where she felt secure and happy.

"I don't pretend to understand the science behind this device, only Maria and her fiancé understood it. But I do know that somehow this ship is powered by the universal lines of force, what the old ones called Vril, which was where we took our name from. And this craft or portal is guided by memories of where you have been and the concentrated will of where you want to go.”

One part of me wanted to grab Sigrun, slap her silly, take her gun and have her take us back. But another part of me couldn't resist the urge to finally get answers to my substantial list of unanswered questions. Keeping hold of Kat's hand, I walked toward Sigrun.

“And how, exactly, do you do this?”

Never losing her benign smile she said, “It is why I had to insist on the company of sweet Katrina. She is the true 'key' to what I want.”

“And why would she care about her? You forget I've—”

I stopped myself from saying “slept with Maria.” I'm sure Kat knew, but I was uncomfortable about being so overt. So instead I finished with, “Spent time with Maria—Ria—and as far as I can tell, she doesn't know Kat from a hole in the ground.”

Sigrun laughed a high, tinkling laugh. “Oh, Christophe, you do amuse me. You have no idea how wrong you are.” And she dissolved into girlish giggles.

Fed up with being the butt of cosmic jokes, I dropped Kat's hand and grabbed both of Sigrun's. “Look, I'm outta of time and patience. Either you stop talking in riddles and cutsie, little inside jokes, or I'm gonna have to stop being the good natured jerk and start breaking things that you will miss.” I tightened my grip on her wrists and bent them back. Pain and fear crossed her face, but soon evaporated as if they'd never been there.

“Of course. But I think it will be more meaningful if I show you what I am talking about.”

Without having a clear idea of what, precisely, she was talking about, I grunted and nodded.

She closed her eyes, tilted her head back, and stretched both of her arms upward, reminiscent of the paintings on ancient Egyptian tombs of people worshiping the sun. Or maybe it was something other than the sun they had worshiped.

Her hands moved in a counterclockwise motion while her fingers rapidly twitched as though she was using some form of sign language while typing in thin air. Suddenly, the mist-covered floor under our feet rippled and she opened her eyes. She held out a hand to each of us.

"Come. Let me show you the true wonders of the Anunnaki."

She walked into the shimmering light now surrounding the enormous room and we followed.

We entered another pool of light that was just as bright but warmer and more soothing. I looked up, blinking. It was sunlight. We were in the middle of lush, green lawns running down to a crystal blue, sun-sparkled river flanked by ancient oaks and shady willows. On the slope of the gentle hill going away from the river were all sorts of fruit trees: apple, pear, cherry, orange, and dozens of others I couldn't identify. And on the other side, sweeping toward a deep green forest, were rows of nut-bearing trees, branches heavy with walnuts, pecans, chestnuts, and almonds. There were also fruits of a more tropical nature such as mangos, bananas, olive, and fig, as well as date palms; all incongruously growing together as if some cosmic force had planned and created the perfect spot to shelter man. Almost like a...

"Yes." Sigrun smiled. "This is the place humans came to call the Garden of Eden; where they were genetically modified and put forth into the world eons ago. They never forgot this place and never understood that they weren't expelled by an angry God, but were seeded in this nurturing setting, made smarter and quicker and bestowed with knowledge that would help them to rule their environment."

Kat and I could only gawk at the incredible place. No wonder we humans never got over having to leave all of this. It was even better than the Medieval and Renaissance painters had imagined. Who wouldn't want to come back here?

"And the people who made this were...?"

"The 'star people,' the 'old ones,' the 'gods.' The Anunnaki."

"Are they...you know...are they here?" Kat asked, clinging on to my hand with a death grip.

A cloud crossed Sigrun's face. "Yes. Perhaps." She looked around uneasily. "But we're not ready to see them yet. We have another stop to make first."

She pointed behind us, and there was the Bell, hovering a hundred feet away. Oddly, it only appeared to be fifteen feet in diameter and not hundreds like when we were inside. I guess when you're the "god-race" you can do anything.

We followed her back through the glowing perimeter, and like before, she stretched out her arms, made some passes with her hands, murmured a few words in an ancient language and the ground shuddered beneath our feet.

She walked to the edge of the wall of mist that defined the interior of the bell but stopped and turned to us. "You'll find things different here, so keep close to me."

"What do you mean by 'different?'" I pulled back on Kat's hand before Sigrun could lead us any further. "Different 'bad' or different 'good?'"

"That depends on your point of view. Many would call it bad, but there are those for whom this place is the fulfillment of all of their goals."

I must have looked as confused as I felt because she sighed.

"What do you know about quantum mechanics?"

"No more than I need to, which is to say, not much."

"Well, here it happens to be very important. It is the basis of the guiding principal of Anunnaki technology and this very device. Very simply stated, it postulates that according to the Everett 'many-worlds theory,' formulated in the mid 1950s, all possibilities described by quantum theory simultaneously occur in a multiverse composed of an infinite number of independent parallel universes. Understand that, in our world, this is only a theory, but for the Anunnaki, its applications long ago opened a gateway, not just into time and space, but every possibility that ever could or will exist."

"Kinda' like that TV old show, *Quantum Leap*."

Sigrun didn't answer. Obviously she was not a fan of re-runs.

"So what you're saying is that this craft, the Bell, is some sort of an inter-dimensional space ship?"

"'Space ship' doesn't do it justice. That's really oversimplifying, but for the purposes of this discussion, it's close enough."

"Then what we're about to see is not really real?" Kat asked, staring uneasily at the barrier of shimmering white.

"No, it is completely real—at least in this universe. But you'll see soon enough. Just keep close to me and let me do any talking."

Sigrun breathed deeply, took us each by the hand, and we stepped through the wall of light.

Chapter Forty-Four

I don't know whether I was relieved or disappointed to see that we were back in Marcel's cellar. "Well that was much ado about nothing," I muttered.

Sigrun gave me a sharp look. "Follow me, and don't touch anything."

We made our way up the stairs and into Marcel's office without seeing anyone.

Hmm.... Did they all kill one another, and if so, who carted off the bodies?

As we passed through the office and out into the main shop, I suspected that something was "off," but I couldn't put my finger on exactly what. It did look like some of the stock had changed, and there were some pictures on the wall that I didn't remember, but Sigrun kept walking and I didn't have a chance to look closer. We got to the front of the shop and paused while Sigrun unlocked the door. I glanced at the objects displayed in the window and my gaze stopped on a set of lamps with some sort of parchment-looking lampshades. I was sure they weren't there earlier. Just before she beckoned us to follow, I peered closer and read on a card lettered in heavy, Gothic script:

Two fine examples of exquisite lampshade art produced by the artist Ilse Koch, crafted while she served the Fatherland at Buchenwald Concentration Camp. Both shades are produced from the skin of a single Jew and represent the highest level in the art of producing beauty from the remains of Untermenschen.

Oh my God.

"Sigrun, where the fuck are we?" I got my answer when we followed her through the door and we stepped onto the sidewalk in front of the shop.

We were in Nazi Germany.

Across the street from the shop, every building was festooned with the infamous red banners of a black swastika in white circle that I'd seen in every old newsreel about Germany under Nazi rule. And from every window and balcony hung smaller Nazi flags bedecked with garlands and flowers just like Berlin was during the Second World War. But this wasn't Berlin. It was Paris! And it wasn't the thirties or forties, it was today.

Or was it?

There was a gendarme on the corner directing traffic, and as we watched, a cavalcade of gleaming black Mercedes and BMWs, all flying Nazi pennants from their fenders, came barreling down the street. As they passed through, people stood on the sidewalk and cheered while the gendarme sporting a Nazi armband came to attention with the straight-armed Nazi salute along with most of the spectators.

When the "*Sieg heil's*" had died away, we walked across the street to one of the classic symbols of Paris, the round, street corner kiosk. At first it looked similar to those found on any street in today's Paris. It wasn't until we got close enough to read the posted notices that the strangeness began to seep through.

Tacked all around the kiosk was a collection of slogans, notices of new laws, and posters publicizing everything from National Socialism, "Good Citizen" awards, along with the times and channels of mandatory state video broadcasts, to an advertisement of a smiling Storm Trooper holding up a bottle of *Hess München Weizenbier*, a beer named for Rudolph Hess, and another with a pretty, Nordic-looking teenager with brown eyes looking longingly at a box on a store shelf labeled: *Dr. Mengele's Blaue Augen in einer Flasche* or "Blue Eyes in a Bottle."

Our train had officially pulled into the Twilight Zone.

Underneath those were dozens of official-looking announcements in the heavy, eye-straining Gothic script favored by the Nazi's, proclaiming upcoming celebrations:

Victory over America Day and the Atom Bombing of Moscow Day
Attendance is mandatory!

But the poster that really let me know that we weren't in Kansas anymore, Toto, was the one that took up almost the entire surface of the kiosk facing the street. It was some type of 3-D holograph that seemed to reach right out and grab you. The image was a Martian landscape of shifting reds and browns interspersed with gleaming cities and saucer-like crafts, adorned with red-and-black swastikas flitting back and forth. The 3-D text read:

Young women – Serve the Fatherland! Mars needs you. Join the virile young men of the SS Mars Division as they prepare to launch the expedition to colonize the Moons of Jupiter. Find fulfillment as a mother of the first generation of Jovian heroes and produce children for the Fatherland!

Sigrun saw my mouth hanging open. "Yes, in this continuum, the Nazis won the war and von Braun put a German man on the moon in 1951 followed by Mars in 1965."

"Is this real or illusion?" I was still trying to grasp the enormity of what was happening.

"Illusion," she replied, adding, "But then, again so is our world."

I continued staring at the poster and trying to wrap my head around the whole thing. She looked around nervously.

"Stop gawking. You're drawing attention to us, and that's the last thing you ever want to do in a police state."

But it was too late. We had already attracted a small crowd of puzzled passerbys who were probably trying to decide if I was some hick from the country or a dangerous radical out to upset Teutonic harmony.

"C'mon, it's time to go," she said.

But we'd stood there too long, practically advertising that we were not part of the happy community of National Socialist *übermenschen*, and in the best tradition of ass-kissing little conformist's everywhere, several had gone up to the Nazi gendarme and were earnestly babbling and pointing to us. Before we could move, the policeman started in our direction. But rather than turning and running, which would have been my first instinct, Sigrun whispered, "Follow me and keep quiet."

That wouldn't have been my first choice, but we didn't have many other options, so we fell in line beside her.

She walked directly to the cop, but before he could open his mouth, she gave a perfunctory, *Sieg Heil*, and loosed a rapid-fire barrage of questions to him in a mixture of French and German.

It was almost too fast for me to follow, but the general gist was that she was asking for directions to her grandfather's shop.

"Why, it is right across the street," he answered, obviously trying to recall if we'd just come from that direction. "But I also have some questions for you, so let us begin by seeing your identity discs."

We were fucked.

But Sigrun had prepared for this possibility. Ignoring his request for identification, she pointed at the shop window. "You mean that one there that says Marcel & Sons?"

He nodded, but then looked at her sternly. "Oui, but what is your business there and who are these people with you? I think you had better come to Gestapo headquarters to sort this out." He reached for Kat's arm and my fingers tightened around the OTF stiletto in my pocket.

Sigrun held up her hand. "I do not have time for this foolishness. I must retrieve my Grandfather's *Pour le Mérite* medal and bring it to him immediately as he is the keynote speaker at today's Victory Over America celebration that is about to get underway at the Arc de Triumph in less than thirty minutes."

The gendarme did a double-take. "What did you say? The only man I know of around here who has that medal is the heroic *alter Kämpfer*, the old-fighter himself: Marcel. And what exactly are you to him?"

Sigrun drew herself up proudly. "*Moi*? I am his granddaughter and that of another hero of the Fatherland, the great Sigrun herself."

The gendarme took a step forward and peered at her. "Indeed. Now that you mention it, yes, you do look like her.

The spitting image. I mean, I have never met her personally, but we do have a framed photograph taken of her with our second Furher Reinhardt Heydrich at his swearing-in ceremony back in 1955 when our dear leader Adolph Hitler passed away after serving the Fatherland so nobly for so many years." He looked her up and down and then stepped back respectfully. "Yes, yes, the bloodline will always tell. Imagine." He beamed with socialist pride. "The granddaughter of one of the leaders of the sacred Vrillian standing right here on my corner. Ah, pure Aryan breeding shines through."

He saluted. "May I extend the congratulations of Paris and the Reich, and of course, if there is anything else that I can do...?"

"*Non, merci.* It is very kind of you, but we need to retrieve the medal and bring it to my grandfather, *très rapidement*, but I do appreciate your assistance." She gave him a friendly *Sieg Heil*, and motioned for us to follow her across the street.

"What the fuck was that all about?" I growled when I thought we were out of earshot.

"Shush, not so loud. There are video cameras and mics everywhere. In this universe, I, as Sigrun, became lauded for helping decipher the Vrillian technology." She unlocked the shop door, and as we turned to head back down the cellar, I saw a sleek, black truck with SS men at the open weapons ports stop next to the gendarme and heated conversation began.

"Uh, oh... I think we ought to get the hell outta Dodge PDQ. Look."

Sigrun turned. "Damn. I had hoped we'd have a bit more time before the local Gestapo office became interested in a granddaughter who doesn't exist. But yes, you're right. We need to be gone by the time they enter the shop."

She led us quickly back down the stone stairs. Halfway to bottom we heard banging on the front door.

"Gestapo! Open up!"

By the time we'd reached the glowing perimeter of the Bell, we could see jack-booted feet descending the stairs. Moments later, amidst shouts of "Halt!" machine pistols opened up, spraying the entire chamber with bullets and some type of laser-like energy flashes.

Fortunately, at the same instant we passed into radiant mist of the Bell and quiet reigned once more.

Chapter Forty-Five

"My God, what was that place?" Kat shook her head the way a wet dog does at the end of an unwanted bath. "Is that one of those alternate realities?"

"Oh, it is real enough for the people of this universe."

"Then why take us here? Did you want to frighten us about what the world would have been like if the Nazis had won the Second World War? I mean, even the Germans like Gram and Uncle Max are glad that the Nazis didn't win."

Kat hugged her arms to her body, but I doubted the chill came from the temperature, more likely revulsion.

Sigrun shook her head. "You're wrong. There are plenty 'true believers,' both fascist and communist inspired, who not only don't share your opinion, but are still actively working to achieve the National Socialist dream. And I'm sure it won't surprise you that foremost among these is Hans Kammler and people like my sometimes-husband, Marcel."

"So this is where Third Reich nostalgia buffs like Kammler and company want to book a first class ticket to?" I asked. Pieces were slowly starting to fit.

"Not just go, they want to bring it back home with them."

"Do you mean that those shits who kidnapped me want to try to set up a similar society in the world we all live in?" Kat was as upset as she was incredulous.

"Not duplicate it; they want to bring it to our reality, lock, stock and barrel."

"How can they do that? We've got lots of self-serving assholes in our governments, but even those who'd offer up dog-crap if they thought it would buy them votes, wouldn't go along with supporting giving the Third Reich another whirl."

Sigrun flashed me a pitying look. "First, I think you're giving the supporters of dog crap too much credit for good sense, but secondly, they have no intention of letting any political discussion or dissensions take place. They intend to rip a hole in the space/time continuum and let the world you just witnessed bleed through to the one we know."

"Well, it wouldn't work!" Kat glared. "Why, the entire world would band together and fight something like that. I mean, every race and religion and country would—"

Now it was my turn as the guy with the bucket of ice-cold water.

"That's a nice thought, Kat, and don't get me wrong, I dig a kumbaya moment as much as the next guy, but we're talking about a world that can't even agree on the right way to walk and chew gum, let alone come together in a unity of race, religion, and politics. Hell, back in WWII, anti-Semitic Muslims under the Grand Mufti formed their own SS Divisions and fought for the friggin' Nazis, for Christ's sake. And we just saw in both worlds how the Nazis had plenty of collaborators, like the Milice in France. Why, there were even Nazi organizations in England, Holland, Hungry, and a dozen other countries, not to mention our own German/American Bund of the thirties, and the skinheads of today."

Sigrun nodded. "And don't forget, using the advanced science in weaponology and rocketry of a Nazi regime that never fell, the countries of our world wouldn't have a chance. Between lasers, Mach 10 aircraft, and nukes that they're not afraid of using, whichever countries of our world didn't surrender immediately would be reduced to smoking, radioactive ruins.”

“Thanks for the boost to our morale.” If it was possible to go beyond depression, I was well on my way. “But why do they have to screw up this world? Why not just hop in the Bell for a one way trip to *Übermensch*-land and leave it at that?”

“Because those nasty laws of physics get in the way. Remember what they say about two objects occupying the same space at the same time?”

“Ummm...not really, but my guess would be that it can’t be done?”

“*Richtig, mein Herr*, absolutely correct.”

“So then that would mean Hans and the boys...”

“Can’t stay in that world because they already exist there. And it has been eating at Kammler ever since he discovered the Bell’s amazing potential during the test flights in Upper Silesia in 1945.”

“How did he find that place? Did he know how to operate the Bell?”

“Only how to activate it. As I said, there is only one of us who is truly adept at *Die Glocke’s* operation. Maria.”

“Yeah, but you seem to know what you were doing just now.”

She shrugged. “I have some small skill obtained mostly by observing Maria, but she is a true Adept of navigating the inter-dimensional cosmos. Originally, that is why the Anunnaki created the order of the Priestesses of the Stars, to instruct handpicked, exceptional young girls, whose greater sensitivity makes them ideal candidates for operating designated pieces of the Vril technology—especially their interstellar/inter-dimensional transportation devices.

"That is what your friend, Max Becker-von Buchholz discovered on the stela they unearthed in the late thirties; the instructions of how to access the Bell transportation apparatus—and the tool to accomplish it."

And it hit me. "The 'key.' Of course. It told them what the key was and how to use it."

She nodded. "They initiated an order of Adepts, who would be able to use the Bell and other devices, to communicate and even visit them in the Aldebaran system and beyond. They gave each of these ancient High Priestesses a remote control, if you will, that allowed them to call the Bell the Anunnaki had created to accomplish this. And to ensure that they could always access it, they gave it to them disguised as a common cosmetic box, and only they would know how to use it to send a signal to the Bell wherever it was. So that no one but their chosen could operate it, they also entrusted each with one of the rings the Annunaki wore, and only by inserting this ring in the box would it be activated."

"So that's why everyone has been so red-hot to get their hands on it."

"Yes, and that is also why they needed both items, because one is useless without the other."

The whole time we'd been talking, Sigrun had been making small gestures with her hands that reminded me of the *Saturday Night Live* spoofs of ancient Egyptian priests and priestesses doing those "Walk like an Egyptian" moves. It had apparently struck Kat too.

"And that's what you're doing with your hands right now," she asked, "–using the gestures and hand movements that were taught to those ancient priestesses to operate this craft?"

"Award yourself a gold star, *chérie*. Yes, and now that you mention it, please remain still and breathe deeply. We are about to arrive."

Before I had enough time to ask "Where?" my stomach lurched, leaving me breathless.

"We're here."

"Where's here?"

But Sigrun had already entered the mist, and a second later, vanished into it.

I took Kat's hand. "Whadda ya say, babe? Up for another adventure?"

She forced a smile. "Why the heck not? 'In for a penny, in for a pound,' as they say. Just one thing…"

"What?"

"When we get home, can we just spend the first night doing something dull, boring and predictable? Maybe like watching the tube in old sweats with nothing more exciting than a bowl of popcorn?"

"Well, I did have my heart set on going after the Loch Ness monster, followed by Bigfoot and the Abominable Snowman, but I might be persuaded if you'd care to make it worth my while."

She kissed my cheek. "Hmmm…Perhaps I could exchange the sweats for a little Victoria's Secret number I've been saving and we could put the TV on one of the 'naughty' channels…"

"Sold!"

And with that happy thought we stepped out into… the same cellar we'd just left.

Chapter Forty-Six

Uh-oh, this can't be good.

"Sigrun?"

We cleared the bright mist and our eyes began to adapt to the dim light of the cellar. It looked like the same Nazi shop we'd just left, but then again, so did the one we'd started from. Which one was it?

I squeezed my eyes closed to make them adjust more quickly. When I reopened them, I saw that we were indeed back where we started, although many of those we'd left here were rather the worse for wear.

The colonel was over by the stairs holding a handkerchief compress to a large and still-bleeding wound in Professor Dombroski's stomach. There were three men down who weren't moving; one of the colonel's men and both of Kammler's stooges. Kammler himself stood next to Marcel, who was deathly pale and gasping for breath, while his son tried to force a small tablet, probably nitroglycerin, into his mouth. Apparently, Kammler had decided that he'd just as soon see Marcel gasp out his last breath without the lifesaving tablet since he was pointing his pistol straight at young Marcel's head.

But he hadn't fired and he didn't look happy about it. So what was stopping him?

"*Guten tag*, Christopher. I told you we would meet again."

I turned toward the sound of the low, soft voice.

Oh, Christ. I should have known. Ria. Maria. The woman/girl who had been the leader of the enigmatic Vrillian during the first half of the last century and who should have been over 115 years old.

Not only was she not, she looked as beautiful as ever. Long, honey-colored hair curled around her shoulders, hanging halfway down her back. Her wide, blue eyes looked at me, and then Kat, and brimmed with sadness. "Oh, Christopher." She sighed.

I didn't have a chance to ask her what she meant because the man standing beside her took a step forward. It was Max.

"You've got a hell of a lot of explaining to do, Max." I said.

"Perhaps." He nodded. "But for now, I'm glad to see that you and Katrina are all right. Thank you for that, Herr Brennan."

"Hey, I don't need any thanks for whatever it was that I was able to do to make up for involving your niece in this crap. Speaking of which, while we're on the subject of apologies, you might wanna throw one in yourself for involving me in a world of shit for the past two weeks."

"Yes, of course, you are right, and I do intend to make it up to you, but I am guessing that you have discovered by now that the issues at the heart of this conspiracy eclipse all of our personal lives."

Sure he was right, but I was fed up with guys with secrets who assumed my life could be thrown away with altruistic phrase that it was "worth it" in the cosmic scheme of things.

Not to me it wasn't.

I glanced at Sigrun. None of this surprised her. I stared at Max and Maria. "These were the two people I saw you talking to on the corner that you said you 'didn't know,' right?"

She nodded slowly. "I'm sorry I had to lie to you, Christophe."

"No, you're not."

She smiled. "You're right, I'm not."

"But I am, Celeste," said Maria. "Or should I refer to you by the name you used when we first came together in Munich after the First World War—Sigrun?"

"Either is fine." She shrugged.

"Celeste..." Marcel was trying to sit up.

She moved to his side. "Yes, Marcel?"

He looked up at her, baffled pain in his eyes. "I'm dying, aren't I?"

"Oui, my darling, I'm afraid so."

"And the Bell... all this time it was a lie. It could not make me younger."

"As I told you, cheri, only if you had accessed it before you started to age."

He coughed and winced with the pain in his chest. "Then why did you not tell me back then?"

"Because summoning the Bell saps an incredible amount of your Vril, your life force. That is, unless you are an Adept like Maria there." She tilted her head towards Maria and Max who had started moving from the stairs.

They stopped next to where Marcel slumped at the table. He looked up at them.

"Save me. Work your magic, call the old ones, take me into the Bell. Help me..."

His eyes franticly flitted from Maria to Sigrun, who slowly shook her head.

"*Je suis désolée ma douce*. I'm sorry. I know that I am not a good person. I have always taken what I want, just like you men do, except that I had a pretty face and a cute derrière, which I knew how to use along with the psychic talent inherited from my gypsy mother."

"Gypsy?" It was Kammler who spoke. He stood there, hand resting on the butt of his pistol in his belt, scowling. "You never told me..."

"No, Hans, I didn't. Neither did I tell any of the fascist Aryans of the Reich, including my 'sometimes' husband, here. As I said, I always had the ability to see the world as it is, and I knew from the first séance of the Vril Gesellschaft I attended back in Munich, that one who had gypsy blood in her veins was going to be categorized as a *mischling*, a half-breed, a mongrel in the coming New Order. My mother had been very careful to educate me at what it meant to be a crossbreed, or even worse, a gypsy in Central Europe in those days." She ran the tips of her fingers over the slowly pulsing blue veins in the back of Marcel's parchment colored hand. "And of course, I was right. The Nazis, like my persistent and boring sometimes-lover, General Dr. Hans Friedrich Karl Franz Kammler," she carelessly gestured towards Kammler who was now staring open-mouthed, "sent the mongrel races like my mother's family to the ovens. *Nicht wahr*—correct, Herr Doctor?"

He clamped his jaw shut and regarded her with an expression that, in a normal, caring human being, could have been classified as hurt.

"Why, even my dear husband, sent his share of gypsies to the Death Camps as part of his Milice duties. *N'est ce pas*, my darling?"

"Why?" Marcel's voice was becoming weaker. "Why didn't you tell me? Maybe I could have saved some of them...at least your close relatives."

"*Ja, natürlich.* I, too, would have spared your family." Kammler said, trying to regain some of his lost confidence.

Sigrun stepped back, her green eyes flashing. "*Mon Dieu* and *Meine Gott.* The two of you would have done that for this poor little *Mischling*? How gallant."

She leaned close to Kammler's face, her gaze hard. "And what would you have done about the other half million who were not part of my immediate family?"

"I-I... You know as well as I that there was no place for them in the New Order."

"Ah, yes. The New Order that Maria, Traute, Gudruna, and Heike and I were supposed to help you and Goebbels, Himmler, and Hitler usher in to rule the world? I just showed those young people that world."

She turned to Kat and me.

"What were your impressions of the Aryan paradise? Did you like it?"

I turned and spat onto Kammler's polished shoe. "What do you think?"

He fumbled for the pistol still stuck in his belt.

"Don't even think about it," the colonel called from across the room. He stood up from where the professor lay, now cold and lifeless, and leveled the big .45 automatic at the center of Kammler's chest. "The boys at the CIA would like to have the pleasure of showing you the methods used to extract information from the Taliban, so don't tempt me."

Kammler's hand twitched as he gripped the pistol butt tighter. His eyes darted between the colonel and me. He glared at me, obviously hoping to see me cringe, as had so many of his victims in those good old days of jack-boots and death camps. I answered him in the same spirit of reason and respect with the universally recognized one-finger salute.

His face turned red and he started to swing his gun towards me.

"Just try it. Please," the colonel said quietly.

Kammler froze.

For a moment I think the SS fanatic weighed trading his own life for the satisfaction of ventilating me—the one who'd thwarted so many of his plans. But in the end, he flashed me a nasty smile as if he had one more ace up his sleeve, and slowly and carefully laid the automatic on the table in front of him.

The colonel motioned to me. "Bring me his gun."

But Kat thought he talked to her, or maybe she was just trying to take control of her life and circumstances, because before I could move, she'd scooped up the gun and was moving toward the colonel.

I swear I saw it coming, but just like in a bad dream, I couldn't move fast enough.

As she brushed in front of Kammler, he yanked her by the hair, forcing her head back into the crook of his elbow and squeezed, almost completely cutting off her oxygen, while he ripped the gun from her grip.

"Now it is you who must lay down your weapon, Colonel."

I thought the colonel was going to tell him to shove it and start shooting. I think he really considered it, but after a few tense moments, he laid his pistol on the rough stone floor and moved away.

"*Sehr gut.* And now," Kammler said with Kat still in his choke hold, "I am going to do what I came here to do, and for that," he pointed the pistol at Maria and Max, "I am going to require your assistance Fräulein Maria."

She shook her head.

"If you do not do what I require, I will begin shooting the occupants of this room one by one, beginning with this lovely young lady."

Max took a step forward. "No, please. I will help you."

Kammler erupted in a short, barking laugh. "You? You are a traitor to every principal upon which the Reich was founded. Even if you somehow knew how to operate the device, I would not trust you. No, it must be Maria. She was, after all, the one who translated the workings of *Die Glocke*. Now." He raised the gun. "*Kommen, schnell.*"

Maria glanced at Max. He nodded slightly and she walked over and stood beside Kammler. He handed her a piece of paper.

"You will program these coordinates into whatever controls determine where the craft will go."

Maria looked at the paper and her brow furrowed. "Are you certain these are correct? I am not a cartographer, but aren't these the coordinates for the South Polar Region?"

"A former German base in New Swabia in Antarctica, to be precise, where important members of the party and government of the Reich have been in exile since 1945. And now, their patience is about to be rewarded. They will become an integral part of our vision of the Thousand Year Reich."

Nothing should have been able to surprise me at this stage, but I joined the others in stunned silence before I mumbled, "Holy crap. Please don't tell me that you've had old Adolph stashed down there for the past seventy years?"

Kammler straightened until he was almost at attention. "Sadly, der Führer passed away in 1955, and Party Secretary Bormann in 1972. But the loyal young women of the *Bund Deutscher Mädel* League of German Girls, the BDM, who heroically chose to go into exile with them, succeeded in bearing the next generations of leaders. It is they who we are going to rescue and see installed in their rightful positions."

"Oh my frigging word." I didn't realize it was me that spoke, but since everybody was staring in my direction it must have been.

Kammler, on the other hand, was done explaining. "Activate the device," he snapped at Maria, "and when we have successfully retrieved our passengers and return here, you and this girl will be released."

All three of them stepped beneath the glowing rim of the Bell.

I wasn't about to let that bastard take Kat again, but when I started to move, there was a flash and a popping sound as air rushed in to fill the vacuum, and the Bell was gone.

"Shit!" I turned back to Max and smacked my had on the table. "Now what are we supposed to do?"

"Wait."

"Oh, great. Thanks for the words of wisdom. How long did it take you to come up with that gem?"

He smiled grimly. "*Ach*, Christopher. The young. They are always so impatient."

"Yeah? Well maybe that's because we don't have age-reversing flying saucers at our disposal, so a few years here and there really matter."

"It will not be that long," was the less than inspiring response from Max.

If anything, it only increased my ready-to-explode irritation.

"You know what, Max? Since the day we met, you've been bullshitting me and using me as a pawn in some high stakes game I don't even know the rules to. And you've used your own niece as well."

He sighed. "Yes, you're right of course—on all counts. You just don't know why."

"All right, since we're probably going to be waiting here for the next couple of days, why don't you take this opportunity to clue me in to the whys."

"First, as I mentioned, it will not be anywhere that long, and secondly, yes. I will do that."

He pointed to the table. "Please, everyone, you all have an interest in this. With the exception of Sigrun." He turned to her. "I suspect you will need some background that, I warn you, will cause you to have to rethink your entire conception of the universe, your planet, and even your very species."

Before he could explain, the air in the cellar began to crackle with static electricity. The Bell was returning.

With a rush of displaced air and a flash of brilliance, it materialized in the same spot it had left. Maria, followed by Kammler, still holding his pistol to the back Kat's head, emerged and came towards us.

Kammler waved the gun at Maria. "Get what you need and be quick about it."

She nodded and walked to the table. "Max, I need the box and key."

"Are you certain that you want to do this, Maria?"

The was something more going on between them, a deeper conversation with hidden meaning, like a secret code that only they were privy to.

But all I was interested in was Kat. They could keep their secret codes and flying saucers. My only goal was getting Kat and getting the fuck outta there.

Maria gathered up both objects. "I'm sorry, Max, but yes, I must. That is the only way that he will release the—the young lady."

Holding the box and the key, she started walking back to the Bell.

"Wait!" It was the colonel. "You don't have to do this. We can insure that if Kammler tries anything, he'll never make it back into the Bell."

The colonel's two remaining operatives had moved to either side and were now pointing their automatics directly at Kammler.

"So let the girl go, Kammler, and place your gun on the floor."

I could see Kammler had no intention of doing anything of the kind. He had nothing to lose. The room was moments away from erupting in gunfire.

"No more bloodshed, please," Maria pleaded. "I must go with him to navigate *Die Glocke* to the place he wishes. And I am the only one who can do it."

"Will you be coming back?" I asked, although I already knew the answer.

"No."

I wasn't surprised. Some inner sense told me that it was going to be a one-way trip.

She smiled at Max. "Farewell, my love. Perhaps we will meet again someday, or perhaps we have already met again, somewhere and sometime."

"Already met?" I said.

"Yes." She turned to me. "Can you recall all the times we met?"

"Ah, yeah."

We'd done a lot more than meet most of the times, but I let that one stay where it was.

"And were you never curious as to why I sometimes appeared to you as different ages?"

"Well, now that you mention it…"

"That is because, young Christopher, as a consequence of having spent so much time traveling in *Die Glocke*, I have become…for lack of a better word, 'unstuck' in time. And now I am doomed to drift, never quite knowing where, when, or at what age I will appear or to whom. The only thing that I do know, is that it will usually be to someplace or someone that I have a strong connection to." She smiled mischievously. "So you should be flattered that we have 'met' so often."

I did something that I hadn't done since the middle school Snowflake Frolic Dance when I spilled a whole cup of Dr. Pepper down the front of Mary Jane Flynn: I blushed.

Then she became serious again. "And so goodbye, *mein Schatz*, and this time, I'm afraid it is for good, so a kiss for luck." But as she brushed my cheek, she whispered in my ear, "You must not continue to see Katrina anymore."

"Why?" I asked.

And she told me.

Maria then spoke a few words to Sigrun that I couldn't quite make out before Kammler cut her off.

"Enough! *Herkommen*. We are leaving right now."

Maria walked back and stood in front of him. "First release the girl."

Kammler looked like he was going to refuse, but Maria planted herself in front of him, her blue eyes glittering like ice chips, until he finally dropped his gaze. He contemptuously pushed Kat away and gripped Maria's arm instead.

Maria glanced once more at Max, turned back to Kammler, took a deep breath, and they both passed into the field of light which grew brighter and more indistinct until, with a whoosh and crackle of ozone, it vanished.

Chapter Forty-Seven

The colonel glared at Max. "Where did she go and when can we get another chance to talk to her?"

Max shook his head. "You can't. She has left this plane and will not be coming back. But she will insure that neither Kammler, nor any of what he plans to unleash on this world, will either."

"Stop talking in riddles, damn you. Where has she taken the Bell and what is she going to do with it?"

"She has taken it to the place where Kammler thinks he will find a hero's welcome, but all he will find there is oblivion. And as for the Bell itself, she knows as well as I that it has outlived the purpose for which it was built. She is going to destroy it."

"How?"

"Have you ever heard of the Pauli Exclusion Principle?"

"Yes, but what does that have to do with destroying the Bell?"

"As you know, the principal applies to quantum mechanics, and simply put it says that no two particles can occupy the same quantum states."

"Yes, or they will annihilate one another. But one more time; what does that have to with Kammler and the Bell?"

"When Herr General Dr Hans Friedrich Karl Franz Kammler meets his doppleganger in the 'Volks Paradise' of the Third Reich that never fell, it will result in a cataclysm that will destroy them and the Bell, as well as all future access to that dimension."

The colonel's eyes narrowed and he leaned forward. "But we need the Bell back here. Do you mean that there will be no way to communicate with those other advanced beings? What about their technology and science? Think what we could do with that to benefit mankind."

He was breathing hard and I guessed that there was more to his consternation than a deep, abiding empathy for the fate of mankind. But if the colonel's concern bothered Max, he didn't show it. He merely shrugged and continued.

"That's what Maria, and those she was in contact with, are thinking about. They've concluded they have already interfered too much over the past million years and mankind will be better off advancing—or not—on their own. The contact with Anunnaki and Vril technology is over."

The tension oozed out of the room. With dull, defeated eyes the colonel motioned to his men to pick up the body of the professor. He gazed at Max and Sigrun. "This isn't over, you know. I still intend to debrief the both of you before we leave Paris, so don't go anywhere. I will have the necessary papers and warrants from Interpol tomorrow or you can just show up at the Sûreté offices in the morning and we can do it the easy way."

"I will be there." Max said.

Sigrun merely flashed the colonel a pouty smile that could have meant anything, and probably did.

"What about him?" The colonel pointed at Marcel, who was sitting quietly in his chair for a change. He hadn't spoken during the entire exchange with Maria and Kammler. "I'm sure the Sûreté will want to speak to him as well."

Sigrun glanced down at him and shrugged. "Then they will have to speak very loudly. He's dead."

Marcel's son stooped down next to him and took his pulse. "You killed him. You bitch!"

"Nonsense, you were standing right here, I never touched him."

"No," he snarled, "You just lied and cheated on him."

"You are wrong on both counts. I never lied to him about my infidelities. And if you knew your father better, you'd understand that faithfulness had nothing to do with our relationship. It was based on mutual interests." She cocked her head, regarding him calmly. "This should be a fulfilling day for you. You, finally, at the age of forty-one, get to become a man in your own right and not an errand boy for your father. And to welcome you into your newfound manhood, I am making you a present of my half of his business. So, *bon chance* and *au revoir*, young Marcel. I think it is time for me to see other parts of the world."

"Just don't wander away until we've had a chance to have our little chat."

"You have no grounds to arrest or detain me on any charges, Monsieur Colonel, or you would have already done so." She picked up her purse.

"I wouldn't try to get too cute with this Ms.—"

"Sigrun. Just Sigrun."

"Well, remember, as I said, we can get a warrant, and I'm sure I can figure out some interesting charges.

"*Bien, mon colonel.* I am always ready to be entertained."

She moved to me and ran one long, painted fingernail across my cheek. "And that is something that I very much appreciate about you, *ma douce.* You do always amuse me."

This prompted the colonel to focus his attention on me.

"And as for you." He waved in my direction. "Don't you go anywhere either until we've had a chance to—"

"Here's everything I have that you don't already know." I tossed him what had been in the epaulet of my leather jacket for the past two weeks. He caught it in his left hand and peered at it.

"The flash drive. Hmmm, maybe we won't need to talk to you just yet, but let me know where you're going to be for the next couple of weeks."

"Boston. As soon as I get outta here, I'm going back to Boston."

"You mean *we're* going back to Boston, don't you?"

Kat saw me hesitate and her eyes filled with confusion.

Then the confusion turned to hurt and anger.

"Don't be so enthusiastic. What is wrong with you? Don't you want me to come with you?"

"Kat, it's not that, it's just that—"

She paled except for the twin flush marks she always got on her cheeks when she was embarrassed or upset. This was definitely upset.

"It's her isn't it?" She gestured angrily at Sigrun. "I've seen the way she looks at you."

She stared at me until I finally had to shift my gaze away.

"I knew it. You've been sleeping with her. The whole time I was tied up in some dingy apartment, you were getting it on with her."

What could I say? She was right.

She rounded on Sigrun. "Well, Missy, isn't that right?"

If Kat expected her to blush and stammer, she didn't know what a century of shifting alliances, artful dissembling, and general duplicities could do to a girl.

"Why yes, of course, *ma petite*. What do you expect?"

Sigrun, with her usual aplomb, threw a little more gasoline on the fire by sliding up close to me. "Le beau Christophe is quite adept at making a woman of any age, feel...well, you know what I mean, *cherie*."

"Knock it off, Sigrun." Ironically, I actually wanted to knock *her* off at that moment. But what could I say that wouldn't be just another lie in a long string of bullshit and tiptoeing around the truth? However, what it was doing to Kat didn't make me feel less like the jerk I was.

Kat turned back to me, tears in her eyes. "Why? And not just the 'why' did you do it. I get that. You're no different than lots of other guys I've known who think with their dick rather than their heart. Why now, after all this and coming to care for each other, have you fallen out of love with me? Please give me that much. Tell me why?"

But of course that was the last thing I could do. I was still trying to wrap my head around what Maria had told me.

I opened my mouth to say something that would make everything ok, but of course nothing would. So, reluctantly I said, "Kat, now this is all over, maybe we need to take a little break from all the intense stuff."

"You bastard." She whispered and ran up the steps. A minute later I heard the shop door slamming and knew that she was gone. Again.

I stood there for I don't know how long, wanting with all my heart to go after her and tell her I loved her, but it was no use. That was the last thing that I could—or should—do. So I stood there and let the misery flow in like the tide and roll over my head.

I sensed rather than saw Sigrun move up quietly behind me.

"Don't take it so hard, *chéri*. Young women seldom know their own hearts. It seldom occurs until they forget about what the head tells them they should do and what the heart tells them that they need. *Très triste*, so sad."

Her pretty lips turned down in a frown but her eyes were filled with jaded amusement and something else; not quiet sympathy or even empathy, but something that said: "Been there, done-that, and sort of wished I hadn't." She was a hard girl to read. All I knew was that she'd played me for a sucker from day one.

So when her lips brushed the back of my neck I whirled around and caught both of her small hands in mine. "Stop it, Sigrun."

She gazed back at me from under long lashes and said nothing.

"I only want to know one thing. Why? Why did you play me for a fool from the first time we met? I got a hunch that our 'accidental' meeting at the airport was not as random as it seemed, was it?"

"What do you think?"

"I think that you and Marcel cooked up the whole thing to get me to reveal the key and the box, and now that I think of it, I'll bet Kammler was in on the whole thing too."

"There. Now that wasn't so hard, was it, chéri? See how easy it is when you start thinking with the right head? Of course Kammler was in on it, but don't think that's because I agreed with his mission. I didn't, but he thought I did. Always the problem of the National Socialists. Everything was black and white to them: for us or against us. No shades of grey."

She stared off into space for a moment. "And what I have discovered about myself over the past hundred-plus years is that shades of grey is all I really am. Like a cat in the night— soft and grey." She moved closer.

I held out my hand to stop her. "That's a good description of you, Sigrun, *le chat gris*. And underneath the soft, little paws are sharp, grey claws."

"Why, that is very good, *ma belle ami*. You have perhaps a future as a poet, *oui*?"

I sighed. This was getting me nowhere. She loved this riposte back and forth and could probably keep it up all day. I, on the other hand, was heartily sick of it and wanted nothing more than to get the hell outta Dodge and try to figure out how my life got so screwed up in such a short period of time. I did have one more question though.

"Then could you have gotten Kammler to release Kat whenever you wanted?"

She shook her head. "No. I tried, but he said only when he had the key, and even then, if things had turned out as he planned, I think he would have killed her—and probably all of us, for that matter. The only thing that mattered to him was the complete and total dominance of National Socialism. Life to them has absolutely no value other than how it can be exploited for the regime. So you may believe me or not, but yes, I used you. But I never wished for you and your amoureux to be harmed in any way." She moved closer until her lips touched mine and her perfume snaked its way through my senses. "Especially you, *mon amour*."

She stepped back and placed her hand on one sweetly curved hip, regarding me with appraising eyes. "Why don't you forget about your flighty young girl and come see the world with someone who knows what really makes it spin."

Her expression held all of her usual amused cynicism, but behind it was something that, had I not known better, I might have called longing and perhaps even—loneliness?

Another couple of months of mindless hedonism and Olympic-quality sex sounded very enticing and, despite how I was trying to distance myself from Kat, I couldn't give up on what I truly felt for her.

"Thanks for the offer, Sigrun but, no. I'm going back to Boston."

She almost looked like she cared and was sad about it, but a second later, the Sigrun who played her life and those around her like a concert pianist was back in control.

"Ah, *trop mal, mon cœur*, too bad. I do think we could have kept one another amused." She shrugged, started for the stairs, paused, and turning back to me said with a wink. "If you ever get bored of being bored, look me up, *chéri*." She puckered her perfect lips into a pantomime kiss. "I think that we will meet again, *mais oui*? *Certainement!*"

Without a backward glance she turned away and walked up the stairs.

The last I saw of her was a tight, black skirt, slim legs rising from 5-inch stiletto heels, and steps on a stone stairway that sounded as hollow as the entire world did to me.

Chapter Forty-Eight

The next day, I caught a flight back to Boston. I slept most of the way back across the Atlantic with only a few thoughts that if some random hijacker decided to plunge the plane in the ocean, he'd get no argument from me.

I arrived safe and sound and in one piece, except for my fragmented dreams rattling around in my brain like old pieces of broken glass.

Since I had nothing to go home to except an empty apartment and some lonely cockroaches, I took the longer and cheaper way out to Brighton via the T. It stopped on every corner and usually took hours, but since it was late on a Sunday and traffic was light, I arrived on my street corner just after 10 p.m. I slung my backpack over my shoulder, turned up my coat collar to the damp wind, and started down the half block to my building. I'd only gotten a few feet when I heard footsteps behind me. Being more tired of running than scared, I stepped into the next flickering pool of sodium streetlight glow and stopped. I was hardly surprised when a figure in a brown tweed topcoat walked up to me.

"*Guten Abend, mein junger Freund.*" Max smiled as he strode up next to me.

"And a wicked pisser night to you too, Max, but you'll understand if your 'young friend' doesn't feel very friendly right now. So if you don't mind, I'm gonna continue on to my apartment where there's a half bottle of inexpensive blended scotch. I'm gonna polish it off if the roaches haven't drunk it all up. Then I'm gonna sleep for a couple of weeks, so why don't you give me a call in a few weeks and I'll meet you for some beer and bratwurst somewhere...or not. I really don't care."

"Here, let me carry that." He reached for my knapsack.

"What part of 'No' don't you understand? Oh, forget it. If you want to share a bottle of mediocre scotch and some bad company, you're welcome to tag along."

"Danke. Maybe I can cheer you up a bit."

I unlocked the outside door to the building and put the second key into the apartment door lock. "Somehow I doubt it, but..."

There was no resistance in the lock from the key. The door was already un-latched. I entered the apartment and saw why.

Colonel Novak was sitting on my living room sofa.

"Wow, should I be flattered I have so many friends, or am I caught in some kind of alien-induced time warp where I keep seeing the same smiling faces over and over 'til we all figure out something better to do with our time? Hey, wait—I've got an idea. Why don't I go get drunk while you guys take a flying leap at a rolling donut?"

No one laughed, least of all me.

"Or not. I really don't care." I took my backpack from Max, tossed it into the closet, then went into the kitchen, got the bottle—and three glasses.

"I have no problem with drinking alone, so if you want any, I'd advise taking it now, 'cause I'm not planning on seeing any of it left when, or if, I wake up tomorrow."

I poured a healthy slug and knocked it back. Neither the colonel or Max made any move toward the bottle, so I poured another, took a swallow, and leaned back in the old, broken-spring armchair.

"Look, Colonel, in a very little while I'm gonna be very plastered. I suggest that if you're intending to get something coherent out of me, you better do it soon."

The colonel took a shiny black object out of his pocket and held it up. The flash drive.

"You lied. You said everything you knew was on this. But it's missing all the crucial pages of the technical schematics. Look."

He opened his laptop, plugged the flash drive into the USB port, and turned the screen. "Do you see the page numbers at the bottom?"

I nodded.

"Then look here. They start with page one and go up to seven." He scrolled though the same sets of drawings and diagrams I'd seen the first time I'd looked at the drive's contents back in Germany.

"So? It looks fine to me? What's your point?"

"My point is that the page after number seven should be numbered eight, but it isn't."

He scrolled back and forth between pages seven and nine. He was right, there was no page eight.

"And the entire drive is like that. All the key pages that tie each technology together and tell the final steps to making it operational are missing. So I'll go back to what I said to you in Paris. We mean to have this for the United States, which means you have two choices. Give me the missing pages or sit in a cell in Guantanamo until you do."

It almost sounded like a step up career-wise. Three squares a day, bed, TV, and probably lots of pick-up soccer games.

"I told you. Outside of having barely glimpsed at what's on there, I know squat."

The colonel stood up, reached into his coat pocket, pulled out two plastic tie cuffs and held them out to me. "I think you know the drill with these."

But Max held up his hand. "Wait. He is telling you the truth. He knows nothing of the missing pages."

"How do you know?"

"Because I have them."

"You? Perfect. After you've spent years trying to convince us you had nothing to do with the project."

"And for the most part, that's true. I was only a very minor player, but from an overall standpoint, perhaps you're right, there were a few things I was aware of that I held back."

"Like the detailed instructions for building an inter-dimensional transport?"

"Yes."

"I suppose I can find room for two bunks at Guantanamo as easily as one. Or the pair of you can stop the bullshit and tell me what I want to know. I've spent the best part of my twenty-year hitch in the Air Force trying to separate the truth from delusion, starting with Project Blue Book."

I couldn't stop myself. "I know I shouldn't stick my hand back into this smelly kettle of fish, but didn't Project Blue Book get cancelled in the late sixties?"

"Yes, in 1969. But of the approximately 20% of the UFO sightings that couldn't be explained away were picked up by Dr. J. Allen Hynek, one of the civilian researchers on the project. He and a few others believed that the hundreds of unsolved sightings and incidents were only the tip of the iceberg. So in 1973, they started the Center for UFO Studies, or CUFOS."

"By a 'few others,' I'm guessing you're including yourself?"

"Let me ask you a question," the colonel began. "Have you ever heard of a program that took place in Antarctica from August 1946 through February 1947 called Operation High Jump?"

"The one organized by Admiral Byrd?"

"Correct. The story given to the papers was that it was to analyze the training of personnel, test equipment in arctic conditions, and determine the feasibility of establishing and maintaining bases in the Antarctic."

"What does it have to do with you? You weren't even born then."

"Correct again. But my father was." Colonel Novak's eyes glowed with some fond memory and then became cold. "He was the officer in charge of liaison between the Navy and the Air Force and a close, personal friend of Admiral Richard Byrd. They both shared the same dream of finding the answer to a thousand questions; from the first mention of the ancient god-kings, to UFOs, and even the secret base the Germans had established in New Swabia during the thirties."

"And did they?" I was getting curious in spite of myself.

"They did. Before he died, my father told me how he and the admiral had sat in on the debriefing of a pilot who swore that he'd found the entrance to a vast underground cavern complex in the middle of the former Nazi occupied territory. Not only were there refugees of the Third Reich, but they were thriving there. They had brought their newly acquired technology, or rather the principles of Vril they'd learned from the Annunaki."

"Hmmm, if that's true, then how come nobody's ever heard of it? Why aren't we buzzing around in our own little flying saucers like *The Jetsons*?"

His hands clenched involuntarily. "Because Truman and the Joint Chief's brass didn't want the public to know. They were afraid that if Joe Six-pack found out the guys we defeated had all this new technology, then they would want to know why the government was keeping it all to themselves. After all, who wouldn't want their own personal flying saucer or jet pack?"

"Why didn't your old man and Admiral Byrd spill the beans?"

"Because after serving with distinction in two wars, they cashiered my father and threatened to make him and Admiral Byrd both laughing-stocks if they breathed a word about what they'd found."

The colonel's face was red and he was breathing hard. I was dealing with a man determined to right a multi-generational wrong. I'd seen enough upright characters and strong silent types who, one day, quite without warning, passed that curve of no-return and went hurtling off the tracks. And when they did, they had a nasty habit of involving innocent bystanders. I was rapidly coming to the conclusion that I'd like to be far away from the colonel when that happened.

"Pop had always wanted me to join the Air Force and uncover the truth of the on-going cover up. That's what I've worked towards over the past two decades." He bit his upper lip. "And now, tonight, I am on the verge of doing just that. So, neither of you are going anywhere until I get the truth." He unsnapped his holster. "And we can do it the hard way or the easy way. Your choice."

Oh fuck! Déjà vu, all over again. Don't you hate being right? Especially when it comes to putting you squarely in the path of a shit storm.

"Hey, I think this is where I came in. How many times do I have to tell you? I don't have—"

"But I do." Max spoke firmly. "Yes, you're right...about the base, the Nazi UFOs, even the Annunaki."

The colonel's hand fell away from the butt of his pistol and stared at Max. Me too.

"Are you saying you know this for a fact, or are you bullshitting me to save your skin?"

"I know, Colonel," Max said confidently, "from first-hand experience. In a few minutes, you'll see why."

I stared at Max. He looked different somehow. I couldn't put my finger on it, but his face looked drawn, elongated, the eyes farther apart, cheekbones higher. He looked... strange, altered.

"You believe there is evidence, both empirical and inferred, that we have been visited by some types of extraterrestrials for hundreds, or perhaps even thousands, of years. Correct?

The colonel nodded.

"What would you say if I said you were incorrect?"

The colonel's face reddened. "You can tell me any denial-laced lie you want, but I've read and seen with my own eyes—"

Max held up his hand. "You didn't let me finish. I didn't say you were wrong. I said the information was incorrect; and it is. This planet has not been visited for hundreds, or even thousands of years. It has been a destination of alien beings for *millions* of years, almost one hundred million, if you're really curious. The Annunaki first discovered your planet more than 65 million years ago."

"Impossible!" The colonel was trying to wrap his head around it, but to me it was all too clear.

"How old is the universe, Colonel?"

As if relieved he'd been asked a question he could answer, the colonel replied, "13.8 billion years."

Max nodded. "And how old is the Earth?"

"4.5 billion years."

"Exactly. So then what happened during those 10 billion years between the forming of the universe and the forming of Earth?"

"I don't know."

"Well, I do." Max said. "Other races arose in other worlds and developed amazing scientific knowledge that was old when Earth was nothing more than a blazing ball of primeval fire and gas."

The normally staid demeanor of the colonel was falling away, like a cocoon as the bright butterfly wings of wonder began to emerge. "These ancient races, you've seen them, met them?"

"How do you know?"

"Because I was there. I am one of them."

Chapter Forty-Nine

I don't know how long we all stood there in silence. It felt like hours but was probably only a minute or two. My pulse raced and my breathing became shallow. The colonel was quiet and pale, but I could see this was having the same effect on him.

This revelation may have shocked the colonel, but from where I sat, everything finally fell into place. Legends where real history and myths were true. Our primordial memories were buried so deep, we didn't even know they were there until something like this came along and released them. The reasons our ancestors believed in the gods, with their powers and abilities to perform things that appeared like divine magic actually had their basis in misunderstood science.

Max looked at the two of us, but we were both lost in expectant silence.

"Let's start with what science accepts, shall we?" he said. "Humanoid man arose several million years ago, but before that could happen, there had to be several convergent events. Things like climate, food supply, and an absence or at least mitigation, of all of the large, nasty things that could swallow them in one bite, like dinosaurs.

"Those ancient visitors needed some kind of a jump-start to bridge the gap between monkeys swinging through the trees in search of food, and a hominid capable of constructing a tool to kill animals and knock fruit out of the trees. But in order for man to evolve a brain capable of abstract thought, he needed protein. He needed weapons to bring down his prey and fire to cook it in order to digest and maximize the calories for brain function. Enter the Annunaki."

For my part, I had seen enough of the impossible turn into the inevitable over the past several weeks, someone could have told me Santa and the Easter bunny were waiting for me outside and I'd have paused only long enough to grab my coat. The colonel, on the other hand, was doing his best Mulder from *The X-Files* routine. I expected him to burst out with "I want to believe" any minute.

Instead the colonel said, "So are you claiming you're an alien being and your people have been coming to Earth for hundreds or even thousands of years?"

"No, not hundreds or thousands—millions of years."

"Impossible! How many 'millions' of years?"

"Almost seventy million."

Now it was my turn to stick my big toe into the murky waters of *The Twilight Zone*. "Seventy million, huh? Well, by my count, your ancestors were here during the reign of the dinosaurs."

"Not only that, we brought it to an end."

"What...? Why?"

"To give the small mammals—your ancestors—time and the environment in which to evolve."

"So you guys paved the way for us becoming human, seventy million years ago, by booting the dinosaurs off of our turf?"

"Something like that, although the final mass extinction was actually sixty-five million years ago."

"Oh sure. Yeah, silly me, I forgot the date. But hang on a sec. Don't the scientists all claim that the dinosaurs were wiped out by an asteroid or something?"

"A comet, and yes…we sent it."

"Holy shit, Max—or whoever you are—you just don't quit. I mean, I've seen a lotta weird stuff lately, but are you seriously asking me to believe your remote ancestors somehow engineered the extinction of a species that had ruled the planet for close to two hundred million years?"

"Yes, and you're making another incorrect assumption. Who said it was my remote ancestors?"

My brain was swimming. What he was telling me was so absurd, I couldn't examine it rationally. The only thing I did notice is that the guy who I'd known as Max was now looking less like him with each passing minute. Even his voice had changed. The heavy Bavarian accent was gone, replaced by perfectly enunciated English, like a voice-over announcer.

"Stop with the semantic games, Max, or whoever the hell you think you are. What are you trying to say?"

"Forgive me for not speaking more plainly. I was trying to gently ease you into the sequence of events for which you lack the scale to comprehend."

"Try me."

"Very well. Our race evolved in the star system of Aldebaran almost a half a billion years ago. We surpassed where your civilization is today over a quarter of a billion years ago. Our progress mirrored your own; succumbing to wars, pestilence, and environmental disasters that caused civilization to stumble, falter and several times teeter on the verge of extinction."

The colonel stared open-mouthed and then I realized I was too.

"Approximately one hundred million years ago, our society had clawed its way back to its highest point. But our age-old ideological differences, which had so often sent us stumbling backwards, were once again on the edge of ripping apart everything we'd struggled so many times to achieve. That's when the committee came up with the idea of The Game."

"The Game?" I said. "You mean as in shuffleboard, football, or cards?"

He smiled. "Probably more like football considering there are two, for lack of a better word in English, 'teams.' Although I suppose there are also elements of shuffleboard as well."

"These 'teams,'" the colonel interrupted "are they like opposing armies?"

"They would be by your definitions. They were actually formed from many groups with opposing viewpoints who had fought and devastated our world many times in the past. To specifically prevent it from occurring again, all of those divergent and often mutually hostile groups were shuffled and assigned, at random, into one of two opposing teams. One team, which for identification purposes let us call the Team of Light, had as its goal the improvement and flourishing of all sentient beings existing everywhere our people had explored in the known universe. The other team, the Team of Darkness, was naturally in opposition to that purpose, and was pledged to return the universe to the state of raw chaos from which it evolved.

"The actual rules of The Game would take a hundred of your lifetimes to explain, but in simple terms, neither side could directly influence events anywhere or at any time. The only way we could affect the outcome of events was by using natural cataclysms: comets, floods, volcanoes, and guide them to influence human behavior much in the same way as you do in your game of chess."

Son-of-a-bitch! "So that's what this is all about? We're all just fucking pawns on your galactic chessboard?"

"That's somewhat of an over simplification, but yes, I suppose so."

"And you're telling us we don't have anything like free will? We're only puppets with you and your friggin' 'god-race' pulling the strings? Christ, Max, or whatever your real name is, no wonder you joined the fuckin' Nazi's. Is that why you gave them the Bell and all the other hi-tech weapons and stuff?"

"In one sense you are correct. The Team of Darkness chose the Germans for a role in The Game, but remember—the other side chose the ones who would become the Allies."

"So Maria was contacted by The Team of Darkness. They're the ones who fed her all the information."

"Some, but the avatars of The Team of Light worked with her too."

"Avatars?" Then it hit me. "My God...you. It's you Max. You're a damn avatar!"

He smiled slightly. "Yes, I guess you'd be correct in applying the term to Maximillian von Buchholz, but technically speaking, I am not the avatar. The avatar, as you correctly identified, is Max."

This time it was the colonel who spoke. "Then that means you—the entity we're conversing with—you are..."

"I am, by your definition, an alien."

"So what are we seeing here, Max or E.T. or whoever—and by the way, what should we call you if not Max?"

"I have no name." He paused. "No, that's not entirely correct. I had a name, but since I discontinued using my physical form, I've found no reason to use it."

"If, as you say, this body you are in is your avatar," the colonel said, his voice quivering, "then what has happened to the human who used to occupy it?"

"Oh, he's still here with me. Although, strictly speaking, not right now, but I can call him back if you'd like to speak to him."

"Back? Back from where? Do you share his body with him?"

"That's a good way to put it. It's more like symbiosis than sharing."

Like a particularly dense student, I raised my hand. "I'm even more confused now, if that's possible. When you say Max is there but not right now, then where is he?"

"Max can use the same astral planes we opened millions of years ago to travel between stars and galaxies. You see, when we discovered that, even beings like us, who had extended their life spans to millions of years, couldn't hope to reach the far ends of the Universe with any sort of physical instrumentation, including travel at the speed of light, we turned inward. We began experimenting with astral projection. Over many hundreds of thousands of years, we mastered it to the point where we no longer need our physical bodies for anything other than an emotional tether to the place we originated from. My own body is lying in a state you would pronounce as death, in a gigantic pyramid-like structure on a world eighty light years away. But it is not dead; merely in a state of suspension that can maintain it for the next billion years should I choose. This is what I meant by symbiosis."

All of a sudden a light bulb went on. "These pyramid thingies. Is your body wrapped up in linen strips and does it rest in anything that might look like a sarcophagus?"

This time he actually grinned. "Bravo, you catch on fast. Yes, the science would appear to an unsophisticated human exactly that way."

"Somehow somebody from the early Egyptian, Sumerian, and Central American native peoples must have seen how you, their gods, had preserved your bodies in pyramid structures encased in some type of coffin/sarcophagus and sought to do the same by preserving their own bodies after death, in hopes they could join you in the stars. I get it. But how did they see it? Did you show them pictures of your world?"

"Once again, you are correct in your supposition as to what they believed. But we did not show them pictures. They saw it first-hand because we took them—royalty, shamans and priests—with us."

"How? You just said you didn't use space ships or saucers or..."

And then it hit me.

"The Bell. That's what you used. The freakin', mother-lovin' Bell! That's why you built it and why you gave the plans for the construction of the Bell, one of your portal devices, to Maria. It was so she could travel to you world!"

"Among many other places, but yes. Our side, those of the Light, wanted to do something to counter the raw, aggressive power being dispensed by our opposition. We chose Maria because, even though neither she nor any human had the foresight to see what harm power beyond human comprehension could do, she, at least, hoped to use the knowledge to better mankind. And for that reason above all, we took her to Aldebaran."

"Take me." The colonel got up and stood in front of the entity inhabiting Max. "You've got to take me to your world."

When the Entity-Max didn't respond, he grabbed him by the jacket. "Don't you understand? I've worked all my life for this. My father knew your people were out there, but you never took him into your confidence. He died discredited, frustrated, and bitter. I won't allow that to happen to me. So I ask you again. Will you take me?"

"No. I'm sorry, but The Game is over on your world, at least for the time being. Though I do admit that events orchestrated by our opposition will most likely call us back again—perhaps even within your lifetime."

"Not good enough." The colonel snarled. "I'm done waiting here, dealing with fools and bureaucrats. I'm leaving with you or..."

Uh, oh. As I feared, the none-too-steady train he was riding was about to go off the tracks.

He pulled the square-barreled automatic. "You won't be leaving here at all. At least not using this body. And I'm betting that while I can't hurt you as the being you are, you're not going to let your loyal avatar be murdered in your place."

The being that I had known as Max regarded him thoughtfully. "You're right of course. I do have an obligation to preserve Max von Buchholz. I cannot let you harm him. But then again, if you check your pistol, you will find the bullets are not lethal."

The colonel pointed the gun at Entity-Max, then me, and finally at the ceiling before firing off two rounds. A pop like that of a cap gun and twin streamers of colored ribbon brushed the ceiling before falling back to the floor.

Desperate anger ran out of the colonel like a punctured balloon. "I should have known. You can do anything, can't you?"

"There is nothing in corporeal existence which is capable of doing everything, but from your standpoint...yes."

"You won't take me?"

"I cannot—at least at this time. But take my hand."

The colonel paused and then stuck out his hand. Max grabbed it and I watched the colonel's eyes roll back in his head. He shuddered and collapsed onto the threadbare carpet.

"Help him up." Max said to me.

I did and he stumbled, barely conscious, to the couch.

"And now, my young friend, who is unaware of how important he really is, I must go. Max will be returning to this body shortly. His memories of what he's seen and where he's been will be confusing and will gradually fade, so please, be a good friend and help him."

"No! You can't go—not without me!"

The colonel was back on his feet again, trying to walk unsteadily towards us. He faltered and sat down heavily. "You can't let me glimpse the wonders of your world and then abandon me back here on this little flyspeck of a world in a remote backwater of the universe."

Entity-Max smiled sadly and shook his head.

The colonel clenched his hands, frustrated. "At least show me. What do you...what did you look like—on your world?"

I watched, trying not to be astounded by yet another astounding thing as the figure in front of us grew one, two, three feet. The face elongated, the cheekbones became more pronounced, large silver-blue eyes set far apart, and long white hair fell around broad shoulders.

"This is how I appeared almost one million years ago."

The colonel stared and then pointed at the being, his breathing shallow. "And this is what I am going to expose to the world if you don't take me!"

Entity-Max smiled almost compassionately. "You must do whatever you think is right. But if you don't mind my asking, what will you use for proof?"

The colonel pointed to the flash drive still sticking out from my computer containing all the Vril plans and drawings that had started this whole thing what seemed like a lifetime ago. He plucked out the tiny plastic oblong and held it up.

"I've looked through it. Even though it is missing the details necessary to complete each device, it still has most of the technical information you gave Maria Orsic. With me to give an eyewitness account of everything you just said, I'm sure our scientists and tech brains can fill in the rest. When the networks and newspapers get a hold of this, it will cause a revolution in the way mankind looks at themselves and at the entire universe. It will not only inspire our scientists to work on it, but those of the entire world!" The colonel's breath was coming fast and his hands shook with an almost religious fervor.

"It certainly might. But have you looked at the contents of the drive recently?"

The colonel paled. "Why do you...what have you...?"

He looked franticly to my old laptop on the end table. He shoved the drive into the USB and watched it boot up. Seconds, later the image of the drive appeared on the screen and he began to scroll through the pages. There were drawings, but they looked crude and unscientific, like something a thirteen-year-old boy would doodle in his notebook. And there were pictures, some grainy, most out of focus, even some drawings of Nazis standing next to flying saucers sporting cannons and machine guns; crude and obviously photo-shopped fake images of the type found on "conspiracy" web sites all over the Internet. It would have been comic if the colonel hadn't been so devastated.

"Noooooo!"

"I'm sorry, Colonel, but there's been enough interference in your world over the past hundred years. Therefore, I hope you understand that we really don't want to add anything more to the many problems your species already has."

"I don't care. I'll show these. Someone will believe me."

Entity-Max shook his head sadly. "I'm afraid not. You know where all of those images came from, right?"

The colonel really didn't need to answer, we both knew.

"The Internet. From tens of thousands of UFO, unexplained and paranormal web sites. And you, of all people, Colonel, should know how easily the government and media establishment dismiss them all as kooks and nut cases. I'm sorry, but it's really for the best."

The colonel slumped back down on the couch and Entity-Max, who was back to looking at least something like the old Max, turned to me.

"I must go now, but there is one thing you should know before I do."

Good God. Was one more nasty surprise waiting for me?

"I know what Maria told you before she left with Dr. Kammler."

"Don't fucking remind me, OK? I've been through enough shit for one day. If I really gave a crap, I'd ask how you know, but then again I keep forgetting, you're kinda like the Great Pumpkin, right? You know everything."

"No. I don't know what you're going to do with this information, but I think I do." He looked at me until I returned his gaze. "Maria told you to never see Kat again because she said that one of the times she slept with you, while drifting through time and space at different ages, the result of your love-making had produced a girl who was your daughter. A daughter whom she named Katrina."

Another sick, cold wave rushed in the pit of my stomach. The same as I'd felt when Maria had told me back in the cellar.

"Jee-zus...back off, I feel creepy and crappy enough already."

"But what you don't know is that she is not correct. There was no child of you and Maria. Her first child was born in the thirties in Germany, and she is the woman who was introduced to you as Katrina's grandmother. Her second daughter, Katrina, was conceived out of quantum time as well and decades before she ever slept with you."

My knees turned into rubber and I sat down before I fell down. "Then who...who is Kat's father."

"I think you know. The person she calls Uncle Max is, in reality, her father as well as the father of her sister—whom she knows as her gran. Now do you understand why we frown on allowing your species to play with inter-dimensional time shifts? It can get quite messy, can't it? It also leaves those humans who spend too much time moving through them feeling...well, let's just say 'confused' about their own chronology."

"Holy crap. So if Kat is really Max's daughter, then there's really no reason why we can't..."

"Do anything normal young couples in a relationship do."

I went from feeling like an incestuous pervert to a horny teenager going on his first hot date. I couldn't wait to see Kat. I promised myself that this time, I was really gonna be straight-up with her and tell her everything. If she let me get that far without telling me to take a hike or kicking my prevaricating ass down the stairs.

Either way, that's where I was headed. I grabbed my jacket.

"Hey, I've gotta split, but you can stay here and discuss the cosmos, UFOs, ancient aliens, or whatever with the shell-shocked colonel over there." I pointed to the figure slumped on the couch. "Just lock the door when you leave."

"One moment please." It was Max, or to be precise, Entity-Max, holding up his right hand.

"I'd appreciate if you could help your friend Max back to his home."

"Huh? You're Max—I mean Max is you or..."

"Now that this part of The Game is coming to a close, we feel it's time for Max to return to exclusive use of his own corporeal body."

Now I got it. Whatever part of the cosmos Max had been hanging out, he was coming home for good.

"Sure, but just out of curiosity, how long ago did you start sharing Max's body?"

He bit his lower lip and looked thoughtful. "Since the spring of 1945, when Maria, Max, and a few others used the Nazi Bell to flee the crumbling Reich."

"Wow. Then, if he's been MIA since 1945, he's gonna feel pretty confused when he sees what been happening over the past seventy years."

"I shouldn't worry about it. He hasn't been excluded from his body. It's sort of like riding on a bus and looking out the window. You still see and hear everything happening, only someone else is doing the driving."

"And what was he doing when someone else was filling in for him? Where did he go? Didn't he get antsy not having his own body?"

"He did have his own body, in astral form, like I have mine even though it's been unused for millennia. Max has seen galaxies and visited worlds humankind can only speculate."

"He's not gonna be shocked when he gets back?"

"Not at all. Perhaps a bit sad that his options of exploration and growth will be limited to his own time, place, and mortality."

"So when Max comes back, you and your UFO posse are outta here, and us poor, little, monkey men are on our own?"

"I didn't say that."

"Then you will continue sticking your cosmic fingers in our pie?"

"As little as possible."

"But you'll be around?"

"Let's just say…look for the unexplained and the unlikely."

He flashed a brief smile then closed his eyes, and Max shivered like he was having an epileptic fit. For a moment, two beings stood there like an old double-exposure photo, Max himself and a tall, translucent, shimmering figure; one of the beings that had shaped our destiny for millennia. A split second later, it was gone and all that remained was an old man with white hair.

"Welcome back Max."

Chapter Fifty

Max looked around confused for a minute or two and then took a deep breath as though sampling the air. He stretched and moved his head from side to side before letting the breath out. Finally satisfied all was as he remembered it, he spoke.

"Thank you. It is good to be back. Strange...but good nonetheless."

"Not a big letdown after bouncing around the universe for a few decades?"

"Now you mention it, Ja. I will miss the wonders of astral travel, but at the same time, over the years I have also come to the conclusion that we humans are not ready to leave our bodies and become beings of pure thought."

"Well, according to our guest-with-no-name, he and his crew have been practicing that since we were ratty little mammals scampering around and hiding from dinosaurs, so I guess we've got time to grow into the notion."

Max smiled.

"OK, ready to go home? I mean your physical body's home, not some distant galaxy."

"Ja, I think I would like that."

"OK, then you've got yourself an escort." I didn't mention my offer was not entirely altruistic. I was counting on him to get me into his apartment to see Kat.

Oops! One last detail.

I turned to the colonel, who had been sitting slumped on the couch ever since learning his goal, at least for now, was unattainable.

"Hey, Colonel. I'm taking Max back to his apartment. If you want to walk along, you're welcome to."

I didn't want him hanging out in my apartment while I wasn't here. Especially since, for all I knew, he might decide to go postal with his service pistol. I couldn't take coming home to cop cars, yellow crime scene tape, and the M.E. scraping the colonel's brains off my couch.

The colonel didn't say anything. He appeared lost deep in thought. Finally, he stood up.

"He thinks I will give up and accept that the greatest discovery man has ever made can be buried again by fear of ridicule? Well, he doesn't know me. My life, and my father's before me, was about finding the truth. I will never give up. He hasn't heard the last from me."

He pulled on his coat and headed for the door. "You wait and see. Soon everyone will know who is pulling the strings of our existence. They will demand full disclosure, I promise you."

With that, he strode purposefully out the door, leaving it open and me blinking.

"Sounds like the colonel is back on his crusade again. Think he'll have better luck this time?"

Max smiled. "If there is one thing I learned in my cosmic wanderings, it is that nothing, *nothing* is impossible."

I nodded and walked to the open door. "Let's go home, Max."

* * * *

As Max fumbled to get his key into the lock of the second floor apartment on Beacon Street in Brookline, I kept rehearsing what I was gonna say to Kat. Every version sounded worse to me than the previous one.

When the door swung open and I saw her standing there, her tousled hair spilling down the shoulders of her powder-blue velvet sweat suit, I froze.

Fortunately, Max was there, and by the time she got through giving him a hug I would have killed to get, I'd found my voice, although what came out wasn't exactly pure gold.

"Uh... Hi, Kat."

Her pretty eyes turned from the warmth of welcome to twin icicles in a split second, like steel shutters slamming shut.

"Look, you've got every right to be pissed at me, and I wouldn't blame you if you told me to fuck myself, but if you'll give me five minutes to try to explain... Then, if you still don't want to see me, I promise I'll leave and never come back."

For a minute I thought she was gonna pick the second option, but finally she opened the door a little wider.

"Come in."

And so for the next hour, while Max wandered around the apartment, looking at things and picking up his pipes to examine, I told Kat everything. And for the first time, I held nothing back, not even the parts that should have gotten me thrown into the nearest rubber room by any practicing psychiatrist. She let me talk and was absolutely silent, no questions or comments. My only hope was that, having seen many parts of it with her own eyes, she'd realize the fantastic and unbelievable was only the starting point for what had happened. Eventually, I ran out of steam like an old teakettle on a slowly cooling burner.

"So there it is, everything right up to the moment I showed up here with Max."

For a moment I was afraid she was gonna point me out the same door I came in. Another minute went by before she drew a deep breath.

"Had you come to me with a story any less fantastic, I would have kicked your butt down the stairs. But after what I've seen since I met you, there's only one thing I can say."

For the first time in a long time, she smiled her big, beautiful, sweet smile.

"C'mere and kiss me!"

Epilogue

So there it is. Probably one of the most unbelievable stories you're ever likely to hear. I know it was for me—and I was there!

I won't say everything in my life immediately returned to normal. My life was far from normal to begin with. But gradually, things began to settle down as Kat and I started picking up the pieces of our bruised, but not broken, relationship.

Three months later, we found a one bedroom on the Cambridge/Somerville line and started doing all those homey little things couples do when they feel secure in a relationship, like spending a Friday night snuggling together, eating good pizza from Davis Square, and watching bad movies on HBO.

One Friday night, about two weeks after we moved in, the doorbell rang and there stood a flower delivery guy with a big bouquet of long stemmed roses with a note.

So very <u>Happy</u> for both of you.
May your love last forever...
Maria

And you thought it couldn't get any stranger?
I had told Kat everything, so the note wasn't a total surprise, but we never saw Maria again. At least, up 'til now, because no one, least of all me, has a clue to what the future holds. So, Kat and I don't think too much about tomorrow. After all, from what we've experienced, tomorrow could be next week, yesterday, or today. I guess our philosophy is: be

happy with what you've got and let tomorrow take care of itself.

The colonel was a man of his word. He did not give up his quest to prove the existence of otherworldly powers, and the complicity of governments, oligarchs, and illuminati in keeping information away from the public.

Shortly after that strange night at my apartment, Colonel Novak resigned his commission, took his pension, and spent several sleepless weeks banging out his own version of events into a very interesting little book that went viral on the Internet, racing to best-seller status on *The New York Times* eBook list in just six days!

He got onto the talk show circuit, and I just saw a new promo for the History Channel where he'll be joining their panel of Ancient Alien Theorists next season. And while Entity-Max was correct that the colonel would be scorned in many circles as conspiracy nut job and a kook, who says being branded as a kook doesn't sell?

Like I said at the very beginning, I started to write the book based on everything I'd learned and what we went through. However, Kat suggested we should hold back a few of the more dangerous and incredible details—as if this wasn't incredible enough! In truth, I really didn't take much persuading.

As for my friend, Kat's Uncle Max—or I guess we should say, her father–though I gotta admit it will take a little while to get used to that one, he went back to living with his older sister, who, of course, we now know is actually his first daughter...

See what I mean? Drifting through time gets confusing, doesn't it?

Be that as it may, I continued to meet Max at his favorite deli for lunch a few times a week, but as time passed, he spoke less and less about what we'd been through and I found myself more reluctant to bring it up. I think we both wanted to let the sleeping dog lie where he was. So I was caught off guard when I went for our usual deli rendezvous a few days after the flowers and note arrived only to find no Max.

I sat down to wait, and as soon as I did, the owner/waiter came over and handed me a folded piece of paper.

I dislike goodbyes, Christopher, so I will say, 'Auf Wiedersehen', until we meet again; of which I am sure. Until then, take care of mein liebstes Mädchen, my dearest Kat, and when the two of you look up at the stars some night, you can perhaps imagine that the old man-in-the-moon is your 'Uncle' Max winking down at you...

You know what? Last night, as Kat and I walked back from our favorite Cambridge watering hole, we looked at one another, and then the moon.

And damned if it didn't wink.

THE END

About the Author

Ric Wasley is a writer and lecturer as well as the author of the popular McCarthy Mystery Series set in Boston in 1968.

Ric has a forty-year professional career history in advertising, publishing, and marketing in Boston, New York, and San Francisco. He has degrees in history and psychology and has been trained in debating, public speaking, and stage acting. A large part of his forty-year career was spent in numerous professional and business settings as a presenter and featured speaker at seminars and professional meetings.

Ric has been a visiting professor at Worcester Polytech Institute. He also teaches a popular course on marketing for authors at prominent venues such as the venerable Cape Cod Writers Conference.

Of the five books in the McCarthy series, which include the first two, *Shadow of Innocence* and *Acid Test*, the most recent is *The Scrimshaw*, the third in the McCarthy Mystery Series, which was released in late 2009. That will be followed by *Black Velvet Band*, scheduled for 2016. In addition to the first two McCarthy Mysteries, Ric has also authored *Midnight Blue,* a quirky vampire tale that combines spectral creatures and nightwalkers with sex, drugs, and Rock & Roll; and *Echoes Down a Dark Well,* a paranormal thriller about reincarnation; *Candle in the Wind*, a twist and turn filled historical mystery; and Ric's newest, *The Girl with Faraway Eyes,* a paranormal historical based on true events!

Ric has also authored the semi-autobiographical novella, *At my Window with a Broken Wing,* and two short stories,

"Embers" and "The Night." Plus a brand new story, "Long Black Veil" that appears in the anthology *Weirdly Vol. 3*.

Just like Mick in his McCarthy Mysteries Series, Ric thrived on music in the sixties and performed as a folksinger and in several rock bands all over New England. He played regularly in the Harvard Sq. folk music clubs in the late '60s where he met music legends such as Bob Dylan and Joan Baez.

Wasley has been involved in both print and broadcast media as well as writing for business and commercial markets for over thirty years and continues to consult for a major media company. In addition to his novels and short stories, he has been published in several literary magazines in L.A. and San Francisco while living in California. Wasley currently divides his time between traveling and his home on Cape Cod where he continues to write, lecture, and create worlds where the unexpected thrives.

www.ingramcontent.com/pod-product-compliance
Lightning Source LLC
Chambersburg PA
CBHW070812190726
48292CB00006B/1985